ANNIE'S GIRL

Audrey Howard

Hodder & Stoughton

First published in Great Britain in 2001 by Hodder and Stoughton
Published simultaneously in paperback by Hodder and Stoughton
A division of Hodder Headline

10 9 8 7 6 5 4 3 2 1

British Library Cataloguing in Publication Data
A catalogue record of this book is available from the British Library

ISBN 0 340 76930 0 Hardback
ISBN 0 340 79452 6 Paperback

Typeset by Palimpsest Book Production Limited,
Polmont, Stirlingshire
Printed and bound in Great Britain by
Clays Ltd, St Ives plc

Hodder and Stoughton
A division of Hodder Headline
338 Euston Road
London NW1 3BH

Chapter One

The chestnut mare, though her brave heart urged her on, helped by the encouraging words of the rider on her back, was beginning to flag. The track she was on led through a vast purple sea of heather in the direction of Ullock Pike, which was over two thousand feet high. It was not really a track but a "trod", walked instinctively by the sheep, and as the animal went up and up she was forced to jump at each stretching stride as though she were taking a hurdle. The muscles in her back legs quivered with the effort of lifting herself and the girl, and the polished satin of her haunches rippled. She was dark with sweat and a great drool of spittle fluttered from her mouth. Her heart pumped and her flanks heaved but her loyalty showed in her willingness to go on despite her exhaustion. At her back, so close they were in danger from her lethal hooves, were two handsome young dogs.

It was October, back-end as it was known in the lakeland and the glory of autumn was spread with a lavish hand on the fells. Colours ranged from the vivid purple of the heather, the red, tawny brown and subtle lemon of the dying bracken, the bright scarlet of the berries on the rowan trees, the blue-black of the bilberry, the yellow of mountain saxifrage. Where the heather and bracken fell away into small clearings there were hummocks, green and grassy, mingled with the whiteness of bents. The autumn sky had turned to flame as the afternoon drew on towards evening, the sun beginning to dip behind Grizedale Pike, its livid colour running into the waters of Bassenthwaite Lake at the rider's back. The flame was slowly dimming to pale rose and on the fells purple shadows began to form but the girl continued to urge her mare upwards.

"Good lass . . . good lass," she whispered in the animal's ear. She leaned forward in the saddle, her nose almost touching the mare's flying chestnut mane.

On the air drifted the distinctive scent of bog myrtle and the pungent aroma of fern and heather which permeated the fells after heavy rain. Mingled with them were the smells of the valley far below, woodsmoke from cottage chimneys and the faint, rank odour of sheep. The long, sweet notes of a curlew lingered across Skiddaw Forest followed by the scream of a hawk.

The mare raced out of the heather, coming to a wide, flat stretch of level ground on which sheep were peacefully grazing, tearing at the sweet grass of the "intakes", the big, grassy slopes where they were brought as winter approached, the fields divided by dry-stone walls. Setting the mare to a new rhythm, horse and rider flew towards the wall, the rider putting the horse to the jump, lifting herself in the saddle and clearing the wall with a foot to spare, landing with a thunder of hooves into the middle of a small flock of sheep. At once they scattered, panic-stricken, going in every direction, followed closely by two dogs who needed no command to round them up and fetch them back, which they attempted to do.

On the far side of the wall, flat on his back, his face a frozen mask of amazement which was rapidly turning to outrage, was a young man.

The mare, as dashing and wild as the girl on her back, skittered madly out of control, striking a ewe a sharp blow to the head. The ewe made no sound as she tottered and fell. A third dog, an older, more experienced sheepdog, ran forward, his belly flat to the ground, his ears pricked, his eyes alert. He sniffed at the ewe, giving her a gentle nudge with his nose, then hesitated, his eyes on the momentarily speechless man, waiting for orders.

"You bloody fool, you bloody senseless fool," the man thundered, getting to his feet, brushing down his breeches, which were old, worn, but beautifully darned, then racing to snatch at the bridle of the rearing horse. "Are you blind? Couldn't you see me or didn't you give a damn anyway? I might have known it was you, you silly bitch, leaping walls, not looking, not caring who is on the other side. You're a danger not only to yourself and that poor sod of a horse you ride but every living creature on the fells. If that ewe of mine is damaged you'll pay for it, you know that, don't you? My God, you deserve a bloody good hiding and why your father doesn't give you one is a mystery to every man who knows him. I've a good mind to . . ."

"To what, Will Lucas? To do what? And you can leave go of my mare's bridle unless you want the skin flayed from your face. Let go of me at once."

The girl lifted the small crop she held in her gloved hand, ready to bring it down across the man's livid face. Her left hand holding the reins was struggling to get her mare under control and the three of them, man, girl and beast, went round and round, the mare's neck arched, her teeth large and ready to bite at the man's hand. Her eyes rolled in alarm, and so they might, for the two humans seemed determined to tear her apart in their identical rage. The two younger dogs belonging to the man were far up the field expertly bringing the scattered flock under control, drifting down the intake in the direction of their master, but the girl's young, untrained animals, no more than puppies, seeing some fun to be had, raced up to meet them. Chaos reigned. The mindless ewes swerved this way and that, defying the desperate nips of the shepherd's dogs which were doing their best to restore order, while the puppies yelped with excitement, the man swore obscenely and the incensed girl did her best to dislodge his hand from the bridle. The older dog lay with his nose on his paws, his wise old eyes following the madness of his master and the horsewoman, then swivelling up to the sheep, an expression that said plainly that he supposed he would have to go up and give a hand. A nip and a growl should see the puppies off and then he and the other two would fetch the scattered sheep down.

The puppies yapped, knowing authority when it bit them on the flank and fled from the flock, then stood beside the wall barking their silly heads off. The tussle between the shepherd and the rider continued but strength prevailed and after a few minutes of circling and shrieking her rage, shrieks that echoed from fell to fell and crag to crag, startling many a shepherd and his dog, the girl was plucked from the mare's back and flung on to her own on the soft grass. The mare, reassured by the man's experienced hand and soothing voice, quietened, dropping her head submissively to crop.

"You've a damn nerve, attacking me like that and your father will hear from mine," the girl snarled as she too picked herself up and brushed herself down. "I shall tell him what you did—"

"Please do and I'm sure he'll only agree with me and everyone living hereabouts that you should be locked up and the bloody key thrown away. What happened to that woman in whose care he put you after you came home from ... was it the fourth or fifth school that declined to keep you?"

The young man's silvery-grey eyes, tilting upwards at the outer corners like those of a cat, glared into hers. He was tall and straight as an arrow, not an ounce of fat on him but a whipcord strength which spoke of long days in the outdoor performance of manual duties, and he had a clever, intelligent face, lean and brown. His hair was brown and curly, a thick uncombed tumble which flopped over his brow and the collar of his faded shirt. His mouth had a humorous twist to it and his teeth were good, white, strong and even, as though all his life he had known only the most nourishing of food. Which he had. His mother, so it was said, was the best cook in the parish of Bassenthwaite and beyond, and had from their birth enthusiastically filled her children's stomachs with her fine cooking: Fig Sue, a kind of porridge made from figs, wheaten bread boiled in ale and seasoned with treacle and nutmeg; clapbread made from oatmeal and eaten with her own butter; crowdy, a kind of nourishing soup; stews made from beef and mutton that had been pickled in brine; herb pudding consisting of the leaves of Alpine Bisort, groats, young nettles, blackcurrant leaves, chives and a beaten egg. Phoebe Lucas had her own pig which she fattened for slaughtering, though she left the latter job to her husband's handyman. There was "tatie pot", neck of mutton chops laid in a roasting tin, covered with layers of onions and potatoes, cooked in the oven until it was crisp. They ate "wangy cheese", dumplings and bacon, rice puddings and fruit tarts with rich cream. She grew her own vegetables, green stuff and salads. She had a cow and from her milk churned her own butter and cheese, and her hens laid more eggs than she knew what to do with. She had a stall in Keswick market where she and Beth, her daughter, went weekly to sell the surplus, for it was a well-known practice for farm housewives to make their "butter money" this way, which was then their own to spend as they wished.

All of which, when added up, accounted for Will Lucas's straight limbs, his clear eyes and his good strong teeth.

"I'm in no one's care," the girl said, haughty as a young queen.

"I can see that, but, by God, you should be. A more feckless, witless female I've yet to meet."

"Oh, and how many of those would that be?"

For a moment Will looked nonplussed. "What?"

"Females! How many females come knocking at Browhead's door, tell me that?"

"Don't be so bloody stupid, and if you don't tie up those damned dogs of yours I'll knock their daft heads together." His voice was flat and so were his grey eyes. Like the lake itself on an overcast day when no wind ruffles its surface, they became as dull as pewter but Briar Macauley scarcely noticed and if she had would not have been concerned. What were Will Lucas's eyes to her, or the expression in them? She was afraid of no one, and her clenched fists, her rose-flushed cheeks, the brilliance of her tawny eyes told him so. When she had set off from Long Beck, though her dander was up, or so Mrs Blamire remarked as her master's daughter flounced through her kitchen, she had condescended to jam a hat on her head, stuffing the mass of her hair beneath it. Even so Mrs Blamire doubted if Reed Macauley would have approved of it. A man's check cap no less, with a peak and a button on the crown which she supposed wryly was in keeping with the rest of her outfit.

In her ride across the footbridge that spanned the tributary of the River Caldew and up through the heather towards the summit of Ullock Pike, it had flown off, releasing in an explosion of bright copper the tangled mass of her tightly curled hair. It hung down her back to her buttocks and tumbled across her face, her eyes peering from it like a maddened she-beast in the undergrowth.

"Stupid am I?" totally ignoring his remark about her dogs. "I'd match my brain against yours any day of the week. I bet I've read more books than you've had hot dinners."

"You're nowt but a bairn. I'm talking about life, real life, not the drifting from one diversion to another that passes for living in your world. The way we live up here. At least most of us. Farmers——"

"I could measure my farming skills to yours whenever you care to challenge me. When I've got them trained my dogs will compare with any."

"You don't mean those scatterbrains larking about over there?" he mocked.

"I'd fetch those sheep of yours down in a minute. Look at them, milling about all over the place."

"Only because of your daft animals."

"Why, when my dogs are trained I'd have then down in a minute. Just you wait. Would you like a bet on it? My dogs against yours, when mine are trained, of course," she added hastily, "and that won't be long. I was up raking the fells only yesterday with Jonty Singleton. We brought down over two hundred between us, some of your foolish creatures among them. I know what I'm doing or at least I would if I was let." A look of misery clouded her eyes but the man appeared not to notice as he continued.

"Briar, *all* sheep are foolish creatures. Don't you know that by now? Almost as foolish as females."

"The ones you mix with might be foolish; in fact Molly Gunson's a simpleton. Oh yes, don't think I haven't seen you making sheep's eyes at her; now she *is* daft."

He began to laugh. "Don't talk such bloody rubbish."

"It's not rubbish. You're sweet on her."

"Fiddle-bloody-sticks."

"It's no laughing matter." Though what she meant by that was not clear to either of them but, her swift temper melting away, she began to laugh too.

"Briar Macauley, will you ever grow up?" he asked her lightly, almost fondly, realising as he spoke that if ever a remark was inappropriate that one was. She was already grown up, her figure that of a mature woman. She was tall, almost as tall as he was, neat-waisted with a full lilting breast and hips that, though they were slim, were rounded and eternally female. Her back was straight, long and supple, and as she moved away from him to stare up the long flank of the intake she walked with the ease and grace of a cat. His eyes moved from the rippling curtain of her burnished hair to the delicate loveliness of her creamy white skin, the soft curve of her apricot mouth, the tilt of her fine eyebrows, the slanting set of her deep golden eyes, and for an astonishing moment he felt a warmth flare in the pit of his belly. How bloody ridiculous, he had time to consider, for this woman, girl really, since she was no more than eighteen, had been part of his life since he had been a little lad. Almost a member of his own family, like his sister

Beth, forever in and out of the farmhouse at Browhead. She had infuriated him, exasperated him, as younger sisters do, irritated him, teased him, quarrelled with him, even struck out at him in temper when he laughed at her, but he had never quite lost that feeling of affection for her that was a family thing. His parents made much of her, perhaps more than they made of Beth, their own flesh and blood, which Beth did not seem to mind, being a placid, even-tempered sort of a girl. Briar's sister had died some years before Briar was born.

And Briar was said to be the image of what Catriona might have looked like had she lived. In looks, his ma said, though not in temperament, for Catriona, Cat as they had called her, had been shy, sweet-natured, a trouble to no one, which could not be said of Briar Macauley.

Turning away, feeling foolish and reluctant to let the girl see his discomfiture, he leaned on his "setting-off" crook and in a low musical voice sent out his commands to his dogs. They began at once to coax the flock towards him. They moved discreetly, making no sudden rushes. There was no urgency in their quiet approach and the sheep moved off warily though not at all alarmed. The girl could not but admire the man's skill and patience. Will pursed his lips, giving a series of whistles and the dogs went, not to their master but to where their master told them to go. Tiny hooves pattered on the track and the flock moved into the small pen erected in the corner of the wall, the wall in which not a dab of mortar had been used.

"That's it, Meggie ... good lass; good lad, Pip." And each dog, as it came to sit beside him, was touched briefly on its silken head and two pairs of bright, intelligent eyes looked up into his with total devotion before settling on their bellies beside old Don, the third dog, now semi-retired. The ewe which the mare had struck got shakily to her feet and tottered to join her fellows.

"Right, my lass, could you have done that with your pair?" Will asked impishly. "Yes, I mean those foolish creatures you brought up with you today."

She turned and grinned affably, knowing no offence was meant and, unusually, taking none.

"These two will be bloody good sheepdogs when I've finished with them."

A spasm of distaste crossed his face. "When are you going to stop swearing?"

"When you do. When *men* do."

"You'd better not let Reed Macauley hear you say that."

"Oh, I can manage my father, thanks all the same. I can do no wrong in his eyes."

He hooted with laughter and the mare shied nervously.

"That's not what I heard and if you believe it you're a bigger fool than I thought." The strange sensation he had experienced a little while ago had gone and was forgotten, and when she hitched herself on to the dry-stone wall, staring out over the splendour below he leaned beside her, his long legs crossed at the ankle, his hands deep in his pockets, his dogs forming a semicircle about his feet. Hers, game and cocky and very young, began some play together, growling and nipping and rolling over. They were watched tolerantly by the working collies as though to say what else could you expect from such droll creatures.

They were shoulder to shoulder, the man and the girl, quiet now as they shared their love for the beauty of the dying day. An early owl hooted from Dodd Wood beside the lake, the sound carried on the wind that blew from there, reaching them through the clear, autumn air. The sheep bleated in the pen. The puppies yelped with excitement, turning their youthful attention to the older dogs, growling in mock ferociousness, jumping and tugging at their silken coats with sharp puppy teeth until a warning growl from old Don made them shy away, their ears and tails down for a moment.

"Those animals of yours shouldn't be out, you know. Not until they're fully trained," Will remarked absently. "They would have that lot" – nodding towards the restless sheep in the pen – "galloping down the fell and straight into the lake."

"Then tell me where and when I can get the chance to train them. You know what Father's like. 'I've got enough damn shepherds, my girl,' he says. 'I'm not about to let you play about with my flock. Get you back to your sampler or your watercolours and leave the sheep *and* the training of the dogs to the men.' Watercolours, I ask you! What does he think I am? One of those mimsy females he gets Mother to trot round to be my companions: Molly Gunson, Charity Mossop, Clara Benson. Just because he does business with their fathers he imagines I would find pleasure in their company and be just like them. Sitting in the parlour—"

"I thought it was a drawing-room at Long Beck." Will raised sardonic eyebrows.

"Well, that's what *they* call it, those stupid girls, and there's Mother still referring to it as the 'down-house' as it was known in her day."

"And what would you have it called?"

"Who cares as long as I don't have to sit in it. It's just that Father wants me to be a lady. Catch a fine husband, preferably titled, for which he's willing to pay. I know he wants me to be happy but that's not what I want. The title, I mean, or the husband for that matter."

She sighed deeply and lifted her gloved hand to push back the heavy weight of her hair from her forehead. If she had her way she would have cut it off, worn it in a fiery cap close to her well-shaped skull, but though she was rebellious of all convention, defiant of all restriction, something, probably her father's wrath and her mother's subsequent distress, kept her from it. She was tied hand and foot, she constantly moaned to anyone who would listen, usually the placid maids in the kitchen, to Beth, to her Aunt Phoebe, who were all used to it and had been since she was a little lass. She didn't want to sit and sew or paint or play the piano. Mother never did, which was true, so why should she? She wanted to be an actress, having seen the travelling theatre when it came to Keswick; a gypsy, for what a fine life that would be living in a caravan and sleeping in a different place each night; a railway engineer; a drover; a soldier. Anything in fact that would transport her from this place where she had been born and bred to anywhere in the world where a bit of excitement might be found. Of her dreams she never spoke since it was doubtful she recognised them herself.

"What's this I hear about – what is it? – a tennis court being laid out at Long Beck?" Will asked idly, his gaze on the golden lake at the foot of the fell. It was as though an enormous candle had been lit beneath the surface of the water, creating an illusion of luminosity which, with the backdrop of the dark fells beyond, was breathtakingly beautiful. Even though he had seen it a hundred times, a thousand times, it never failed to raise what his ma called "goose pimples" on his flesh. This place, these fells, this land of the lakes was in his blood, in his soul, and he could not imagine, nor even, if he was honest, consider leaving it. Not like the wild girl beside him.

She turned eagerly, glowing with excitement as she did at the mention of anything new, anything novel, which a tennis court would be in this farming community, something that other folk in the parish knew nothing about. Last year a committee of the Wimbledon Croquet and Lawn Tennis Club had drawn up certain rules regarding the playing of the game by ordinary folk. She had seen the game played on a trip to London last year with her mother and father and now, it seemed, because of these new rules, every good-sized suburban garden could match the resources of the great country houses which alone had been able to possess such a marvel. At once she wanted a lawn tennis court and had plagued her father until he had given in. If it would keep her at home instead of roaming the fells, bringing in the young gentlemen and ladies with whom he wished her to mix, then he was all for it. She was a bored, restless, young woman, always wanting to be "doing something".

Lately she had been badgering him for a "safety bicycle" which she had seen being ridden by an eccentric-looking gentleman on a visit to Keswick. They had been strolling, she and her mother and father, up Market Place, just passing Moot Hall which is situated in the centre of the road when the sound of a furiously tinkling bell had made them stop and turn, as it did every other pedestrian in the vicinity. Horses neighed shrilly and pulled at their reins and folk stared, open-mouthed, as a strange machine whizzed past. It went no faster than a galloping horse, which they had all seen at one time or another, but it had seemed to go by so rapidly that ladies stepped back in alarm, their hands to their breathless bosoms.

"What the devil ...?" her father began.

"What is it?" her mother asked, interested, as she always was at something new and not at all afraid.

"It's a bicycle, Mother. I saw one in a magazine."

"What bloody magazine?" her father asked ominously.

"Oh, Father, does it matter? Just look at it, isn't it wonderful?"

"I am looking at it and what in God's name has the fool got on?"

The bicyclist wore tight knee breeches, gaiters and ankle boots, a jacket somewhat like a soldier's with a high buttoned collar and a round cap called a "pill-box", and from then on Briar had wanted a bicycle. So far ladies – and not many of those – could only ride tricycles since a tricycle, which had three wheels, one at the front, two at the rear, accommodated a full skirt but Briar had nothing but contempt for these ladylike contraptions.

So far, hoping to satisfy her with the game of tennis which could be played in the seclusion of her own garden where he or her mother could be on hand to oversee what went on, he had managed to distract her from her longing for a bicycle, a so-called "safety bicycle".

"Mmm," she said now in answer to Will's remark. "The land at the back of the house is being cleared. The only thing is ..." Her bright face fell and he turned to look at her, amused by her childish enthusiasms and disappointments.

Dipping his hand in his breeches pocket, he drew out a packet of cigarettes and a box of matches. Selecting a cigarette, he placed it between his lips. Cupping his hands to shield the flame from the breeze, he struck a match and put the flame to the end of the cigarette. She watched him curiously. She was well used to the cigars her father and the gentlemen with whom he mixed smoked but this new-fangled thing between Will's lips diverted her attention. Cigarettes had been smoked for many years now by the working man, the habit brought back by soldiers of the Crimean War it was said, but she had never seen Will smoke one before.

"I didn't know you smoked those things," she said.

"There's a lot of things you don't know about me, lass." He grinned amiably.

"Can I try one?"

"Your pa wouldn't like it."

"My father isn't going to smoke it."

"It'll probably make you sick." But nevertheless he offered her the packet, lit the cigarette she placed between her lips and placed his buttocks against the cam stone at the top of the wall, watching her reaction.

She puffed and coughed but, knowing she wouldn't give in to it, he was not surprised when she smoked it to the end.

"Your pa would go mad if he saw you now. Anyway, what were you saying about this tennis court?"

She drew in a deep lungful of smoke and her eyes watered, but she managed to gasp out a few words.

"It won't be ready for this season."

"What season's that, then?"

"The tennis season, idiot. Don't you know anything about what happens beyond the boundaries of the lakes?"

"Not about bloody stupid things like tennis, I don't, and, might I ask, is there anything on your mind but the pursuit of pleasure or the satisfaction of your own desires?"

"Oh, don't be so bloody stuffy."

"You say you read books but what about newspapers?"

"Yes, I read newspapers."

"So, if that's the case, what do you reckon to the situation in Zululand?"

The expression on his face was triumphant and hers was a picture of astonishment.

"Zululand?"

"There you are, you see, you've never heard of it," he said, jubilation in his voice.

"Of course I have and if I was a man I'd be off to join the army and give that Cetewayo a damn good hiding. It's all very well that chap ... what's his name?"

"Sir Bartle Frere?"

"Is that it? Well, it's all very well talking of negotiating about boundary disputes but they should listen to him when he asks for extra troops. My father says—"

"Aha, so you're speaking the words of your father, Briar Macauley?" He smiled, knowing she would take the challenge he had teasingly flung down. If he was amazed, and he was, that she knew so much about the situation in South Africa, he did not let her see it.

Leaping from the wall, which was easy in the outlandish outfit she wore, she turned to face him, her eyes narrowing menacingly, her quick temper running like fire through her veins.

"No, I'm not, you impudent bastard. I've been able to read since I was five years old and when I was ten my father put *The Times* in my hand. 'Leave that rubbish Miss What's-her-name gives you and read this every day instead,' he told me, so I did. I know all there is to know—"

"So I have heard." His mouth curved in a wide grin but there was no animosity in his expression.

"What the hell does that mean?"

"It means there isn't a girl in the parish who has as good an opinion of herself as Miss Briar Macauley."

Again, and surprisingly, she grinned. "That's true and why not? Tell me if there is any female who does what I do?"

He pulled a face ruefully and leaned away from the wall to stand beside her and at once his dogs stood up, watching him intently.

"There isn't one, my lass, and, by God, there isn't one father who doesn't feel pity for Reed Macauley. From all I hear your mother was a wild one until your father tamed her and now, just when most men of his age are looking forward to grandchildren, a bit of peace at the back end of his life, he has you to contend with."

Briar Macauley's face softened and her eyes turned the colour of warm honey. There wasn't a man, or woman, in the world she loved as she did her father. Her mother was respected, admired, loved, of course, but not with the strength of emotion she directed at her father. He was wealthy, which mattered not one whit to her; he was arrogant, which was as it should be; he was proud of his heritage, as she was; and he cared not a fig for the opinion of others, and she was the same. She had heard tales of her mother, the woman from Browhead they had called her. A strong woman, an independent woman and Briar could think of nothing she would rather be.

"And another thing," Will was saying, not looking at her but with an air about him of some tension, she couldn't think why.

"What now?"

"That Jonty Singleton."

"Jonty? Don't tell me you've something to say about him? But then, why not? You're fond of criticising."

"I mean it, Briar. He has a reputation for . . . wenching."

She hooted with laughter. "Wenching! Is that what it's called?"

His tone turned surly. "You know damn well what I mean. Every girl from here to Keswick and beyond seems to have captured his attention. The good-looking ones I mean, but he hasn't marriage in mind, just . . ."

"Go on."

"He's . . ."

"Go on, tell me."

"He's . . . oh, hell and damnation, what's it to me what you do, or who you do it with?"

"Exactly. Now, Will Lucas, if you'll untangle those damn dogs of yours from mine, I'll be off." Her manner was lofty, making it sound as though it were *his* animals who were causing the swirling commotion. "And let me say this. If Jonty Singleton were to lay a hand on me I'd give him wenching!"

With a piercing whistle to her dogs, a sound that lifted the head of every shepherd and his dog from Hause to Keswick, she leaped on her mare's back, setting the animal to the wall. Amazingly, the young dogs followed and Will watched her thunder down the fell in the direction of Long Beck. For some reason he sighed.

Chapter Two

It was almost dark when Will pushed open the door of the small, sturdily built farmhouse that overlooked the lake at the north end of Bassenthwaite. He ducked under the low door frame, stepping over the threshwood into the hallan, a passage between the front and back doors, and from there moved into the warm and welcoming heart of the house. Entering any farmhouse on the fells of Cumberland necessitated a careful ducking of the head and the picking up of one's feet, for the threshwood, an oak beam four or five inches thick, was let into the floor and secured to the walls on either side of the door.

A plump little woman was stirring something in a pan on the open fire which was situated in what was known simply as the "house". She turned round as the door from the hallan opened and an expression of irritation, almost of offence — which was totally false, since the lad was the apple of her eye — crossed her well-scrubbed, plain and rosy face.

"Come in, lad, come in. Don't stand theer ditherin'." Though he was doing no such thing. "An' close door, will thi'. That there bottom wind fair gets in thi' bones this time o't year. See, get them boots off an' all. Trekkin' half the mud off't fells on me clean floor an' me just off me knees after scrubbin' out hallan."

Will amiably eased off his boots using the toes of one foot against the heel of the other and letting them clatter to the shining slate slabs on the floor. In his stockinged feet, the warm and serviceable stockings knitted by his mother of a night, since Phoebe Lucas could not abide idle hands, he threw himself down on the sconce, a fixed wooden settle that ran at right angles to the hearth. Under the settle was stored the kindling for making the fire and in the lidded seat was kept the family's bed linen. Various small cupboards were built into the thick walls where spices and salt were kept, since the warmth of the fire kept them dry. Above the hearth was a huge canopy which extended out into the room and it was under this the family gathered at night, as it was the warmest place in the farmhouse. Against the wall opposite the hearth stood a large and impressive piece of furniture, a carved oak bread cupboard, so sturdy it had survived even the great flood. On it were the initials SA and the date 1723.

Over twenty years ago, it had been, the great flood, which had swept away much of Browhead Farm which had stood for generations, nobody knew exactly how many, and when it had been rebuilt, though some modernisation had been possible, Will's mother would not have a stick or stone altered. She had cooked for years over an open fire, she said stubbornly, good nourishing meals with nowt wrong with them and she could see no reason to change, though eventually she had given in to her friend Annie's insistence that a small oven, heated by the fire, should be let into its side. She was used to it now and though she wouldn't admit that Annie was right and she was wrong she confessed to herself it was very useful. But she still did much of her cooking over the open fire as housewives down the ages had done. There were cast-iron, copper and brass cooking utensils hanging neatly and handily on the wall, shining like the crown jewels, and in the hearth on a chimney crane was a complex arrangement of bars and hangers ornamented with wrought-iron swags and touches of brass. There was wood, stacks cut into neat logs and stored beneath the sconce, but Phoebe was a thrifty housewife and unless there was a need for it she saved the logs for what she liked to call *best*! The peat fire was good enough for cooking over and a sight cheaper an' all, for all she had to do was take the sledge – when her husband or son weren't looking – up on to the fell and cut herself a stack. As if she hadn't enough to do, her mild-mannered husband scolded her, but years of living with Phoebe had taught Charlie Lucas that she'd have her own way, choose how, especially if she was sure it was the right way.

"Sit thi' down, lad, an' get thessen to't fire. I've set some spiced ale ter warm. See, Beth, pour our Will a glass, there's a good lass," turning to a young woman who was the image of herself in everything but the colour of her eyes and who was setting out the well-scrubbed table with plates and cutlery. "Then run ter't barn an' fetch tha' faither. That there Clover's ready ter drop 'er calf an' 'e will keep fiddlin' about wi' 'er. If I've told 'im once I've told 'im a thousand times the lass'll do it wi'out 'im standin' over 'er. But will 'e listen, will 'e heck as like. 'E'll catch 'is death an' then where'll 'e be? Six feet under, that's where. Now wheer's tha' bin, our Will?" She turned her sharp gaze on her son as though accusing him of being up to no good.

"I'd tell you if you'd take a breath, Ma." Will's voice

was filled with his amused affection for his mother. She frowned warningly, ready to give him a piece of her mind but instead she turned back to the fire and continued to stir the contents of the pan. It was broth, chicken broth in which the whole of a chopped-up fowl, one that was no longer a good layer, herbs, onions and peppercorns were simmered for several hours, and which would be the "starter" to their evening meal. At breakfast, at five o'clock summer or winter, Phoebe put before them a good plate of eggs, bacon, mushrooms she herself had gathered, with plenty of her freshly baked bread, but at midday, since her men were away from the farm for much of the time, they had to make do with a "noon-piece" as Phoebe called it. This in itself would have fed a family of half a dozen but Phoebe would have it that when they came in at night they were starving so she set a "decent" meal in front of them. It was a wonder they weren't all as massive as the pig who rooted in the pen at the back of the farm, her husband said to her, the one she was fattening for the winter months ahead. He himself was as thin as a thread – Phoebe's words – and she did her loving best to get a bit of weight on him.

"Go on then."

"I went up Ullock Pike raking in the sheep for the gathering at the weekend and guess who came thundering up on that bloody mare of—"

"Will Lucas . . ."

"Sorry, Ma, but she's enough to make a churchman swear."

"Briar Macauley?"

"Who else?"

Phoebe turned from her fire, her unlined face red and damp with sweat, putting her fists on her plump hips, the spoon still clasped in her right hand, staring in dismay at her son.

"Eeh, that lass," was all she said, shaking her head, but there was a wealth of sadness in her voice.

"Aye, that lass, and still dressed up in that daft outfit she's taken to wearing. Breeches, a long hodden-grey coat and no hat, her hair all over the damned place and as mad as a fighting cock." Though he spoke disparagingly of the girl he had argued with this afternoon there was a certain amount of admiration in his tone of voice and his mother did not miss it. She loved Briar Macauley as she loved her own good daughter, Beth, the girl who was just entering the house, her arm through that of her father, perhaps even more, for it was often the case that the naughty child has more charm than the good. But she didn't want her Will mixed up with her. Even if Reed Macauley was the wealthiest man in the district and even if Annie Macauley was her oldest and dearest friend.

"An' after all our Annie's said to 'er. Not ter mention 'er pa. Eeh, she wants a good leatherin'."

"What's this then?" her husband asked her, moving across to the small, earthenware sink that stood in the corner of the room. He turned on the tap from which ran clear, fresh water, Phoebe's only concession to modernity and convenience – apart from the side oven – when the farmhouse had been rebuilt. Charlie filled the sink with cold water and, taking the soap, made by Phoebe, washed his hands, then reached for the snowy towel that hung at the side of the sink, turning to look enquiringly at his wife as he wiped his hands.

"Will saw Briar up Ullock Pike." Her words, though innocent enough, spoke volumes.

"Dressed like a lad?"

"Aye, what else."

Both Phoebe and Charlie sighed with what seemed great weariness and Will exchanged a glance with his sister who, as yet, had not spoken. He shrugged his shoulders then settled down with his warm ale, drinking it with great enjoyment.

Phoebe shook her head and, unexpectedly, for his mother was not known for demonstrations of affection, she moved to her husband and put her forehead on his chest. She was considerably shorter than he was, for not only was Charlie Lucas lean and straight, even at his age, he was over six feet tall, like his son. His arms rose to enfold her and they stood for a moment or two in wordless comfort.

"I can't 'elp but think on our Cat," Phoebe murmured.

"I know," Charlie answered, "but what else can you expect when the lass has Annie and Reed Macauley for parents and is allowed to go where she pleases."

Phoebe pulled away from him abruptly and looked up into his face, her own stormy.

"Nay, Charlie Lucas. Cat were a little angel even if she did have Annie fer 'er ma. Poor little lass had nowt all 'er short life but she never took on like that there Briar."

"Lass, you know you love 'that there Briar', as you call her."

"Even if her pa is Reed Macauley." The quiet voice of her daughter spun Phoebe round to face her.

"Nay, I've nowt against Mr Macauley, girl." Phoebe was clearly piqued. "Years ago afore thi' were born me an' Annie an' Cat would o' been sorely tried, at least until tha' pa came on't scene, wi'out 'im. 'E thinks the world of our Annie, does Mr Macauley. Tha' pa wouldn't 'ave

24

bin able ter buy this farm from 'er wi'out 'is say so. Tha' knows it were in 'er family fer many a long year."

"Aye, Ma, we know," Will said, sighing deeply, raising his eyebrows in the direction of his sister, for had they not heard the tale of Annie Abbott and her elder daughter and this farm, which had once been theirs, a hundred times or more. But he should have known it was the wrong thing to do.

"Now you look 'ere, my lad," his mother began, her face like thunder. "Them were 'ard times, times tha' can't imagine when me an' Annie an' Cat 'ad nowt ter eat but turnip bread and there's not much nourishment in that. Tha'd soon 'ave summat ter say if I was ter put it in front o' thi'."

"Now then, Ma, I didn't mean—"

"I don't care what tha' meant, Will Lucas—"

"Jesus, how did this start?" Will clapped his hand to his forehead and the basket in which a mother cat and her four kittens lay snug and warm before the fire was given a smart, but inadvertent kick with his stockinged foot. The mother cat hissed in anger and the kittens miaowed piteously.

"Nay, Will Lucas, 'ow can tha' take the name o' the Lord in such a way, an' don't tha' kick them kittings or I'll tekk tha' faither's belt ter thee."

Will turned imploringly to his father, the expression on his face saying that he'd meant no harm, to his mother, to his mother's defence of her dearest friend, to the long dead Catriona, or to the kittens in the basket. He was beginning to be somewhat irritated himself, for, along with his father's sweetness of nature, he had inherited Phoebe Lucas's touchiness, which manifested itself now in her absolute belief in and conviction of the rightness and goodness of her friend Annie Macauley. If it had not been for Annie's spirited defence of her many years ago Phoebe Lucas — who had then been only *Phoebe* with no knowledge of who she was or where she had come from — would have ended up in the poorhouse, or worse, in a brothel. She wouldn't have a word said about the Macauleys and though she was aware of the self-willed, stubborn, headstrong nature of Annie's daughter no one, not even her own son, was allowed to criticise her.

Charlie, who was as peaceable as the placid Clover who was at this minute struggling to bring forth her umpteenth calf in the barn, clutched his wife to him and held her firmly against his chest. Charlie Lucas was a clever, well-educated man, come from what was known as a "good" family in the south, though where that might have been he had never mentioned. Once he had been a fighter in the Chartist cause but that had been scourged out of him years ago with the downfall of Feargus O'Connor and others who had thought the same way as he did. He was not really a farmer but in the twenty-five or so years since he had drifted into the lives of Annie Abbott, as she was then, and Phoebe, at Browhead he had learned to become one. Sheep farming mainly, for that was what Browhead was, a hill farm, a sheep farm with some arable and dairy farming. There were hundreds of sheep on the high ground, over two thousand feet up where they had spent the summer, but which would soon be brought down to the intakes, big, grassy slopes fenced by dry-stone walls, and below them the "inlands", small, rich enclosures about the farmhouse itself where the sheep would winter. They were Herdwicks, small, agile, wiry, goat-like so that they could survive on the craggy tops of the high fells, with deep, round bodies and rough white faces, thick-boned with sweet flesh and a thick fleece. They were perfectly suited to the climate and conditions of England's highest mountains and Browhead could be said to be a thriving and prosperous farm.

"Now then, sweetheart," Charlie said to his little wife, holding her struggling figure close to his chest. "Our Will didn't mean anything and I don't think he kicked the basket of kittens on purpose, do you?"

No, she didn't, for there was no better man with animals than her lad but nevertheless she was mortally wounded by his lack of understanding, or even interest, in the terrible times she and Annie had suffered a long time ago. Of course, it *was* a long time ago and the young couldn't have old heads put on their shoulders, could they? Besides, she loved this man who held her close to him, loved him with a passion no one, least of all him, knew about. She had been second-best years ago when he had married her and she knew that his heart still belonged to Annie Macauley, and always would. But they had a good marriage and she knew, in his own way, he loved her.

She let herself be petted and soothed for a while, since it was very pleasant, then pulled away sharply in case he thought she was "soft". At once she began to bustle round the fire, pushing Will's legs to one side as she reached for the bubbling pan of chicken broth.

"Well then," she said, apropos of nothing, missing the wink Charlie gave his son as they were told imperiously to get to the table.

She would have eaten her meal in silence but Charlie Lucas was a man who liked a bit of conversation over a meal, for he had come from a family who were well accustomed to such things. Both his children, even Beth, had gone to the grammar school in Keswick. They were intelligent, like he was. They enjoyed reading and had been brought up with the habit of discussing what they had read. They were not animals, he often said, to eat and work and make love — this last not voiced to his children — and spend their days in silence. He had, at first, confounded his young wife by talking to her when he made love to her, telling her she was a lovely woman, which she didn't believe but she was not to know that he meant it. She was sweet and smooth with soft, contoured breasts, a solid, sweetly curved waist and rounded hips, fragrant with the smell of the lavender she put in her cupboards and the fresh bread she baked every day. It had been no hardship to make love to her and he told her so, though not in those words. She had brought him joy when he had expected none and their shared pleasure in the act of love was still warm and living.

But she could not leave the worrying subject of Briar Macauley alone. It niggled at her thoughts and she wanted to share them with her family. A trouble shared is a trouble halved, they said, and though she knew there was absolutely nothing anybody could do about the lass, even her parents, she suspected, she longed to set it to rights. Still, it soothed her to see to the appetites and wellbeing of her family, moving round the table with the pan in her hand, encouraging each of them have another mouthful of her soup, the tatie-pot she drew from the small oven at the side of the fire where it had been warming, the apple tart she had baked and the thick whipped cream she had churned herself.

"Sit down, my lass, and let Beth get the apple pie," Charlie had told her as she fretted at the oven where the pie was keeping hot, but at last, with a cup of refreshing tea in her hand, she consented to sit with her family at the enormous table, so enormous it had had to be built in the room, which stood beneath the window.

"Did she say what 'ad upset 'er, our Will?" she asked at last, and they knew what and who she meant, for there was always someone upsetting Miss Briar Macauley.

"Nay, just the usual. She wants to train those dogs of hers to shepherding but it seems her pa won't let her."

"I know what's up wi' 'er. She wants ter be 'er ma all over again. Annie were that independent. She were well known fer it and the lass wants ter be't same, but wi' Reed Macauley at back of 'er tryin' ter turn 'er into a lady there's not much 'ope o' that."

"Ma, I just don't understand why Mr and Mrs Macauley won't allow Briar to . . . to do what she really wants to do." Beth's voice, which no one had ever heard raised in temper, was soft and perplexed. Beth Lucas was as even-tempered, as sweet-natured as her father. She was inclined to be merry in a quiet sort of way, seeing humour perhaps where no one else did. She was generous and loyal, devoted to her family and to her friend who was, surprisingly, the dashing Briar Macauley. Though there were seven years difference in their ages it did not seem to matter, since Briar was bold and confident, dazzling in her beauty, danger-loving, rebellious and fearless. Everything in fact that Beth was not. Briar had visited London and had even been to Paris with her parents. Beth had been no further than Keswick with her mother to stand behind the stall on market day. Beth was well-read and well-mannered and could have run the domestic side of Browhead as easily as her mother and yet she had never been outside the shelter of her family's home alone. Beth was shy of strangers, unworldly. Her upbringing had kept her young for her years whereas Briar's travels, the many schools she had attended where she had created havoc, her indifference to the conventions of the day, her total belief in the rightness of what she wanted from life

29

gave her a vigorous self-assurance which Beth admired at the same time as it made her fear for Briar's future.

"What she really wants to do? And what is that, lass?" Beth's father asked her, his voice mild, ready to smile at this plain but beloved daughter of his. She was short, inclined to be plump, with his long, silvery-grey eyes — her one real asset — and heavy, ruler-straight hair which she strained back into an enormous coil on her sturdy neck.

"Hmmph, dost think she knows?" Phoebe began, but her husband lifted his hand. For all his mild manners Charlie Lucas commanded the respect of all who knew him and at once his wife, for the moment, subsided.

"Well, I'm not even sure she knows it herself, Pa, but she loves the land, the lakes, the farm, Mr Macauley's farm at Long Beck and instead of sitting on her behind doing embroidery, as *he* wants her to, she's off on her mare doing what she would do if she was his son instead of his daughter."

"You're saying she wants to be a farmer?" her brother asked incredulously. He leaned his elbows on the table then reached for one of his mother's fresh-baked clapbread. He lavished butter on it and took a huge bite while his mother looked on approvingly. His lean brown face wore an expression of amused disbelief. The mother cat, sensing something that she might find tempting, wound herself round his legs and he leaned to pick her up, settling her in his lap and stroking her silky fur. She purred loudly and her kittens, waking up and finding her gone, began to miaow. She took no notice but daintily accepted a morsel of the oatcake Will absent-mindedly offered her.

Beth sighed. "Well, I do know this, she doesn't want to be a lady of leisure. You know how active she is . . ."

"Well, happen her new tennis court will keep her

occupied and entice to her side all the *gentlemen* her father wishes her to meet."

It was said sourly and if Charlie Lucas, who was more astute than his easy-going manner seemed to imply, wondered at it, he said nothing in front of his wife. She had, no doubt, some worthy, suitable young lady already picked out for her son, probably Anne Singleton whose family farmed Upfell. Brought up to farming ways was Anne, her dairy work the best in the parish. A good sensible lass who would fit in right well with Phoebe. Much as she loved Briar Macauley she'd not do for Phoebe Lucas's son.

"A *tennis court*! What in 'eaven's name's that?" Phoebe exclaimed, her eyes wide with horror as though her son had said Briar was to have a music hall erected for her pleasure at Long Beck.

"Oh, it's some nonsense them up in London play about with," her son said contemptuously. "They knock a ball over a bit of netting with a racket and the one on the other side has to knock it back."

"Well, I never! 'Ave they nowt better ter do with their time than play games like bairns? I'm surprised at Annie fer allowin' it." Phoebe was red-faced with indignation.

"Sweetheart, you know that Annie . . . well, it's probably something to do with Cat."

Phoebe turned in astonishment to her husband. "Cat! Poor bairn never 'ad no daft games ter waste 'er time with. She worked as 'ard—"

"Don't you think that's why Annie is so indulgent of Briar?" Charlie answered gently. He leaned across the table and took his wife's work-roughened hands in his. Though a lass no bigger than a happorth of copper, or so he described her, came up each day from Hause to help Phoebe with the scrubbing, the peeling of vegetables, the endless washing and ironing that took place at Browhead, somehow Phoebe's hands were never less than red and rough. Charlie suspected that she favoured the child, Minnie, who was no more than twelve and the eldest of eleven in the family, and gave her the lightest jobs about the farmhouse. Soft as clarts, was his Phoebe, though she would die rather than have anyone recognise it.

Phoebe's face softened and though she would normally fling him off with a tart remark she let her hand rest in his, for she knew it was the truth. Annie Macauley's first daughter had lived a life of almost unendurable hardship while her mother struggled to bring back to life the farm her father had left her almost thirty years ago. She had worked beside Annie and Phoebe, making swill baskets and birch twig besoms to sell at the market, digging peat for the fire, collecting rushes to make rushlights which were all they could afford, working, as they did, despite her young age, from cock-crow to nightfall. She had died knowing nothing of luxury or even of some of life's necessities which most took for granted. She had known only the love her mother and Phoebe had given her, and hard work, and it was this that urged Annie on to the almost wicked spoiling she showed to Briar. And Reed, who might have stopped the girl's headlong flight in her restless search for pleasure, could deny his beloved wife nothing.

"Aye, tha're right, lad, poor little Cat ..."

"And poor Briar, for if this goes on much longer she'll grow up one of the most spoiled lasses this side of Ambleside."

Will got to his feet, putting the purring cat back in her basket with the kittens. "Grow up." *Grow up!* What a way to describe the luscious young woman he had argued with this afternoon. And she was luscious and she *was* a young woman, at least physically. In his mind's eye he studied the high round exuberance of her breasts, with nipples standing out like cherries, straining against the linen of the shirt she wore beneath her hodden-grey coat. The boisterous rolling of her hips and buttocks which were round and tight as she leaped over the wall. The long slenderness of her legs, whose shape was revealed beneath the skin-tight kid breeches she wore, the rich and creamy rose of her wide, laughing mouth which, when she was pensive, was full and pouting as a child's. The almost transparent gold brown of her eyes starred with dark brown lashes which, he remembered noticing, were tipped for half their length with gold. A beautiful woman, or a beautiful child, he pondered, as he made his way up the narrow staircase to his bed.

"Now don't tha' stay up 'alf the night readin', our Will," his mother shouted up after him, longing, he knew, to come and tuck him up as she had done when he was a child.

"No, Ma." But it was not his books that kept him awake that night but the wild rose beauty of Annie Macauley's girl.

Chapter Three

There were great country fairs held twice a year at Cockermouth, Kendal, Keswick, Penrith and Ulverston, the first at Whitsun and the second at Martinmas in November. It was here that servants and farm-hands who were not "stopping on" for another six months, perhaps wanting a change if they were young and adventurous, gathered to put themselves on show with the intention of being hired by another master. A straw stuck in a hat or in the corner of his mouth indicated that a labourer was for hire and on completion of tricky and yet careful negotiations, for the Lakeland man was known to be canny, between master and man, hands were struck and the hired man received a shilling as "arles" or earnest money as a token of his hiring. That was all that was needed, a handshake and the man, or woman, passed, like the slaves of the southern states of America before they were emancipated over twenty years before, from one master to another. Of course these men and women were paid wages, unlike the slaves, men £10 to £12 per half year with board and lodging included, women £7 to £9.

The serious business of the fair being completed, the

next two days were regarded as a holiday, a festival for the masses, for the lads and lasses with their wages and "arles" money in their pockets out to enjoy this respite from their drudgery.

Briar slipped from her bed on a cold November morning, shivering across the thick carpet to the smouldering fire which was almost out. As soon as her young mistress rang her bell Nan would come bustling up the stairs with a basket of kindling and some hot coals on a shovel to speed up the process of rebuilding the fire. But on this particular morning Briar Macauley was, as her father would have put it, up to no good and if she called Nan to help her she might get stopped by her parents, whom Nan would be bound to call, or, if not that, held up arguing with Nan, and then Jonty would go without her. She had been to many country fairs and sports occasions before, ever since she had been old enough to accompany her parents. She had walked beside them, going where *they* wanted to go, seeing what *they* wanted to see, dressed in the lovely little dresses, the fur-trimmed cloaks, the expensive boots which her mother and father thought appropriate, held back by her father's restrictive hand from dashing here, there and everywhere to see all the wondrous things that were on view, things that her father thought unsuitable for a female child to see.

But today, St Martin's Day, she was to go with Jonty Singleton, he in his best "setting off" suit, she wearing her breeches and hodden-grey coat, her hair tied up and stuffed beneath what was known as a "wide-awake" hat with a low crown and a wide brim. It had belonged once to her father, headgear he had worn when he went shooting twenty years ago. It was battered and stained with something, she didn't know what and didn't care, since it shadowed her face.

She must remember never to take it off, she thought as she jammed it on her head, for there would be bound to be folk at the fair who would know her and her family. Farmers, shepherds, country folk, but also men of a higher station with their families, for this was a day out to which they all looked forward. It was fine – she had ascertained that when she peeped from the window – but she thought it might be windy by the way the trees surrounding Long Beck were threshing about.

Dawn was only just lining the peak of Ullock Pike, a silvery-blue line which was slowly turning a faint and rosy pink, heralding the sun as Briar crept into the stable and tiptoed towards Flame in her stall. Victoria whickered as though offended by this disturbance at such an early hour, and Briar hesitated and held her breath, for two of the stable lads slept in the room over the stable block and the last thing she wanted was for one of them to come down and investigate what Victoria was up to. It so happened that Briar was one of the few human creatures Victoria was prepared, in her irascible way, to accept, since Briar was not afraid of her and Victoria knew it. She blew through her nostrils a time or two as though to remind Briar that she could be awkward, then quietened.

Briar saddled Flame in silence, then led her out of the stable, keeping to the grass verge at the edge of the cobbled yard. The gate, as all Reed's possession were, was well looked after and oiled regularly and made no noise as she lifted the latch and crept through it, closing it carefully behind her. When she was well clear of the house, and in growing daylight, she leaped on to Flame's back and, putting her heels to the horse's sides, urged her into a gallop. She had a joyous urge to shout and whoop but instead she clamped her mouth tightly shut, making her way down through the bracken and heather by the side of Salehow Beck to where she could see Jonty and his cob waiting for her.

He shouted and, taking off his low bowler hat, stood up in the stirrups and waved to her.

"You're late," he bellowed, disturbing a small flock of sheep who were sheltering from the wind beside the wall, causing them to scatter like the daft creatures they were.

"I had to be quiet and it slowed me up," she cried, "but I'm here now and, let me tell you, I'm famished, since I've had no breakfast."

"Neither have I but we'll soon rectify that, my lass. We'll stop off at the Dog and Duck and persuade Rosie to cook us a hearty breakfast. Ham and eggs would go down very nicely with some mushrooms. What d'you say?"

Their mounts were picking their way delicately down the steep slope towards Applethwaite and the road to Keswick, and as the quiver of excitement raced through her Briar felt Flame respond to it as though Briar had transferred the feeling to her mare. Excitement, that's what she wanted, adventure, something to stir up the day and carry her forward to some wonderful future, of what sort she had no idea but, if she had anything to do with it, it would not be dull. First there was today when she would stride through the fair with Jonty beside her, two young men, or so it would seem to the other fair-goers, out for a day's lark as young men are wont to do. As long as this fierce and cutting wind didn't blow off her hat no one would know the difference between them.

"I could do with something to tie on this bloody hat. If this wind blows it off no one will mistake me for a lad."

Jonty, riding easily in the saddle, turned to grin at her, the expression on his face audacious. "Lass, the hat hides your hair, certainly, but the rest of you's a bit of a giveaway."

"What d'you mean?" Her tone was truculent. She had gone to a great deal of trouble to hide her femaleness, wrapping a scarf round and round her neck, and with the hat pulled well down to her ears and only her tawny eyes glowing between she was pretty sure no one would recognise her for what she was.

Jonty's smile was impish and he let his gaze drop to her breasts which thrust disconcertingly forwards. It was her habit to walk and ride with her back straight, tall and proud, her head held high, but this action made it very obvious that beneath her coat she was not what she seemed, or what she *hoped* to seem.

"You'll have to slouch a bit if you mean to hide your . . . ahem . . . shape, Briar."

"What's wrong with my shape?"

"Absolutely nothing, lass. Any man would tell you that but it's not exactly . . . boyish which is why it's so splendid."

"Jonty Singleton, you take your eyes off my shape or my fist will make your ears ring." Nevertheless she knew what he meant and for the rest of the ride until they reached the Dog and Duck she did her best to slouch in the saddle.

It was almost full daylight by this time and the road to Keswick was filling up with people on the way to the fair. Waggons piled high with saleable goods, eggs and cheeses, butter, and plucked and trimmed fowl, the well-polished farmwives striding out beside them. Pedlars' carts stuffed with all manner of marvels such as shepherds' bells and leather gaiters, bridles, saddles, whips, padlocks and saws, tea trays and cough drops, corn plasters, pots and pans. They would set up their stalls among those already there, those who had been wise enough to get to Keswick early and have first choice of the best positions, vying with those offering gingerbread, gauze from Italy, ribbons and lace from France – or so they *said* – hats and caps, cloaks and brooms, beehives and baskets.

"What have you got in that bag?" Briar asked Jonty as they dismounted in the noisy yard of the Dog and Duck, pointing to the carpetbag which hung on his pommel and which he was lifting off to carry inside the inn.

"I'm going to do some wrestling. There'll be a few prizes to be picked up so I thought I might as well bring my costume."

Briar lifted her shoulders in childish delight, grinning with anticipation and eyeing Jonty's broad shoulders and muscled back.

"Does Mrs Singleton know?" For it was well known that his mother did not approve of her son's activities.

"She doesn't even know I'm off to the fair."

"She'll be furious when she finds out, and your father."

"Like your pa, you mean."

"It'll be too late then. The fun will have been had."

"That's just how I look at it though Pa will probably threaten to take the skin off my back."

They strode into the inn, two young bucks on an outing. It was a working man's inn where those who had done business at Keswick stopped off for a pint or two of ale on their way home. Normally it would be closed at this time of the morning, barely past seven o'clock, but today it was packed with those on their way to the fair, many of them travelling overnight and in need of a good breakfast before they tackled the day's business.

"Let me do the talking," Jonty advised in a soft voice, bending his head to Briar though she was almost as tall as he was. "And keep your hat well over your face."

Pushing his way to the bar and drawing Briar behind him, he turned his charm on the overworked barmaid, evidently well acquainted with her, for she responded at once, leaving some truculent fellow who begged all those around him to confirm that he was here first.

"Do us a bit of breakfast, Rosie, my love," Jonty whispered in her none too clean ear. "Me an' my friend are famished."

Rosie wiped her none too clean hands on her none too clean apron and eyed Jonty's friend with interest. Jonty Singleton was an old customer, and not just at the bar, but the tall chap with him might be worth getting to know. She worked hard in the bar for Jed Postlethwaite but she had a nice little business of her own which, as long as it didn't bring disrepute on his inn, Jed was prepared to overlook, and besides Jed had a wife who was cold and mealy-mouthed – though she was a dab hand with pies and such which made her worth keeping sweet – and Jed often sampled Rosie's wares, free, of course.

"'Oo's tha' friend then, Jonty?"

"This is . . . is Bertie, a lad I used to go to school with, Rosie. Bertie, meet Rosie." He winked at Briar while Rosie was busy appraising the tall lad with the lovely eyes which was all Rosie could see of Briar's countenance above the scarf. Briar deepened her voice, wishing Rosie a very good morning, choking on her own laughter, since it seemed likely that with a small amount of encouragement, or none at all, Rosie would drag her across the bar and ravage her.

"Ham and eggs, Rosie, there's a good lass, and some mushrooms to go with it. In the meanwhile Bertie an' me'll take a tankard of ale apiece."

Those in the snug who knew Jonty Singleton watched him and the young man with him as they swayed helpless with laughter across the room and almost fell on to the settle that stood to the side of the enormous fireplace. Jonty was known for a fool, with a sense of humour that was inexplicable to everyone but himself or so his pa said of him bitterly, but his hilarity, and that of the lad with him, was surely verging on the lunatic. Some of the men had a strange feeling they knew the lad, nudging one another and staring at him curiously.

It was warm by the fire and Briar longed to throw off her scarf which she had pulled down slightly in order to eat but she knew it would be inadvisable. She would have to be careful or one of these men, Sammy Garnett who stood in the corner and whose family had, years ago, owned Upfell, the Singleton farm, and Joey Addison, a shepherd from a farm up Uldale way who had once worked for her father, might recognise that beneath the shapeless coat was not a lad larking about with Jonty Singleton but Reed Macauley's wild daughter.

They rode into Keswick, she on her skittish, long-legged mare which had obviously come of good stock and Jonty on his sturdy cob, tethering their animals outside the Packhorse, where, though Briar was unaware of it, her mother had once worked as a barmaid. Even so early they were subjected to a great deal of pushing and shoving, for the market-place and every street leading off it were jammed wall-to-wall with a laughing, excited press of people come to buy and sell their own goods and to watch the variety of entertainments which had already sprung into life. Slack wire balancing, the wire slung between two houses, impeded the progress of waggons and pedestrians. A sad and frightened bear, well muzzled, pranced to the prodding of its owner's stick. Travelling quacks sold elixirs from the back of a cart, guaranteed to cure anything from bile of the liver to warts on the nose. From somewhere came the "oom-pah-pah" of a brass band and a man holding aloft a banner proclaimed that the wrestling was to start at ten of the clock, urging folk to get there early so as not to miss the giants of the sport of Cumberland wrestling.

To the side of the market-place stood those who were for hire, patient row upon row, some already wreathed in smiles for they were the strongest, those more "likely-looking" and had already been "taken on".

After drinking another jug of ale, the Packhorse's finest, the landlord told them, and then another, Briar and Jonty made their giggling way to the field where the wrestling was to take place, Briar feeling decidedly light-headed, though the strong brew did not seem to have affected Jonty. She felt herself to be grinning in a most friendly fashion at every passer-by and indeed, that is how she felt, friendly and carefree, telling herself that this was the life, the life of a young man who has no need to be "proper" but can please himself what he does and where he does it. She was so blissfully careless Jonty had to remind her more than once to keep her scarf up about her mouth and her hat pulled well down. Somehow it would keep slipping to the back of her head in a style that could only be called jaunty, tendrils of soft curls wisping about her ears and neck.

"Now you wait here and don't speak to anyone, d'you hear. Even if you see someone you know just ignore them. *Especially* if you see someone you know. Now promise me." Jonty looked down into the deep tawny eyes of the girl, the mad, delightful girl with whom he was half in love, at least what *he* called love which did not include marriage, of course. She was quite dazzling in her casual indifference to what other girls of her class might call danger, and, by God, she was fun to be with. She charmed him with her lively wit, her loveliness and her total disregard for any of the conventions that restrained other girls. But he thought she might be ever so slightly tipsy, since she was not used to the strong ale they had drunk in the Packhorse. He supposed he should have allowed her to drink only a half-tankard but then it was difficult to get Briar Macauley to do, or *not* do anything she wanted, which included being careful. Her face beamed up into his, her peach-ripe mouth wide over her straight white teeth and he once more put up a hand to cover the lower half of her face with her scarf, a movement that surprised passers-by, for you didn't often see one man doing such a thing to another.

"Why, where are you going?"

"I'm going to that tent there to change into my costume. Now promise you won't move." He felt rather pleased with the idea that for the moment Briar was in his care, if you could call it that. No one knew where she was and if the day went well and she continued in such a blissful mood he knew a shepherd's little hut on the way back to Long Beck where . . . well, first things first. He wanted to impress her with his prowess in the roped-off ring and perhaps with another tankard of ale inside her, to celebrate his win, she would be even more amenable to a bit of . . . he got no further than that, for he did not seriously consider the *total* seduction of Reed Macauley's daughter. Just a bit of a kiss and a cuddle, perhaps.

No one knew exactly how long the sport of Cumberland wrestling had gone on but it was a tradition that was carried out at all the fairs. It was a sport that required no equipment, just two sporting young men prepared to throw each other to the ground with a series of skilful moves. There were two judges and a referee, for everything had to be seen to be above board as the two protaganists wrestled for the best of three falls.

Jonty stepped into the ring, dashing and handsome in his costume, aware that there were more than a few pretty girls sighing over him, looking round to make sure Briar was watching him and was slightly nonplussed, as were those standing beside her, when she waved to him, which, in their opinion, was not the sort of thing one young man would do to another. Jonty wore a pair of long drawers, tightly fitted to his legs, which were tucked into stockings, a white sleeveless vest and over his drawers a pair of vivid blue velvet trunks embroidered at the back with hearts and flowers and his initials. The excitement became intense, for Jonty had won several belts and his opponent, a giant from the other side of Ullswater, looked very impressive which would make for a good bout. They faced one another, then in a swift movement, having "tekken hod", each one grasping the other with locked arms around the body, each one with his chin on the other's right shoulder, they began to move, crab-like, about the ring, sizing each other up. A fall would be given when any part of one man's body touched the ground and expressions such as "blown out", "swinging hypes", "cross buttock", "hank and twist" and "dog fall" were bandied about furiously among the crowd as they compared one man's move with the other.

Briar screamed with excitement, shouting Jonty on, capering about like a child when he threw the giant from Ullswater. It seemed to go on for ever but although the giant *was* a giant he could not compare to the skill and stamina of Jonty Singleton who won the match, and the leather belt which was presented to him by the wife of a prominent businessman in Keswick.

But disaster struck when Jonty stepped out of the ring, surrounded by a jostling, shouting pack of male spectators, all doing their best to pat the winner or even shake his hand, for Jonty was a popular figure in the sport. They were considerably startled, falling back in sheer astonishment, silenced by the sheer effrontery of it, when a young chap squirmed his way through the crowd and fell upon Jonty with a shriek of delight. The hush deepened as the lad began to kiss the winner, hanging round his neck so that his feet were lifted from the ground. His hat fell off and from beneath it streamed a curtain of hair which shone like copper in the fitful sunshine, reaching his ... her – it could only be a *her* – buttocks.

"Jonty," she was screaming. "Jonty, you did it. That was bloody marvellous ..." Several ladies on the fringe of the heaving crowd were seriously offended, not only by the language but by the fact that it came out of a female mouth.

"Dear heaven, it's Annie Macauley's girl," one whispered to another, before Jonty Singleton, who swore later that he had never been so amused in his life, almost carried the deliriously screaming girl to a spot at the back of the tent and proceeded to kiss her with great vigour. He would have gone on doing so, since she seemed willing, but the voice of Reed Macauley thundering directly into his ear made him spring away from her as though he had been shot.

She moped about her bedroom, dressed now in her bedrobe because her father had insisted that her breeches and all the paraphernalia with which she had disguised her gender were to be burned, a task he would personally see to.

"I'm not going to lock you in, my girl," he had told her quietly, a quiet that was more threatening than his first roars of outrage, "but let me say that if I see you outside this room until I give you permission I shall pack you off to a boarding school which will make the ones you have already attended seem like a holiday in Paris. It will be more like a prison. I shall personally make sure of that. Now stay here and try to behave yourself. Nan will bring you something to eat."

"But, Father—"

"Don't. Don't, Briar. I am not to be got round as I have in the past. If I hadn't at the last moment decided to go to Keswick and have a look at that ram of Seth Cartwright's God only knows what you would have got up to."

"I wasn't getting up to anything, Father."

"You call kissing Jonty Singleton behind the tent at the wrestling *nothing*? It was all over the bloody town, what Reed Macauley's girl was about. I have men telling me they saw you in the Dog and Duck."

"Oh, Sammy Garnett."

"Aye, Sammy Garnett and others who made it their business to inform me, in the nicest possible way, naturally, that my lass . . ."

Her father had actually shuddered before he turned away and strode to the bedroom door. She was sorry really, for she loved her father and she could tell that he was not only angry but distressed. She often wondered what her mother made of all this, it normally being a girl's mother who made the rules for her daughter and saw that they were kept to, but hers seemed to have a more casual approach to the conventions – or the slighting of them – that appalled her father. She supposed it was due to her mother's own background which had forced her, years ago, to ignore what folk said about her as she carried on the business of rebuilding and running the farm at Browhead, of keeping a roof over the head and putting food in the mouth of the daughter she had borne illegitimately and who had since died. Do you give a damn what folk think of you when you are struggling to keep your head above water or do you continue to strike out for the side where safety and your future lay? She often felt her mother sympathised with her, Briar, and would possibly have been more lenient but she would not go against Briar's father, as Briar had recognised years ago.

Pity about the fair though, and Jonty Singleton. She had been having such a good time. She had protested forcibly as her father dragged her through the crowds, standing with their mouths hanging open, she had seen that, to where her mare was tethered. She had wanted to see some more of the wrestling and planned to watch the start of the hound trailing, and the finish as well! She had been told that there might be fireworks and a travelling theatre was to perform *The Merchant of Venice* and there was to be dancing in the square when the market stalls were taken down. There were all manner of sights still to be seen, freaks such as the pig-faced lady and the hairy man from Morocco, she had protested, childishly, uselessly, she knew that now, but the smell of ale on her breath had so incensed her father she wondered how he had held in his temper until he had got her home.

So she had been dragged ignominiously through the shocked and delighted crowds, put on her mare and led away at the back of her father's horse like a naughty child.

Flinging herself on her bed and staring mutinously at the shadows dancing on the ceiling, she sighed. She knew she would never be any different and she wondered why her father didn't realise it, then, turning on her side and moving her narrow-eyed gaze to the fire, she began to plan how and where she would find herself a new pair of breeches. Perhaps there might be something in the innumerable boxes and trunks that lay in the attic above her head. She had heard her mother talk of Grandmother Macauley who had been known for the sort of woman who would cut a currant in half, thrifty and not one who would be inclined to throw out good clothes that might have become too small for her son, Briar's father. She'd like to wager that they were all packed away up there, carefully stored in lavender to keep away the moths. She smiled and turned on to her back.

Tomorrow, or perhaps the next day, when her father had got over today's brou haha, she would make it her business to climb up to the top of the house and see what legacy Grandmother Macauley had left for her granddaughter.

Chapter Four

The wild dashing of hooves on the rocky track at the back of Browhead was a familiar sound to its occupants, since it was the only way down to the main road from Upfell Farm and Long Beck. Reed Macauley had a fine, spirited black mare, tall and dangerous, the only one who was not afraid of her apart from his daughter who was afraid of nothing was Reed himself. As a lad of twenty, over thirty years ago now, his father had given him the present mare's grandmother whom he had christened Victoria in honour of their then young Queen, and the one he rode now was named for her as had been the mare in between. Mind you, his sense of humour was known to be wicked and those who knew him had not been surprised. A beautiful, well-bred animal with a coat like satin but with a disposition that boded ill for those whom the animal took against.

Jonty Singleton from Upfell, whose pa's pocket was not as deep as Reed Macauley's, rode a young cob, stocky and strongly built with black and white markings and, being another with a sense of humour, he had christened the sturdy animal Firefly. Firefly was not as good-looking as Victoria, nor was he as graceful in his movements but he was dependable, and though Jonty would have liked a dashing mount with which to show off his riding skills to the young ladies, his father, being practical, somewhat taciturn, a blunt-spoken and independent fellsman and certainly not one to listen to the youthful pleas of his son, had brought home Firefly, telling the lad he was lucky to have a mount at all.

The third animal that came at a gallop, never less, down the track belonged to Briar Macauley and it was Flame, the chestnut mare, with Briar astride, which was her usual mode of riding, who startled Beth this Sunday morning as she placidly moved about the yard in her task of feeding the thirty or so hens which pecked the cobbles. There were half a dozen ducks squabbling, their wings outstretched, over the same handful of corn and several geese which honked in alarm as the thunder of the mare's hooves lifted over the back wall.

"Good morning, Beth," Briar shouted, then reined in her mare, for she was genuinely fond of Beth and had a few minutes to spare. She leaped nimbly from the animal's back and fastened the rein to a handy cam stone at the top of the dry-stone wall, then jumped over it as a lad would, one hand on the top, landing gracefully in the yard, scattering the geese and hens and ducks, only the rooster standing his ground.

"Briar, where on earth are you off to this early? It's only just light." Suddenly Beth's sweet face assumed an exasperated expression and she moved towards the wall, swinging her bucket. The hens, sensing no danger, began to follow her, cackling furiously, making so much noise the mare did her best to back away from the wall. "You're never going to the hunt?" Beth protested, her hand to her breast as though Briar had declared she was off for a night's roistering.

"And why not?" Briar's voice was defiant but at the same time she was ready to laugh, for this was all a huge joke.

"Why not? *Why not?* You know your father will be furious especially after what happened at the fair. It was all over the fells, the way he dragged you through Keswick, and now here you are galloping off again on your own and dressed in ..." Her eyes sharpened, going over Briar's outlandish but familiar outfit, the outfit that, or so the rumour went, her father had burned in the yard at Long Beck.

"Where did you get those breeches and jacket? Your father destroyed ..."

Briar casually inspected the polish on her leather boots, the ones that Wally had brushed vigorously this morning and the only part of her apparel that her father had not chucked on the fire.

"Oh, I raided the attics and found ... well, I suppose they must have belonged to Father when he was a lad. They're a bit short, the breeches I mean, but when I tuck them in my boots they fit perfectly, and as for the jacket I'm not sure who wore that but I found it in a trunk with this hat" – which was stuck jauntily on the back of her head – "and here I am." She grinned impishly.

Beth sighed. It seemed that no matter what Annie and Reed Macauley said to her – well, what *Reed* said to her, for Annie was much more tolerant of her wayward daughter – she still went her own road, as Beth's mother described it.

She glanced round her, hoping her mother was occupied in the kitchen and had not noticed the sound of the mare, nor Briar's cheerful voice, or she would be out here giving her friend what for. Though it was none of her mother's business what Briar did, nor what her parents allowed her to do, Phoebe could not resist having her say. She sighed with relief when her mother did not appear, turning back to Briar.

"Don't go, lass. Stay and—"

"What, Beth? Have you some exciting alternative to tempt me with? Collecting the eggs or weeding the herb garden perhaps? Really, I don't know how you stand it. I know ..." Her face lit up and she grabbed her friend's arms. "Why don't you come with me? I could give you a lift on Flame and we could ..." Her face fell as she held out Beth's arms and looked her over. "But you couldn't walk far in that skirt."

Beth pulled herself away and for once she was not her usual placid self. "Really, Briar, even if I had the clothes I wouldn't want to come and stride up the fell after a fox with all those men looking."

"But that's half the fun, don't you see, watching the expressions of disapproval and listening to the muttering going on which they daren't say to my face. Oh, do come, Beth."

"Don't be foolish, Briar. You know I can't. Besides, Will's already gone."

"Has he? Damnation, I'd best be off then or they'll start without me."

"Briar ..." But Briar was already over the wall, her long legs flying, leaping lightly on to Flame's back and with a shout of something or other which Beth didn't catch she was off down the track.

"Who were that?" Beth's mother called out from the doorway, then, seeing her daughter's face, her own darkened. "As if I didn't know. First our Will an' now her. Look sharp with them hens." She went inside and banged the door.

*　　*　　*

The sound of the huntsman's horn rang high up the slopes of Orthwaite Bank and the hound pack began its full-throated baying. It was early and the mist lay thick and white in the dale as though the cumulus clouds had fallen from the sky. There were thin wraiths about the lakes and tarns as if the waters were warm and the cold air had turned them to steam, but the upper slopes were already sunlit, bleaching the coarse fell grasses almost to the same colour as the sky. The low sun touched the black outcropping of rocks, outlining them against the mist from which the pack then emerged. The huntsman strode out in front with his terriers at his heel, his firm voice keeping the hounds together. At their back was the whipper-in. Following in a long straggle were the huntsmen, and one woman!

Dragging to locate the scent of the fox had taken place earlier, preliminary to the hunt, and now the hounds, having picked up the scent, were in full cry, ready and willing to follow the cunning animal over the most difficult and hostile terrain, up to a distance of fifty miles in the day if necessary. The canny fox had been known to run along a dry-stone wall in its attempts to throw off its pursuers, to hide on a roof or window ledge, or even in a stream, but the hounds, whose upkeep was paid for by the local farmers, were as stubborn and steadfast as the dalesmen and fellsmen themselves. The fox was the farmers' natural enemy, taking newborn lambs and losing them profit; besides, the sport of fox-hunting was greatly enjoyed by most of them. During the winter months from October to May it was said, and perhaps with some truth, that a man from the lakes loved the hunt better than taking his wife to bed!

Lakeland fox-hunting bore little resemblance to its namesake down south; indeed the men of the lakes looked with a certain amount of contempt on what was considered the niminy-piminy ways of the squirearchy. None of their huntsmen wore the dainty pink coat and black hat of the men who rode to hounds in Leicestershire and thereabouts. To follow their hounds they required not a glossy, well-groomed hunter but a stout pair of well-made boots and a sturdy stick. Hodden-grey coats and breeches were almost a uniform, the wool from which they were made coming from the backs of their own sheep and woven by their own wives.

There was a sudden stillness among them when they saw who was to accompany them, and what that huntsman wore. A lass, Reed Macauley's lass who had a reputation for being wild, dressed just as they were with her long elegantly turned legs on full view for all to see. Indeed they were scandalised but Reed Macauley was a man of wealth, a man with a great deal of influence in these parts and they had no choice but to fall in alongside the splendid figure of his daughter. Her laughter rang out and it was seen – and disapproved of – that her companion was none other than the parish's other rebel, Jonty Singleton. It looked as though there might be some sort of hullabaloo when young Will Lucas, who was known for a steady sort of a fellow, spoke quietly to Reed's lass, perhaps telling her that this was no place for a woman, which was as it should be, but Jonty Singleton whispered in her other ear and she only laughed that high laugh of hers and pushed past young Will. She and Jonty strode out, still laughing, not even glancing at Will, who looked as though he'd like to give someone a good leathering, preferably her! They'd alert the fox, way they were going, the pair of daft wights, their high jinks and its accompanying merriment ringing from high fell to high fell so that even the raven that roamed the peaks on the lookout for some tempting morsel drifted away. Aye, a right pair they were, well suited was the general consensus, and what the devil Reed Macauley was thinking of letting her out on her own dressed in that outrageous rig was beyond them.

They climbed high that day, clambering over rough and rocky, grey-pitted outcroppings, sliding on the screes over which the fox and the pack led them, doing their best to get a purchase on the moving surface. Their breath steamed about their heads, not just the farmers and shepherds who were after their natural enemy, but the miners, the factory lads, the mill workers who were always glad, not only of a day out in the sweet, fresh air of the environment of which they saw or smelled little from one week's end to another, but for the few bob they might earn for the head of the vermin, fox, or marten or wildcat.

It was noon when Briar picked up a stone in her boot. It had rubbed a blister and though she had refused at first to acknowledge it every step was agony and she was sure she could feel blood running down inside her boot. They had been walking and climbing for the best part of four hours and though she could go on all day, she told Jonty, who had stayed by her side ever since they left Hause, she thought she had better stop and take off her boot. Aggravating as it was to let these frozen-faced men see her bested, even she knew her heel was going to get worse if she continued. To be stopped by something as foolish as a blister was mortifying and she would probably have to make her way back down to Hause in her stockinged feet, but she was determined she was not going to let these sniggering males have the satisfaction of seeing her limp on beside them. No, she'd make the excuse that she'd had enough of the hunt and meant to sit in the sunshine and eat the pasties and clapbread Mrs Blamire had reluctantly wrapped up for her at daybreak.

"I don't know what your father will say to this, Miss Briar," Mrs Blamire had told her disapprovingly. "I shouldn't be surprised if he gives me my notice for encouraging you in one of your daft schemes." Mrs Blamire had been at Long Beck since before Briar was born and with the familiarity of an old servant felt she could speak as she pleased. "You don't think of that, do you, when you go off on one of your jaunts?" Her eyes ran up and down the absolutely appalling outfit her master's daughter had on, lingering at her bosom which peeped out ... well, it *thrust* itself out of the opening of her coat.

And after all that trouble at Martinmas an' all. She herself had watched the fire in the yard when the master had tossed Miss Briar's breeches and hodden-grey jacket, and the wide-awake hat into the flames, standing to watch them burn. And now here was the lass, dressed in the very same outfit, or so it seemed, and off on some jaunt which Mrs Blamire knew would not please the master. So where had she got the outfit she now had on, and did the master know that, even after such a drama as had occurred in November, his wilful daughter was off again? Dear God, there would be the devil to pay when he found out and she only hoped she or any of the other servants would not get the blame for it. The whole outfit, a replica of the last one, was a disgrace, really it was. She had a knitted jersey on which clung to her shape, and Nan and Betsy, the two kitchen-maids, though they had seen their young mistress in a similar rig-out many times, could not keep their eyes off her, and young Wally, who cleaned the boots and anything else Mrs Blamire put him to, was quite mesmerised, his eyes ready to pop out on stalks.

"See, you two, get on with chopping those mushrooms. And if you've nothing to do, Wally Hardcastle, I'll soon find you something." Her voice softened. "Eeh, Miss Briar, won't you ... well ..." She was trying to say "find something decent to put on" but she knew she might as well save her breath to cool her broth, for if the lass took no notice of her father what chance had she, Cissie Blamire of influencing her? Mr and Mrs Macauley were still in their bed and she'd like to bet they had no idea that their daughter, their only child, was off on this crack-brained jaunt. There'd be hell to pay when they did!

She, and they, would have been mortified if they could have seen Briar Macauley, her boot and stocking off, her bare foot in Jonty Singleton's enquiring hand, their laughing faces close together. The shocked men watched for a minute or two, not knowing what to make of it, some of them with daughters of their own somewhat worried, for would they like their lasses to be left alone with such a womaniser as young Jonty Singleton, but if her pa didn't stop it, who were they to interfere? There was a look about the girl they didn't quite like, a look that seemed to suggest she was game for anything that might be pleasurable.

But the rest of the huntsmen, after another appalled look at the couple who seemed to be sprawled, there was no other word for it, on a soft cushion of tufted grass, strode off after the pack with that easy, rolling gait of the true fellsmen. It was noticed that Will Lucas had hesitated, hanging back irresolutely, then with an expression on his face that seemed to ask what the hell was it to do with him, and did he care anyway, he followed the rest.

"They'll lose the fox if they don't get after those hounds," Briar said casually, biting into the crisp apple Mr Owen, her father's gardener, had sent into the kitchen from the orchard only that morning. She was well aware that Jonty was watching her, his eyes narrowed, his hand still caressing her foot and smoothing her ankle. It made her want to shiver, whether with delight or repulsion she wasn't awfully sure.

"Mmm," was his only answer. He smiled most agreeably. They had been playing this game for weeks now, ever since she had ridden up Ullock Pike in an attempt to train her young dogs and had found him raking in the sheep, most belonging to his father but a dozen or so to other owners. These would be taken to the "meet" which was a social gathering from where they would be collected by the farmers who owned them. A sheep will normally stick to its own "heaf" or the pasture where it was weaned but there were always exceptions to this rule, recognised by the "smit" mark on their fleeces.

They had continued their game at the fair in Keswick, both of them delighted with the "lad" Briar had become, which was in itself a titillation, at least to Jonty, and had it not been for the arrival of Reed Macauley, who knew where it might have led. Now, it seemed, Jonty was to have another chance.

"Why don't you catch up with the others?" she asked him smilingly, knowing there was nothing further from his mind. She knew herself to be what was known as a "good" girl from a decent family and would allow no man to take liberties, but was Jonty Singleton aware of it or did his masculine arrogance believe she would simply lie down and accept his advances?

Jonty Singleton had only one idea in his mind and that was somewhat blurred. She was so bloody beautiful and so bloody contrary, saying something with those incredible eyes of hers that might mean "yes", but at the same time laughing up at him. Might she not suddenly become awkward as many girls did when he got to a certain point in his wooing? But somehow he could not help himself, nor keep from trying. As yet he had done no more than kiss her but was she not promising him something more today, allowing him to handle her flesh, stroke her foot and ankle and even a bit higher. The swelling in his breeches was becoming painful but still he held himself back, for he did not want to spoil his chances by going too quickly. He had almost had her – at least she had not objected – at the fair but on that occasion she had been slightly the worse for drink. Then her pa had come and dragged her away and that had been the end of it.

"I can't leave you on your own," he murmured, wondering if he dare chance putting his warm mouth to the tempting arch of her foot.

"Don't be daft. What harm can I come to up here?"

She smiled into his deep, chocolate-brown eyes, so brown they were almost black. His hair was very dark, smooth, straight and shining, and his face was a rich amber. His mouth curved in a merry smile but there was a sensuality about it she did not recognise. He was very handsome and she knew all the girls in the parish of Bassenthwaite yearned after him, for not only was he handsome he was also a good catch because Upfell, thanks to his father's hard work for the past twenty-odd years, ever since he had taken it over when the last owners left, was prosperous. A good catch was Jonty Singleton, and he knew it. His shoulders were broad and he was tall, but there was a certain insolence about him which women found attractive and men took exception to.

He had pushed up the leg of her breeches the better to ascertain the prospect of her being able to walk home, he had told her softly, and his hand continued to smooth the white flesh of her calf. He kept his gaze on her, noting the slight widening of her eyes and a sudden drawing-in of her breath which, as a lover of some considerable experience for the past nine or ten years, having been obliged by a milkmaid from up Orthwaite way when he was fifteen, he recognised.

"God, you're a beauty," he murmured, "and I've half a mind to . . ."

She smiled somewhat shakily, for she had the feeling she was getting out of her depth here. She knew she had only to tell him to get his damned hands off her and he would do so at once but the trouble was she rather liked what he was doing to her, and being ignorant of men and what they did to women she was curious to find out.

"What? Half a mind to what?"

"Come on, sweetheart, you know what I mean. How old are you, sixteen, seventeen? Don't tell me you've never . . . ?"

"I'm eighteen, Jonty Singleton and I know what goes on," she said stoutly though she didn't. Her voice trembled a little, for she was totally ignorant of physical desire. She had heard remarks made by the stable lads when they had thought themselves alone but they had made little sense to her. Being a country girl she was knowledgeable about the breeding and birth of animals but that was the true extent of her comprehension.

"Do you indeed, then what I'm going to do to you won't come as a shock, will it?" His voice was silky and his hand caressed the back of her knee, and though some female instinct warned her that she should stop him now while *he* was still capable of stopping, was her name not Briar Macauley and when had a Macauley ever been known to resist a challenge.

He had kissed her before at the fair in Keswick but she had been somewhat tipsy, she remembered, and though she had been aware that she had not objected it was all rather fuzzy in her memory. Jonty was very attractive, he made her laugh as he was never serious. He was charming and, she was inclined to think since he had never given her cause to think otherwise, he was harmless and by that she supposed she meant easily handled.

"And what might that be, pray?" She said, smiling and leaning back against the tall rock where, she wasn't quite sure how, he had propped her.

"This." His open mouth was half an inch from hers. His breath was sweet and not the least bit offensive but suddenly, contrarily, she was offended. She put her hands against his shoulders and pushed but Jonty Singleton, though he was not a molester of women and indeed had never forced one in his life, since he had not needed to, was not to be pushed. His mouth, hot and vigorous, came down on hers and without thought she bit down on the bottom lip, bringing blood to it, blood that smeared her own mouth as well as his.

"So, that's it, is it," he snarled, his male body, fully aroused, and his hasty temper, which his father despaired of and his mother worried over for would it not get him into trouble, getting the better of him. "Well, we'll see about that." And with a strength gained in the wrestling matches where he pitted it against men as big and bigger than himself, he bore her to the ground. His mouth took hers again and his body strained itself against her, his knee between her legs.

For a moment she managed to free her mouth. She was as furious as he was and not the slightest bit afraid, for this was only Jonty Singleton and could she not get the better of him any day of the week. Indeed could she not get the better of *any* man.

"Get ... off ... me," she gasped. "Take ... your ... filthy ..."

She was astonished when Jonty's thrusting body "got off" hers but did so with a speed that was quite unexpected. She had thought she might have to shriek at him, claw at him with her nails, lift her own knee and drive it into his ... private parts, which she had heard was most effective in disabling an amorous man, though who had told her she couldn't at this precise moment remember.

She sat up and pushed back her flowing copper mane and was further amazed to see Jonty lying on his back a couple of feet away and, bending over him, his hands curled into fists, the most amazingly beautiful young man she had ever seen in her life. Jonty was handsome, big, strong, dark as a gypsy, but this man was just the opposite. He was tall and fair and loosely put together, his good breeding showing in every line of his body, the personification of the young English gentleman: the straight patrician nose, the long elegant mouth which even now had a half smile about it, fair hair falling in thick waves over his high forehead, blue, blue eyes that were long-lashed and set wide apart. As he looked at her quizzically she found herself, for the very first time in her life, wishing she was correctly dressed as a young lady of her station in life should be dressed. She felt a strange and perplexing need to act like a lady, to be as the young ladies, she was certain, would be in this gentleman's world.

"Is this fellow annoying you, madam?" he drawled. "Because if he is it would afford me the greatest satisfaction to give him the hiding of his life. I see you have blood on your mouth which is further proof that he is no gentleman."

He held out his gloved hand, taking hers solicitously, helping her to her feet, doing his well-mannered best, she could tell, to hide his own amazement at the sight of her trousered legs in their hodden-grey. His eyes wandered in consternation to her free-flowing hair which was tangled down her back to her buttocks and did their gentlemanly best to avoid the heaving swell of her breasts which flaunted themselves from the unbuttoned opening of her coat. He was a gentleman and gentlemen did not stare at ladies, but then, was she a lady, his speculative expression asked, or just a woman? And yet she could see the admiration, the interest, the excitement, the curiosity in his eyes and was glad but, dear God, why the devil hadn't she worn something decent, as her father described it, as indeed everybody described it instead of this outfit which she insisted on wearing on most days. But then if she had on the wide-skirted fashion of the day she would not have been up here on the fells and would therefore not have met this ... this dazzling creature, for he was certainly that.

Her own admiration and curiosity flowing free, she heard Jonty snort with disbelief then he sprang to his feet, and had the stranger not neatly side-stepped would have knocked him all the way down the fellside to Orthwaite. Jonty Singleton was the son of the man who had once been her own father's yardman and his mother a housemaid, neither of whom could read nor write, but Jonty had had the excellent education of Reed Macauley, of Charlie Lucas, of Will Lucas and was certainly not the hobbledehoy this handsome young stranger clearly thought him to be.

"What the bloody hell do you think you're up to?" Jonty spluttered, still, at this moment, in somewhat of a daze, since he could not believe what had happened. A moment ago he had been deep in the delights of Briar Macauley's body which had fascinated him for a long time now. He had sincerely believed that she was to allow, amazingly, the seduction ... well, perhaps not that, but at least some of the liberties his masculine senses had considered to be his. Now, from nowhere, this insolent fool – and he *was* a fool if he thought he could get the better of Jonty Singleton – had interrupted them. He had ridden up unheard on the handsome hunter which was cropping the grass nearby, and was actually smiling at what Jonty considered to be *his*.

"I'm not up to anything, my good fellow, unless you can call rescuing this lady from the unwanted embraces of an oaf such as yourself as being up to something."

Jonty's roar of rage echoed to the top of Dead Crags where Will lagged behind the rest of the hunt, stopping him in his tracks and even turning the heads of the huntsmen who were somewhere on the path in front of him.

"What the bloody hell?" one of them said, remembering perhaps that they had walked off and left Reed Macauley's daughter in the persuasive hands of a well-known philanderer. They could hear the screams of a woman which *must* be her and though the pack was ahead of them and presumably the fox, half a dozen of the most responsible turned back, running after Will Lucas as he cascaded down the fell.

It took several of them to separate the two men, one of them Jonty Singleton, the other a stranger, though the daughter of Annie Abbott, as many of them still thought of her, was doing her best to get them apart and had a raw swelling about her eye where she had apparently got in the way of an enthusiastic fist. She was sobbing, not, as they all thought, with fright but with temper, since in this, the first instance where she had wanted to make a good impression, she had failed dismally.

Chapter Five

They had named her Briar after a bright copper-red rose with very prickly stems, a particular favourite of her mother's, and by God could any name be more appropriate, her exasperated father was fond of saying, nay, thundering, as she stood before him in his study, which she did at least once a week, if not more, in the aftermath of some mad escapade or other.

"You're a female, my lass. A lad might get away with it but never a lass."

"Mother got away with it when she was a lass no older than me."

"We're not talking about your mother and you'll oblige me by listening and taking note of what I say. It's not the first time, lass, that I've had to speak to you about your outrageous behaviour and I'll not have it, d'you hear? Your mother is at her wits' end trying to turn you into a lady."

"I don't want to be a lady, Father," she had always answered mutinously, meaning it, but this time she said nothing, merely leaning her shoulder against the window frame and gazing in a somewhat disconsolate manner at some spot beyond the turning point in the gravel drive that led up to the front door of the house.

"Are you listening to me?" Her father reached angrily across his desk, opened the lacquered cigar box and took out one of his favourite cigars. Crossing to the fire which blazed in the grate he took a spill from the mantelshelf, and after putting it to a flame, placed the cigar between his lips, lit it and blew a perfect ring of smoke into the air before turning back to his daughter.

"It's that Singleton lad who eggs you on to this outrageous junketing, for it seems he's always the one who's involved and I shall see that it's stopped. Mind you" – his voice was bitter – "I don't suppose you need much encouraging. Like you, he's wild and feckless and if his father can't keep a check on him then I'll have to see what I can do. Perhaps if I were to whisper in his ear that the name of Reed Macauley carries a deal of weight round these parts he might do something about it. A bloody good hiding might do the trick. Are you listening to me, girl?"

"Yes, Father."

"Then you will oblige me by answering."

"I'm sorry, what was the question?"

If he was surprised by her listlessness where he would have expected defiance he did not let her see it, or if it showed perhaps she did not notice it.

"There was no question. I'm just telling you, and your mother agrees with me, that you are far too wild and have far too much freedom. The only thing to decide is what is to be done with you. You went too far this time, my lass. That black eye of yours is the talk of the parish, as is your behaviour yesterday. Everyone has heard the tale of Reed Macauley's daughter who had two men brawling over her."

"One of them wasn't brawling, Father," she said for-
lornly. "He was ... he was helping me ..."

"Helping you to do what, may I ask?" Reed Macauley's
face was as cold and hard as the stone from which his fine
mansion was built, just as though he sensed some mischief
brewing, which was usually the case with this headstrong
daughter of his.

"I had a ... a blister on my heel. I had removed my
boot and all he did was bend down to assist me to my
feet." Though she had been offended by Jonty Singleton's
treatment of her she was honest enough to realise that she
had brought it on herself and she knew if she told the exact
truth to her father he would go rampaging down to Upfell
Farm with his horse whip ready to lay it about Jonty's
shoulders. The blame did not entirely lie with Jonty and she
was aware that if hard feelings were aroused between Reed
Macauley and Jake Singleton there would be hell to pay.

"Then why in God's name did Jonty take exception to
that?" Her father was clearly suspicious, and astonished.

"I don't know. Perhaps he thought that the ... the
young man meant me harm and so ..."

"And so the pair of them set upon one another and
somehow *you* got that black eye. Who is this fool who
would get in Jonty Singleton's way?" For Jonty was
well known for his strength and courage in the field of
Cumberland wrestling.

"I don't know, Father." Briar sighed deeply and for the
first time Reed became aware of his daughter's strange
apathy and, what's more, the elegance of her afternoon
dress, eminently suitable, not only for the time of day,
but for a young lady of her class. It was of unwatered
moire, soft and light, the colour of old ivory which was
a marvellous contrast for her hair which had been brushed

and brushed by Nan and then plaited, the plait as thick as a man's wrist hanging down her back to her waist. It curled at the ends and was tied with a tawny waterfall of ribbons the colours of autumn. The bodice of the dress was tight and plain, sculpted to her magnificent breast and fastened in a row of tiny pearl buttons at the front finishing at a pointed waist. The sleeves were also close-fitting. The skirt was flat at the front but was intricately swathed to the back where it was draped over a small bustle and fell in what was known as a "waterfall back", a series of short flounces to the floor, each one edged with tawny brown velvet. Her ankle-length kid boots had been dyed to the same shade of tawny brown. She was as vivid as the autumn colours of the leaves on the trees, her skin warm and clear with a touch of peach at her cheekbones. She was the exact age and was as beautiful as her mother, his wife, when he had first met her, though Annie told the tale that he and his black mare had nearly run her down when Annie was a child and he an arrogant youth. What a woman she had been, and still was so was it any wonder that between them they had bred this lass whose will was as strong and defiant as her mother's had been at the same age. She looked quite glorious, he marvelled, or would have if her expression had been livelier, and for a moment or two Reed was of the opinion he would rather have his argumentative, self-willed, noisy daughter than this submissive young woman who leaned at his window.

"What's the matter, lass?" he asked her gently. "You know I'm only thinking of what's best for you. If only you would ... well, if only you would consent to wear what you have on today instead of creeping out in that ridiculous outfit that somehow or other you've found after I burned the last one."

Suddenly, as though she had heard the thoughts he had harboured before he spoke, Briar burst into an explosion of unparalleled joy, a joy so luminous it heightened the loveliness of her face.

"Dear God ... oh dear, dear God," she shrieked. She whirled away from the window, then back again, her hands to her cheeks, her eyes like golden stars. An expression of unbelieving rapture glowed about her, a radiance that lit the rather dim study like a candle and for a moment her astonished father thought she was about to break into a jig. She swivelled from foot to foot, capering, he could call it no other, like a child, into the centre of the room and then back to the window for another look at whatever it was that had caused her intense excitement.

"Oh, I mustn't let him see me peeking from the window. I must sit down, calm myself; he is a gentleman and will expect ... Oh, Father, tell me I look—"

"Lass, lass, what the devil's the matter with you?" Reed felt a prick of irritation and yet was not this lovely girl of his always the same. Lit up like a beacon over some bloody thing, like the tennis court that was to be put in, or cast down into despair over nothing at all. She had never had a moment's hardship in her life, just the opposite, for her mother, and himself as well he supposed, had indulged her from the moment she came into the world lustily yelling her displeasure. She was demanding, exasperating, intractable, brave as a lion and with a loving, generous heart which made those she offended forgive her everything. So what was she up to now? For a start she was dressed as a young lady should be dressed which was suspicious in itself and now she was flushed and luminous with some ... what the devil was it?

He moved to the window, ignoring Briar's pleas to come

away and was in time to see Percy, one of the stable lads, run round from the side of the house and take the bridle of a rather fine bay from a tall, well-dressed young man who had just jumped down from the animal's back.

"Well, lass, you evidently know him or you wouldn't be in such a dither. Who is he?"

"Oh, please, Father, don't let him see you spying on him," she begged from the other side of the room. "He's . . . he won't expect . . . faces at the window."

"If the day ever comes when I can't look out of my own damned window," her father growled, drawing furiously on his cigar, "I shall be ready for my grave." Reed Macauley's fine blue eyes, that even now in his fifties were as keen and sharp as when he had been in his prime, flashed their message of amazed disapproval at his daughter then turned back to study the stranger who was at this moment lifting a hand to knock at Reed Macauley's front door. "Who the bloody hell is he?" he demanded, peering at the young man who was now, having removed his hat, smiling engagingly at the housemaid who had opened the door to him.

"Please, Father, come away from the window," his daughter implored him, having sat down hastily in the leather chair beside the fireplace.

"What in hell's name is wrong with you?" but the knock at the study door brought his daughter to her feet again and her hand went to her mouth.

The door opened and Nan, one of the fresh-faced country girls Annie liked to have in her kitchen, popped an intrigued face round it. She had an air of excitement about her, smiling broadly so that her apple cheeks plumped up beneath her pale blue eyes.

"Yes, what is it?" Reed asked her. "Or should I say, who is it?"

"Oh, sir, such a lovely young gentleman and with such lovely manners. He said—"

"Bloody hell, girl, what's the matter with everyone today? First her" – nodding at his mute, frozen daughter – "and now you babbling like a fool and grinning like some monkey with a ... Who is it and where have you put him?"

"If tha' please, sir, 'tis Mr Henry Saunders an' I've put 'im in't drawin'-room. 'Ave I ter fetch Mrs Macauley only he said he wanted a word wi' you. That's what he said. A word wi' Mr Macauley."

"What about, for God's sake?"

"Nay, I don't know." But her smile twinkled in Briar's direction.

"Henry Saunders, do we know him?"

"Yes." A gasp, no more, from Briar, but both her father and the housemaid turned to her enquiringly, waiting for enlightenment.

"Well?" her father asked truculently.

"He's the gentleman who ... who helped me yesterday."

"So what's he after now? A bloody reward?"

"Oh, Father ..."

"Well, I suppose we'd better see what the devil he wants. Nan, you'd best fetch Mrs Macauley from wherever she is."

"In't parlour, sir, wi' Mrs Blamire."

"Well, ask her to come here and then ... well, I suppose we'd best see what this feller-me-lad wants."

"Yes, sir, an' will I fetch owt?"

"Owt?"

Nan, like the other servants in Mr and Mrs Macauley's employ, was well used to Mr Macauley's ways. He did his best to make them all believe he was a hard taskmaster with no time for anything that smacked of tender emotions but in reality he was soft-hearted and would give a helping hand to anyone who needed it from a hurt child or an injured dog to an old soldier knocking at the back door for a bowl of broth.

"Aye, coffee 'appen?" Nan asked.

"Aye, happen." He sighed as though he were hemmed about by idiots who were ready to hand out charity to all and sundry who passed his gate then he began to pace the carpet, waiting, as he had always waited and always would, for the footstep of his beloved wife.

The young man rose to his feet as Mr and Mrs Reed Macauley and their superbly beautiful daughter entered the drawing-room but Annie Macauley noticed that though his eyes went at once to her and Reed as was correct it took no more than five seconds for them to fly to Briar. She also noticed that, again correctly, he had laid his hat and gloves on the carpet beside his chair indicating, as was only proper by the rules of good society, that he expected to remain no longer than the fifteen minutes that should be allowed him. He had probably had to tussle with Nan who would have tried to take his hat from him, since this was a house in which trifling matters such as the rules and proprieties of the gentry were not applied.

"Well then, what's this?" her husband growled, ready to withhold his hospitality until he knew what the devil was going on. A perfect stranger coming into his home uninvited was not something he cared for.

"Sir, madam," the young man said, bowing his head after he had managed to tear his gaze away from Briar, whose own eyes were modestly cast down in the most amazing way. "I beg you to forgive this intrusion which I know is an unforgivable breach of etiquette since we have not been introduced but I felt I must come and enquire after your daughter's health."

"My daughter's health! Good God, man, what the devil . . ."

Annie Macauley put a soothing hand on her husband's arm, then moved forward with him across the luxurious carpet.

"That is most kind of you, Mr . . ."

"Saunders, madam. Henry Saunders, known as Hal to my friends," glancing again at Briar with a look that said that with all his heart he hoped she would be counted among that number.

"Mr Saunders, won't you sit down and tell us why you feel the need to enquire after my daughter's health. As you can see" – turning to smile at Briar – "she is blooming."

"Yes I can, madam, but . . . her eye . . ." And it was all there for anyone who cared to look, the interest, the attraction, the excitement effervescing inside him. His spectacular blue eyes, strangely like those of Reed Macauley, were brilliant with his feelings, for he was young and had not yet learned to hide them.

"Her eye will heal, Mr Saunders, won't it, my dear," she said to her husband, making nothing of the shiner that adorned her daughter's face.

"Hmmph," Briar Macauley's father said, a vast disapproval in his tone which asked what the bloody hell was going on here, and, Annie knew, he would voice it out loud if not cautioned.

"Then . . . ?" Her hand remained on her husband's arm as she led him to the sofa which stood at an angle from the merrily blazing fire. She indicated to Mr Saunders that he was to sit opposite. With some small movement of her hand she also indicated that Briar was *not* to sit next to their guest but was to find a chair elsewhere.

Mr Saunders gingerly sat, his reverent gaze slipping as though he could not help himself, no, not if he were put to the torture, from Briar's parents to Briar herself. Briar kept her gaze on the carpet, as modest as any girl of her age and station in life should be. Annie smiled but Reed did not though he consented to sit beside her. Annie rang a bell and when Nan came, bobbing a curtsey, she ordered tea. She kept up a polite thread of conversation in which Reed took no part. He lit another cigar without asking his wife's permission and when the tray came took a cup unsmilingly from his wife's hand, all the time his keen blue eyes never once leaving Mr Saunders's face. The young man, though it was obvious he was nervous, did not falter.

"And where are you from, Mr Saunders?"

"My father has a property in Gloucestershire, Mrs Macauley, but at the moment I am staying with my aunt and uncle at Middlefell Hall. Do you know it?" He courteously included Mr Macauley in the conversation, who at last deigned to speak.

"Aye, lad, we do. Would that be Sir John and Lady Sutton?"

"Yes, sir," Mr Saunders answered eagerly. "Lady Sutton was ... is ... was sister to my mother. My mother died some years ago and ... and my father married again. A ... a nice young lady ..." Here he stumbled somewhat, his smile tightened, his manner became awkward and his face lost something of its boyishness. But he went on bravely. "She is ... with child, my stepmother," not adding that she was a year younger than he was, "so when my aunt invited me to ... she is very kind, my aunt, I mean. I spend a lot of time at Middlefell Hall and she felt that with the impending birth I might care ... I have been here for three weeks now. I like to ride, you see, but when I came upon your daughter ..." His voice became indignant. Briar had as yet not uttered one word except to thank her mother for the cup of tea Annie handed to her. Briar lowered her face into her cup, trying to hide the bruise on her face, but it seemed Mr Saunders thought she was quite splendid, with or without the black eye. He looked at her gown with approval, as she had known even yesterday that he would, then turned back politely to his hostess.

"My aunt has expressed a desire to call on you, Mrs Macauley," not adding that he had driven his Aunt Agatha to distraction until she agreed to do so. It would not be correct for him, a guest in her house, to deliver an invitation to the young daughter of a neighbour, particularly as his aunt had admitted that she did not even know the Macauleys, but being a correct woman with a fondness for her dead sister's son she had finally given in. There was to be a ball the following week at Middlefell Hall in honour of his cousin Clarissa's engagement and it was to this that his aunt was to extend her invitation. But first, she said firmly, she must call on Mrs Macauley to ascertain if they were the right sort of people. Yes, they were well aware that Reed Macauley was a wealthy and influential gentleman in these parts with a hand in many projects but he was a *farmer* when all was said and done, and she would not invite him or his family to a ball to which half the gentry of Scotland, Cumberland, Westmorland, Yorkshire and Lancashire were invited. Not until she had made sure that this girl about whom her nephew eulogised and her parents were fit to mix in good company.

"Well, that is most kind of her, Mr Saunders. I'm afraid we live very simply here, and do not pay much heed to the conventions, but do tell your aunt I would be pleased to see her whenever she cares to call."

Hal Sunders was not sure what his aunt would make of this since in her world the paying and receiving of calls had a strict set of rules to which every lady in good society adhered, but it would have to do, for how else was he to make the acquaintance of this intriguing young goddess under whose spell he had fallen. When he had first seen her yesterday her beauty had distracted him from her unconventional dress and the man who had been ... well, he could only call it "handling" her. She had been struggling with the ruffian and all his young gallantry had leaped to defend her. He had been not exactly shocked, for he was not a prude, but surprised by the way she was dressed; but now would you look at her in her lovely gown, her hair restrained, her modesty and innocence, coupled with something else he failed to recognise, set his pulses racing all over again.

He drank his tea which Mrs Blamire, as had Mrs Macauley, thought more suitable for an afternoon social call, and with the help of her mother did his best to draw out the stunning young woman under whose spell he had completely fallen, but she would not be drawn, smiling when it was appropriate but allowing her mother to do all the talking. Both Annie and Reed Macauley were bewildered by her quietness, her decorum, her dreamy expression, her ladylike attention to her cup and saucer, and when their guest rose to leave, having got no more than a shy smile from her, she stood beside them and allowed him to bow over her hand and express the fervent hope that they would meet again soon, with no more than a nod of her head.

"Well, what the bloody hell was all that about?" her father demanded as Hal Saunders galloped off down the drive and on to the track that led down towards Hause. He took his wife's arm and followed his daughter through the wide hallway to the drawing-room. "And what, my lass, are you up to? I've never seen you so well behaved in my life."

"Leave her alone, Reed," his wife remarked mildly, for there was something in her daughter's manner that alerted her to the true state of affairs. When had Briar ever sat still for a whole half-hour while her mother entertained the ladies with whom she was acquainted? Indeed when had Briar even been present on these occasions? Tomorrow Reed and his shepherds would be up on the fells drafting the ewes for breeding and there was no doubt Briar would manage to go along, dressed, naturally, in the breeches and greatcoat, which had mysteriously reappeared, her hair in a wild tangle about her head, for she invariably lost the ribbon with which she set out. Her young, untrained dogs, Blackie and Bonnie, who had been named for two merle collies Annie herself had once owned at Browhead, would race beside her, getting in everyone's way, barking and nipping when they should be quiet and careful. Reed would come home in a tearing rage and the shepherds would take home tales of the maister's daughter who needed her behind tanning. But today she had been the perfect lady and it could only be because of the perfect gentleman who had called this afternoon.

✻　　✻　　✻

It seemed that Lady Sutton, after a successful visit to Long Beck, must have approved of the Reed Macauleys and their beautifully behaved daughter about whom her nephew couldn't stop talking, and the day after she called there came an invitation to the engagement ball of her ladyship's daughter, Clarissa Mary. Miss Sutton was to marry the Honourable David Cameron whose father had an estate in Scotland, an excellent marriage and one that accorded well with the Sutton family pedigree. Sir John Sutton had a hereditary baronetcy and Lady Sutton was from a titled family. Their son, John Peregrine Sutton, Perry to his family and friends, though somewhat wild, would inherit Middlefell Hall and the wealth – or what was left of it – that went with it so what the bloody hell were they getting themselves into, Reed demanded as he wrestled with his tie on the night of the ball.

"Darling, you can be wonderfully obtuse when you want to be," his patient wife said to him as she went to his aid. "This young man seems to have taken a fancy to our Briar and—"

"And what are his intentions? That's the question I want answered." But it was obvious that though he did not mean to bow and scrape to his hosts this evening, for he considered his background to be as good if not a shade better than theirs, he was not displeased. What had once been a plain farm, solid and built into the steadfast earth and rock above Bassenthwaite Lake, had long been renovated and built on until it could only be called a mansion set in vast gardens, with enough flowerbeds, lawns and rose arbours to prove to anyone that he could afford to waste land as he pleased. He had acres of ploughland, a peat moss, woodland, rough pasture, dozens of small fields, several farms, valley bottom land and even a moor over which he and his friends might shoot. His flock of sheep was over two thousand or more at the last count and his herd of cows were of the finest breed. He had a stable of which any gentleman might be envious, stocked with fine thoroughbreds. His family had lived at Long Beck since the days before the reign of James I and the union between England and Scotland. His forebears had been granted privileges, most of it land, when they had answered the call to arms to defend the borders between the two countries, which, he was willing to bet, was long before the high-falutin' Suttons had settled in the land of the lakes. His forefathers had been "estatesmen" or 'statesmen, wealthy yeoman farmers who were the most socially powerful in Cumberland, and he was not about to be looked down on by these titled folk who had condescended to invite the Macauleys to their ball.

"Well, promise me you'll watch that temper of yours, my darling. I know what you are like if you imagine you are being patronised."

"They'd better not try," her husband said ominously. "I know what these wild-riding, hell-raking young lordlings can be like and I'll not have it, Annie. I've seen the way they go galloping across any field they take a fancy to, flattening the crops and stampeding the sheep."

"They are not going to be riding down your crops or distressing your flock tonight so please, for Briar's sake, and mine, be polite."

"I am always polite," he grumbled, which wasn't true, as he took her arm and prepared to lead her from their bedroom. "Sweet Christ, Annie, you look no older than Briar in that frock."

"Frock . . . ?" She raised her eyebrows.

"Take it off and come to bed."

"Reed Macauley, this is your daughter's night so take your hand out of my bosom and come downstairs. The carriage has been waiting for half an hour and so has Briar. She's striding up and down the hallway like a caged animal."

"Dear God, would you believe it?"

Chapter Six

There were several gentlemen there that splendid evening
who were acquainted with Reed Macauley, mainly through
his business enterprises, those who lived in and around
Keswick, Carlisle and even as far away as Ambleside and
who, in various ways, had heard of this difficult daughter
of his, but could the exquisite, well-mannered creature who
danced with the nephew and the son of their host, and their
friends, be her? It hardly seemed likely, for Reed Macauley's
lass had been described as a hoyden, headstrong, wilful,
beyond even her father's power to restrain her. This young
person would have graced the drawing-room of any of the
privileged ladies who had been invited and who had heard
whispers of her indecorous lifestyle and, though they did
not know her personally, began to believe their husbands
guilty of exaggeration. She held her head high, her back
straight and yet not stiff. Her manner, as she was introduced
to the guests of Sir John and Lady Sutton, was pleasant
but by no means meek, and her smile polite. Where had
she come from, they asked one another, knowing of her
humble background, on her mother's side at least, and from
where had she inherited that air of polished graciousness,

of great breeding that said she believed herself to be no less than a duchess? It was well known that Mrs Reed Macauley, who was Macauley's *second* wife, had once been plain Annie Abbott from Browhead Farm, which was bad enough, but years ago she had borne an illegitimate daughter who had, thankfully, some said, died in an accident. The Reed Macauleys were not much in society, probably because of it, for though it was a long time ago such a thing was not forgotten. And then there was the question of his *first* wife, whose whereabouts were a mystery. There had been whispers of a divorce but then as none of them knew anything about such scandalous things and had certainly never known a divorced person they were none the wiser.

But this girl of theirs was superb, unique one could almost say, and though they let no one see it, her parents were astounded – and delighted – by her behaviour. Reed, who liked to dance only with his own wife, to Lady Sutton's vast displeasure, could not get over it, he told Annie, and if he had not ridden over with her in his own carriage from Long Beck to Middlefell Hall could well have believed that Briar was someone else's child.

"What's got into her?" he growled into Annie's ear as he led her in the waltz. It was many years now since the popular Austrian folk dance was adapted to what it had become, the waltz, for the position taken by the dancing couples – their arms about one another! – had so shocked the public sense of decorum that the waltz itself had not been accepted for many years. Which was another reason Reed Macauley danced only with Annie, since no other man was to be allowed to hold his beautiful wife in his arms, as the waltz demanded.

"I've never seen her so well behaved," he went on. "Not that I'm complaining, mind. This is how I've always wanted her to be. What's the point of having a good-looking lass like Briar if all she wants to do is gallop about the parish dressed in a lad's clothes. But I'm not sure I like the way that lad of Sutton's is clasping her. It's not decent."

"Darling, there are a hundred people watching them. What harm can she come to?"

"I don't care for him, Annie and that's a fact and if he doesn't . . ."

"The waltz is ending, dearest, and here comes Mr Saunders to claim her. He seems very smitten."

"Well, that's as may be but that lad of Sutton's is too wild by half for my liking and I shall say so if he doesn't stop mauling her about. By God, the pair of them look as though they are going to fight over her like two dogs with a bone."

"Please, Reed, Lady Sutton has seen them and is going across to smooth it over."

"*I'll* smooth it over in a minute and it won't be with a quiet word, I can tell you."

But he could not deny that his daughter, his treasure who came second only to his wife, his lovely Briar was the sensation of the evening, overshadowing to a great extent, which did not please her, the pretty Miss Clarissa Sutton whose engagement party it was.

"She looks well, Annie," he said with great satisfaction, meaning Briar, of course, "though that girl of Buchanan's is a good-looking lass. Takes after her mother, I suppose," peering short-sightedly across the room to where a handsome couple, both dark and striking, stood with a young woman obviously their daughter. Reed Macauley was a proud, even a vain man and though he wore spectacles in the privacy of his own home he would not dream of wearing them at a function such as this; consequently he often overlooked gentlemen he knew, causing offence at times.

"I think we'll go over and have a word," he continued. "You'll like Mrs Buchanan. The gossip is that she was a bit of a handful herself when she was young, like you, my darling," smiling fondly into his wife's lovely face. They sauntered arm-in-arm across the ballroom and when the introductions were made it was seen that Mrs Reed Macauley and Mrs Alex Buchanan, both the wives of wealthy businessmen, landowners with much influence in their respective parishes but really not of the class of the Suttons, were soon deep in animated conversation.

The Suttons had spared no expense. The ballroom was like a vast flower garden, hanging with exquisite arrangements of blooms which had been grown especially in their own hothouses for the occasion. Miss Sutton, as dainty and fragrant as a rose, wore a gown of delicate gauzy pink set about with silver ribbons and bows. Her dancing slippers were of silver kid and her blonde hair, fine and silky, had been arranged artfully to hide the fact that there was not a great deal of it. Her future husband, the Honourable David Cameron, whose credentials were impeccable, was heir to a hereditary chieftainship and a vast estate in Scotland. A most satisfactory match, it was agreed. A somewhat vapid young man with little or no chin and who looked as though he couldn't fight his way out of a paper bag, or so Reed whispered in an aside to his wife. Which could not be said of Sir John's own handsome son who, it was rumoured, was much addicted to cards and bare-knuckle prizefighting, to fast horses of the expensive kind, to pretty women and fancy wines. He certainly consumed a vast amount of champagne and seemed to consider that Briar Macauley was his own exclusive property!

At the interval the guests sat at small, round tables on fancy gilt chairs which did not please Reed, for he was heavy-set and liked a chair to be a chair. The buffet was excellent, served, naturally, with vintage champagne which Sir John had laid down when his son was born for his son's twenty-first birthday which had taken place four years ago, and on his daughter's birth for her engagement party. The supper table was placed in the dining-room, reached from the ballroom through open doors that folded back on themselves, and looked absolutely splendid, a work of art and a credit to her, many ladies told Lady Sutton. Again it was decorated with flowers, pink rosebuds, fern and trailing ivy, with scented candles set in silver candlesticks down the length of the table. The Sutton Crown Derby ware and silver cutlery had been got out, with the exquisite crystal glassware, and set along the length of the table was the buffet supper prepared by the Suttons' French chef. There was a boar's head garnished with aspic jelly, mayonnaise of fowl, hams, tongues, raised chicken pies, a galantine of veal, roast pheasant and larded capon. Lobster salads vied with prawns, all ornamented with cut vegetable flowers. Compotes of fruit, dishes of fresh fruit, bon-bons and tipsy cakes alternated with raspberry creams, fruited jellies and charlotte Russe, meringues smothered in whipped cream and strawberries, and all arranged so artistically the eye was as gratified as the palate. Lavish indeed but then this was a very special occasion, one not to be repeated for a long, long time, if the tales of the wild ways of Perry Sutton were to be believed. A feckless young man and one no woman would care to be left alone with if she was in her right mind, let alone marry, or so it was said. But he certainly seemed taken with the Macauley girl.

The Macauley girl! She sat at a table with what looked

to be a dozen young men about her, all of them begging to be allowed to fetch her a little more lobster, another glass of champagne, both of which she had scarcely touched, for though no one had ever told Briar that ladies were known for their birdlike appetites, she picked at this and that with a delicacy that would not have displeased any of the mamas at the party with marriageable daughters. She was dressed in white gauze over a skirt and bodice of embroidered white silk with tiny puffed sleeves and a low, square-cut neckline edged with silver rosebuds and sequins. It was styled in the very latest "sheath", copied, though no one was aware of it, from one that had been worn by Mrs Lillie Langtry and it hugged Briar's magnificent figure in the same stunning way it had hugged Mrs Langtry's, which her father was not awfully sure he approved of. The back of the skirt was draped over a very small crinolette, for the bustle was going out of fashion, falling in a train of flounces, each one edged again in silver rosebuds and sequins. Her vivid copper hair had been brushed up into an enormous coil in which silver rosebuds and sequins were scattered.

She had not seen *him* – she hardly dare speak his name – since the day he had called at Long Beck and though it was certainly not discernible in her cool composure as she had entered the ballroom – which had hushed almost reverently as she and her handsome parents stood for a moment in the doorway with their host and hostess – she could feel a dithering and churning inside her, just below her ribcage, a sensation of being thin-skinned, raw almost, so that she thought she might flinch if anyone should speak to her. Her mind was empty of everything but equal measures of fierce joy and fright when she saw Hal striding across the ballroom floor towards her. At his approach the joy bubbled up inside her like the champagne in the glasses held by the guests, for she had waited to see him again with bated breath ever since he had ridden away last week. Then the fright slid through her veins, freezing her to a state that was almost paralysis in case he should not be as she remembered him. It had seemed to her in the intervening period that she must have imagined him, and her feelings for him, made him up, since not once in her life had a man stirred her to more than a certain lazy laughter. He was a stranger to her. His background, his culture were totally unfamiliar to her so what was it that had drawn her so violently to him, and he to her?

"Miss Macauley," he said, and the hundreds of candles that illuminated the room glowed even more fiercely with the shared force of their desire. He was exactly as she remembered him. Tall and gloriously handsome in the black and white of his evening dress, a pleated shirt and a red sash that marked him as a man ahead of fashion. His hair, which must have begun the evening brushed and smooth, fell in a soft, pale tumble across his tanned forehead. His long, elegant mouth was smiling whimsically, probably at his own haste in reaching her, and he held his hands out – to the amazement not only of the assembled company but his relatives, and hers – to capture those she held out to him. It was an instinctive gesture.

"Mr Saunders." Her voice was soft with her love, though she did not recognise it as such, and her eyes smiled into his.

And so the evening began, an evening of magical wonder which was only interrupted when, reluctantly, he surrendered her to other young gentlemen who wished to take her round the floor.

"The devil take it, Hal, where in hell did you find *her*? She's the most glorious creature I've ever seen," Perry Sutton said to his cousin, his eyes narrowed with careful appraisal, watching as Job Buchanan, another young man with a reputation for fast living, whirled past with Briar Macauley in his arms. Perry's voice was rich with the long vowel-sounds of privilege but it held a certain coarseness as though he were speaking of an actress or a shop girl, of whom he knew a great many. "Mind you, that girl of – what's his name? – the chap talking to Miss Macauley's father ... right, Buchanan, would be worth investigating. What a matching pair of beauties they are, difficult to tame, wouldn't you say, but what a pleasure in the trying."

"That'll do, Perry," his cousin answered sharply, his eyes on Briar. "Miss Macauley's a lady, and so is Miss Buchanan."

"Really?" Perry drawled. "I've just been discussing her with Freddy Palgrave. Miss Macauley, I mean. Freddy's papa has property Kendal way and does business with hers. It's said she rides round in *breeches*, my dear fellow, and astride! Dear God, I wouldn't mind seeing that. I might make it my business to ride over to – where is it she comes from? – and make her acquaintance. But why wait? I think this dance is over and I'm having the next with—"

"No, Perry, you are not. It's mine and if I hear you say one more disparaging remark about Miss Macauley I shall be forced to give you a damned good hiding." The cold voice and eyes of his cousin caused Perry to splutter in astonishment.

"Hey, hold on, lad, there's no need to—"

"There is every need, Perry. Let me make it quite plain. You are insulting the lady I mean to marry, though if you breathe a word of it to Aunt Agatha, or indeed anybody, I shall personally see that you don't ride Oscar for a very long time." With that Hal walked away from his cousin, across the ballroom and bowed to the seated Briar.

The polished floor was filling up again, couples dipping and swaying, the gentlemen's stark black and white emphasising the vivid colours of the ladies. The orchestra, since this was such a special event, had been brought from Carlisle, and when Hal put his arms about her and began to lead her round the edge of the floor, couples already dancing seemed to scurry out of their way, since they were a beautiful pair and oblivious to others. The lilt of the music, the heady scent of the flowers, the enchantment of being in this man's arms, looking into this man's magnetic blue eyes, dazzled Briar and she could not speak. She had barely uttered two words to him, despite the half a dozen dances they had shared and he did not seem to mind. She did not even feel the need to be witty, nor her normal vibrant self.

"Will you ride with me tomorrow?" he asked her abruptly, startled and further charmed by the darkening of her eyes and the sudden flush of delight that tinted her skin.

"Of course, Mr Saunders. I'd be—"

"Hal, please."

"I'm not sure . . . ?" Again it seemed he was enchanted with her hesitation, since they barely knew one another and was it proper to be on first-name terms so soon?

"Please. And may I call you Briar?"

"Of course."

He smiled, his mouth curling up at the corners in a way that made her heart skid and thump in her chest.

"May I ask how you came by such a name? Not that it isn't ... lovely" — for how could anything about her be anything else? — "but it is unusual." His smile asked for forgiveness if he had overstepped the mark of good manners.

"My mother ... there is a rose, copper-coloured, of

which my mother is particularly fond. I believe my grandmother planted it many years ago but it has . . ."

"Yes?"

She dipped her eyes then glanced up mischievously,
herself for that moment. "It has very prickly stems." A
dimple appeared in her cheek then disappeared as she
became serious again. Being in love was a very serious
matter, at least for the moment. The candlelight danced
on her skin and dazzled her eyes and she thought she had
never been so happy in her life, wondering at the same time
where this unfamiliar woman who danced in Hal's arms had
come from. She knew it was totally unlike her real self who
had been left somewhere up on the slopes of Ullock Pike
but she knew, wondering how she knew, that she must be as
this man wanted her to be. As *she* wanted to be for him. Her
mother and father were watching her, she was well aware,
astounded by her ladylike behaviour and she wondered idly
who they were talking to: an attractive lady and gentleman
about her parents' age and a lively-looking girl, dark and
glowing with brilliant blue eyes and honey-coloured skin,
probably about the same age as herself.

She and Hal danced in silence, their bodies almost
touching, so close in fact that Lady Sutton hissed to her
husband that really he would have to speak to her nephew.
Just look at them, tranced the pair of them, she whispered in
his reluctant ear, since he and a number of other gentlemen
were about to escape the tedium of the dancing and retire
to his smoking-room for a game of cards.

"What d'you expect me to do, my dear? Hal is not my
son, he's your nephew and if he wants to make a fool
of himself over a pretty girl then that's his affair. He's
not a boy."

"That's just what he is, a boy. He's had no experience

with chits like that one and I'm only sorry I let him persuade me to invite these people. They are not our sort, John, and my sister would turn over in her grave if she thought I was allowing her son to become embroiled—"

"Oh come, Agatha! Embroiled, I ask you, and, besides, the family seems to be perfectly respectable and—"

"Now, perhaps, but I was just talking with Abby Armstrong and she tells me the mother's background is highly suspect."

Sir John, whose own son was not involved which would have been another matter altogether, and wanting to join his guests in the smoking-room, patted her arm and edged away.

"Now then, my dear, you're making a mountain out of a molehill. It will come to nothing, believe me. She is an exceedingly pretty woman and has caught Hal's eye. This time tomorrow he will have completely forgotten her."

Sir John was mistaken. His nephew presented himself the following day at Long Beck, so early Reed Macauley was seriously offended, not as he pretended at the unearthly hour but at the sudden premonition that he was going to lose his little girl, his only child, his treasure.

"He has only called to take her for a ride, my darling," his wife murmured soothingly, knowing what was in her husband's mind.

"Hell's teeth, Annie, we've only just finished breakfast. Has the young puppy no manners?"

"He has perfect manners, Reed. The manners of a gentleman."

"That's what I'm afraid of," her husband growled cryptically.

At Briar's frantic insistence her mother had produced from somewhere a dark blue riding habit with tight trousers beneath the skirt, not quite the modest outfit she desperately needed but adequate and decorous enough to please Hal Saunders. Certainly more so than her riding breeches and jacket! It had been made twenty years ago when her mother had married her father and, to please him, since she was not a horsewoman, she had promised to ride with him. She had worn it no more than a couple of times, long enough to convince her doting husband that what she said was true. She was not a horsewoman but her daughter was and the habit fitted her as though it had been made for her. It was daring, what with the breeches and all, but it was still out of date. Nevertheless it would do until Briar had her own made up. Her hair was plaited and twisted into a rope which Nan anchored to the back of her head and she had to be satisfied with that for there was no hat. Hal seemed to find it suitable which was all that concerned her. He would take her hunting one day, he told her, not specifying when or where that would be, expecting her to understand, which, of course, she did.

They rode together every day, climbing to the peaks of the bold Lakeland fells, their horses racing one another, Briar's dogs at their heels, sitting, when they arrived, shoulder to shoulder and looking out over the landscape where winter was rapidly setting in. Above them the fells wore their first cap of snow and below them a haze of mist and rain drifted across the lake. The feast of colour which autumn had created in the woodlands and on the fellside was dying and the far side of the lake was almost invisible. It was damp and growing colder as December drew on but they did not feel it and if they did it did not concern them. They were in love. It had not been spoken of, not in so many words but Briar understood this man she unexpectedly loved. She moved quietly through the days, waiting, astounding her family and the servants with her stillness, waiting for the day when Hal would *say* the words. He held her hand when they sat and looked out over the high, grey-green landscape and she knew, by his quietness, the intensity with which he looked about him, that he shared her primitive love for this hard, enduring earth interwoven with tumbling rocks and tumbling water. That though he might come from a flatter, greener, quieter landscape he could settle here with her. She did not even know *how* she knew these things only that something inside him spoke to something inside her, breathing the truth of it. She knew he had just finished his education at Cambridge, as young men of his standing did, but what he meant to do with that education she could not imagine.

"Briar . . ."

"Yes?"

"I'm the most unsettled sort of a chap without the least idea what I'm to do with my life."

"I know."

"Yes, I thought you would. You seem to . . . well, the thing is, I think you know *exactly* what you want."

Yes, she knew what she wanted. How could she possibly not know when this part of England was part of her and all she required from life was to be here, on this shelf of the fells with, somewhere, a place of her own and Hal by her side.

She waited.

"I'm not . . . I have no *work*. Oh, I have an allowance from my father, quite a decent allowance since he has money and property but there is . . . his wife and the child she is to bear him and so that must be considered."

He was telling her that he would never be rich. That he could not give her the luxury her father gave her and to which she had been accustomed all her life.

"Of course."

She sat quite still and watched a sparrow-hawk sketching a blur across the pale blue-grey of the sky. She had nothing to say. She could feel his eyes on her and the desire in him, hot and needing and it was echoed in her and she had time to wonder at the speed with which she had reached this moment in her life. A few weeks ago she had been heedlessly arguing with anyone who crossed her path, not knowing where that path would lead. Her father, her mother, Phoebe, Will, Jonty Singleton, Beth at Browhead had all felt the edge of her sharp-tempered tongue and now she was moving steadily towards a future which, back then, would have horrified her.

"Briar?"

She did not speak.

"Briar?"

She turned her face to his so that he could see into her eyes. She was *there*, her expression said, waiting, the woman he wanted, ready, should he speak the words, to be taken.

"I think . . ." His voice was unsteady.

"Yes?"

"We had better get home. It . . . it looks like rain."

She nodded submissively, controlled by the need to let him see, not quick-tempered, defiant, self-willed Briar Macauley, but the woman he wanted her to be, yielding, his to do with as he pleased.

"My love . . . my love," he suddenly breathed, then swept her to him and kissed her, the hard, crushing embrace of a man who can no longer hold himself back.

He kissed her again and again and she gloried in it, and

in the pain it caused her as he bore her back to the rocky ground. His kisses became deeper, more sensual, savouring her mouth and her skin, his hand moving to her breast, stroking it with enquiring fingers, teasing the rock-hard nipple through the silk of her shirt. She arched her back into the caress and his mouth slipped down until his mouth burned through the thin fabric of her shirt, his eyes glazed with wanting, beginning to make a faint sound in the back of his throat.

"Briar . . . sweet Jesus . . . stop me . . . don't let me . . ."

He was making a tremendous effort to edge away from her, appalled, as the gentleman he was, as the lady *she* was, that he might hurt her, straining, she could see it, to break the instant desire that had welled up in them both.

"Briar . . . what a brute I am. Dear God, I do beg your pardon."

"No . . . please, Hal, I'm not offended."

"What a marvellous girl you are."

"Not really," smiling.

"You are so beautiful." And taking her hand he turned it palm upwards and put his mouth to it, warm, tender, so that it melted the bones of her and made her shiver with delight. She was dizzy and bemused with her love for him. She adored him and would do or be anything he wanted or needed to please him. She knew he was hers, though he had not yet said so but that would come. She loved him and because of it her patience was, and always would be, unending. She loved him. It was enough.

Chapter Seven

"What's to do wi' our Briar? She come pickin' her way past here on 'er 'orse all dressed up in that frock thing lookin' like the Princess of Wales herself. I nearly dropped me bucket I were that flabbergasted. 'Good morning, Phoebe,' ses she, 'lovely morning, isn't it?' which it wasn't, but she were smilin' an' noddin', lookin' like the cat what's swallowed the cream. Now I've 'eard rumours . . ."

"They're true, Phoebe." Annie Macauley sighed deeply, leaning back on the settle. She had a cup and saucer in her hand which she placed on the seat beside her before bending to remove first one and then the other of the stout boots she had put on to walk from Long Beck to Browhead. Annie had never taken to horse riding, preferring to stride out as she had done as a girl. Years ago when she had lived at Browhead she and Charlie had captured a wild fell pony and trained him to the plough and she had ventured to ride on his back but she had always said she would rather walk than ride and she still did.

She put her feet on the small tuffet before the blazing fire, curling her toes in the heat. One of the kittens, of which there were usually half a dozen or so around the

97

farmhouse, jumped gracefully on to her lap and she pulled its ears and smoothed its fur until it purred in rapture.

"What! Tha' mean she's set on 'avin' this chap she's met at Middlefell Hall?" Phoebe turned to stare in astonishment at Annie, her hands still deep in the bowl in which she was mixing up a batch of scones. She was so astonished her hands actually became still, something that happened only when she was asleep.

"Well, she didn't actually meet him at the Hall, she met him at the hunt. She was with Jonty Singleton, it seems ..."

"Eeh, not again?" Phoebe was deeply shocked, for who in the parish of Bassenthwaite had not heard of the "to-do" at Keswick on the day of the Martinmas Fair.

"Yes, again. Reed was ... well, I've never seen him so livid, even in the old days before we were married when it was directed at me. Anyway, it seems Jonty was ... misbehaving."

"That don't surprise me."

"And this young man came to what he thought was the rescue but you know Briar ..."

"Aye." They both sighed sadly and deeply.

"It seems she didn't want to be rescued and there was a scuffle."

"Aye, I heard."

"Well, this young man, the one who was bent on rescuing her from Jonty Singleton's harmless attentions, appears to have fallen in love with Briar and his feelings are returned."

"But?" Phoebe was clearly perplexed, so much so that she sat down in the chair opposite her friend, her hands still sticky with the dough of the scones.

"He's a gentleman, Phoebe."

"So I 'eard."

"So nothing will suit but that our Briar becomes a lady, hence the riding habit. He's said nothing to Reed yet but it's as plain as the nose on your face what his feelings are for her so it seems that, with him being a gentleman, his intentions are honourable."

"Nay."

"You don't believe they are?"

"It's not that, my lass. I just canna see our Briar changin' from't tomboy she's allus been into one o' them ladylike creatures tha' see ridin' about in their carriages with their parasols ower their 'eads to keep off't sunshine."

Annie had a moment to wonder when Phoebe, who rarely strayed far from Browhead except to stand behind her stall at Keswick, caught a glimpse of these delicate ladies whom she seemed to despise. They certainly did not frequent the market.

"I know, lass, it's hard to picture but ever since she met him, and I must admit he's a likeable chap, she's been the model daughter Reed has always wanted. He's away at the moment visiting friends, this young gentleman I'm talking about, down south somewhere for the hunting, which is very different from ours, and she's moping about the place like a sick cat. I wish she'd put her breeches on and go for a gallop up Ullock Pike but she's determined to be as she imagines Hal – that's his name, Hal Saunders – would wish her to be. Next thing she'll be sitting in the parlour with a bit of embroidery in her hands."

"Dear Lord!" Phoebe was clearly appalled, not at the image of a young lady at her embroidery but at the idea of their Briar engaged in such a pastime.

"She's been brought up with men who are ... are single-minded, like her father and other farmers and

99

businessmen of our acquaintance. Somewhat ruthless and tough, with a purpose in life but this Hal seems to have none. He has an allowance from his father and a charming nonchalance to go with it. He's handsome, humorous, *very* likeable and seems kind but he's not . . . our sort. Oh, he's a country gentleman, used to country ways, riding, fishing, shooting, that sort of thing but not, I fear, as Charlie is, or Reed, or Jake Singleton. Not that I would want her to marry Jonty Singleton but Mr Saunders is gentry and we're not."

"Mr Macauley's a gentleman farmer an' not wi'out a bob or two."

"Aye, I know that but it's nothing to do with money, Phoebe. It's a way of life and I'm not sure our Briar is suited to it. The lady of the manor and all that."

Phoebe stood up and moved back to her scone mixture. She attacked it with vigour, knowing as she did so that the scones would be as hard as rocks, for this was not the way to go about it but unable, in her alarm for their Briar, to stop herself.

"What will tha' do then?" She gave the scone mixture another good wallop.

"What can we do? Reed's not against the match, if there is to be one, for the lad's from a good family, though whether he'll get much from his father's estate is doubtful as it seems there's a new Mrs Saunders, young and pregnant and if the child's a boy it will be bound to interfere with Hal's expectations."

"Eeh, I dunno what ter say."

"What is there to say, my lass?" Whenever Annie Macauley was disturbed she reverted to her old way of speaking. She was upset now, not for herself or her husband, for hadn't they got through a lot worse than this, but for her daughter. She didn't know why she had this strange and mysterious feeling that this was not the right thing for Briar, since the lad was all that any mother would want for a son-in-law. She could understand why Briar was so obsessed with him and that was another thing, using a word like *obsessed*. The lass was changed, which should please her, but it seemed to her she had changed for the wrong reason. Beneath this demure – dear God, when had she ever thought to use such a word in connection with Briar Macauley – this demure demeanour, the real explosive young woman was still lurking, not far from the surface and if anything should occur to . . . to prevent her daughter from getting what she longed for, yearned after, craved, what would be the outcome? She didn't want to see her lass suffer and yet what could she do, for there seemed to be nothing *against* the lad.

"He's such a pleasant fellow, Phoebe, you can't say he's not . . ."

"An' yet tha's not easy in tha' mind is tha', our Annie?" Phoebe lifted the scone mixture out of the bowl and slapped it down on the floured table top, pressing it into a round with the heel of her hand. She began to roll it out ready for cutting into shapes to go into the oven. Beth was down the field picking rushes which would be made into rushlights, for though the Lucases were not impoverished and could afford candles, or even the oil lamps that lit many homes, Phoebe could not throw off the old ways, the ways of the thrifty, and the rushlights were the cheapest way of doing so. Charlie and Will, after threshing the oats in the barn had taken them down to the mill to be ground, the cart which had seen many such journeys pulled by a horse that doubled up with the plough at ploughing time. It was three thirty and already beginning to grow dusk and she glanced out of the window, watching for her family.

Annie pushed the kitten to the floor where, offended as its kind often were, it stalked, tail straight up in the air, towards the basket where it and several others slept in the cosy nook by the fire. Annie pulled on her boots and reached for her warm, fur-lined cloak, throwing it about her shoulders, and for a minute Phoebe was transported back in time to the days when Annie Abbott, as she was then, had nothing to keep her warm but a threadbare shawl.

Phoebe was so troubled she allowed herself to be pulled into Annie's arms where her head barely reached Annie's chin. She loved this woman deeply and if Annie suffered so did Phoebe, but with a comforting pat on Annie's back she pulled herself away and her hands rose to fiddle with her hair as though Annie's embrace had loosened it.

"Nay, my lass, it'll be all right, see if it's not. It could be worse."

"How?"

"She could've tekken a fancy ter Jonty Singleton."

Annie was smiling to herself as she strode up the track towards Long Beck.

The scones were as dreadful as Phoebe had envisaged, though Charlie protested when she whipped one off his plate and threw it into the fire.

"What was wrong with that?" He was clearly astonished, not only by his wife's high-handed disposal of a perfectly good scone, or at least he thought so, but the way in which she seemed to be crashing around her kitchen, which was not a good sign. She was not exactly *crashing* but whatever task she set herself to she did it with such force it was as though she were mad about something and had to take it out on the inanimate objects she handled. She thumped down his big mug of tea with a thud that slopped the liquid over the lip on to her fresh white tablecloth. She flung the soiled dishes into the sink in such a way they seemed in imminent danger of breaking and gave the harmless tabby an irritable telling-off for getting under her feet.

"Lass, lass," her husband said at last. "Whatever's the matter? What's happened this afternoon to make you so . . . so . . ."

"So what, Charlie Lucas?" She put her hands on her hips and glared at him as though he were the offender and Will and Beth exchanged puzzled glances.

"Well, you're upset about something, that's very evident."

"And so would you be if you'd heard what I heard this afternoon."

"And what's that, my lass?" Charlie took her hand in his as she flounced past him and drew her to the table, urging her to sit down. "What is it?"

She didn't know herself why the news Annie had told her this afternoon should have upset her so. She loved Briar and she loved Annie. They were both as dear to her as her own family and though she would be the first to admit that Briar was a proper handful, a right little madam who needed her ears boxing, she could not bear to think that the child was doing her best to turn herself into something she wasn't. She had never met this Hal Saunders and he might be exactly the right man for their Briar, but what if he wasn't? She was worried and when Phoebe was worried about one of those whom she loved she became sharp-cornered, argumentative.

But Charlie loved her. He loved Briar and Annie and would understand how concerned she, Phoebe, was, and how the whole thing just didn't set right. Then again the whole thing might come to naught and she would have worried for nothing. Annie hadn't seemed too anxious but then she was married to Reed Macauley who would welcome an alliance between his beautiful daughter and a sprig of the gentry. Though Annie had been fiery-tempered as a lass she had mellowed in the years since she had married Reed and was inclined to let him have his way.

"Well . . ."

"Go on, love, tell us."

"'Tis Briar."

Charlie and his daughter were so focused on Phoebe neither of them noticed the sudden stiffening in Will's lounging figure. His elbows were on the table, which, if his mother had not been so absorbed with Briar Macauley, she would have berated him about. A mug of strong tea was between his hands and very carefully he placed it on the table.

"Aye, go on."

"Well, it seems lass has got 'erself mixed up wi't lad from Middlefell Hall."

"Not bloody Perry Sutton?" Will's voice was harsh, horrified and he half rose from the table.

His mother again failed to remonstrate on his use of what she called "language". "Nay, lad, not 'im. T'other 'un. Annie said 'e were cousin or summat."

"In what way 'mixed up'?" Charlie asked her gently.

"Oh, nowt bad, so Annie ses, but it seems lad wants 'er an' she wants 'im."

"But what's wrong with that, Mother?" Beth asked.

"Nay, they're not our sort, lass." Her mother contemplated her daughter, her face twisted into a frown. "Gentry they be an'—"

"But Briar's well brought up and Reed Macauley's very rich. And if the man is decent what is it you have against it?" Charlie asked. "Perhaps Briar needs someone . . . someone who's . . ."

Will stood up abruptly and pushed his chair back with a violence that astonished them all.

"Someone who's a gentleman, so-called, is that it?" His voice rose in a tide of something none of them recognised. To tell the truth he did not recognise it in himself, he only knew that the thought of Briar marrying some . . . some sprig of the gentry was anathema to him. He had watched her grow, seen the tantrums, laughed at her fierce temper, her vigorous determination to be herself, whatever that might be, and gone whistling on his way, for it was none of his concern what Briar Macauley did with her life. He was dallying with the idea of courting pretty Jenny Bracken whose father had a nice little farm just beyond Orthwaite. Not as big a farm as Upfell but prosperous. Jenny was an only child and with no sons to inherit Jacob Bracken would look with favour on a chap such as Will who could take it over when Jacob was six feet under. He and Jenny had exchanged smiling, speculative glances at several of the social gatherings that took place in the Lakeland dales. Auld Wives' Hakes when the farmers' wives would get together over a cup of tea and local gossip and Farmer Bracken's wife had brought her pretty, fresh-faced daughter when it was held at Browhead. There had been festivities at Christmas, at clipping time and harvest when a "kern supper" usually took place. Cards were played, three card lant, whist, brag and nap, but at many of the "merry neets" those who were invited often liked to listen to music, to dance, or just have a "crack" with their neighbours. Will and Jenny had partnered one another in the Cumberland Square Eight, the Long Eight, Ninepins Reel and the Circassian Circle which resembled Scottish country dances. It was said that the poet John Keats, when he witnessed the dances at Ireby, had remarked that the difference between our country dances, meaning those of Cumberland, and Scottish figures is about the same as leisurely stirring a cup of tea and beating up a batter pudding! After they had danced he and Jenny had walked down the path a little way into the privacy of a stand of trees, exchanging shy kisses and he had gone to his bed telling himself he could do a lot worse for a wife than Farmer Bracken's lass.

Now, for some ridiculous reason, the idea of Briar Macauley, whom he had always thought of with amused tolerance and a certain amount of affection, marrying a gentleman, marrying *any* man filled him with an explosive madness which, if he didn't get out of his mother's down-house, would burst from him in a torrent of chaotic outpourings.

With a sound that had no words in it, with no excuse, with no reason that might satisfy his bewildered parents and sister, he strode to the door, wrenched it open and flung himself outside, banging it to behind him. In the yard his dogs rose from the ground where they had been dozing, thinking he was about to put them into their corner of the barn where they spent the night, but with a muffled oath he jumped the wall in front of the house, landing in the frost-rimed field and began to run. Ewes, brought down for the winter, scattered in alarm. The dogs followed silently, ignoring the sheep, for they had had no orders from their master. They followed him down the long slope of the pitch-dark field and when finally he settled himself on the wall, his elbows on his knees, his head hanging down, they nudged against him in sympathy. He reached out a hand to each one in turn, smoothing their domed heads.

"Sweet Christ, what the hell's up wi' me?" he groaned out loud. The dogs looked up at him and old Don licked his hand, then laid his head on his knee.

She was walking, well, *strolling* along the bank of the stream at the back of Long Beck when next he saw her. There had been a light fall of snow during the night, no more than an inch or two and the hem of her skirt brushed it, leaving a faint tracery in its purity. For a moment he was not sure it was her, for when had Briar Macauley ever walked *anywhere* and worn a gown to do it in, then she lifted her head and smiled up at the ice-blue sky as though at some private thought that pleased her. She wore blue, the blue of the hyacinths that bloomed in the bowls his mother set in the window bottoms just after Christmas. Though he could not see the bodice, the skirt was simple without a train or a bustle but with a certain amount of fullness and as she moved a fraction of her snowy-white lace petticoat showed beneath the hem and the stout black boots she had on crunched in the frozen snow. Over the gown she wore a three-quarter-length sleeved cloak in the same colour as her gown, lined with a pale grey fur. The cloak had a high collar and the fur framed her face which was rosy with the cold. Her abundant hair had been plaited and looped to the back of her head, held there demurely with a knot of blue ribbons. Even from where he stood frozen next to the wall he was about to climb over, he could see the brilliant softness of her golden-brown eyes, the smooth texture of her creamy skin, and her beauty struck him a blow that dumbfounded him. His heart surged in shock, then raced along at a beat he had never experienced before, clattering in his chest, stopping his power to breathe for several long seconds.

It was her young dogs who alerted her to him and at once they began to race about the river bank as though beseiged by a pack of wolves, lifting their fine heads to the heavens and barking lustily.

She turned, not in apprehension, for Briar Macauley had found nothing in her life that had ever made her apprehensive, but with surprise. Was she not on her father's land, in her father's world where nothing could ever hurt her and if he had turned out to be a vagrant or one of the many itinerant travellers who crossed this bit of Skiddaw would she not give him the length of her tongue.

"Will Lucas, what the devil are you supposed to be doing, hanging about up there like a lost soul? Have you lost something? Your flock perhaps?" She smiled to take the sting out of her words, turning to stroll towards him and again he was struck by the dream-like quality of her movements. The dogs pranced beside her, baring their teeth, pretending to be fierce and he was amazed at his mind which, even at a time like this, had a moment to despair that she would ever train them to discipline. He supposed, his thoughts turning bitter, that she would have no use for such things now, now that she had taken up with a man whose profession was *gentleman*.

"Don't be daft." His voice was flat and expressionless.

"I was only joking, Will. You just surprised me that's all. I thought I had the fell to myself."

"Aye, that was obvious, way you were smiling at nowt."

Her mouth dropped open. She and Will had often tangled with one another, exchanging sharp words, quarrelling over nothing at all really, but it had all been done without malice. So what was wrong with him today? He was scowling fiercely, his brows dipping over his eyes, his mouth twisted into a grimace of what looked like distaste. He had his shepherd's crook with him and for some reason he gave the dry-stone wall a crack with it, almost dislodging the cam stone. Behind him she could hear the racket of his sheep which were being kept in check by his dogs and across the stream where she had walked were a couple of strays which he had evidently been about to retrieve.

"What's the matter with you, Will Lucas?" she asked him, her voice sharp, her own face beginning to frown. "Got out of bed the wrong side this morning, have you, or is Jacob Bracken proving difficult to woo? Oh, yes, I've heard that you have your eye on his lass."

Will leaped over the wall, barely touching it with one hand, and for a moment she felt compelled to back away from him, almost tumbling into the stream. He advanced towards her, and her dogs started a caterwauling that could be heard in the yard at Long Beck where Billy was currying Flame. He lifted a hand to shade his eyes, looking up the fell where Miss Briar, to the amazement of them all, had decided to climb.

"You keep your nose out of my business, my lass, and I'll keep mine out of yours. Oh aye, we've all heard of the fine gentleman" – his voice rose to a sneer – "who came a-courting at Long Beck but who's mysteriously disappeared again. What was it? Your father's high-handed refusal to allow his daughter to be married for his money, or was it you with your breeches and your hair flying loose which no *lady* would dream of doing. I see you've taken to putting on a frock and—"

"Don't you dare speak to me like that, you bastard."

"Ah, so Briar Macauley's still in there, is she? The one who insists that ladies, or rather *females*, which you undoubtedly are" – raking her body with insolent eyes – "should be allowed to use the same foul language as a man. Bastard, am I?"

"You're worse than a bastard, you're a jumped-up clodhopper who wouldn't know how to treat a lady."

"And I suppose that's you, is it? Some milksop ninny has flattered you into believing that you were meant to be a part of his fatuous way of life and instantly you put on a dress and drift aimlessly about."

"You don't know what you're talking about, you ... you ... It's you who are the ninny, gabbling on about something you know nothing about. He's a gentleman, d'you hear, a gentleman and he treats me—"

"Like a lady! Is that it?" He had advanced slowly towards her, his face twisted with his rage, his frustration, his need to hurt this woman who was hurting him so badly, not stopping to consider why he was in such pain. She refused to back up, even when they were standing almost nose to nose. Her dogs had run off, alarmed by the madness that swirled about their young mistress and the man she had met. They knew him but they were afraid of him and not old enough to stand and defend their mistress against what they recognised as real danger.

"Where is he then?" he snarled. "Where is this fine speciman of the English gentry? I suppose he got you up on the fell and seduced you into allowing him a few liberties and then—"

"Don't, Will, don't! He loves me, I know he does. Don't say these things." Tears stood in her eyes and she dashed them away with the back of her hand. "We love each other and we will be married."

Will's face spasmed. His eyes changed from the normal lovely silvery grey to the darkness of pewter, flat and dangerous.

"Really, and when is the wedding to be? In the spring perhaps, or perhaps never, which is more likely. His sort don't marry, Briar, at least only their own kind, though, of course, your father is very rich."

"You bastard . . . you evil bastard . . ."

"You've already told me that and—"

"He's away . . . hunting but he'll be back."

"Hunting, is it?" His voice was mocking. "Well, until his return perhaps, as he has already sampled it, you will not mind if I do the same."

Before she knew what he was about he swept her into his arms which were like a vice closing about her body. Her arms were captured at her sides. His mouth came down on hers, hard and oppressive, smashing her lips against her teeth until she tasted her own blood. His lips ground down, so painful she moaned in the back of her throat, then suddenly they parted, soft and sweet, and so did hers. His tongue touched hers delicately and to her utter horror she found herself respond, then he stepped back and laughed. A harsh and arrogant laugh that seemed to echo about the hillside.

"Well, well, what a lucky chap he is to have a woman as responsive as you, my pet. I wish him well of you, I really do."

He touched his hand to the tumble of brown hair on his forehead, turned and jumped the wall as lightly as a feather. The sound of his laughter followed him up the hill but his face, if she could have seen it, was not even smiling.

Chapter Eight

"I think it might be prudent to invite the Suttons to dine," Annie announced suddenly one evening, warily eyeing her daughter who was picking at the excellent glazed breast of lamb and Brussels sprouts which Mrs Blamire had sent to the table. The lamb, naturally, had come from the Macauleys' own flock, as tender and succulent as only good English lamb can be, and the sprouts, picked only that afternoon, were from Mr Owen's splendid vegetable garden. The Macauleys seldom ate a meal which their own land, their own dairy, their own orchards or their own greenhouses had not provided.

At once Briar's head rose from her indifferent contemplation of the food on her plate and her face coloured into a rosy smile.

"Oh, Mother, would you? Would you really ask them? D'you think they'd come?" She leaned forward, her elbows on the table one on either side of her plate, in her eagerness nearly knocking over the half-glass of white, chilled wine her father allowed her.

Immediately, though he had begun to frown, since he could see no reason why they should entertain a man who thought himself several cuts above the Macauleys of Long Beck and, more to the point, was of no earthly use to Reed Macauley in the world of business of which he was a part, Reed was distracted by his daughter's last question.

"Not come? Why the hell shouldn't they come? They might be the Suttons of Middlefell Hall but that doesn't mean they are anybody special, my lass. They imagined they were doing us a favour when we were asked to that affair before Christmas but I only went because you wouldn't let me alone until I agreed." His tone was ominous and he attacked his lamb as though it had personally offered him an insult.

"But you would have no objection if I were to invite them, would you, darling? After all we should return their hospitality and to make it seem more—"

"More what?" Her husband's tone was truculent, since he could not see why they should need a reason to entice the Suttons to his home.

"Well, less . . ."

"For God's sake, woman, what are you trying to say?"

"As though . . ." It was not often that Annie Macauley was lost for words – ask anybody who had known her years ago when she was a young woman – but she was well aware of her daughter's feelings for this undeniably suitable young man and the only way to . . . well, *bring it along*, meaning the romance, the courtship, whatever it was going to turn out to be, was to bring her family and his, meaning his aunt and uncle, together. Briar was watching her, her eyes wide, her breathing almost at a standstill, the *new* Briar, that is, the one who desired nothing else but to be what Hal Saunders wanted her to be, waiting for her mother to persuade her father that this was the right way to go about it.

"We need to let them see that Briar is a perfectly acceptable young woman."

"Perfectly acceptable!" Reed roared. In the kitchen where she had just returned after serving the main course, Nan cocked her head and raised her eyebrows. Mrs Blamire was stirring the custard which would be served with the apple and raisin tart she had in the oven. Her hand stilled and she turned to Nan while the other maidservants lifted their heads from the different tasks Mrs Blamire had put them to, waiting for Nan to speak.

"'Tis about them Suttons," she whispered, just as though those in the dining-room could hear her.

"What?"

"About them comin' ter dine."

"Eeh, never."

"Aye. Master's in a right to-do."

"Why?" Then, as though she had just become aware of the eagerly listening ears about her, Mrs Blamire signalled to Nan that they would continue their conversation later.

In the dining-room Reed glared at his wife, then at his daughter, for who in the wide world could not believe that his beautiful, clever lass, for she was clever if somewhat unconventional, was not fit to be allied to the very highest in the land. Well, perhaps unconventional was too mild a word, for he knew the lass was inclined towards downright and undisguised rebellion. She had a wilful determination to have her own way which a husband, or any of the society from which Hal Saunders came, would not find acceptable but despite these flaws in her character she would be a prize any man would treasure.

Reed Macauley's temper, easily slipped, was straining at the leash and knowing she was the only one who could soothe it to manageable proportions, his wife put a hand on his arm then slid it down to clasp his fingers. His face was still furious, wanting to think ill of all those who believed themselves better than him. He wanted to curse, to explode with resentment, which he did whenever he felt like it, and since they were all used to it, even the servants in the kitchen, they showed no surprise nor offence when he did. But today, perhaps because it was his wife who was asking it, or perhaps because he knew that Briar wanted this and if there was anything he could get her he would, he clamped his mouth shut.

"Go on," he almost snarled.

"This . . . this young man . . ."

"Who's buggered off God knows where."

"Reed, please. It is the hunting season and in the hunting season this is what young gentlemen do."

"They want something to occupy their bloody time *properly* instead of traipsing up hill and down dale after a poor beast who's done them no harm." His wife smiled quietly to herself since the fox was a predator Reed himself did his best to eradicate.

"And tell me this," he continued. "If the lad's so taken with our lass what's he doing down in damned Gloucestershire?"

Briar stood up and began to stride about the room, swirling her skirts and kicking them to one side at every turn. Her amber eyes flashed, her breasts heaved and her bright copper mop of curls rioted in a wild explosion about her head and down her back, freed by her nervous energy from its neat ribbon. If the truth were told she had the same question in her own mind that her father was asking. Why, *why*, after all that had passed between herself and Hal, had he gone off with his cousin with no more than a brief note to tell her that he would be back soon. She had understood, or so she told herself then, but it was becoming increasingly difficult to keep up, indeed to remember that perfect certainty that had filled her heart and stilled any anxiety she might otherwise have had.

"Darling, you know what these people are like," her mother was saying, "hunting and shooting is part of their lives, indeed they have not much else to fill it. They have no need, as you and I did, to earn a living, to prove ourselves, to build up something in our lives, something important to us, so they spend their days doing these, what are to us, strange things and . . . you know what I'm talking about, so don't pretend you don't. You liked Hal, didn't you? And for goodness sake, Briar" – turning abruptly to her daughter – "sit down and eat your meal. It will do no good striding about like that. He will come back, my lass, so stop fretting."

For a brief moment Briar halted in her circle about the table then sank down again into her chair. "Mother, how do you *know*? Why did he not speak before he went?" Her voice ended on a kind of wail, for Briar Macauley was not accustomed to being thwarted, to being denied something for which she longed with all her young and aching heart.

Her father looked at her in astonishment. This child of his had cared for nobody in all her young life. Not deliberately unkind but unthinking. Now she was in a state of the jitters because some lad who she had taken an inexplicable fancy to had ridden off to hunt the fox, which he and she knew very well was what gentlemen of his sort did.

"Perhaps he felt the need to talk to his father, darling," her mother said soothingly.

"About me, d'you think?" Briar asked hopefully.

"Well, it would seem to me that if he intends to ask for you—"

"*Ask for her?*" Reed clattered his cutlery to his plate, making a great deal of noise so that Nan, who was just entering the room to clear the plates, since Mrs Macauley had rung the bell, melted slowly back into the hallway, closing the door behind her.

Again Annie sighed and took her husband's hands between hers.

"My love, you must realise that—"

"Stop trying to soft-soap me, Annie. I don't know what this young squireen's up to but he'd better not be trifling with my daughter."

"Which is why it might be a good idea to entertain the Suttons." She held on to his hands lest he wrench them irritably away, since she knew he would rather sit comfortably by his own fire with her beside him than make polite conversation with strangers. "And if we are to entertain we might as well invite others. How about the Buchanans?"

"Well, I suppose if it has to be somebody it might as well be a man with something to say for himself other than the balderdash those friends of the Suttons prattle on about."

"And I like Mrs Buchanan. Shall I ask Alice?" turning to Briar who was sitting on the edge of her seat as though waiting for her parents to cut through all these trivialities and get to the important question of Hal Saunders.

"Yes, if you want." Who cares, her manner said.

"Very well, I'll send invitations, but don't be disappointed if the Suttons make some excuse not to come."

"They can please themselves," her husband said ominously. "Now ring the bell again and get that bloody girl in here to clear these plates."

*　　　*　　　*

Briar ordered Percy to saddle up Flame and went wildly racing up the steep fell to the front of Long Beck, her dogs at her heels. At the top she looked out over the folds of the fells below her, Jenkins Hill to the south, Little Man to the north, leaning her back against the cairn piled there, keeping in the lee to avoid the biting wind which crept into the bones of her. It had, for the Lakelands, been a mild winter without the usual blizzards that made life so hazardous at the beginning of each year. Today there was snow up here, a couple of inches deep, but not enough to impede her mare. It spread an icy beauty on the land, the land stretching upwards to the peak of Skiddaw, down the vast slopes and deep crevices, the narrow ravines and grey pitted rocks, the rich copper of the winter bracken until it reached the denuded black tracery of the trees of Dodd Wood and the strip of velvet green beside the deep blue waters of Bassenthwaite Lake. There was smoke rising as straight as a pencil from the chimneys down in the dale where it was sheltered and here and there a huddle of slate-grey roofs where farms lay. Shadows the colour of ripe plums lay on the snow where the sun did not reach and all so heartbreakingly beautiful she felt it reach down into her soul. Blackie and Bonnie huddled against her, both of them attempting to lick her face, whining softly as though they sensed her unhappiness. She wrapped her arms about them and tucked her chin into her collar, brooding on the whereabouts of Hal Saunders, her lovely, usually vivid face sombre with unaccustomed sadness.

*　　　*　　　*

Hal Saunders presented himself at Long Beck at the beginning of February. It was a measure of his love for the daughter of the house that though the season, the hunting season that is, which was the unchallenged and exclusive heritage of the leisured classes, was only halfway through, he had left it to come north.

"Is Mr Macauley at home?" Hal asked the trim house-maid who answered the bell, smiling in that shy, good-humoured way he had, bringing an answering smile to Nan's face.

It was a Sunday and Nan knew that her master was at this moment ensconced in his study, yesterday's *Times* in his hand, his feet up to the roaring, leaping fire and would any moment be ringing for her to fetch him coffee. This was a time in the week that he savoured, for though a farmer worked seven days a week her master was a gentleman farmer with men to labour in his stead and his Sunday morning with his newspaper was sacrosant, even from his beloved wife. Mr and Mrs Macauley were devoted to one another and what's more they allowed that devotion to be seen by others no matter where they happened to be. It could be quite embarrassing sometimes for those who were not used to it, a secret smile that hinted at something that only they knew about, the touch of a hand across a table, even in company, but no matter what, even Mrs Macauley kept away from him on his Sunday morning perusal of *The Times*.

"Well ..." she answered hesitantly, keeping a firm hold on the doorknob as though afraid Mr Saunders, for she knew who he was, might try to storm the hall.

"It is of the utmost importance ... er ..."

"Nan, sir, but I'm not sure Mr Macauley'll like bein' disturbed."

"Perhaps if you were to tell him that Mr Saunders is here to speak of . . ."

Hal moved awkwardly from one foot to the other since he was very nervous, and had even removed his hat as though Nan were a lady. He was determined to see Reed Macauley no matter how much it might annoy the father of the girl he loved, but he could hardly tell this maid what his business was about. She was standing her ground, though her rosy face was soft, eager to do what he asked, but at that moment light footsteps sounded on the parquet flooring which edged the carpet of the hall and Annie Macauley appeared behind Nan. Nan sighed with relief.

"Who is it, Nan?" Her mistress smiled, a smile that deepened with evident pleasure when she saw Hal.

"Why, Mr Saunders, how nice to see you. Won't you come in? I'm afraid Briar has gone . . ."

Hal's face, from its smiling effort to persuade the maid to allow him in to see the master of the house, became stern, guarded, almost grim as though the task he had ahead of him was something that was not to be trifled with.

"I'm not here to see Miss Macauley, madam. I wish to speak to Mr Macauley, if he could spare me a moment."

"Come in, Mr Saunders, please. Nan, take Mr Saunders's hat, if you please and then fetch coffee to my parlour."

"Mrs Macauley, please," Hal said desperately as though not another moment must be wasted, not another moment squandered in case his courage deserted him.

"I insist, Mr Saunders." And Hal had no choice but to follow her across the fine carpet, his boots clattering and scattering snow on the parquet flooring as he allowed her to lead him into a small, cosy and littered room at the end of the hallway. It was homely, a room where work was evidently done, not the neat and tidy place where a lady might engage in embroidery or watercolouring, but with books, some opened lying face down, with what looked surprisingly like basket weaving. He had never seen a lady of his acquaintance weaving baskets and his face must have revealed his surprise. Annie saw it and smiled.

"I used to make swill baskets when I was younger, Mr Saunders, and sell them from door to door. I can't seem to get out of the habit, not selling them, of course," she added hastily, "but my servants find them useful for various purposes. The best swills will hold water and I pride myself that mine are the best."

"My word," he said faintly. "I had no idea."

"No, I suppose not. I have not always been the wife of a man with means, Mr Saunders. Once I had to earn my own living. This" – indicating the coracle-shaped basket – "was one way of doing so and now and again I get the urge to see if I still have the knack."

Hal didn't know what to say. It seemed that the girl he loved and whom he was determined to marry came from an extraordinary family. He sat where she told him to, perching on the edge of a sturdy, well-cushioned chair, listening with amazement as she beguiled him with tales of when she was young, no older than Briar it seemed. She had had a sheep farm; she had worked on the fells, she had tramped to places he did not know such as Whitehaven, where she had sold the swills she had made, the woollen stockings she had knitted and the besoms – sweeping brushes – and indeed earned an honest penny wherever she could, little knowing, either of them, that Annie Macauley's daughter would have been mortified to hear what her mother was divulging to the man Briar loved. But then, much as she loved him, Briar knew Hal Saunders hardly at all.

"Now then, Mr Saunders, I believe you want to see my husband?"

"Indeed I do, Mrs Macauley." Hal was mesmerised by this splendid, astonishing, still lovely woman who was Briar's mother, a woman who had had to fight every inch of the way to be as she now was. He felt the wonder of it surge through him, for if the mother was so magnificent surely the daughter would be the same.

His feeling of hopeful bemusement was somewhat diminished by the sight of Reed Macauley's frowning impatience as he rose from his comfortable chair by the fire.

"Good morning, sir," he said, his voice steady none the less.

"Is it, I hadn't noticed," his host growled. "Well, I suppose you'd best sit down, lad. I hope this won't take long. I've things to do that won't wait, but I suppose I'd best give you a few minutes or my wife won't like it." A fond expression flitted momentarily across his face as he lowered himself into the chair from which he had risen. "Well?"

"Well, sir, it's—"

"Cigar?"

"Cigar, sir?"

"Do you fancy a cigar, lad?"

"Thank you, no, I really want—"

"I think I'll have one if you'd be so good as to pass me that box on the desk."

"Of course, sir." Hal sprang to his feet, lithe, supple, young, eager, and behind his back Reed smiled, for wherever he came from the lad was good-natured. He took several long moments to light his cigar and get it burning to his satisfaction, then he turned a calm expression on Hal and, as though he hadn't the faintest idea why he had called, politely asked him to state his business.

It took him no longer than five minutes to decide the boy was genuine. A bit too well-mannered for his liking, and by that he meant easy-going, but then he *was* a gentleman and Briar would soon knock him into shape. He had spoken to his own father, he said, who was to increase his allowance so that he might support a wife as he should, and Reed let him babble on, watching him, liking what he saw and heard, though he wouldn't for a gold clock have told him so.

He interrupted him only once.

"And where are you to live, my lad, tell me that, for I know that if you took our Briar from this land of the lakes she would fade away. Oh, I know she has plenty to say about adventure and travel and all that sort of twaddle but it's all hot air, you must realise that."

"Oh, I do sir." Hal smiled. "I knew from the start but I didn't voice it. She thrives here since she has her roots planted exactly where they are most needed. She gets nourishment from the good soil, the high fells, the becks and tarns and the constant sound of tumbling water. She's a woman of the north, a country woman but then I'm a country man and I reckon we'll do well together. Until we have decided where we are to settle permanently my aunt has offered the gatehouse at Middlefell Hall. It is quite spacious and I believe Briar will be—"

"You mean to wed her then?" Reed blew smoke lazily into the already smoke-laden air, his face stern as though he had previously believed the lad was toying with his daughter's affections.

Hal looked amazed. "Wed her? Of course I mean to wed her. Why do you think I'm here?"

"Nay, you haven't said yet, and our Briar's not mentioned it."

"Mr Macauley, I felt it was only right that I ask your permission before I approached Briar ... Miss Macauley."

"Well, you have it, for if I said no my lass would make my life hell and I must admit that lately I've a yearning for the quiet life. I had enough of the other with her mother."

"D'you mean ...?"

"Bloody hell, lad, how many times do I need to say it? Go and find the lass and get it over with and then perhaps we can all have a bit of peace."

The dinner party that Annie had spoken of a few days earlier became another engagement party to which not just the Suttons and the Buchanans were invited, but half of the Vale of Borrowdale, Keswick and Bassenthwaite and not many of them were gentry. Men, farmers with whom Reed shared a "boon clip" in midsummer, when every sheep farmer helped out another. Men such as Charlie Lucas whose plain-spoken wife Phoebe was Annie's closest friend, Jake Singleton, the small sheep farmer from Upfell, of whose sweet-natured wife, Maggie, Annie was inordinately fond. Beth and Will Lucas, Jonty, Davey and Anne Singleton who were their offspring. Reed's solicitor, his banker, all the men with whom he did business and their families, packed into his luxuriously appointed dining-room whose table was capable of seating forty guests.

Long Beck was situated on a crest of the land, the grounds falling away from it like the wide tiers of a crinoline skirt, lawns and flowerbeds and elaborately clipped box hedges with here and there the white gleam of a garden statue. There was a summerhouse, a covered trellis walk festooned, in season, with hanging baskets filled with flowers, and at the back of the house the cleared land where the tennis court was to have gone. Its future was now uncertain. Soon there would be a carpet of daffodils beneath the trees that Reed's grandfather had planted to protect the house from the fierce winds, forsythia, lilac, massed hedges of rhododendron. There would be roses and carnations later but now the house and gardens bloomed with coloured lanterns which led from the start of the track, up behind Browhead and Upfell to guide their guests to Long Beck itself.

The hall was wide, vivid with blooms from Mr Owen's hothouse, and warmed with an enormous fire which flickered its dancing flames on the polished wood panelling. The folding doors between the drawing-room and the hallway had been opened out, the room's huge windows allowing guests to look out on to the illuminated gardens. There were wide sofas in deep blue velvet, cabinets of dark wood, glass-fronted to display the fine porcelain of Coalport, Meissen and Sèvres which several Long Beck mistresses, including the present one, had collected. The enormous dining-room was high-ceilinged and on the panelled walls were two oval portraits, one of Annie Macauley painted soon after her marriage to Reed, her magnificent shoulders framed in a cloud of gauze, her vivid copper hair, caught carelessly with a bright green ribbon, curling in profusion about her face and down her back. The other was of Briar as a young girl. The artist had tried to paint her as a young girl should be, demure, virginal, wide-eyed, but her spirit, which would not allow such a deception, shone out wickedly so that her tawny eyes, so like her mother's, had a fire in them that was quite glorious.

Everywhere was displayed the evidence of Reed Macauley's wealth: crystal lamps, silver, porcelain, delicate ornaments which had come from the four corners of the earth, crafted by famous names and all treated with careless indifference as though, should one break, another would replace it at once.

It was evident that the Suttons, Sir John and his wife, their daughter and her recently acquired fiancé, thought it all too ostentatious for words, though naturally they were too well bred to say so. They had come for the sake of Lady Sutton's nephew, her dead sister's only child who was to marry the daughter of the house and though they deplored the union, no matter how rich the bride-to-be's father, they were prepared, for Hal's sake, to see it through. Only their son, who the moment his foot was inside the door made a beeline for the stunningly attractive Alice Buchanan, thoroughly enjoyed himself. He would not, naturally, in the normal course of his daily life mix with any of these yokels but he made himself pleasant to Maggie Singleton and Phoebe Lucas, to their daughters Beth and Anne, before sweeping Alice Buchanan into a dark corner of the hall where he tried to kiss her. He was rewarded by a slap to his head which made his ears ring and himself even more determined to pursue her until he had what he wanted.

The only ones unaware of anything, of anybody, of any undercurrents, of any offence given or taken, were Briar Macauley and Hal Saunders who drifted through the evening on gossamer wings of enchantment, dancing only with each other, wrapped in one another's arms in what Lady Sutton obviously considered quite an indecent manner, their young bodies swaying to the lilting rhythm of the music and their own hearts.

Chapter Nine

She was surprised the next morning when Nan came to her room to tell her that the young gentlemen were here and asking for her.

She had slept well as the young do, no matter what the circumstances. She had been excited, quivering with radiant happiness after bidding Hal and his somewhat straight-faced aunt and uncle goodnight at well after midnight. She had been positive that she wouldn't sleep; how could she with so many fascinating, exhilarating, brilliant thoughts swirling round her brain like silver fishes in clear blue water? But the moment her head had hit the pillow she had dropped into what was almost a state of unconsciousness. No dreams, even of Hal, and she had woken at seven, refreshed and ready for the day which would surely contain Hal.

Ringing the bell for Nan she had sat up against her pillows, smiling and stretching, drinking the hot chocolate that Nan, smiling herself, brought her. Her curtains were drawn back on the sunny, frosted day, a vivid winter blue sky. Her eyes had become unfocused as she dreamed her dreams so that when Nan came bursting in again, her rosy face even rosier with excitement, for a moment she was confused.

"Young gentlemen?"

"Lass," said Nan, beginning to laugh, "what young gentleman is it likely to be but Mr Hal. And that there cheeky young varmint with the glint of pure mischief in his eye who—"

"Perry?"

"None other."

"But . . ."

"Are tha' ter see them or not? Nay, not dressed like that, my lamb. They're ter be off ridin', ses they, an' will tha' come with 'em. Tha' pa's with 'em, glarin' at their muddy boots on 'is carpet."

"Oh Lord, Nan, quick, get me dressed." Since she had met Hal she had made a determined effort to curb the language Will Lucas had complained about but which until recently she had been unable to stop. "Lord" and "Dear heavens" were all she allowed herself now except in the most extreme moments. "Just brush my hair and stuff it in the net. That's it and reach for my hat, will you?"

Dressed in the smart riding habit, correct in every detail, that she had had tailored for her by her mother's dressmaker in Keswick, she floated down the stairs. Three faces were turned up to watch her and on those three faces were three very different expressions. Hal Saunders's expression was soft, gentle, rapt as though he looked at an angel, his love for her shining from the brilliance of his blue eyes. It said that he loved her beyond all reason, without reservation, without qualification, purely and yet intensely. She saw it, recognised it and something inside her slipped, dissolved into a tenderness so exquisite it pained her to draw breath. She could not tear her gaze from his and both of them for that moment were unaware of the other two men. Perry was grinning engagingly, for this escapade was of his making but his grin drifted away as though even he knew he was in the presence of something not quite of this world. Something special. Reed Macauley, having known as great a love as his daughter shared with Hal Saunders, though somewhat more tumultuous, for his Annie had been wild, turned away and fumbled almost blindly with the handle of the breakfast-room door. There was the sound of housemaids in the drawing-room and beyond in the dining-room where they were cleaning and polishing and returning it to its usual perfect order after the party the night before. One was singing softly and another called out that someone should see to that stain on Mrs Macauley's rug.

"Well, you'd best come in here," Briar's father said grimly, acting as though these two young pups had got him out of his bed and he was not at all pleased about it. "My lass can't go gallivanting off without something inside her. Ring the bell, Briar, and have some coffee sent in and happen some toast."

"Oh, Father, I'm not hungry," Briar complained, her hand reaching of its own accord for Hal's which was waiting for it.

"Then you'll not go, my girl. Eat something or get back to your room and these two lads can do as they please." They were not his responsibility, his manner said, but she was.

They ate the hot buttered toast Nan brought in and dutifully sipped the scalding coffee while Reed Macauley hung broodingly over them. His daughter was still his daughter never mind the family ring that had once belonged to Hal Saunders's mother and which was now on Briar's finger. He was not at all sure he liked the idea of his lass going off with these two young squireens but she was to marry one of them, a fact declared the night before in front of dozens of friends and neighbours so what harm could come to her. Hal Saunders was a sound young man, sensible, a gentleman and though Reed was loath to give up his protection of his daughter to another man he would have to accept that this was the way of it.

They escaped at last, galloping madly along the track that led from Long Beck and down the relatively gentle slopes of the western side of Skiddaw towards Latrigg. They reached Keswick, still urging their mounts at a breakneck speed so that folk going about their daily business turned in alarm at the sound of the horses' hooves on the road.

"Where are we going?" Briar shouted, her face rosy, her tawny eyes like iced gold, her lips parted across her white teeth. Flame's nose was but an inch from the tail of the bay Hal rode and leading was Perry, wildly excited about something, his fair hair in a disordered mop of curls about his head.

"We're going to meet Alice Buchanan." He allowed her to draw up beside him where the track widened, turning to grin over his shoulder and Briar had a brief moment to dwell on the wonderful, magical life she would lead with this man beside her.

"Alice?"

"Perry arranged it last night. He's very smitten with her, didn't you notice?"

"No, my darling, I was too busy being smitten with you."

"If we weren't going so fast I'd kiss you. As it is we're going to lose Perry if we don't keep up."

Alice Buchanan was dressed in a duplicate of the outfit Briar herself wore, though she had abandoned the hat, a smart bowler, with which she had set out, tossing it to the back of a gate as she left the stable yard. She was waiting at the side of the road at a place called High Bridgend, no more than a cottage or two at the north end of Lake Thirlmere, which was approximately halfway between Ambleside where her family lived and Long Beck.

"Good morning, Briar," she called, holding the reins of her restive and obviously well-bred roan. She nodded pleasantly at Hal and gave Perry a conspiratorial smile which was as vivid as it was mischievous. "I'm sorry I didn't have the time or the opportunity last night to discuss today but Perry is very demanding and ... well, you and Hal had no time for anyone but each other. I do hope you don't mind being roped in for what Perry calls 'a bit of fun'. He's a rogue, really he is." She turned her gaze on Perry and it said that whether a rogue or not she liked what she saw.

"No, I'm glad to be included," Briar said, though to tell the truth she would rather have gone riding alone with Hal. Still, she was rather intrigued by this handsome girl whose search for something other than sitting at home with her embroidery matched her own.

"I had the devil's own job to escape the chains my papa would like to fasten me in but here I am." Alice smiled a brilliant sapphire-blue smile and in her eyes something said that she was as ready to be friends as was Briar. "Perhaps you could come over to Hollin House for a few days before you and Hal are married. It would give us a chance to get to know one another without these gentlemen forever butting in. We could go into Ambleside which has the most fashionable little milliner's who makes hats that are the very latest thing and Mother's dressmaker has lately come from London to set up her own business. She trained in Paris and, since you will need so many new gowns and pretty things for your . . . Dear God, will you listen to me babbling on when these two are patiently waiting to climb to the highest peak."

"Not patiently, my pet," Perry quipped, "though I must say the thought of all those pretty things is most intriguing."

"Oh, ignore him, Briar. Do say you will come."

"I'd love to." The thought of having a friend who was as outgoing and as fun-seeking as Alice Buchanan was very appealing. All her life she had had no close friend but Beth Lucas of whom she was very fond, but Beth was dutiful, placid, content to live her quiet life at Browhead with no thought for the "fun" that Briar sought. Briar knew that should she be in trouble, of any sort, Beth would be the first to rush to help her. But this Alice Buchanan was lively, adventurous – hence this ride out this morning – and though she lived twenty miles away from what would be Briar's new home they both rode decent horses and would soon cover the distance. Of course, once she and Hal were married they would be able to entertain their own friends and the idea that one of them would be Alice Buchanan pleased her.

The two young women eyed one another approvingly until the heavy sighing and fidgeting of Perry Sutton broke the spell.

Above them towered the peak of Raven Crag to the west and Great How to the east and stretching as far as the eye could see to the south lay the beautiful water of Thirlmere. It was heavily wooded on both sides of the lake.

It was a perfect winter's day, hard frost, bright sunshine and the snow that had fallen a few days ago, a mere inch or two, was crusted and crackling under their feet as they left the track and began to move up among the trees. They walked their horses, four handsome young people who knew, particularly the gentlemen, that by the precepts of the day, at least in their society, they were doing wrong, for these were gently bred young girls from good families and should not go about unchaperoned with gentlemen who were unmarried, and not related. As they left the cover of the trees the tussocks of heather sparkled and winked and a small flock of Herdwicks scattered as they approached. High up, over two thousand feet, the peaks of the fells, Dale Bottom, Bleaberry Fell, High Seat and Raven Crag, were deep in snow but here it was almost mild.

Alice Buchanan, Ally to her friends and family, was deep in conversation with Perry who was making her laugh, a laugh that rang out, echoing from crag to crag and disturbing a fine stag that had come down from the snowy heights to feed, but the foursome did not see him, for each man was absorbed with the lady of his choice and each lady enchanted to be that choice.

A waterfall thundered down a deep ghyll to the left of the sheep trod they were on, the white water as pure as untrodden snow but lit by a rainbow, its colours clear against the water. Briar and Hal halted for a moment, their hearts stopped by the beauty of it, silent, hands clasped as she leaned against his shoulder, then they moved on following the other two who seemed oblivious to anything but each other. For some reason, though it was not her nature, Briar felt a prick of alarm, not for herself, since was she not with a man who loved and respected her, a man her father approved of, a man whom she was to marry, but alarm for the careless Ally who seemed unaware of anything but the charm of laughing Perry Sutton.

"When was all this arranged?" Briar asked Hal, wondering what Mr Buchanan, who had looked as fierce as her own father, would think of his daughter dallying up here with Perry Sutton whose reputation was not the sort any father would care to have his daughter's name linked with.

"Last night. I think you and I have been invited to act as chaperones, though I must say she seems to have taken a great liking to you, but I don't think Alice cares a jot for chaperones. She's like a wild, untamed bird who has been caged and is now let loose which is why Perry is so taken with her." He smiled down into her pink-cheeked face, his eyes telling her that he was glad she was more decorous than the wild Ally. Again, as in the past few weeks, Briar was bewildered by the change in herself. Once she would have been as delighted as Ally to be the focus of a mercurial young man's attention. It was different now, *she* was different now. After all she and Hal were betrothed and her father knew she was with him.

For a brief moment she felt her heart move frighteningly in her chest for fear Hal should ever learn that only a few weeks ago this was the sort of adventure she herself would have gloried in. In fact she had, with Jonty Singleton, enjoying every moment that was a defiance of the rules of the world she lived in.

She stopped and Hal stopped with her, and stretching up she placed a soft kiss on the corner of his mouth, moving into the shelter of his arms, tucking her head beneath his chin so that he would not see the expression on her face.

"Darling, darling, I love you," he murmured against her hair, for, like Ally, she had abandoned her hat.

"We will be married soon, won't we," she whispered,

afraid suddenly that something appalling would come along and take away this wonder that had been given her. Snatch it out of her grasp before she had a firm hold on it.

"As soon as I can persuade your father." He strained her to him and she could feel the maleness of him hard against her and at the same time was aware he was making a decent attempt to keep some space between them.

"We'd better catch the others up," he said, his voice harsh with his need and obediently, like a child, she put her hand in his and, catching the reins of their mounts which had begun to wander, they moved up the trod after Ally and Perry.

When they reached the shelter of a high group of scattered boulders Perry pulled his black hunter into the lee of them, fastened the animal to a firm rock and removed the pouch that was slung to his saddle.

"Sit down, if you please," he commanded, and when their horses tethered, they were seated, their backs to the rough stones, he opened the pouch and produced a bottle of wine, a cooked chicken, fruit, cheese and a freshly baked loaf of bread.

"A picnic!"

"Yes, I persuaded Cook to get it together, even to baking the bread last night, then raided the pantry and father's wine cellar."

Briar had the thought that whatever Perry Sutton wanted from life, even something as simple as this picnic, there would always be some woman ready to provide it. She smiled at Ally who winked audaciously and Briar relaxed, since it seemed her new-found friend was aware of what she was thinking. She accepted the glass of wine Perry handed to her and nibbled on a chicken leg, and when Perry and Ally wandered off on their own she forgot her misgivings,

misgivings that were really not hers to harbour, turning into Hal's arms to receive his kisses.

They were married on the first day of April and, as the bride had been certain it would, the weather gave them one of those perfect spring offerings that catch at the heart. Around the little church of St Bridget's, close to the sparkling blue waters of Bassenthwaite Lake where her parents had been married, spears of late crocus, yellow, purple and white, threw a drifting carpet of colour which vied with the proud trumpeting of wild daffodils and the delicacy of primrose. It stretched down to the lake's edge, inviting the guests to wander there after the service as though the day, the wedding, the radiant couple who were now man and wife, had cast a magical spell on even the most earthbound. Or perhaps it was merely the happy realisation that winter and the late snow which had held back the blossoming of the spring flowers had finally gone. The sunshine had warmth and guests who sauntered in it seemed inclined to smile and nod and exchange a greeting with other guests who they would not in different circumstances have even deigned to notice, since there was a great mixture of the classes.

The senior Mr Saunders and his new wife were not present since Mrs Saunders was considered to be too near her "time".

The bride wore white lace and a cloud of embroidered chiffon, white rosebuds in her hair, looking quite magnificent. White roses were heavily massed at the altar and baskets of white rose petals were scattered at the bride and groom's feet as they drifted back down the aisle, gazing into each other's eyes as though they were totally alone.

She wore diamonds at her neck and in her ears, a gift from her doting father who, at the last moment before handing her over to Hal Saunders, had frowned, wondering perhaps whether he was doing the right thing, stepping back to take his wife's hand for comfort. The church bells pealed across the water as Mr and Mrs Saunders came out of the porch and into the clear, spring, sunshine-filled air to climb into the carriage lined with white silk and driven by high-stepping white horses. There was to be a wedding breakfast at Long Beck, a marquee on the lawn with a bride cake which weighed two hundred pounds. The two bridesmaids, dressed in the palest ice-blue silk, were Beth Lucas and Alice Buchanan with whom the bride had struck up a promising friendship, both of them being kissed enthusiastically by Perry Sutton who promised to be a nuisance. The bride and groom scarcely noticed, for it was very evident, at least to the bride's father who had once had similar feelings himself, that they could not wait for the whole thing to be over so that they could be alone.

Now that the ceremony was reverently done with there was a certain division of ranks, the landed gentry, friends of the Suttons, installing themselves at one end of the marquee, the working men, many of them wealthier than they were, at the other. Sheep farmers discussed lambing as they drank Reed Macauley's expensive champagne, businessmen spoke of the rising cost of this and that, and Reed Macauley's labourers, servants and farm workers celebrated raucously their little mistress's nuptials in true country fashion, ready, if given the slightest encouragement, to see the young couple to bed and throw the bride's stocking as it had been done in the old days.

A carriage took them to the gatehouse at the top of the lake where Middlefell Hall was situated, the gatehouse that was to be their home, for neither of them could, at that moment in their lives, concern themselves with wedding journeys. She had been to Paris and London, as he had, and they could see no reason to go again, they told one another, since it only meant that it would postpone the moment they both longed for: the moment when they would climb into the snow-white, lace-trimmed bed that awaited them at the gatehouse. She and her mother, with Phoebe Lucas to help them, had turned the somewhat drab rooms into a home that was light and airy, their choice of colours the palest peach toned with beige, soft green and delicate cream; thick carpets, deep comfortable chairs fit for a gentleman to sink into, silkwood furniture gleaned from the attics of Long Beck and polished to a gleaming shine by Phoebe, flowers in crystal vases, watercolours on the wall, and plain velvet curtains to shield the young bride and groom from the eyes of the world.

Even Lady Sutton had approved!

Briar turned to wave at the great gathering of people who stood on the forecourt at Long Beck to see them off, again the gentry somewhat languid, looking about them in amazement at the enthusiasm shown by the lower classes. She would be happy now for ever, the expression on her face said. She and Hal stood in the centre of the world that was to be theirs, an enchanted silken world of jewel colours and textures. The day had turned cold now as evening drew near but she did not feel it, for was her hand not in Hal's, warm and joyful, desiring nothing more than to be there for ever. She had nothing more to wish for.

The lamps had been lit at the gatehouse by the house-maid, who bobbed her curtsey to her new mistress, her smile shy and respectful. Their new home stood at the entrance to the great park in its own walled garden. It was only temporary, that was understood, for Reed Macauley was eager to build his daughter and her well-born husband a home that befitted their station. Hal had nothing but his allowance from his father which was enough for their needs but certainly not sufficient to build the house that was due Briar Macauley, or Saunders as she was now. The gatehouse was small by comparison to Long Beck but, thanks to Annie Macauley, comfortably furnished. A dining-room of good proportions, a drawing-room with low oak beams and thick stone walls, two large bedrooms above, one of which would be shared by the women servants, a modern kitchen, thanks to Reed this time, though of course his daughter would never enter it except to give orders to her cook, to the shy housemaid or the skivvy, all three of whom her mother had found for her. There was a man to see to the horses and another to tend the pretty garden though it was discovered that, surprisingly, Hal was fond of gardening!

In the rich firelight he undressed her and himself and for several minutes they knelt before the fire and adored one another, adored their nudity, adored the freedom of their unfettered limbs, and when at last his hand reached out to touch her breast the sensation of his skin against hers was so exquisite she moaned softly in the back of her throat. She put out her own hand to smooth tentatively the silken width of his shoulders, letting it trail down the coarser feel of his chest with its scattering of fair hairs, and with growing desire they moved towards one another, their hands eager, greedy now, for the sensations they had longed for ever since that day of the fox-hunt on the fells. She watched, fascinated, enraptured, by the emotion her body visibly caused in him. He entered her at last, his body tight inside hers and her body closed on his, holding it, holding him fast, fusing them together with love and need and self-abandonment so that at last she was totally his, he was wholly hers. He groaned and trembled with the helpless passion she had aroused in him and so great was her need to intoxicate him her own fulfilment did not concern her.

"Briar, I love you ... I love you," he groaned, falling heavily to lay his fair, tumbled head on her breast and she held him, loved him, soothed what seemed to be his pain until he slept. She was content.

It was the same the next morning, almost before it was light, their bodies easily aroused to sensuality and tenderness, and this time he held himself back until that sweet filament at the centre of her womanhood, which she had felt stir the night before, came alive and flamed through her and she called out his name as though in a dream.

"So, wife, you're a woman now," he told her smilingly, knowing he had made her so and he was content.

They spent the next seven days, which was the time Ally Buchanan and Perry Sutton had decided was long enough for any newly married couple to be totally alone, walking hand in hand first through the meadows which were white with daisies, with blue violets and silver-white lady-smock, then up through the spring forest at the back of Middlefell Hall. The light had a translucent quality at this time of the year which touched the lovers, one so fair, the other so fiery, to a beauty which no one beheld but the lovers themselves. The beeches and hornbeams which had been bare all winter appeared to be a bright and glorious green with their new leaves. Thrushes sang and the ground beneath the trees was turning to the palest blue as bluebells thrust up their spears. Primroses tufted under the hazel trees and Hal pulled his wife down into the softness of them to make love to her, knowing there was no one to see but the blackbird with its liquid song who swung upon the branch of an ancient oak.

They walked every day, though Flame and Max, Hal's grey, dozed in the stables for want of exercise. On horseback they could not pause every step or two to touch hand to cheek, to lay mouth to mouth, to kneel down in the heather to study with delighted enchantment the nest of a red grouse in which six young cheeped.

When they returned to their home he would carry her up to their bedroom, to the delighted embarrassment of their housemaid, bending his head to negotiate the low doorways.

"Let me get out of this gown first . . ."

"I'm not sure I can wait that long, my darling . . ."

"Yes, you will and you must remove your boots at least . . ."

"Undress me, sweetheart, I have a fancy to own a slave . . ."

And she would do so, layer by layer until he was naked, turning back the cover of the deep feather bed which the housemaid, whose name she had forgotten, had scented with lavender. Under his loving gaze she would undress herself, slowly, languorously, shaking loose her hair, offering herself to him inch by inch until he reached out and pulled her on top of him.

"You're a wanton, Briar."

"Is that bad?"

"No, it's glorious."

"I love you."

"I love you," they would tell each other, entranced almost to the point of what could be described as a drunken state, drunk on love, on need and on the wonder that out of all the world they had found one another.

Chapter Ten

Hal Saunders astonished them all one evening by leaning back in his chair and asking casually of his father-in-law, "Sir, would you say I had the makings of a farmer?"

Briar and Hal were dining, as they did now and again, with her parents, driving over from Middlefell Hall gatehouse to Long Beck in the carriage her father sent for them. The nights were drawing out now and they could have ridden Flame and Max for the journey up to Long Beck but Reed Macauley had, over the years, developed a liking for the custom of dressing for dinner when he and Annie had company and, as he growled to his daughter, who would have been happy to sit at table in her riding habit, she could hardly ride her mare in a full evening gown, could she? She looked particularly well this evening in a sheath-like dress of gold silk which was draped at the back into a small bustle. It was low-cut, revealing the fine, creamy smoothness of the top of her breasts, with short sleeves and a well-fitted bodice. Her hair was artfully arranged to give a look of rumpled curls tied up casually with gold ribbon. The weeks she had spent as Hal Saunders's wife had smoothed the sharp corners from her and though she had always been quite exquisite, now she looked sleek, polished, her tawny eyes soft, narrowed, glowing with sensuality so that her mother would not have been surprised to hear her purr like a well-satisfied cat. She herself knew the feeling well!

They all looked up in astonishment, their soup spoons halfway to their mouths and at the back of the smaller but still very elegant dining-room where the family ate when alone, Betsy and Ellen, who stood waiting to serve more soup to the master, who had a hearty appetite, exchanged a sharp look. Betsy, who had taken over from Nan – gone quite recently to take up residence at the gatehouse as the new Mrs Saunders's lady's maid – and who was now head parlour-maid at Long Beck, raised her eyebrows, for there was no gentleman of her acquaintance less suited to be a farmer, in her opinion, than Mr Hal. He liked country pursuits, true, and in the weeks he and Miss Briar had been married had been known to shoot, fish, take part in fox-hunting, on foot and mounted, tramp the fells with his new bride and generally idle the days away in the pursuit of country gentleman pleasures. It was said he had a flair for gardening and had been seen with his shirt sleeves rolled up, turning over the soil in his own bit of garden, to the amazement of those passing by who had received a cheerful greeting from him. He was to plant, God love him, his own vegetables, and there was talk of asparagus, artichokes, celery, leeks, onions, peas and cabbages. There was a small orchard he was tending where he was to grow apples and pears and plums to fill the pies his wife's cook baked for them. He had a fondness for roses and carnations and dahlias and meant to make his wife a garden fit for a princess, which he obviously thought her to be. Such a lovely gentleman, ready to smile and have a bit of a chat with anyone, no matter what their rank, and every one of them had grown so fond of him but, Landsakes! a farmer he was not.

The master choked on his soup, blinked, then put his spoon carefully into his soup bowl before wiping his mouth with his napkin and sitting back in his chair. Miss Briar's face was a picture and it was evident this was the first she'd heard of it, and the mistress sighed and shook her head, for if Mr Hal had some plan in his mind that he hadn't discussed with Miss Briar there'd be hell to pay. At least it would have been so in the past.

"Did I hear you aright, lad?" the master said disbelievingly. "A farmer! What in God's name put that idea in your head?"

"I'd like to know that too, my darling," Miss Briar said, her voice deceptively mild. At once her husband turned to her and took her hand, smoothing the back of it with his thumb and as though she were an animal that has been spooked by something but was now in hands she trusted she relaxed and was even ready to smile. Honestly, the look that passed between Betsy and Ellen said, could you believe the change in their little mistress and all because of the young man who was gazing at her as though she were the most incredibly precious thing in his life, which it seemed she was.

"It's an idea I've had in my mind ever since we married, my darling," he told her earnestly. "It seems I'm not one of those chaps who can sit about and drink claret or do nothing with their days but spend them shooting at everything that moves, not that I don't enjoy it," he added hastily, "and I'm particularly fond of riding to hounds or even walking with the fox-hunt. But you know how partial I am to seeing things grow, though where it come from I've no idea since I'm not from farming stock, but I thought, since you are and have farming in your blood, I mean, and seem to ... to know something about it, we might ... well, let's hear what Mr Macauley thinks." He turned courteously to his father-in-law still holding his wife's hand as though afraid, should he let go of it she might explode into laughter, or dismay, or anger.

"Well," Reed Macauley spluttered at last. "I admire your zeal in wishing to do something worthwhile with your life but, lad, you've not the faintest idea what farming's about. You can't lie in your bed until you feel like getting out of it nor look out of the window and decide you don't fancy the look of the weather so you'll stop indoors."

"I realise that, sir," Hal said somewhat stiffly. "But surely determination and a love of the countryside count for something. With your guidance ..."

"And my money, likely."

"Sir, if you are to be offensive before I've even outlined my ... our plans, then there is no more to be said."

"Nay, lad, I'm not meaning to offend but it's true, or have you a few thousand tucked away you've said nowt about?"

Hal looked ready to spring up and stride from the room but this time it was Briar who held on to him, her hand soothing the hurt pride, the smarting indignation that stiffened the muscles in his face.

"I have nothing but my allowance, as you well know, sir," he said at last through tight lips, "but you tell us you are determined to build my wife and me a house, a home of the sort to which she is accustomed and, though I am quite happy in the accommodation I have provided for her, and I think she is too, I have said nothing on the matter. Now, when I suggest you spend your money on something that will not only allow me to earn a living, and give us both a challenge in life, you are against it."

"Nay, lad, have I said I'm against it?" Reed asked grimly. "You take offence where none is meant, but you must be prepared to admit that, since it is my money you are asking for, I have a right to speak up about it?"

"Yes, sir, I admit that, but it seems to me you don't mind spending your money on Briar or myself as long as it's something you think we should have, not something *we* want."

"Does Briar want it? She's had little to say on the matter."

Reed turned enquiringly to his daughter, his face unsmiling, and only his own wife knew he was actually made up with the idea and also that his son-in-law had just gone up several degrees in his regard. He had expected and even been prepared to like supporting his engaging young son-in-law for his daughter's sake. You had only to look at the full and contented look about his lass to realise that it had been put there by Hal Saunders. Though he was, or rather he considered himself to be, detached from sentimentality – except where his wife was concerned – his heart was overwhelmed by what he knew was the perfect joy in which his daughter lived, and it was thanks to this young man who was ready to glare at him, unafraid and defiant. He liked Hal. Who could not help but like him? What sort of farmer Hal Saunders would make was open to comical conjecture, but at least the lad was eager to have a go at something and not sit on his behind like many of his kind did and could you not but admire him for that?

"Darling," his wife said soothingly, "don't you remember the days before Briar married Hal when she drove you demented begging to be allowed to train her sheepdogs?

And remember how she was always willing to go up on the fells with the men when it was lambing time."

"Aye, I do." Her husband's voice was irritable. "She was a right bugger at times but there was no need for her to do it, you see, Annie."

"Not like when I was a lass?" She smiled lovingly and the two maidservants exchanged another look, for if anyone could sweet-talk the master it was the mistress. Happen Mr Macauley was remembering the days, before *their* time, when Mrs Macauley had been forced to work her own farm, refusing Mr Macauley's help with a vigour that had driven him to madness, or so they had heard. Now he wanted his daughter, Annie Macauley's daughter, to be a lady, married to a gentleman, which she was and here was the gentleman himself wanting to be a farmer. Or that's what he seemed to be saying. And there was Miss Briar turning a lovely shade of rose, her excitement at the idea warming the cockles of your heart. She was leaning towards her husband, her lovely bosom threatening to fall out of the top of her gown in her rapture and himself hardly able to keep his hands off her, to everyone's embarrassment.

"You're talking about Bracken Ridge, aren't you?" she said ecstatically, glowing into his face, ready to kiss him right there and then at the table and the damned soup turning cold as Christmas. Mrs Blamire would be giving Moll, the kitchen-maid, the rounds of the kitchen, berating the cat, hanging over the roast pork and moaning about the potatoes and veg which would be ruined, wondering what the devil was going on in the dining-room and ready to blame Betsy and Ellen. They shifted from foot to foot, doing their best to draw Mrs Macauley's attention to the meal which was spoiling but even the mistress was mesmerised by her daughter's words.

"Not that bloody run-down place at the back of Browhead," Reed Macauley roared, pushing his half-empty soup bowl away from him so violently the soup slopped over the edge on to the tablecloth. The two maids sighed. "Old Croxley's been dead for two years and his wife gone to Carlisle to live with her sister. No lads to take over and the whole place gone to rack and ruin. I bought some of the livestock myself."

"Good land though, Reed," his wife said placidly. "When I was at Browhead—"

"When you were at Browhead has got nothing to do with it, my lass. That was twenty years ago and since then—"

"Father, it could soon be got in good heart again. A small flock . . ."

"And some cattle," from Annie. "A good dairy . . ."

"And with the new farming methods, rotating crops and such we could grow—"

"You've read a book or two, I see, lad. But that doesn't make a farmer out of you," Reed snarled. "And how much is this lot going to cost, tell me that?"

"Not as much as the mansion you intend building your daughter, sir. I've done some calculations—"

"Oh, you have, have you?"

Patiently Hal ignored the interruption. "And after consultation with a chap I know whose father owns thousands of acres of mixed farming in Cheshire—"

"This isn't bloody Cheshire, my lad." But they all knew that Reed Macauley was beginning to weaken. He was shouting the odds, as his wife called it, because that was his way. He knew best, always had done, unaware that behind his back his wife and daughter had led him on a thread of cotton so fine and gentle he hadn't even been aware of it.

"Please, Father, listen to Hal." Briar now turned to her father with the same rapturous regard that she had shown her husband. "You know I've always been interested in the flock. How many times have I tied to go up Ullock Pike and teach my dogs—"

"Those bloody dogs. I've said time and time again they'd never make decent sheepdogs. They'll have been lying on the rug in front of your fireplace just like the lapdogs you've let them become."

"That's not true," Briar returned hotly. "Hal and I take them out every day, don't we, darling, but it's damned difficult to train a dog to sheep when you've no sheep."

Hal put his hand on his wife's arm and as though pulled by invisible strings she at once calmed, turning to him, her look softening, and Annie and Reed exchanged a disbelieving glance, for it seemed their daughter was now handled by this man who had married her, tamed her, loved her with less trouble than it took to smooth down a nervous kitten.

Annie smiled, a smile that was very similar to her daughter's, for she had loved Reed Macauley since she was a lass of no more than eighteen or nineteen. She had defied him, fought him, hated him, vilified and almost destroyed him in their early days, as he had her, but since the day they were married had accepted his love, and returned it, as her daughter did with Hal Saunders. Which was why she understood it.

"We could all go up and have a look, surely?" she asked, turning her smile on him and they all watched its effect, even the two housemaids.

"It's a ruin, my lass, and the land gone to seed. It'd take a lot of money."

"But you *have* a lot of money, my love." And in her eyes

he read the message she sent him. It had been a source of great sadness to her that she had not given him a son, only this one rebellious daughter. But wasn't this, if it worked to everyone's satisfaction, the answer to that sadness? A daughter who already loved this land her father farmed and a son-in-law who seemed to be telling them he wanted to be the same. They were so right together, Briar and Hal. He held her in the palm of his hand, which was unbelievable when you remembered her childhood and young womanhood, leading her heart into quiet waters, and she had responded and become the very lass any man would be proud of, husband or father. This marriage had been the making of her and this man and his grand idea would set their future to a steady joy which was wondrous to behold. It would be a hard life, Briar knew that if Hal did not, but it would be a good one. A sound home, days filled with completeness, nights overflowing with love, that was obvious to see even now, children and best of all, which she knew Reed would especially savour, their lass close to them and not whipped away into the indulgent life gentlemen like Hal took for granted.

Reed grinned. "Eeh, Annie Abbott, tha've allus knowed how to get round me," breaking into the dialect that had been his mother's. "Well, young man, how about you and me going——"

"My wife must be included, sir." Hal's voice was very stern and Annie hid a smile, for it seemed young Hal Saunders was not to be pushed in a direction he did not want to take. This was a joint venture, his manner said, his and Briar's, and Reed Macauley was nothing but the investor. If there was anything to be done, or anywhere to go, it was him and Briar together.

Again Reed grinned, well pleased it seemed. "Lad, if you

can get the better of me, you'll go far, and it seems you can. Now then, what the devil are those two women supposed to be doing lurking about at the back of the room. Stop hanging about and let's have some warm soup, Betsy, or whatever your name is, and at once if you please."

From where they stood they could see right down the sloping fellside to the far shimmer of the lake at its foot, Bassenthwaite Lake which, in Briar's opinion, was the most beautiful of them all. There were those who considered Ullswater to be unsurpassed, others favoured Windermere or Derwentwater but this was her lake, her mother's lake, her father's lake where all three had been brought up and it was a magical place in which to settle. Her father was prodding round the back of the farmhouse, begging her mother to look at this and that and could their lass be expected to settle in such a ruin, but she knew he was not unimpressed. It did, as Hal said, need a lot of money spending on it but this was to be her parents' wedding gift to them to set beside the exquisite family silver that had come only a few days ago from Hal's father. Her father would not be outdone. The Saunders' silver was hundreds of years old but it held no particular value for Briar when compared to this, this life, this land, this future which she and Hal were to share.

It was a blue and silver day, still and without wind, and on the far side of the lake the wooded heights of Wythop Woods were reflected in perfect symmetry in the deep water. An upside-down exact copy of the world above it. As they watched, Briar's hand in Hal's, a breeze ruffled the lake, shattering the mirror image. Each tiny wavelet was tipped with light and each tiny trough a blue shadow, the whole surface moving from one side of the lake to the other. They both sighed with the perfection of it.

Below them, sheltering their backs against the protective sides of Little Cockup were two farms no more than a mile or two apart. One was Browhead which had once been the home of her mother's family, the Abbotts, and which Phoebe and Charlie Lucas now farmed. The other was Upfell from which Jake and Maggie Singleton wrested a living. The sun lit up the pristine whitewash of the mighty stone walls, their roofs strong against the winds which swept down the fells, tinted a slaty blue. Their chimneys were low, almost level with their roofs, cylindrical in shape to prevent the wind from driving the smoke down into the "house". All around the farm buildings, barns and outhouses were neat green fields slashed by squares of dry-stone walls, the fields dotted with the ewes and their new lambs which, if the weather allowed, would soon be taken up to their own heafs.

Hal put his arm round Briar's shoulder, then dropped a kiss on her windblown hair. She leaned against him for a moment then, at an irritated shout from her father behind them, they smiled into one another's faces and turned, still hand in hand, and began to trudge up the field towards where he stood with his wife.

"Don't those two ever leave go of each other's hands?" he was heard to say to Annie, then, grinning, his still fine teeth a white slash in his weatherbeaten face, reached for hers.

"Well, I don't know," he grumbled as his daughter and her husband reached the front of the building, "it'll take a deal o' work to get this tumbledown place into something like."

"But it can be done, sir." It was not a question but a statement.

"Aye, I suppose so, that's if you're set on it."

"We are, Father."

"Then we'd best get that building chap up here to have a look at it."

"We'll want it to look as it did when it was built, Father, won't we, Hal?"

"Oh, you will, will you?" Her father was looking about him with what appeared to be distaste and she was not to know that this farm reminded him of Browhead where he had fought so hard to win her mother, days he did not care to remember. The front door of the farm, which stood wide open having been unlocked by the key fetched up from the solicitors in Keswick in whose hands the sale of the farm lay, opened into the hallan, which divided the house. The threshwood was at least five inches high so that entering the house was somewhat tricky. There was a big living-room, a small parlour with low windows looking out down the fell to the lake, a dairy behind it facing north, a buttery which could be made into a decent, modern kitchen, her mother murmured, and above, leading from the house by way of crooked, winding stairs, four large bedrooms. The farm buildings consisted of a barn, cow houses and stables, all of them well built to withstand the rigours of the Lakeland winter, especially up here clinging to the hillside.

They wandered about, the four of them, peering into this and that, the pale morning light, dim and hazed as it did its best to get through the dirty windows, revealing the dusty shapes of the old furniture discarded by the farmer's wife when she left to live with her sister. It was two years since a fire had burned in the enormous hearth and the damp chill entered their bones.

"A good fire will soon remedy that," Briar said as

though someone had complained. There was a musty smell of herbs, hay and buttermilk, but overlying it was the faint memory of fresh bread and lavender from the polish with which the farmwife had attacked her furniture. Every surface was thick with dust. There was soot two inches deep on the hearth and cobwebs drifted lazily from oak beam to oak beam but Briar and Hal gazed sublimely about them as though they were viewing Her Majesty's drawing-room at Windsor Castle.

In one corner, wreathed with cobwebs, stood a piece of furniture that had evidently been well used over several generations since there were gouges and scars in the glossy wood from which it was fashioned. Applewood, it was, ancient and sadly abandoned by the farmwife who had no children and, one supposed, no use for it: a hooded cradle carved with the initials C and W on the headboard and underneath the date 1753. The initials and the date were carved painstakingly with what looked like flowers and small birds.

"Oh, Hal, look," Briar breathed, kneeling down reverently, the full skirt of her fine riding habit disturbing the dust of two years.

"Darling ..." He crouched beside her on his haunches and both of them put out a gentle finger and ran it over the wood, leaving two marks in the dust.

"It's beautiful."

"Isn't it."

"It must have been fashioned by a new father long ago."

"D'you think they know that ..."

"I'd like to think so."

"It could be lined with some fine material."

"And fresh initials carved on it. A *B* and an *H*. Would that be all right, d'you think?"

"Yes, of course. It would be perfect. It must have broken their hearts to have nothing to put in it."

"They left it here for us, didn't they?"

"They did, my love."

Reed and Annie Macauley watched bemused and then at the same time enlightenment shone in their faces and lit their eyes and lifted the corners of their mouths. They turned to look at one another then he held out his arms and she stepped into them, overcome by what she knew she had just heard.

Hal and Briar stood up and turned, their own faces trembling with some emotion, then Briar burst out laughing and Hal looked somewhat embarrassed.

"We were going to tell you, really we were, but so much was happening and then seeing the cradle ..."

But it would not be the true nature of Reed Macauley if he did not have something to say on the matter.

"And you still riding that bloody mare out there," he roared, nodding his head to where Flame was placidly cropping the sweet grass outside the door. He turned his indignation on his son-in-law. "And you're as bad, risking my grandson in such a careless fashion." The child, would, of course, be male. "I'm surprised at the pair of you, really I am, and I shall have something more to say on the matter when we get this lass home with her feet up where she belongs."

"Reed, Reed, darling," his wife spluttered, "Briar is a strong, healthy woman and the child will ..."

But Reed was deeply offended at what he saw as the cavalier attitude they were taking towards this, his first grandchild, but as the three of them smiled at him with affectionate goodwill he began to smile too and the glow of joy in his eyes was clear to see. He dropped a kiss on his wife's head, swept his daughter into his rough embrace and clasped the hand of his son-in-law.

"Well, we'd best get this place into a home fit for the lad," he began, striding about the down-house with a purposeful air. "We'll need a nursery and a place for Briar to have for her own without the servants bothering her."

"Father, it might be a girl," Briar ventured, turning to put herself in the welcoming arms of her husband. "Hal and I would not mind and there'll be plenty of time for others."

"Fiddlesticks! A boy first to take over the farms, then perhaps another for there's room for two and then you can start with the lasses, eeh, Annie?"

"Darling, it's nothing to do with you and me." But she herself was shining with happiness. She put her arm through that of her daughter, leading her towards the side of the house and they were soon in deep discussion on the furnishing of a small parlour, the engaging of more servants, the colour of curtains and carpets, while her husband and the father-to-be wandered towards the barn and cow house as Reed Macauley began the task of turning Hal Saunders, gentleman, into a farmer.

Chapter Eleven

Alice was with her when her waters broke. They had been eating strawberries from her father's hothouse and she had put down the cramps she had been experiencing to the fruit, so that the rush of hot dampness between her thighs took her totally by surprise.

"What is it?" Alice asked her, for though she was a country girl and had been present when her Border terrier bitch gave birth to three delightful puppies she had never actually been privy to the onset of a human labour.

"It's the baby, you fool, and a fortnight early or Hal would not have gone up with Dobby to fetch down the ewes." Briar gasped and leaned into another sharp pain.

She and Alice were in her little parlour off the house, the main room where Mrs Evans was preparing the gargantuan meal that her master's working men, shepherds, labourers, cowmen and stable lads, expected when they finished their day's labour. It would be dark by four at the latest and looked like snow, for it was January and the time for blizzards in this part of the high Lakeland. There had been hard, stinging frosts and light falls of snow dusting the peaks but Dobby, who was experienced in such matters, said a blizzard was coming as sure as eggs are eggs and he and the men had been busy these last few days battening down the hatches, as Mr Hal put it, though they were not quite sure where he had got the expression. Dobby was so old there was no one who could remember where he came from, only that once he had worked for Reed Macauley's father, then for Reed and now, since he was an experienced shepherd, had been loaned to Reed Macauley's son-in-law until the lad got the hang of things. With Dobby's consent, of course, for the old shepherd heeded the word of no one, not even Reed Macauley. He was withered and wizened and wiry, with a cap of white grizzled curls on which he slung his cap every morning though there were those who believed he never took it off even to get into his bed. You had to keep on the right side of Dobby, *and* his equally ancient black and white collie dog, who slunk a bare inch from the back of Dobby's leg unless directed elsewhere by a series of whistles only he and his master understood. Dobby had been given a snug room above the tack room, one with a small grate with a fire in it on which he could boil a kettle for his cup of tea; otherwise he ate what the other men ate, hot plates of Mrs Evans's substantial food brought over by the kitchen-maid. They liked their own company did he and his dog and they made it plain that it was not to be interfered with. Mary had scoured his room once when he was up on the fells and had been reduced to tears by the old man who told them plainly that if the operation was repeated he would be off within the hour!

It had taken Briar and Hal a maddening three months before the farm at Bracken Ridge was considered by Reed Macauley to be fit for his daughter to live in. She would have argued but her husband agreed with her father, saying that with the baby coming it would be too much for her to live in the chaos the alterations to the farmhouse were causing. There were walls to be knocked down and walls to be built up, an extension to the back of the farmhouse which had been turned into an elegant dining-room and a study for Hal. A new range, the very latest, was installed in the kitchen, window frames repaired, chimneys swept, slates to be renewed on the roof and a hundred and one other things and, in Hal's opinion, and after all his was the opinion to which she listened, it would be best if she remained in the gatehouse until it was all done. Lady Sutton had agreed with him, not for Briar's sake, despite the coming child, but because, since Hal and Briar had moved there, her son Perry had lost some of his wildness, spending time in the company of the newly weds. She was not to know that the reason he visited his cousin and his cousin's wife was the bewitching daughter of Alex Buchanan with whom Briar had become so friendly and who often stayed overnight!

In those three months, glad of Alice's fondness for Briar, Hal had been out every day with the shepherds and the other men who worked for Reed, learning the intricacies of becoming a farmer. Long Beck was a large and prosperous farm, but despite its size it was bound to the cycles of the seasons like any other. Reed Macauley was somewhat of a local squire in his part of the world but his cattle and horses, of which there were a great many, had to be fed and groomed. His men milked the cows and taught Hal the way of it, though many was the time he came home with bruises from the menacing hooves of Clover who was known for a bugger. Her tail caught him many a clout across his shoulders too, but he stuck at it, to the approval of his wife and her father. He learned the art of grooming the enormous horses who would pull his plough, though he would have his own carter at Bracken Ridge, but more than any other part of the world of farming he learned about sheep: Herdwick sheep. With his father-in-law's help – and cash – he went to the market on the first Saturday in October not only to purchase the start of his flock but to hire a ram to service them. The best rams, or "tups" were "spoken for" in advance but with Reed's influence Hal hired a new tup, one that had "good" blood in its veins. Then he drove his flock, with the help of Dobby and his dog, with Blackie and Bonnie doing their enthusiastic bit, back to Bracken Ridge where Briar, who was banned, not only by her husband but by her father, from walking the miles from Keswick Back End Fair and then up the fell to the farm, was waiting.

She was six months by now, radiant with good health, bonny with the size of the child growing within her. She was sitting on the wall watching for him and as he came over the brow of the hill, Dobby at the rear of the small flock, she jumped from the wall like an excited child, flying down the slope with her extended belly bouncing before her to fling her arms about Hal's neck and cover his face with kisses. Her hair hung down her back and even Dobby had a hard job to hide his admiring smiles, for if ever a woman suited her approaching motherhood, it was Briar Saunders.

"How did it go?" she shouted into Hal's ear, making him wince, flinging herself about to stare in wonder at the start of their flock, just as though she had never seen a ewe before. Her dogs, which she and Hall had tried patiently to train over the last few months, though young and as excited as she, were behaving for once in exemplary fashion, swinging wide at Hal's whistle to fetch back a stray. The walk had been long and difficult, for the tup knew it was mating time and fought to get at the ewes.

"Fine, fine, but let's get these bloody hoggs in the pen or the tup will fight the lot of us." Hal had learned the difference between a gimmer and a hogg, between a twinter and a two shear and also the many diseases that can strike a sheep, such as black disease, a rapidly fatal infection of an adult sheep, foot rot, head fly, lamb dysentery, liver fluke and others. He was learning to shear, to deliver a lamb, to work the two dogs, but at this moment his concern was for his wife who seemed determined to help in rounding up the wandering ewes.

"My love, what in hell's name are you doing lumbering up and down this slope in your condition," he grumbled at her. "See, get inside. Nan is waiting for you."

"I know, but, darling, this is our first flock, the beginning and I don't want to miss a moment. Did you get as many as we wanted?"

"Yes, I did, thanks to your father and Dobby who have both forgotten more than I'll ever know, but we can talk about that later."

"And the tup! He looks a strong one. This time next year he will have given us twice as many."

"Aye, he's very ... eager." He grinned then gave her a gentle push towards the lighted doorway where an exasperated Nan waited for her mistress.

Every night Hal tumbled into his bed like a felled log. He was a strong, muscle-hardened young man by now but he had never before in his life indulged in such vigorous manual labour.

"I'll be able to help you as soon as this baby comes," Briar promised him, her hand smoothing his flat stomach and tangling in the wiry blond pubic hair that protected his flaccid manhood. Though she was big with child they had so far managed to manoeuvre themselves, with a great deal of muffled laughter, in order still to enjoy the physical love that was so important between them. Position was the thing, Hal whispered in her ear as he turned her this way and that, or twisted himself into a contortion that would have won him a job in a circus, he told her. Even naked she was as beautiful to him as on their first night together, her growing belly a joy to him. He kissed it and the child inside at every opportunity, his hand caressing the darting leaps and capers his child performed in the snug security of its mother's womb, but sometimes, as on this first day as a sheep farmer with his own flock, the attention she craved was beyond him.

"Darling, if only I could," he groaned.

"I see, you're tired of me already, is that it? Or is it that you have become one of those farmers who love their dogs better than their wives?"

Challenged, he showed her vigorously that he was not!

"But you will let me be a part of it, won't you," she begged him later, knowing that if his promise was given he would not go back on it. He was already half asleep and scarcely knew what she was saying as he promised that he would. He had walked and climbed nearly twenty miles that day in an effort to keep up with Dobby, checking on their flock and the recalcitrant tup, and when he finally reached the farmhouse had soaked in a hot bath before their bedroom fire knowing, and wondering how he did it, that the little man would not be experiencing the ministrations he himself was enjoying at his wife's hands.

Now it was fierce winter on the hills. The white bowl of the valley below them had glistened that day under a blue sky edged with inky, threatening clouds. Against the thin

layer of snow that had fallen the night before, a dark ribbon
of Hal Saunders's sheep moved towards the home paddock
and tomorrow would be the turn of another score or so.
When they were safely fenced he and Dobby slung flaps of
hay from bales carried from the barn, while down the slope
in the farmhouse Briar Saunders began her own travail.

Alice supported Briar as she gasped her way through
another spasm, shouting through the closed door of the
parlour for Nan.

"I must have been in labour for a while," Briar said
slowly, endeavouring to straighten up. "You'd best get
Nan to send for Doctor Burbage from Hause and my
mother and see if . . ."

She bent over with a strangled gasp.

"What, darling . . . what?" Alice questioned.

"Hal . . ."

"Of course . . ." And then Nan was there, with Mary
and Mrs Evans to help her up the crooked stairs, pausing
for a moment as she communed with the pain for a long
moment. They were all women and though none had borne
a child they waited in awed silence. Even before they had
reached the bedroom which was cosy with firelight and
sparkling with cleanliness, they heard the rattle of hooves
in the yard as Chuckie, the stable man, clattered towards the
open gate. He would shout out his message at the doctor's
front door, making sure it was heard before riding on to
Long Beck to fetch Mrs Macauley. He had been astounded,
as were two of Hal's labourers mending a wall, to see the
grand Miss Buchanan with only Mrs Evans's warm shawl
about her, her silken skirts up about her knees, taking the
wall towards the fells where the "maister" was on the bare
back of Mrs Saunders's chestnut mare.

The three women moved slowly about their task, for

Nan was the eldest of nine and Mrs Evans and Mary, who had both come from large families, knew that their mistress had a long weary way to go yet. They put her in a clean nightgown, Mrs Evans and Mary politely averting their faces, though Nan was well used to the sight of Briar's naked body. When she was comfortable, or as comfortable as could be arranged in the circumstances, Nan sat down beside the bed and held her hand.

"It'll be a while yet, my lamb, but we're all here an' someone's gone fer tha' mam, an't doctor," though what use he would be she couldn't imagine. Giving birth was women's work and though it was 1880 and rumoured that the Queen up in London had a doctor to attend her at the birth of her nine children, the last twenty-three years ago, country women were not convinced this was necessary. Still, Mr Macauley had insisted that Doctor Burbage be called the moment his daughter went into labour.

"Mary's settin' little clothes out, lass, so's ter be ready fer't bairn," wincing as her mistress gripped her hand in a vice, gasping out loud for Hal.

"I can't manage this without my husband, Nan."

"Nay, my lass, tha'll not want a great hulking man gettin' in't road," Mrs Evans told her cheerfully, chucking another shovel of coal on the already leaping fire.

"Nan, please send for him, please." She bore down on another pain, doing her best not to cry out.

"Lass, give us a yell, if tha' want—"

"Nan, get Hal for me ... please ..." This last on a long wail of agony.

Mary bustled in with a kettle of hot water and Mrs Evans took it from her, putting it on the fire before settling herself comfortably in a second chair, for she might as well have a rest while she could. Mrs Evans had what were called "dairy-maid's legs", for in her youth and young womanhood she had done dairy work which meant standing for hours each day on a cold flagged floor. They were knotted with veins which sometimes ulcerated, though she told no one of it, just sitting down, as her position allowed, and gave her orders to Mary who was young and lively, treating the agony with a poultice of lesser centaury or feverwort, which grew in the hedges and was known for its efficacy against varicose ulcers, when the rest had retired.

Doctor Burbage, Annie Macauley and Hal Saunders all arrived together, the three of them pushing one another aside to be first up the stairs, but the husband, being stronger, younger and quite frantic with fear, won the day. He had seen Alice Buchanan galloping up the fellside on Briar's chestnut and had for a moment been paralysed with shocked astonishment.

Dobby removed his clay pipe from his mouth to remark shortly, "Looks like bairn's on't way," before turning back to more important matters like the movement of the flock down the fell before the blizzard struck.

Alice shrieked that the baby was coming, so frightening Hal he pushed her off the mare and leaped on to its bare back, thundering away from them, scattering sheep in all directions to which Dobby muttered an oath or two.

"Well," said Alice.

"Tha's a fair walk, lass," Dobby advised her before whistling up his dog, watching her as she began to make her way in her house slippers down the track to Bracken Ridge.

The farmhouse was in uproar, each man shouting to the next that the little mistress had "started wi't bairn", those who lived down in Hause and who walked the mile up to the farm each day hanging about to see if there might be news to carry back to the missis. They grinned and nudged one another as the young master came tearing down from the fell, telling one another that he'd not be so eager when it got to the second or third or fourth.

"Nay, lad, tha' canna come in 'ere," Nan told Hal sternly when he tried to shoulder her aside, quite enjoying the power she had suddenly been given and unwilling to let it go.

"Bugger it, Nan, get out of my way," he snarled and with a cry of compassion fell to his knees beside the bed he had shared with Briar for nine rapturous months and wrapped her in his arms.

"I'm here, my darling, I'm here."

"Hal, don't leave me."

"I won't."

"Oh yes, you will, sir," the doctor, who had reached the bedside by now, told him but, as Nan reported to Chuckie's wife later on, he might just as well have addressed his remark to the chair. Mrs Macauley was behind him, clucking her tongue and doing her best to separate husband and wife but it did no good, and two hours later, when Master Thomas Saunders roared his way into the world, Hal was still there, his wife leaning against him, his arms about her shoulders while at the other end the doctor delivered the child into the waiting arms of his grandmother. Deeply offended he was, for not once in his long career had a husband been in the room when a child was born, never mind almost in bed with the mother. Mind you, it did seem to comfort Mrs Saunders who did exactly as he bid her with no fuss, not even when he sewed up the inevitable birth wound. A big boy, despite being two weeks early who, when put to his mother's breast without even a wipe round his red face, sucked heartily to what seemed the great pride and pleasure of his mother and father. When he was full he burped politely and fell into a deep, contented sleep, not even awakening when Mary bathed him in front of the bedroom fire.

There was a great cry from the farm folk when they were told of the boy's arrival, for it seemed a new line had begun. The name of the line might not be Macauley but already his proud grandfather, who could scarcely be persuaded to let the boy's own father have a hold, was talking of changing his will, making the lad the heir to his own farm. Mrs Evans's elderberry wine was passed around the workers, with ale for the men and the little lad's head was well and truly "wetted", although the grandfather professed a fancy for a glass of brandy, if his son-in-law had such a thing.

"Brandy! Brandy! It's champagne for my son, Mr Macauley and I have a bottle ready and waiting for this day."

Briar sat up in the big bed, her copper tumble of curls which Nan had brushed and brushed tied up with emerald-green satin ribbons. She was propped against the immaculately laundered white cotton pillows, the sleeping child in her arms. She looked so beautiful it just about stopped her young husband's heart and he leaned over her and his son, kissing them both with awed tenderness. The other occupants of the room, Doctor Burbage, Annie and Reed Macauley watched bemused. The firelight and lamplight fell in a golden swathe across the parents and child, turning the copper of Briar's hair to a tawny gold which was copied in the fluff of hair on the boy's head. The new mother and father seemed unaware of the others, circled in a moment so unique, so special, Annie took Reed's hand and, nodding to the doctor, led the way from the room.

In the kitchen there was great confusion and joy with what seemed every worker on the farm, even Dobby deigning to take a sup of ale, crammed inside the walls.

"Eeh, and me with nowt for supper," Mrs Evans was crying, her bad legs forgotten. "Mary, see, run an' fetch that cold leg o' pork from pantry. It'll be short commons this night what with little lad comin' early." But they all sat down to heaped plates of potatoes and sweet cauliflower grown by Mr Hal himself in the little vegetable garden he had created at the side of the house. And him with a farm to run an' all! "What a good job I made that fruit cake with this lot to feed," as though she didn't do it every day of the week. In the little dining-room the grandparents sat in style at the polished dining-table until, with an oath, Reed Macauley stood up and, taking his wife's hand, led the way back into the kitchen.

"Bugger this," he cried. "If I'm not to celebrate the birth of my grandson with his people then it's a poor do," wiping his eyes and handing his handkerchief to his wife. They roared their approval while upstairs their mistress sat up in bed like a queen with her son in her arms and her husband's head against her shoulder and thought, no, she *knew* that she was the happiest, luckiest woman in the world.

"I love you, husband," she whispered, smiling at the old-fashioned phrasing.

"And I love you, wife."

"Put Tom in his cradle, Hal."

"It's Tom, is it." He smiled, taking his son in his arms then placing him carefully in the warm cradle, the one they had found when they had first looked at Bracken Ridge. It had been lined with muslin backed with the soft fleece of one of Reed's sheep. Beneath the original initials C and

W had been carved two more, B and H, and a space left for the date.

"I'll get Jack to finish that tomorrow," Hal said absently, putting a strong, loving hand on the fragile dome of his son's skull.

"Never mind tomorrow," Briar called softly, "come over here and put your arms round me. I'm in need of some attention."

Two smaller bedrooms had been knocked into one to make a decent bedroom for Briar and Hal. Briar, against her father's wishes, for he liked new and expensive furnishings, had kept the decor simple and as it had been when the farm had been newly built. The bed was of mahogany with a high, padded headboard and the foot to match. Bare floorboards with a rag rug or two would not have been suitable so she had compromised with a plain turkey-red carpet an inch deep in pile with pretty sprigged wallpaper and curtains to match. There was a handsome wardrobe in the same warm wood as the bed, with a dressing-table and a chest of drawers. The washstand was draped with white muslin and on the bed an exquisite white muslin and lace bedspread fell gracefully to the floor. Pictures of Lakeland scenes, soft, dream-like watercolours, adorned the walls, and the balance between comfort and simplicity had been achieved. There were massive oak beams to hold up the roof, under which Hal had to bend his head, and the window bottom was filled with pots of vivid geraniums. The rest of the house was the same, a compromise between the old and the new.

Hal moved slowly across the room to her, sitting on the bed and wrapping her in his arms but that was not her intention. She had borne a son this day and though she knew it was too soon for the resumption of their loving, she wanted what she had had every night ever since the day they were married: her husband in her bed, their bodies close together, their breath mingling, their lips ready to touch, warm and sensual, though it could lead nowhere tonight.

"Take your things off, darling," she murmured, holding out her arms to him. Her nightgown, which she had undone to feed the child, slipped from her shoulder revealing the creamy satin of her skin and the full globe of her breast.

"Sweetheart, should we not wait?" Hal was hesitant, for this woman of his looked as radiantly ready for their vigorous lovemaking as she always did.

"For what?" She pulled the ribbon from her hair and it fell over her forehead and streamed down across her breast as she sat up.

"You must be tired." But he began to pull his shirt over his head and tussle with the buckle of his belt. The child in the cradle made soft plopping sounds and Hal was distracted, turning towards the cradle, but his wife was determined.

"You were mine before you were his and I was yours," she said softly, peering at him from beneath the curtain of her hair, "and I want you in my bed, tonight, as you were last night, and as you will be until the end of our days. I shall not sleep without your arms about me, you know that, and I need sleep, so are you going to hop up here or must I come out and get you."

They heard him laughing, even in the kitchen, the women exchanging looks which said surely to God they weren't at it already! The child no more than two hours old and the pair of them giggling like two youngsters in a hayrick.

It was to be three weeks before Briar was healed enough to allow her husband to "claim his rights" as she laughingly called it, but that night, the night Tom Saunders was born, he held her and stroked her — though it did him no good — soothing her to sleep, loving her, being loved and soothed in return. Their son slept on as though he knew they needed these few hours together to renew the strong, precious bond that had held them in thrall since their first meeting on the fells, and the farmhouse settled itself down about them and slept.

Chapter Twelve

Alice hesitated for a brief second, looking round the cosily glowing kitchen where she had spent so many happy days of her childhood and girlhood. It was as though she were saying goodbye, which she was; as though she were printing every detail in her memory to take away with her but if you had asked her if this was so she would have vehemently denied it. After all she was not leaving for ever. She would be back as soon as . . . well, *soon* and then all would be well. She loved her family and her home and she hated to hurt them as she knew they would be hurt but what she was about to do was inevitable, her parents should have realised that by now. Besides, it was so much more exciting and if there was anything she loved it was excitement. And she'd certainly had that since she met Perry Sutton.

It was almost the end of January and though it was warm in the kitchen, since the fire in the range was never allowed to go out, she knew it would be cold beyond the kitchen door. She was dressed for riding. A warm blue woollen riding habit under which were trousers of the same colour. Over her habit was a hooded cloak, again in blue, a dark blue lined with a rich sable. She wore no hat. Perry had once remarked in that husky voice she loved that her hair should never be covered, that it should be allowed to hang down her back to the cleft of her buttocks, thick and silken, dark, shot through with the tones of russet and chestnut, just like her mother's. It fell over the thrown-back hood of the cloak in a heavy mass, curling loosely at its ends, springing back from her broad forehead as she lifted her head to listen to the sounds of the house. A cat dozing in a basket by the fire lifted her head and stared balefully at her then comforted herself by mewing plaintively and proceeded to give her kittens a good washing.

Alice slipped quietly across the shining flagged floor and lifted the latch, then remembered that at this time of night the door would be bolted. Gingerly she drew the bolt back, praying it would not squeal. It didn't, for was not her father's house well maintained by her father's servants and it would be woe betide any of them if things weren't exactly as he liked them to be. Hinges oiled, windows well fitted and shining with cleanliness, woodwork freshly painted, a place for everything and everything in its place, the men and women he employed meticulous in the following of his orders.

She closed the door softly behind her and stepped out into the winter's night which was almost as bright as day. There was a full moon riding the sky, trailing a thin line of cloud, with a circle of light about it and a solitary star glittering above it. The sky was a silver blue, as were the roofs of the stables which shone wetly in the luminous light. She drew in a deep breath and keeping to the periphery of the stable yard stole round it, hugging the wall. The small bag containing a change of undergarments she had hidden earlier in the day in the corner of the tack room behind a pile of sacks was still there. Gathering it up she whispered across the room to the door and let herself out into the yard again. She heard a horse wicker and a thrill ran through her, for she knew it was Perry's hunter which he would not leave behind.

"But we'll be back soon," she had told him, frowning, since they had argued about this before and would it not be more practical to take one of the steady, sturdy mares from the Sutton stables. If he was to take Thunder why could she not take Charlie, her roan, but Perry had kissed her arguments away, as he usually did, winning the day, as he usually did, saying that Thunder was fast and could move freely even with two riders. He could gallop and jump and his brave, confident character was just what was needed to get them far away before her disappearance was discovered.

He was at the outer farm gate, Thunder tethered to the gate post, he himself stamping his feet and blowing on his hands in the whippingly cold air.

"Good God, woman, where have you been? I though you'd got caught or had changed your mind."

"Changed my mind! Changed my mind! Don't you know by now that I never change my mind. I'm not one of your shilly-shallying females who dither about saying one thing and meaning another."

"Yes, yes, my sweet, I know but let's not hang about here or your father, who I swear has eyes in the back of his head and ears pricked for any suspicious sound, will come growling out of the house with his shotgun and dispose of me as he would like to do."

"Don't be silly. You know he likes you really," she answered untruthfully. He had sprung into the saddle in that easy, athletic way he had which was the mark of a true horseman, and she allowed him to haul her up to sit before him. Thunder jibbed at the extra weight, dancing sideways in resentment but Perry held him strongly, setting him to a trot and then a canter, not asking too much of him with his double burden.

"I know nothing of the sort, my love. He has made his feelings quite plain about my wooing – what a quaint word – of you. I am nothing but a fortune-hunter in his opinion."

"And are you?" she taunted him, turning her face to his. His mouth came down on hers, fiercely, and one hand moved inside the bodice of her habit and cupped her naked breast, his finger and thumb pinching the nipple. He squeezed it, hurting her, but she arched her back against his chest, thrusting her breast more strongly into the palm of his hand, biting at his lips, and both of them were savagely aware that tonight they would lie together at the inn where he had secured them a room. Tomorrow they would be man and wife! He had a faint regret about that, for Perry Sutton was not the marrying kind, but to get his hands on Alex Buchanan's money, which he needed desperately to do, he must marry his daughter. He liked Alice, she was great fun and it would certainly be no hardship to make love to her. In fact he was looking forward to it, since no matter how he persuaded her she would allow him no further than the fondling of her magnificent breasts, deep, hungry kisses, and the smoothing of her leg as far as her knee. She was as eager as he to go further but, though he was not aware of it, Alice Buchanan had the measure of Perry Sutton and she knew that without marriage she would have no hold on him. She loved him. She wanted nothing more in this world than to be his wife but she was, despite being ill-advisedly in love with him, wise enough to know that to keep him, even to *get* him, she must not let her rashness get the better of her. She would be his wife, or nothing, and she had told him so.

She moaned deeply in the back of her arched throat.

"Take the reins," he said hoarsely in her ear and when she did, automatically controlling the hunter, Perry's hands lifted the hem of her skirt about her waist and slipped inside the top of her trousers. They found the crisp curling brush of her secret womanhood which he divided, dipping into the hot, wet, slippery centre of her, disposing of her virginity with a swift and cruel thrust of his fingers. When, ten minutes later, they reached the inn on the edge of Keswick the groom's mouth fell open in astonishment as the lady and gentleman leaped from the back of the hunter and threw the reins in his direction. The landlord was equally amazed as the handsome young gentleman hurried the stunningingly beautiful, *flushed* young woman up the stairs before him.

"Excuse me, sir," he protested, receiving nothing but a snarling demand for their room number.

They took each other like two snapping animals, their desire almost vicious, and when it was done they slept for an hour in one another's arms before beginning again. She was already pregnant by then.

Briar had just been allowed out of her bed by the grim-faced nurse hired by the doctor and was standing at the window of their bedroom, her two-week-old son in her arms, when Alex Buchanan rode hell for leather up the rocky track that led from the back of Browhead where the Lucases farmed to Bracken Ridge.

"Please, Mrs Saunders, I beg you to get back into bed before you have a relapse," the nurse protested, seeing the comfortable five weeks she had promised herself with her latest patient disappearing like the coating of snow the housemaid was vigorously brushing from the front step. Ladies, real ladies that is, kept to their beds for a properly decent three weeks, avoiding putting a delicate foot to the dangerous floor until she gave them permission to do so. Then, depending on herself and the doctor and the new mother's constitution she spent several weeks reclining on a suitable sofa, or, in the best circles, a chaise-longue. Five, six, even eight weeks was quite normal, and yet two weeks after the birth of her son here was Mrs Saunders racketing about her bedroom like any common working woman, jigging baby up and down as though he were a puppy. These modern mothers! Really! She didn't know what the world was coming to.

Briar, who had just fed her son, pressed her face closer to the window, watching with amazement Mr Buchanan's precipitate dash up the moorland track to the front gate that opened on to the front entrance and path to the farm. She had what Hal promised her would be a pretty garden just to the right of the cobbled pathway. She and Hal had spent hours poring over books on horticulture, their particular favourite being *Beeton's All About Gardening* which was most informative on what to plant, when and where. Dahlias, they thought, which were bright, showy and hardy; delphiniums, tall, blue to make a rich background against the mellow stone walls; clematis climbing the walls of the farmhouse; plenty of daisy-like flowers in yellow and white, a real English country garden. Lavender edges to the beds, and roses, sweetbriar, moss rose and white damask side by side with sweet William, peonies and pinks, wallflowers and Canterbury bells, and it was often remarked by those who had known her before her marriage that if they had been told that Miss Briar would ever concern herself with such a mundane task as gardening they would have believed the teller had lost his wits.

So, a splendid setting for his beautiful wife, Hal said tenderly as he drew their plans, and for the beautiful children they would surely have. How many? A dozen would be nice, he said, grinning impishly. Eleven more to fill the nursery so perhaps, planning so many, they had best skip up to their bedroom while Nan wasn't looking and waste no more time!

Now what was Mr Buchanan up to, coming at full gallop up the front drive instead of proceeding round the side of the house to the stable yard as those on horseback normally did? Instead he leaped awkwardly from the back of his tall bay, flinging the reins in the direction of the startled Chuckie who had hurried round the corner of the building to ascertain whose animal was clattering up the track. Mr Buchanan crashed open the garden gate and limped quickly along the garden path to the front door. Mr Buchanan had been involved in a serious accident in his copper mine near Coniston many years ago and it was said he still suffered with his back, which caused him to walk with a slight lurch. His knock thundered through the house making even the baby twitch in his sleep.

"Goodness me," squeaked the nurse, peering over Briar's shoulder. "Someone's in a hurry." She was considerably startled when Mrs Saunders, who really was not dressed for visitors, thrust the sleeping child into her arms and crossed swiftly to the closed door of the bedroom. She opened it and was out on the landing and halfway down the twisting staircase before nurse could do more than gasp and hold out a beseeching hand of protest.

Nan at the front door was almost knocked off her feet by

Mr Buchanan's forceful advance into the narrow hallan, her face a picture of astonishment, his drawn into an expression that might have been anguish.

"Sir . . ." Nan began, then Briar was at her elbow, for in her heart she had a good idea why Ally's father was thrusting his big frame over her threshwood, his face turning from the scarlet of his dash over from Hollin House to the pasty sweated hue of dread.

"Mr Buchanan. How can I help you?" She turned to Nan. "It's all right, Nan, you can go. Give us a moment or two and then fetch some coffee."

"A brandy would be welcome, Mrs Saunders. Briar . . ."

"Of course. We'll find it in Hal's study."

If Mr Buchanan noticed that Briar was wearing a morning gown, no more than a wrapper really and fit only for wear in the bedroom, which was doubtful in his present state, he did not remark on it, though Nan did when she re-entered the kitchen.

"Dear Lord, what's up now?" she cried to the bewildered servants, her hand to her breast.

"Why? Who was that at the door?"

"Mr Buchanan, that's who."

"Not Miss Ally's father?"

"None other an' in a right old state an' all."

"What d'you mean?" Mrs Evans pushed the cat from her lap where it had been purring contentedly under her hand, and stood up anxiously. That Miss Ally was as wild as Miss Briar, or as Miss Briar had been before her marriage to Mr Hal, was well known and there had been talk about her, Miss Ally that is, and that wild limb of Satan from Middlefell Hall.

"An' Miss Briar with nowt on her back but her morning gown," Nan fretted, more concerned with her mistress's

unconventional attire, it seemed, than the purpose of Mr
Buchanan's visit. She shook her head in disbelief though
they all knew that Miss Briar was, or had been, a flouter
of the rules of society. Mary, who was kitchen-maid and
only recently come from a farm up Bridekirk way where,
until she was fetched by Mrs Macauley, she had slept in
her undergarments, changed once a month and who had
no idea what a morning gown might be, crept up to the
kitchen table, curiosity creasing her apple-cheeked face, for
the ways of the gentry were a fascination to her.

"Never! What would her ma say?"

"Sometimes I don't think Mrs Macauley cares all that
much. Not about Miss Briar but about the customs of
society. They say she went about in trousers in her day."

"Aye, so I heard. They'll be wanting coffee then?" Mrs
Evans said, nodding in the direction of the study and
beginning to bustle about her stove and her coffee pot,
her position in this household giving her an importance
that she liked to display.

"No, Mr Buchanan craves a brandy, or so 'e ses."

"What, at ten o'clock in the morning!" Mrs Evans was
deeply shocked.

"Aye, it must be somethin' bad. Eeh, I don't know what
ter make of it all. It must be something bad," Nan repeated.
She sighed deeply and shook her head before reaching
for the teapot and a comforting cup of tea, the panacea
for all ills.

It was bad.

"Mrs Saunders ... Briar," Ally's grim-faced father was
saying, his hand steadier now that he had drunk down one
glass of brandy and accepted a second. "It's Alice. She's

gone off with that bloody swine. I beg your pardon, but who else could it be? Her mother is off her head with worry. We wondered ..."

"Gone off!" Briar was open-mouthed with shock. She was well aware that Ally was infatuated with, no, more than infatuated with the devilish, charming rascal Perry Sutton, but surely, surely even she couldn't have ... no, of course not. But then what was Mr Buchanan doing tearing over to Bracken Ridge as though the devil himself were at his heels?

"She left no note, not a word and took nothing but her riding habit which seemed to point to Sutton's lad. I've been to Middlefell Hall where I nearly got the door slammed in my face just as though the very idea of their aristocratic lad consorting with my lass was anthema to them. He was a gentleman, they told me and would no more run off with a *lady* than fly to the bloody moon. But I know better. My God, I nearly punched that sod Sutton on his smirking mouth. I do beg your pardon, my lass ... my language ... Oh aye, that's who she's with. Perry bloody Sutton. Last night they went and God knows where that bastard's taken her or what he's — Jesus God — what he's done with her, though I'm inclined to think the worst."

"But ... !"

"I'm sorry, Briar, but you are her friends, you and that husband of yours who is cousin to ..."

"To Perry?"

"Aye, none other, and we were wondering, did she say anything about ... about plans, what they meant to do? Well, some place they ... he ... might have mentioned, where he might have taken her. The Suttons had nothing to say on the matter so I thought ... I've been everywhere I could think of. Her mother's distraught ..."

Alex Buchanan was a strong, proud man but his head fell to his hand as he bowed it in despair. Briar, who hardly knew him, barely restrained herself from putting out a compassionate hand and laying it on his thick, greying hair. He was very like her own father whom she loved dearly and though he was gruff and not a great one for displaying his emotions she knew he cared deeply about his lovely daughter. And Ally was just like she herself had been before she married Hal. If Hal had asked her, Briar, to run away with him, desert her family, her friends, her home, her life in this world of hers, which she took for granted but in her heart she loved and thrived in, she would have gone running off with him in her petticoats. Followed him anywhere. Believed whatever he promised her and it seemed Ally Buchanan felt the same about Perry Sutton.

Hal had heard a whisper, come no doubt from his aunt who would trust him to keep it to himself, that though the general belief hereabouts was that the Suttons were wealthy, a couple of generations of young sons of the family, including Perry, had been gamblers. They had land, true. They had that great house, a splendid stable, but maintaining the Wentworth hunt, feeding fifty couple of hounds, the salaries of huntsmen and all the other men needed, would be likely to exceed £3,000 a year. There was the expense of preserving game birds on their land and had Briar noticed, since others had, it seemed, that Lady Sutton was wearing last year's wardrobe, or could it be the year before that? Briar could not believe that Ally was not loved for herself but her father's fortune would make her all the more attractive to a rogue like Perry Sutton. Ally had confessed to her that her father was suspicious of Perry whose reputation as a wild-riding, hell-raking philanderer would not endear him to the father of daughters no matter what his pedigree. It would not concern Alex Buchanan that the woman who married Perry Sutton would one day be *Lady* Sutton, the mistress of an ancient seat, one of the oldest in the district of the lakes. Middlefell Hall was a beautiful house with a great stone-flagged hallway, oak-ceilinged, a long gallery lined with an impressive array of ancestral portraits, none of which would impress Ally's father. The inbred arrogance of the Suttons would only serve to set his teeth on edge. Briar had the feeling that if this man believed that Perry Sutton genuinely loved his daughter he would swallow his antipathy towards him and allow the match but he didn't. He believed that it was his, Alex Buchanan's money he was after. No matter how much Ally wanted him Alex Buchanan would find some way to prevent it. If it was not too late!

"Where would he take her, d'you think?" Mr Buchanan agonised, running his fingertip around the edge of the glass, staring into the fire that blazed on the hearth, and Briar was aware that he was not really asking her so much as thinking aloud. "North if he means to marry her, I suppose, or would it be south where his fox-hunting friends reside? Where young lordlings play with not a thought for the reputation of the daughter of a mere manufacturer. Where she might be seduced rather than married but then how would he get his hands on her money? My money? God knows ..."

There was a great banging of doors and clattering of footsteps on the stone-flagged floor of the hallan and, his face ruddy with the intense cold outside and the exertions of his morning, Hal strode into the room. He had put on weight since his marriage, not fat but muscle, for his days were spent in physical labour and his splendid masculine strength and beauty seemed to fill the small room. Briar stood up at once, her face assuming that loving, yearning expression which only he awoke in her. It was a mixture of adoration, sensuality, sweetness, an almost maternal tenderness and awe that somehow this man had chosen her above all others. Often it made those in their company feel somewhat ill at ease as they strained towards one another though they did not actually touch. Alex Buchanan also stood up and Hal turned to him as though in surprise even though Nan, as he came through the kitchen, had told him of their visitor.

"Mr Buchanan, sir?" Hal said cordially, and it was clear he was mystified as to the reason for the visit.

"Hal, Mr Buchanan is ... well, he's looking for Ally."

"Ally?"

"Aye, and that young sod, Perry Sutton." Alex Buchanan's face became even grimmer, for was this man not the young sod's cousin and were they not all tarred with the same bloody arrogance of their rank.

"Perry?" Hal turned in bewilderment to Briar then, suddenly aware that his wife was dressed only in her morning gown, he frowned. He had been brought up to respect a lady and no lady of his acquaintance would be seen by a gentleman not her husband in the flimsy garment his wife was wearing. Briar saw his expression and knew what it meant.

"Hal, for goodness sake take that look off your face. Can you not see that Mr Buchanan is almost out of his mind with worry?" So forget about my attire for the moment, her unspoken words seem to say. "Alice and Perry have ... have disappeared."

"Disappeared! You mean together?"

"Yes, and Mr Buchanan was wondering if we might know where ... well, where he might have taken her."

"Taken her?"

"Dear God, Hal, this is serious so will you stop repeating everything I say as though I were speaking in a foreign language." It was not often that Briar spoke so sharply to her beloved husband who could say or do no wrong in her eyes, but Perry Sutton, though he was of the same blood as Hal, had a bad streak running through him and if she was any judge of character would have already seduced Ally Buchanan. What other reason would he have for running away with her? He would need to make sure of her before returning her to her father or perhaps they were already married. She thought, knowing him, he would have had the parson arranged, the church somewhere on their escape route prepared, a ring on Ally's finger and a marriage certificate in his pocket to show her father before Alex Buchanan, and his three great sons, set about him with the thrashing he deserved.

"Do you intend going after them, sir?" Hal asked politely.

"Lad, if I knew where they were I would. Do you think I want my daughter married to that blackguard?"

Despite his knowledge of Perry's reputation Hal's face reddened with anger. After all he was related to the "blackguard" in question.

"Sir, I'm sure my cousin has nothing but honourable intentions towards your daughter—" he began.

"Don't talk daft, lad," Alex said flatly. "If he'd had honourable intentions why didn't he come to me, as you did to Reed Macauley, and make them known? I swear I'll thrash him to within an inch of his life when he brings her back, married or not. Well ..." He turned away towards the door which Hal held open for him. "I'd best get back to my wife and hope to God he brings my lass back with a ring on her finger, for her reputation's worth nothing now. Hell's teeth, I wanted something better for her than a rake like Sutton but it seems beggars can't be choosers." His face was set in grim lines of despair.

There had not as yet been a great deal of snow, despite Dobby Hawkins's forecast. Just an inch or two to cover the ground, freezing where it fell, but as Alex Buchanan mounted his horse which Chuckie held for him, watched by Hal and Briar, great soft snowflakes begin to drift by the window, floating as gently as feathers to the ground where they began to form a steadily thickening carpet of pure, unsullied white.

He was not to know that it would be another season, a long and interminable six months before he set eyes again on his daughter.

Chapter Thirteen

It was August. A warm, bright day with a breeze from the south-west, a pleasant change from the normal, biting wind that swept across the land of the lakes and mountains even in summer. The field below the farm where Hal had hopefully planted corn was starred with the vivid scarlet of poppies, and growing in the field banks were harebells, blue as the sky above. The honeysuckle burgeoning on the farm-house wall filled the air with its heady aroma, causing the senses to reel, and in the cradle beneath the shade of the vast horse chestnut tree, the child waved his fists, doing his best to capture the sunbeams that dappled the leaves above him. He babbled cheerfully, then, gripping the sides of the cradle with two chubby, dimpled hands, pulled himself to a wobbly sitting position. Amazed and delighted with himself, he grinned at the two women who gazed at him in wonder.

"Dear Lord, he's sitting up," whispered his awestruck mother, the expression on her face declaring that no child, ever, had been as clever as hers.

"My dear, I believe they do at his age," Annie Macauley said smilingly, "but he really is a dear little imp, and so even-tempered, just like his pa."

"Yes, isn't he, though that red hair comes from you and me."

The two women contemplated the handsome boy, their expressions similar ones of doting fondness. They were very alike, mother and daughter, the mother, despite her approaching fiftieth birthday, still supple, slender, her skin firm and creamy, her face serene in the knowledge that her husband loved her as much, if not more, than he had when they first met so long ago. Below them lay the well-cared-for roof of the farmhouse in which she had been born and in which she had spent so many years of drudgery, first in the hands of her hard and hard-working father, then when he died on her own behalf, in an attempt to win a life for herself as an independent farming woman. All about them, scattered in the surrounding intakes and up on the fells, were the sheep which were the livelihood of the upland farmers of Bassenthwaite. Herdwick sheep, small and agile, with the reputation for the sweetest mutton ever tasted. They roamed the heights in the summer, clipping the heather and fine turf right down to the soil and needing no extra feed.

Over the winter Hal Saunders's small flock had been depleted by heavy snowstorms. Big snows, even in April, were not unusual. Under the expert guidance of Dobby Hawkins, Hal's lambs were dropped in February and March and kept to the inlands about the farm until the danger of snow was over. But Hal had other things to contend with beside the weather. Foxes had made raids on his newly born lambs and in his newly emerging occupation of farmer Hal had been horrified when ravens had torn the eyes out of half a dozen of his tottering, vulnerable little newborns. He had been incensed when he had watched an eagle carry off a small white bundle in its talons, sprinting

to fetch his shotgun but too late to save the frail lamb. He
went fox-hunting right up until May, helping the fell packs
as they did their best to rid the land of the predators.

But now it was shearing time and from the yard at
the back of the farmhouse Briar could hear the voices
and laughter of the dozen or so men, come from farms
within walking or riding distance to give a hand in the
communal clipping. They brought their own hand clippers
and, seated astride their own wooden clipping stool, a good
shearer, with a boy to bring the sheep to him, would clip
between seventy and eighty sheep a day. Before the arrival
of her mother Briar had been out in the yard watching
Hal attempt to shear a struggling, bleating ewe. She had
him over half a dozen times, scampering about the yard,
avoiding his determined hands with a determination of her
own, causing great merriment among the men. But, give
him his due, despite being a "gentleman", he didn't let
the ewe beat him, hanging on to her at last and making
a decent fist of shearing her. He had finally managed to
tuck the little pointed head under his arm, clipping away
at the underpart of the wool as instructed by Dobby when
all four feet were tied together to allow him to shear her
back. The beast had a few nicks in it, as did he but they
were both daubed with the same foul-smelling ointment,
beast and man, and he seemed none the worse for it. An
amiable sort of lad, they all agreed.

When his flock was finished he and his men, including
Dobby Hawkins, who was worth half a dozen, would help
out those who helped him. Then, when every sheep was
sheared and marked with the respective farmers' coloured
"smit" and the lambs earmarked, when the naked, scrawny
ewes and their lambs were returned to their own heaf, the
merrymaking, the "merry-neet" of dancing and drinking

and celebrating would begin. Until then Nan and Mary were kept busy fetching out great jugs of beer, laughing and being teased as they walked through the mass of men and animals in the yard, the purple hills above them, the calm lake below.

A light haze slanted across the far end of the garden and Briar looked about her in deep content. Her world, her life, her husband, her son satisfied her in a way that she had not believed possible even on the day she was married. The windows behind her were wide open on to the garden and the scent of the full-blown roses drifted through them to mingle with the perfume of the potpourri which she — amazingly, remembering her love of other, more active, more exciting pastimes — had mixed herself. A huge, overburdened bee blundered against the window, there was birdsong in the elm trees at the edge of the garden, and she and her mother were sitting in pleasing accord, drinking tea.

"He's settled then, your Hal?" Annie remarked casually, taking a sip from the fine bone-china cup Mrs Evans, in the absence of Nan and Mary, had brought out to them. She had baked dozens of great loaves and made as many cheeses from their surplus milk, her experience as a dairy-maid years ago standing her in good stead, and with thick slices of bacon, these had been sent out to the men; but Mrs Macauley and Miss Briar were presented with wisps of macaroon, slices of seedcake and coconut biscuits. Her legs were a throbbing misery but Mrs Evans's pride would not allow her to present anything but her best to her mistress's mother, despite the extra work.

"Doesn't he seem so, Mother?" Briar asked lazily, watching her son's small fists grapple with the sides of the cradle, intent, or so it seemed, not only in sitting up but climbing out of the thing.

"Indeed he does, but what about you, lass? I thought you were to work beside him on the farm. I heard you say so a dozen times before Tom was born."

"Ah . . ."

"And what does that mean?" Annie replaced her cup and saucer on the small table set between them, watching her daughter who watched her son.

"It means that soon . . . when Tom is . . ."

"When Tom is walking, or has gone to school, or is perhaps leaving home you might consider turning your hand to sheep farming? I can't quite see it happening, not just yet. It seems to me you have, to your own and everyone else's surprise, taken to motherhood with great enthusiasm." She shook her head smilingly. "Who would have thought it?" She put out a slender hand, one that had touched neither spade nor shearing clippers, neither plough handle nor scythe, neither mixing spoon nor scrubbing brush for many, many years and placed it on her daughter's bare arm. "Not that it's a bad thing, my love, for there is nothing sweeter than the love of, the loving of a child. I know, for I've experienced it twice."

Her face closed up suddenly and her great golden eyes, so like those of her daughter, became flat and unfocused. Her voice was low as she continued.

"And there is nothing more devastating than to lose a child. I know that too, for when Cat . . . went, I wanted to die. So make the most of this precious one and all the others who are to come. Oh yes, I've seen the way that husband of yours looks at you and I've also seen the way you return his look and I would be surprised if Tom didn't have a brother or a sister this time next year. Let the men, for there are plenty of them, work the farm with Hal, while you do what you seem good at. Being a mother."

They were both laughing when the carriage drew up at the gate at the bottom of the long garden. Hal had planted the two acres with laurel hedges that, when grown, would curtain the rough dry-stone walls surrounding it. Terraces had been dug out of the sloping land, each one formed into a smooth lawn. As he had promised, with the help of Mr Owen, the gardener at Long Beck, and his lad, Sandy, he had filled beds with roses, sweet William, lupins, iris, peonies, pinks, wallflowers and delphiniums, making an explosion of colour running like bright ribbons beside the stepped paths leading to the front door of the farmhouse. Against it stood the ancient and massive horse chestnut tree which shaded his wife, his son and his incredibly young-looking mother-in-law.

Briar shaded her eyes, then narrowed them as she studied the figure of the woman who, helped by a solicitous coachman, climbed heavily down from the carriage. It was evident that she was expecting a child.

"Who can this be?" Annie asked curiously, surprised when Briar leaped to her feet and, slowly at first then more quickly, began to move down the path. From over the roof of the farmhouse came the clamour of the men at work and the frantic baaing of the frightened sheep, and from his cradle where his hands clung for dear life to its side in his effort to stay sitting upright, Tom jabbered and chortled, watching his mother dart down the garden.

It was Alice Buchanan.

"Alice . . . Alice," Briar shrieked, and to the coachman's amazement, since he was not accustomed to such demonstration among the society he served, fell on his passenger's neck and hugged her. Both young women, bewilderingly, had unshed tears in their eyes.

"Well . . ." Ally managed to say at last, half crying, half laughing. "I'm glad someone's pleased to see me, especially considering the state I've got myself in."

"Oh, Ally, I'm absolutely delighted to see you. Where on earth have you been all these months? Why didn't you write? You look wonderful. Why didn't your mother let me know you were to have a baby? When did you get back? Where are you staying and—"

"Hold on, hold on, will you? Let me answer one question before you ask another."

"Ally, I'm sorry but I've missed you and worried about you but see, come and sit down."

Briar held her friend's hand and led her gently up the first set of steps, treating her as though she were made of spun glass, forgetting how strong women with child can be. She herself had not ailed a day, not even the dreaded morning sickness which seemed to afflict most women, and almost up to the day Tom was born strode about the farm and the surrounding fields, escorted by her anxious husband who beseeched her to rest as the doctor told her.

She was afraid to ask the next question that bubbled to her lips, for not one word had been heard of Alice and Perry since their elopement six months ago. Of course, the word "elopement" signified a wedding and how could she question Ally on whether there had been one? And if there had been, where was Perry?

Ally seemed to read her mind and though her lips continued to smile her eyes were flat and expression-less.

"But where is Perry, you were about to ask?" she said

lightly as though his absence were of no consequence despite the bulge of her belly.

"Well ..."

"Set your mind at rest, Briar, for I have a husband though he has deserted me ... oh, only temporarily, my love, or so he says. He is not a domesticated kind of a husband as I suspect your Hal is by the radiant look on your face, so you see he sent me on to ... well, not exactly set up home for our child, since Middlefell Hall is already set up, so to speak, but to make peace with Lady Sutton and to bear his child, which he imagines might be a tedious procedure. The hunting season will begin in a few weeks and his friends in Leicestershire begged him to stay on until ... until October at least. He wants to hunt with the Quorn."

"October?"

"When the baby is due. Or perhaps November."

"Oh, Ally ..."

"Don't you dare pity me, Briar Saunders, or I shall turn right round and get in that carriage." Ally's voice was fierce. "As much as I detest my mother-in-law I would rather be with her than stay here and be ..."

"I am not pitying you, Ally, honestly." Though of course she was.

More tea was ordered. Ally admired the handsome boy in the cradle who obliged by showing his new tooth, struggling energetically to retain his unsteady sitting position. Yes, she had already been to see her parents who had received her gladly.

"But why shouldn't they, Ally?" Briar poured her friend a second cup of tea while Annie Macauley watched the two young women with clear, shrewd eyes. She felt great compassion for Ally Buchanan, or Sutton, as she supposed she must call her, and for her family. She knew from Christy Buchanan that she and her husband had been out of their minds with worry over their missing daughter. They were aware that she had gone with Perry Sutton and though Alex had travelled down to Leicestershire, to "hunting" country, in an effort to trace the couple, had even begged names of Perry Sutton's friends from his parents, names of his hunting friends, his school friends, they had been of no help whatsoever. And Hal, who was Perry's cousin, had not moved in the same circles and had been unable to shed light on where he might be. Lady Sutton had merely confirmed coolly that her son – this was January – was staying with relatives during the hunting season but she had declined to name them, since she could not believe that her son had taken the daughter of a prominent business gentleman with him and indeed had no knowledge of the whereabouts of Mr Buchanan's – "what was her name? Alice" – none at all. Her attitude implied that if he could not keep a rein on her then he deserved to lose her and that she was not surprised to hear that she had wandered off.

So, the Buchanans could only *assume* that Alice was with Perry, much as they disliked the idea. Meanwhile Alex had hired men to search for her among the gentry in Leicestershire but to no avail. People of their class were close-mouthed about their own.

"Oh, Briar, surely you must realise how much I hurt them. I admit I wanted to write to tell them I was safe, and married, but Perry, for some reason, wanted to keep it secret. He's going off to Scotland, he says shooting grouse or stags or something and obviously I couldn't tramp about the moors so . . . I came home. I wanted to stay with Mother and Father at Hollin House but . . . well, it appears the heir must be born at Middlefell. It's a . . . a barn of a place and when I'm Lady Sutton I shall . . . Papa says he will . . ." She shook her head and laughed merrily, a false laugh. "Will you listen to me? I've only been home five minutes and already I've killed off Sir John. Oh, Briar . . ."

Briar exchanged an anguished look with her mother. The despair in Ally's voice was so apparent she was not sure how to continue. It made no sense really, not if Briar believed what her father had said often enough. That Perry Sutton was a rogue who had got his hands on Alice Buchanan for the sake of her father's money. Ally was lovely, high-spirited, her effervescence, her humour enough surely to attract any man to her, but if all Perry wanted from her was the wherewithal to continue his pleasure-seeking, sybaritic style of life then why, if they were now married, had he not brought her home to claim what was hers — her very substantial dowry and the allowance her father, in view of her condition, would undoubtedly give her?

The noise from the yard at the rear of the farmhouse continued. She could hear Hal shouting with laughter, the sound lifting the corners of her own mouth, though she did her best not to let her friend see it. *Her* life was so perfect. Her and Hal's love, with time, had deepened and strengthened and though she had come to realise that she was the more iron-willed of the two of them, that her nature, which had always rebelled against restraint, was the stronger, it made no difference to their relationship. It was not that she was the more serious, for she found her husband could make her giggle like a helpless schoolgirl, but her temperament had in it the solid resolution of her farming forebears. Forebears on both her mother's and father's sides had known hardship and the need to challenge life and take it by the throat until it was beaten. Their resolve had been passed down through the generations until it reached herself. Hal was flippant, sunny-natured, blithe as the skylark hovering in the arc of the sky, and though he was determined to make a farmer of himself and was succeeding in the undertaking it did not for a moment alter his good heart nor impair his even-tempered ability to laugh at life and somewhat ruefully, at his failures. He kept her and himself busy with the many schemes he had brewing. He laughed at her and with her. He pampered her adoringly then abandoned her for his farming duties. He indulged her, amused her, entertained her, made love to her until she was exhausted. He exasperated her and excited her with his boyish enthusiasm and though they were husband and wife they were friends and lovers.

Of course, in all this it was easy to see that he was not totally dependent on the profit he made to keep himself and his family with a roof over their heads, clothes on their backs and food in their mouths, as so many fell farmers were, which obviously made an enormous difference to his easy-going attitude to their lives. The knowledge that his own allowance, which came from his father from money left him by his mother and which, when he was twenty-five, would pass on to him to do with as he liked, was a buoy to keep them safely afloat

And now here was Ally, who had been so like herself before she was married, evidently made deeply unhappy by the way Perry was treating her. She had loved him and had been determined to have him. She had known his faults – if his wild behaviour could be so described – and, like women before her, had believed he would change on marriage. Not exactly settle down, become domesticated, since she was not, but cleave to her as her father did to her mother. Christy and Alex Buchanan had not been the conventional married couple, like Briar's own parents, but their relationship was strong and loving. It seemed that the same could not be said about Ally and Perry, and Briar found she was not surprised.

Annie Macauley stood up and smoothed the full skirt of her light muslin gown. It was a pale apple green trimmed with creamy lace at the wrist of the full sleeve and at the edge of the low neckline. Her hair, the russet of which had hardly faded since she was a girl, was carelessly looped to the back of her head with a knot of green satin ribbon and a stranger, on seeing her with her daughter, might have been forgiven in believing they were sisters. Briar was similarly dressed, her misty-blue dress tightly sashed about the waist in wide blue satin ribbon. Neither lady wore a hat, for they had both been reared outside the strict conventional mores of the day where a lady would not even venture into her own garden with her head uncovered.

"Well, my dear, I must go or your father will be up here demanding why I have deserted him for over an hour." She looked somewhat embarrassed as she realised what she had just said might be construed as a criticism of Perry Sutton's behaviour, showing up poor Alice's predicament in an even worse light. Hastily she bent to kiss her daughter's proffered cheek then impulsively did the same to Ally. She bent her head into the cradle to tickle the chin of her crowing grandson who grabbed at her hair in great delight.

"What a poppet you are," she told him, smiling then bending again to kiss his round and rosy cheek.

As though his training and years of serving the gentry had given him a sixth sense to their needs, Percy, the Macauleys' coachman, appeared round the corner of the farmhouse on the high seat of the carriage which had brought his mistress to visit her daughter. He leaped down and gave her his hand, fussing about her until she was settled, much to her annoyance, for Annie Macauley had climbed these fells about her from the moment she could toddle and would have preferred to walk the couple of miles to her home at Long Beck.

With a smart "get on there" to the horses the coachman guided the carriage down the drive. Annie waved to Briar and Ally. In her heart she thanked the fates that had sent Hal Saunders to them. Knowing her daughter as she did and her attraction for the wild and unusual, it might have been Briar crumpled in the wicker chair, six months pregnant and deserted by Perry Sutton!

Briar watched her mother's carriage until it was out of sight and then turned back to Ally. She wasn't quite sure how to proceed, for she had never been called upon to deal with the pain, distress and unhappiness of another. She had never, in her wilful, self-centred young life, given much thought to what others might be feeling. She conceded and was glad of it that she had not on any occasion knowingly hurt or deliberately turned away anyone when she might have given help. It was just that no one had ever asked for her help, and when she looked back to the way she had been before Hal's loving and calming influence, she could see why.

"Is there some way I can . . . I can assist you, Ally? Don't try to pretend you are . . . that everything is exactly as it should be. I can tell it's not but if there is anything . . . anything at all that Hal and I can—"

"Unless Hal can go to Leicestershire or Scotland or wherever he is and drag his cousin back to my side – where he should be right now – then there is nothing." Ally's voice was hard and clipped. She shifted in the chair that Mrs Evans had earlier brought out for her, her hands protectively over her belly, for though she might not want this child it was her instinct, as a mother-to-be, to protect it. Like Briar and her mother she was dressed in a misted pastel shade which was fashionable for summer wear but she had a fine shawl draped about her to disguise her swollen figure, no doubt at her mother-in-law's instigation.

"But, Ally ..."

"Besides it would do nothing for my pride to know that he had to be forced to come home. Oh, I know he will rush back when his finances make it necessary. He sold my jewellery, did you know that? No, how could you. Bring what you can, he told me, for I want them all to see what a splendid wife I have found for myself, but within a week he had them off me to pay a gambling debt which a gentleman is compelled to do. He promised me others, bought with *my* money or should I say the money he hopes to pry out of my father, which he will do, for my father won't see me without. His luck with cards, for the most part, is phenomenal and living in other people's houses as we have done for the past six months it has cost us nothing for what he laughingly calls our 'board and lodgings'. So, at the moment, he has enough for his needs and ... and when that comes to an end, as the allowance he initially had from his father came to an end, he will play his ace! Yes, darling Briar, that's what I am, and my child makes me doubly valuable." She lowered her head, not in defeat, but in bitterness, studying her hands and her full belly.

"Oh, Ally ..."

"Yes, a thing of sniggering pity, that's me, but, by God, let me get rid of this burden, which, the number of times he had me on my back. I swear he got on me to pin me down and keep me out of his way and his own enjoyment of life. But I promise I shall not be the prisoner he thinks to make me. A ready source of income is what he imagines me to be but when the heir is delivered and I am myself again I shall go to Papa and tell him that ..." She paused.

"Tell him what, Ally?" Briar put out a gentle hand and placed it on the two Ally clasped about her child. As she did so, just as though Briar's compassion was too much for her, her defiant courage defeated at last, tears gathered in Ally's eyes, brimming over and dripping from her eyelashes. They were warm on Briars hand.

"I don't know ... damnation, I don't know. A wife's place is at her husband's side," she continued. "I've made my bed so I must lie on it. All the old clichés that are trotted out on occasions such as this and I suppose when I am Lady Sutton which, by the look of the poor old man, won't be too long away, I can make a life, with my father's money, up at the Hall. I was married for my money, Briar."

"Oh, surely not, Ally. Perry loved you."

"Wanted me, Briar, wanted me in his bed and I admit I was just as mad for him, but when I see you and your son and know what you have with Hal ... Darling, you absolutely glow with it, as does your mother and, come to think of it, mine. I can tell the difference."

"Won't you stay here with us for a while, Ally? You and I are friends and—"

"What for? I have to face the life I have, the husband I have, the child I am to have, since I went into it willingly. My father knew but I wouldn't listen to him so I can only hold myself to blame for the ... the pickle I've landed myself in." She laughed tonelessly at her own choice of words then heaved herself to her feet. "Well, I must be off or my mother-in-law will make my life even more miserable with her admonishments about mothers-to-be and how they should act, at least in her world. Thank God Clarissa was married while I was away and has gone off to Scotland with the Honourable! Perhaps she'll have her bastard of a brother to visit her. I believe the Honourable is keen on murdering stags though I'm not sure he will care for his brother-in-law's free and easy way with the ladies."

Briar watched the expression that clouded Ally's vivid blue eyes and though she didn't want to believe it she was aware that Ally was telling her that Perry Sutton had already been unfaithful to her.

"Ally, I can't bear it. To see you like this when ..."

"When you are living in paradise?"

"I didn't mean that."

"Yes, you did, but don't worry about me, darling." Ally's voice became flippant. "I come from strong stock, just as you did. This won't get me down, I promise you. Now, where's that carriage?" And like Annie Macauley she was not surprised when it turned elegantly round the corner of the farmhouse.

"Thank God, at least, the Suttons have a decent carriage left, even if the rest of the estate is falling apart."

They kissed one another's cheek in the way of ladies taking their polite leave, then, again to the amazement of the Sutton coachman, flung their arms round one another for several seconds.

Without another word Ally, with the help of the coachman, conscious of the precious Sutton burden she carried, clambered into the open carriage and was carried off to what she had called the life she had, the child she would have and the husband – God help her – she had.

Briar swept up her boy and, to the bewilderment of the kitchen servants and the men in the yard, summoned her husband to her on the back kitchen step where she flung herself into his astonished arms and wept noisily.

Chapter Fourteen

Will Lucas was at the lower edge of the coppice wood when, pausing to wipe his sweating face on the sleeve of his shirt, he saw Briar Macauley, or, as she was called now, Briar Saunders, moving slowly towards him down the gentle slope of the land behind Browhead. At once something inside him – he supposed it was his heart though he did not consider himself to be a romantic sort of a chap – lurched and began to trip in the most foolish way. He felt his breath quicken, due no doubt, he told himself as though he needed to justify it, to her extraordinary beauty. She had been beautiful, God knows, before she married but now, perhaps because she was a mother as well as a wife, and was fulfilled as both, she was quite magnificent.

The term "coppice" when translated meant grown for cutting. Bark that was intended for the tanneries was cut in late spring since the rising sap of the trees allowed the bark to be cut out more easily. The felling and splitting of the coppice poles was hard, manual work but Will, though lean, was strong, tough, well accustomed since a lad to working beside his father, who had learned the art from the mother of the young woman who was approaching.

The wood covered no more than one acre, but being well managed by himself and his father was capable of producing ten thousand poles at every cutting which was a valuable source of income to his family. There were oak, ash, birch and sycamore, beech, hazel and alder, evergreen holly, pine and yew, all raw material for bark tanneries, swill baskets, which Beth and his mother sold at Keswick market, gommets, hoops, charcoal and bobbins. The Lucas family were not involved with such industries, only in as much as they sold their crop to those who were.

Briar had her child with her, a sturdy, tumble-legged boy of about fifteen months who, no matter how many times he tripped on tussocks of rough grass, measuring his length, his legs flying up in the air, picked himself up with gusto and great good humour and carried on. Though the slope was not steep he gathered momentum as he descended, his arms whirling in his effort to keep his balance, his rosy mouth open in a wide grin of enjoyment, a babble of words floating from it which she seemed to understand perfectly though to Will they were totally incomprehensible.

He watched her approach with mixed and painful feelings. There was a man's appreciation of a beautiful woman, a male regret, if that was not too bland a word, that she belonged to another, two if you counted her son who obviously held her undivided attention, and that hidden and terrifying knowledge that though she was married to Hal Saunders she still had the power to affect him in a way he knew would never die. A year or two back he had entertained the idea that he might court Jenny Bracken, the daughter of a small but prosperous farmer up Orthwaite way. Sadly he had given it up, to her disappointment, he knew, and her father's disapproval, since Will had made it plain he had a fancy for her. But could a man take a bride on whose face would always be imprinted that of another woman? He knew he couldn't and in wild despair, on the day Briar had married Hal Saunders, had come to the wretched conclusion that it would need a very special woman to cut Briar Macauley out of his heart and fit herself in the space Briar left, and where, he asked himself, was he to find such a woman?

Briar's two dogs, who had never been properly trained, and never would be now, to control her husband's sheep, lolloped about the child, doing nothing to help him stay on his feet. They were just as daft and excitable as they had been over two years ago when they had flung themselves up the fellside with her and indiscriminately scattered his sheep in all directions.

"Blackie, Bonnie," she called out as she had then, "come here, you crazy animals, and leave poor Tom alone. He has enough trouble staying upright without the pair of you tripping him at every step. Tom, wait for Mama, darling. If you keep up this pace you'll end up in the lake."

It was a dull day, the clouds hanging so low that the peaks of the mountains on the far side of the lake were invisible in the heavy mist. The lake was flat and a leaden silver grey, the newly greening pussy willows dipping their golden catkins over the edge, ruffling the waters into tiny wavelets. The heather and bracken were beginning to thicken and colour up the fellside, vying with purple mountain saxifrage among the damp rocks. There were early purple orchids clustered under the trees in Will's woodland, and water avens, sweet woodruff and red lungwort doing their spring best to brighten up the day. Ravens called, frolicking against the heavy skies and from the chimney of Browhead smoke stood straight as a ruler for lack of wind.

Both mother and child were well wrapped up with scarlet knitted scarves about their necks and mittens worked by Nan and Mrs Evans during the winter. Stout boots protected their feet though Tom's tripped him up each time one of the dogs nudged him.

Will dropped his lat-axe, smiling, unable to resist the appeal of Hal Saunders's son, and holding out his arms caught the child as he ran helter-skelter to him, swinging him upwards and outwards, round and round in what his own mother called a "twizz". The boy squealed with delight and when Will stopped shouted for "more", a word even Will could understand.

"You'll be sick, lad," Will protested, setting Tom on his unsteady legs. "There, take this" – handing the boy a smooth piece of wood – "and throw it for't dogs."

Distracted, Tom began a game with Blackie and Bonnie, the stick going no more than a few feet but the dogs patiently brought it back to him in turn, while Will's own collie, old Don, watched with rheumy eyes from the patch of soft grass where he lay, too old now for fetching sheep, never mind sticks.

"So what brings you down here, lass?" Will said carefully at last, for never, not if he could help it, would he let Briar know of his true feelings for her. He watched the boy, avoiding Briar's gaze lest she see what was in his eyes and recognize it. "It's not exactly a day for a stroll. There's rain about an' it'll be on us within the hour."

"You sound just like old Dobby," she said, laughingly referring to the old man's readiness to prophesy doom and gloom in the weather conditions. "Bottom winds" which plagued his creaking rheumatic bones, though he would never admit to the last, and rattled the windows of the farmhouse. "If Skidda wears a cap" meaning the messenger clouds that hid the summit, rain would fall in the central fells. He would pull his lip and assume a doleful expression if the sun rose red in the east, for surely it would herald a shepherd's warning of a bad day. Should the sun not shine on Christmas Day woe betide the coming apple crop, and "if the cock crows on going to bed it rises with a watery head", and a dozen other sayings with which he alarmed his fellows.

"And he's usually right," Will said unsmilingly.

She grinned and reached to tie her scarf more tightly about her. She flung back her long plait which hung almost to her buttocks. Will watched her, hypnotised by the movement of her graceful body, the polish on her hair, which when it was dragged back from her face became as smooth as silk, losing its tendency to curl except at the ends. Her lips, as red as a hedge berry, parted on her grin to reveal the curl of her pink tongue and the gleam of her white, even teeth. She appeared to be oblivious to his gaze or at least unaware of its nature, swinging about to watch her son's antics with the dogs.

"So he is," referring to Dobby, "but Tom has been cooped up all day so I decided to brave the weather and take him for a walk. I've been told I should hire a nursemaid to care for him and after the fuss I made when I was married about working with Hal on the farm I suppose it's true but I enjoy looking after him myself, at least for the time being. And Hal doesn't mind. He really is the most agreeable of men."

She shaded her eyes and looked down the field to where Tom was now rolling in the grass with the dogs, having abandoned the stick. From over the wall that divided the field from the farmyard, Phoebe and Beth popped surprised but delighted heads, brought by the noise the

dogs and the child were making. At once Tom struggled
to escape the mêlée, calling in his own particular language
to the two women, knowing that he would be lifted over the
wall, petted and kissed and carried into "Feefee's" house,
cuddled on "Beff's" knee and fed the delicious biscuits
or small cakes which Feefee or Beff always had on hand
for him.

"Bye, Mama," he called out, waving his hand over Beth's
shoulder, his transparent blue eyes shining with merriment.
Wherever Tom Saunders went he was loved and spoiled,
though as Phoebe said fondly, it was really impossible to
spoil him since he was such a sweet-natured little lad. The
image of his da in temperament and in looks except for the
riot of pale auburn curls on his head which he got from
his ma and his grandma. A great favourite was Briar's lovely
boy and Will found himself turning to smile quite naturally
at Briar when the two women and the child disappeared
into the farmhouse.

He shook his head. "There'll be no work done in the
kitchen while the lad's there. Mother is longing for one of
her children to give her a grandchild and until that happens
she'll take over young Tom there."

"And what are the chances of that happening, Will? A
grandchild, I mean." Knowing her son was in safe hands,
she leaned her back against the trunk of a tree and settled
herself for a good gossip with Will. "I seem to remember
you were sweet on Jenny Bracken a while back. Has she
rejected your advances or——"

She was surprised when Will interrupted her shortly,
his face losing its smile and closing up grimly.

"There'll be no grandchild from me, Briar Macauley, so
I'd be obliged if——"

It was her turn to interrupt. "What! Never! Come on,

Will, there must be a dozen pretty and amiable girls who would be glad to—"

"That doesn't concern you, even if there are."

"Well, there's no need to snap my head off, Will Lucas. I was only saying—"

"Well, don't. It's nothing to do with you or anybody."

Will turned away from her, aware that he was making too much of his aversion to marriage and fatherhood if it was not to be with her. He did his best to make light of it. "Besides, I'm not ready to settle down."

"Indeed, I can see that but let me tell you I can highly recommend it," unaware that she was stabbing at his heart which had settled down to a solid, uneasy thump. "Well," she said, changing the subject, feeling somewhat awkward, though she didn't know why, "that seems to be the end of our walk." She laughed, turning to look about her at the straight stand of trees that Will was cutting. He watched her, holding his breath and then, furious with himself for being so affected by her after all this time and by his own foolish words on the subject of grandchildren, he frowned and turned hastily away, shouldering his lat-axe.

"Well, I'd best get on ..." he began but a sudden commotion at the top edge of the wood, a great "hullo-ing" and the crash of horses' hooves, a man shouting and another shrieking with laughter, made them both turn in bewilderment towards the direction of the hullaba-loo.

"What the ..." Will lifted his lat-axe and took a step up the slope and Briar followed. Neither of them thought that there might be danger, for the laughter coming through the trees sounded in no way threatening, and they were right. Crashing through the wood, crushing the tender young spring flowers, lifting old Don from his feet and caring not a whit for any damage they might cause were three horsemen. One was Perry Sutton.

"Where in hell's name are we?" he shouted over his shoulder to the two horsemen behind him, neither of them known to Briar, and had old Don not begun to bark furiously, might have ridden straight on, down the field and over the wall into Phoebe's farmyard.

"Hold on, chaps," he continued, his drawling, long-vowelled voice setting Will's teeth on edge, or so it seemed, for he began to employ his lat-axe in a most ferocious manner, holding it in a two-handed grip just over his right shoulder. "It appears one of the yokels has taken exception to our riding over his vegetable patch and I do believe he means to give us all a thrashing."

"Does he indeed?" the second horseman tittered. "Well, we'll have to see about that." His laughter rose, a high neighing laugh which seemed to come through his nose instead of out of his mouth.

Will waved the axe, then realising how foolish he must look dropped it to his side and advanced towards Perry Sutton's horse, a well-bred and very evidently expensive hunter.

"I'll tell you where you are, you nincompoop, since you ask. You're on *my* land and if you don't turn round and get yourself off it I'll have you from that bloody animal and, as you said, give you the thrashing of your life. Now, bugger off."

"Well, will you listen to the yokel," Perry drawled to his grinning friends. "He's going to give me a thrashing and I'm not sure I would object to him trying, what say you, chaps. Shall we let him try ..."

He did not finish his sentence. Giving him no time to set himself Will leaped up and, grabbing the lapels of his smart hunting jacket, dragged him from his hunter and threw him to the ground where he landed on his back in a patch of churned-up mud.

"Will, don't you think you should—" Briar began, moving forward and taking Will's arm, but he threw her off as though she were no more than a weightless child, incensed, beyond reason, not only by Perry Sutton's insolence and contempt but also by the feelings aroused in him by the despairing knowledge that the love – yes, he admitted it at last – he harboured in secret for Briar would never be returned.

But Perry Sutton had more than a little experience in bare-knuckle prizefighting and with an oath he leaped to his feet and before Will knew what he was about had landed a sharp blow to his shoulder, a blow that had been aimed at his chin but luckily had fallen short. Will staggered back in surprise, for he had been of the opinion that the likes of Perry Sutton were not given to fisticuffs. All he had wanted to do was to throw the man to the ground, show him up for the braggart he was, shame him in front of his friends, then force him to limp from Will's land with his tail between his legs.

"Good fellow," roared one of the horsemen, "show him his place, Perry, and if you need a hand you have only to say. The insolent dog needs a lesson in manners."

In a moment the two adversaries were circling one another just like the fighters Perry Sutton had taken on in the prize ring, but Will Lucas had a black surge of anger in him, a maddened need to take out his frustration, his unreturned love, his determination to show the blackguard that despite his pedigree he could not ride roughshod over Will's land, and it drew him into a fog of rage which blinded him to any consequences.

Briar began to scream, surprising not only herself and the two horsemen, but Perry Sutton as well and as he turned to look at her in astonishment Will's fist caught him on the point of his jaw and he went down like a felled tree. And stayed down. Will continued to circle his prone body, blood on his fist where he had hit Perry, his face working, his feet scuffling in the muddy patch, longing, his expression said, for Perry to get up so that Will could hit him again and again. Perry Sutton meant nothing to him. He barely knew him but he had heard farmers grumble about his tendency to ride roughshod over their crops and through their farmyards, scattering their livestock and frightening their women. He was married to Alex Buchanan's lass and had a baby daughter which folk thought might settle him down, *should* settle him down but it hadn't. Now the insolent bastard was treating Will's land as though it were a public highway that was his to ride over as he wished and, the madness still in him from his conversation with Briar, Will longed to do some damage to someone, and Perry Sutton seemed the obvious person.

"What the devil . . ." one of the young men said, the one with the neighing laugh, leaping from his own hunter and hurrying to Perry's side. Briar moved too, kneeling down in the mud, putting a trembling hand to Perry's face, her own as white as the stock at the throat of Perry's friend, since she thought Perry had sustained a serious injury, indeed perhaps was dead. The second horseman hurriedly dismounted, his eyes wide with shock, then he turned on Will, his thoughts the same as Briar's.

"By God, you've killed him, you ignorant sot. You'll bloody well swing for this." But from the ground a groaning voice told him to "put a sock in it, Percy", and Perry Sutton was seen to attempt to sit up. His companion helped him to his feet, looking round him desperately as though for some conveyance to get poor Perry back to Middlefell Hall, but Perry threw him off, swaying slightly as he looked towards Will who still had his fists up menacingly as though he longed to go on and beat Perry Sutton to pulp, and Briar wondered why. She knew that Will was enraged by Perry's high-handed riding over *his* land but there seemed to her to be more to it than that.

"You'll pay for this, my yokel friend," Perry said pleasantly, just as though he were expressing a comment about the weather. "I'm afraid I haven't the pleasure of your name but . . ."

"Will Lucas and any time you want a replay I'd be happy to oblige. I must say I enjoyed it enormously."

"Did you indeed. Perhaps I'd better warn you that you won't enjoy it the second time we meet. If I hadn't been distracted by the luscious Mrs Saunders I doubt you would have got that blow in. Of course, I had no idea that you and she were . . . well, I will say no more but . . ."

"You offensive bastard. Briar had nothing to do with this."

"Really . . ." Perry put a hand to his face which was already beginning to swell. He moved his jaw from side to side as though testing it was not broken, then he smiled. "I wonder if my cousin, her husband, will see it in that light. His wife lolling against a tree in a most provocative pose laughing with a neighbouring farmer."

"You rotten, lying sod," Will roared, ready to surge towards the man who was taunting him, but a shriek from down the field brought him to a standstill and turned all five heads towards it. Phoebe Lucas, her face as red as a turkey cock's, her greying hair escaping from its tight bun,

her immaculate pinny all over the place, was floundering up
the slope, and on the other side of the wall, an amazed Tom
in her arms, was Beth. Her face was as white as her mother's
pinny and she clutched a protesting Tom to her as though
her brother threatened him and not Perry Sutton.

"What's goin' on 'ere, our Will?" Phoebe shrilled. "I've
never 'eard such a commotion in me life. Tha'll 'ave folk
from all over't fells runnin' down ter see what's up." She
stared suspiciously at the three horsemen who had invaded
her husband's land, looking them up and down as though
she reckoned nowt a pound to the three of them, then
gasped when she noticed the swelling on Perry Sutton's
face. She knew who he was, of course. Hadn't everybody
hereabouts heard of his exploits, gambling, drinking and
other things which decent women scarcely dare whisper
about and him a married man with a bairn.

"Ere, 'ave thi' bin fightin', our Will?" For it was obvious
somebody had and the two men who were supporting Perry
Sutton could not be involved.

"Mother, stay out of this. It's over now," Will began
but Perry Sutton smiled lopsidedly.

"I don't think so, lad." Had Briar not put a restraining
hand on Will's arm, he might have surged forward for
another punch to Perry's jaw.

"I'm sure you are right to protect your ... er, friend,
Briar, but there will be a reckoning."

"Fiddlesticks, Perry. Will was protecting his land, as all
farmers are entitled to do."

"His *land*?" Perry smiled nastily and again Will would
have gone for him had not his mother shrieked her
displeasure.

"I don't know what the 'eck's goin' on 'ere but it'll stop
right now, dost 'ear me. See, Briar Macauley," calling her

the name she was still known by, for was she not Reed Macauley's lass and would remain so until the day she died. Phoebe was convinced that Annie's girl was somehow behind this rumpus, she didn't know why, for hadn't Briar been as good as gold ever since she married that nice lad and settled down to being a wife and mother. Folk couldn't believe she was the same lass who had run wild on these fells, but here she was, mixed up in some free-for-all in Charlie's coppice wood and Phoebe meant to get to the bottom of it if it was the last thing she did. She ruled the roost in her small world. Her word was usually law, with her husband, her daughter and her son, though at the moment Will looked as though for two pins he might turn against her.

"See my lass," she went on, "tekk tha' lad an' get off 'ome while me an' Will sort out this pother."

"Pother! What a way the lady has with words, don't you think, chaps, but really, madam, we have not the time nor the inclination to stay ... chatting with you. I presume this bumpkin is your son but let me say this before we get on back to the Hall. He's not heard the last of this and if I were he I would—"

"You're not me, you rutting bastard and if I were you I'd get on that bloody animal of yours and get out of here while you still can. I swear—"

"Theer's bin enough swearin' round 'ere, our Will, an' I'd be obliged if tha'd get thessen down ter't 'ouse afore any more—"

"Go along like a good little boy, our Will. Go with your mama and—"

"Perry Sutton, will you get on your horse and ride off home before you cause any more damage. You really are the most offensive, derisory fool and your liking for stirring up trouble will get you deep into it one day. This is just a storm in a teacup." Briar turned to Phoebe, putting a placatory hand on her arm. "It really is, Phoebe. Two foolish men taking exception to one another. Oh, I know you were incensed because of the way Perry rode on your land, Will, but really, is it any reason to come to blows over it? See, go down and let Phoebe put something on your hand."

"That's right," Perry jeered as he was hoisted into the saddle by his two companions. "Run away with Mama and—"

Briar turned savagely away from where Phoebe was reaching out to her son with every intention, it seemed, of dragging him down the slope towards where Beth still stood dithering with Tom. She rounded on Perry, taking his booted foot in her hand, ready, in *her* rage, to drag him from the saddle.

"Leave it, Perry, just leave it. You're like a bloody schoolboy who hasn't the sense to know when enough is enough and must be forever taunting others into fighting so that you might prove how much better than they you are. You go home to your wife and child, if you can remember where you left them and do your best to be a man. Grow up. Try to be like your cousin who is twice the man you are and then perhaps someone will respect and love you as Hal is respected and loved. And not just by me. Now, go with your friends and forget all this nonsense."

"Forget! *Forget!* Not as long as I live, my dear. You have made a mistake today taking the side of this yokel instead of your own kith and kin. Your own class but then you yourself are no more than the middle-class daughter of a self-made man and why my cousin deigned to marry you will forever be a mystery to us all. But then, your prowess in bed is probably phenomenal which, I'm sure, is why my cousin chose you. That and your father's money."

He turned his hunter and, followed by his companions, began to thunder up the slope in the direction from which he had come.

"Dear sweet Lord," Phoebe whispered, holding her son's arm, whether to support him or to prevent him from racing after Perry Sutton not awfully clear.

Chapter Fifteen

"What on earth have you said to Perry? He was in a tearing temper and actually informed me, as though I were some submissive little wife who obeyed her lord and master's slightest command, that I was not to see you again and that if he heard that I had disobeyed him he would beat me within an inch of my life. I laughed, of course, which made matters worse but then matters are so bad between us how could they be worse."

"Dear God, Ally, he's not been hitting you again?"

"No, he can hardly do that since his mama would tell his papa who notices nothing that doesn't slap him in the face, and his allowance would stop. Besides, if I appeared in public sporting a black eye as I did in March – d'you remember? – her precious son would be totally ostracised. I never thought I'd see the day when I'd be thankful for the presence of old Lady Sutton but she seems to be the only one he listens to. So tell me, what happened? I know it involved that chap from the farm . . . I can't remember his name."

"Will Lucas."

"Yes, well, Perry came home sporting a very splendid

black eye of his own which he seems to think you had a part in. He was in an icy rage and informed me that you are as much to blame as this Will."

"How ridiculous. Will did nothing. It was Perry who was objectionable," Briar exploded, feeling the edge of her own temper begin to sharpen. Mind you, it had been simmering ever since the episode in the coppice wood last week when Perry's odious remarks regarding her and Will had caused such resentment. Treating Will as though he were no more than a half-witted, unwashed peasant into the bargain and no wonder Will had taken exception to it and given Perry the thrashing he deserved. Perry's insinuations had shocked and upset Phoebe and Beth who had both been close to tears, though given time Phoebe's distress had turned to anger, and it had taken all Will's power of persuasion to prevent her from marching up to Middlefell Hall and giving the young rogue, as she called him, the length of her tongue. Fierce was Phoebe in defence of her young. She could not understand his nonsensical and nasty insinuations about Briar and Will, she had raged, frightening the boy who cowered back in Beth's arms. Will had been unable to look Briar in the face he had been so shamed and who could blame him? To be accused of dallying with another man's wife was not something a man of pride and honour, which Will was, could stomach and she could tell by the way he had stumbled away from her that he was livid. He was followed by his mother who wanted nothing more than to put her arms about him and tell him to "tekk no notice" as though he were a child again.

Briar had been in two minds whether to tell Hal about the incident, since after all Perry was his cousin but then Hal was well aware, surely, by now, of the bad streak in

Perry and would not try to defend him? The strange thing was, she felt a reluctance to speak to Hal of herself and Will in the same breath, linked together, so to speak and she wasn't sure why. She and Will had grown up together and she was enormously fond of him as she would be of a brother, as she was fond of the Lucas family as a whole, but there was a tiny core inside her, a woman's instinct which told her, which *whispered* to her, a whisper to which she preferred not to listen, that there was a puzzling anomaly in Will's attitude towards her. For the past couple of years whenever they met he was brusque, not casually scornful, as once he had been, laughingly jeering at her as a girl who was beneath his young male's consideration, as older brothers do. Lately he appeared to be dismissive, almost rude, whenever they met, which was not often, gazing over her head into the distance as though she were invisible, or unworthy of his notice and it had, for some reason, piqued her, again she did not know why. Now this fight with Perry Sutton had brought something to the surface that she would have been glad to see left where it was. And what was it, her mystified mind asked, and why should she not tell Hal of the whole stupid affair? Because whatever it was that was ... hidden, might it not be brought out into the open, was that it?

She had told Hal, of course, making light of it, avoiding the mention of Perry's nasty innuendo about her and Will. Instead she made a great show of heartfelt indignation regarding Perry's rudeness, his contemptuous remarks about Will's background, which was quite legitimate, and was gratified when Hal, the least aggressive of men, agreed with her that Perry deserved the beating that Will had given his cousin.

"I should warn Will, though, my pet. Perry has a long

and unforgiving memory and if he can do this Will a bad turn he will."

"Oh, Will can take care of himself, Hal," she had told him airily, believing it, for though Will had not the experience in the prizefighting ring that Perry Sutton had, he was strong, tough, as all men of the fells were and in a fair fight could well hold his own with the likes of Perry Sutton.

They had tumbled into bed together, she and Hal, and, as they did most nights and sometimes in the dawn of the day, made love, she the aggressor, with a passion and fierceness that had surprised and delighted Hal and left them both sweated and gasping, and convinced Briar that at last she must be pregnant with their second child. She did not connect it in any way with what she and Hal had been discussing as they made ready for bed.

"What was that all about, my darling?" Hal had cried, collapsing against her.

"Am I to take it that you have a complaint?" She wrapped her arms about his beloved head and held it closely, possessively to her heaving breast.

"My love, the only complaint I have is against myself. I just wish I had the strength and stamina to do it all again."

"Perhaps I might be able to help you with that," she said, smoothing her hand down his flat stomach until it found the object under discussion.

"Hell's teeth, you're insatiable." He smiled against her breast then arched his back and groaned.

"And you are not?"

"Dear God, I love you . . ."

"Then love me . . ."

*　　*　　*

She had been in the barn with Hal and Dobby Hawkins when Nan had come to tell her that Mrs Sutton was in the "drawing-room" as Nan insisted on calling it. It was a comfortable room, furnished with many pieces of furniture from the attics of Long Beck where they had been stored for years. Furniture that had once been used by her father's mother and grandmother, country pieces that went well with the decor she and Hal had decided upon. Deep comfortable sofas and chairs in durable material of ox-blood red, a couple of bentwood rockers with plump cushions in bright colours, the old fireplace in which a good fire always burned, a decent patterned carpet — at her father's insistence since he knew how cold stone flags were — and rich woollen curtains at the window to keep out the fierce winds that shrieked over the mountains in the winter. There were plants growing in the window bottom, hyacinths in the spring and geraniums for summer, and a few framed prints, birds and clouds and silhouetted trees hanging on the plain whitewashed walls. A family room in which Tom spread his toys and books and nobody minded if it was untidy but by no stretch of the imagination could it be described as a drawing-room.

She and Hal were kneeling in the straw studying a couple of lambs, orphans which, with a few shepherd's tricks he knew, Dobby hoped to introduce to a ewe who had lost her own. Lost to the ravens and eagles that swam the sky searching for the weak and vulnerable, and to the foxes that were the bane of the sheep farmer's life. Two lamb's fleeces, taken from lambs who had perished through having their eyes pecked out, hung on the side of the pen. Their mother could be heard bleating in the next pen but if the lambs could be kept alive until their new "mother" accepted them mother and lambs might survive. It had been known for a ewe whose lambs were born dead or who had lost them to scavengers to die of it, pining away for the loss of her babies.

"I'll feed them with the teat and bottle, Dobby," Briar was saying eagerly, putting out a hand to the two feeble little creatures.

"It's night an' day, missis. Every 'our an' then they might pike away."

"And what about Tom, darling?" Hal asked, knowing how adamant she was about caring for her own child.

"Nan can take over for a few days, sweetheart." Behind them Dobby shuffled impatiently. Everyone knew these two doted on one another, an emotion Dobby had never experienced. Women were just something that interfered with a man's natural life and he'd no time for them. Never had. Would you listen to the pair of them going on and on about the bairn, her making out there was no one else to see to the bloody lambs when a lad, one of the labourer's lads could do the job just as easily.

"Mekk tha' minds up, wilta," he said sharply, for if they'd time to waste he hadn't. "Lambs'll be dead an' buried way pair o' thi' carry on."

It was at that point that Nan came to say Mrs Sutton was in the drawing-room and Dobby sneered in disgust as Reed Macauley's lass stood up and swung round as though to go with Nan.

"Ay up," Dobby exclaimed. "Ista nursin' them lambs or not?"

So it happened that the two men had gone about their separate business, Dobby to check on the still pregnant ewes in the inlands, Hal to stride up the lower fells, when Ally Sutton was shown into the barn where Briar held a lamb in a stranglehold, doing her best to encourage the little creature to keep the teat in its mouth. Hal had his own dog now, which he had trained with Dobby's help, running at his heels, her belly low to the ground. The dog was just under two years old, sold to him by Dobby who had come by him from a farmer whose own bitch had given birth to three pups and had needed only two. The dog was called Fancy, a funny name for a dog, Dobby had grunted, but then Mr Hal was a funny chap, though he had turned out to be a decent farmer and a bloody hard worker. He was searching for any ewes that might have wandered off the inlands, scraping through a hole in the wall on to another man's heaf, daft as sheep are, and might now be in trouble bringing forth a lamb.

"Can't we go indoors and sit in comfort with a cup of tea, Briar?" Ally had complained at one point, looking about her at the straw, the dust, the mess the ewes and lambs had produced, at her own dainty boots which were not made for this kind of wear.

"I'm afraid not, Ally. I've promised I'd help these lambs to survive and Hal is depending on me. Besides, that old bugger is convinced—"

"Which old bugger?"

"Dobby. He believes I can't keep them alive and that at the first diversion, like yourself, for instance, I shall wander off and leave them to die. So, you'll have to make do with me here. Now then, tell me more about Perry."

"What is there to tell? He hinted – well, he did more than hint – that you and this Will person are having an affair and he means to make trouble. I know you and Hal are solid as a rock and the way you feel about each other is legend but if Perry can put a worm of doubt in Hal's mind, he will."

"I've already told Hal about the incident." Briar soothed the wriggling lamb, holding it more closely to her chest, one arm about its fragile body while her other hand held the lamb's mouth and the bottle which was plugged firmly between its lips.

Ally lifted one foot out of the muck which sucked at it, looking at it with distaste, then retreated to the door and the cobbles just outside.

"But did you tell him everything Perry said? About you and Will. He was quite explicit, Briar."

"He was lying." Briar's voice was flat and cold.

"Lying! You don't even know what he said."

"I can guess. He might be your husband, Ally, but the man is a bastard."

"I know that, Briar." Ally's voice was patient. "Of anybody I should know that but if he can cause trouble, for you and Will, he'll do so. I beg you to warn Hal. I'm surprised Perry hasn't been over before now but he will as soon as his black eye has gone. His pride won't allow anyone to see him with a 'shiner'."

"I don't care what he has to say to Hal, Ally. Do you honestly imagine that Hal will believe that Will Lucas and I are ... are ..."

"Having an affair? Of course not but if you don't tell Hal everything that was said he'll think it very strange. And then, of course, it puts him at a disadvantage when eventually Perry spreads the word."

"Oh God, Ally, why the hell did you take up with that swine in the first place." Briar lowered her face for a moment, resting it on the lamb's soft fleece.

"What difference would it have made?"

"None, I suppose." Briar sighed deeply, distressed and angry that this cloud should have come to blight the enchantment in which she and Hal had drifted and dreamed for the past two years. It wasn't blighted, of course, not really, but the sheer nastiness of Perry's accusations, which she had put to the back of her mind this past week, hoping Perry would have forgotten, tinged the shining perfection with a faint grey shadow.

Ally stood for a moment, hoping that Briar would give the blessed lambs to some passing stable boy or labourer but Briar continued to squat against the barn wall, one lamb on her knee, the other beside her waiting its turn with the bottle.

"Well, if you can't offer me a cup of tea I might as well go home to my daughter. Not that I'm allowed to do much with her since Nanny took her over when she was born. Her grandmother saw to that. I think she imagines that if I have anything to do with her upbringing she will grow up as wild as her mother, and her grandmother on her mother's side. There are still tales about rebellious Christy Buchanan."

Briar kept her gaze on the lamb in her arms and wondered when it was that she and Ally had grown apart. They had been so alike before Briar married Hal, loving freedom, rebellious of the chains society and their families tried to put on them. She had once been taken with the idea that she and Ally might become good friends but something, she was not sure what, had driven them apart. Perhaps it was Ally's indifference to her child which contrasted so strongly with Briar's own maternalism. Ally didn't seem to mind that her baby daughter was being brought up in Lady Sutton's care while Ally drifted about searching for diversion, though not with her husband. Perhaps it was Briar's own fault. She had, she supposed, withdrawn from her, as she had withdrawn from everybody in her obsessive love for Hal, though she did not use the word obsessive. She had no time left in her life for other people, not even her own mother and father, though naturally she visited them and they her. She had committed herself totally to Hal, and to their son, and it seemed to have left no room for anyone else. She was longing for another child and though she admitted to a certain fondness for Ally, she found that what she once thought of as "fun" and attractive in her friend now irritated her. Particularly Ally's attitude to her own baby.

"I don't know why you allow it," Briar said somewhat distantly.

"I often wonder about the change in you, Briar, since you and Hal were married. I had heard you were always ready for a bit of a lark but now you seem to want to do nothing but play at 'house' which I find to be a bit of a bore. And we can't all be endowed with that sense of motherhood you have in abundance, my girl." Ally's voice was sharp. "Verity is a perfect darling and I'm very fond of her."

"Fond! You make her sound like a puppy."

"Don't, Briar. Don't criticise me. We can't all have the perfect—"

"I'm sorry. I didn't mean it."

"You're worried, aren't you? About you and this Will man?"

"Don't be ridiculous. Will is nothing to me, but I'm afraid that Hal might be furious.

"That's why you must tell Hal immediately. Get it out in the open. Now I must be off."

"Yes. I'll be over to see you when the lambs ..." Her voice trailed off miserably.

"Ah, the lambs."

That night she waited until she and Hal had spent an hour in one another's arms in the big bed then, as she

felt him relax in that posture before sleep, confessed that
she had not told him everything about Perry Sutton. That
Perry had said some unpleasant things about Will Lucas
and herself and that that was why Will had thrashed him.
She could feel the sudden stiffness of his body but she
waited, her arms still wrapped tightly about him and when
he tried to roll away from her she wouldn't allow it.

"Don't, darling, don't move away. I'm sorry I didn't
tell you the whole truth but I was afraid that you might
go over to the Hall and give Perry another dose of what
Will had already meted out. You would, wouldn't you?
Any gentleman would, but he's a troublemaker, sweetheart,
you know that, and cannot bear anyone to have what he
lacks. He and Ally are ... not as we are and though I'm
not saying that is what he wants, for he'll always be wild
and unsteady, but he resents the fact that you have married
me, a woman from a lower class, with money – no, don't
pull away. I know that didn't concern you one jot – and
you are happy. We have a son, which he wants."

Hal relaxed against her, his whole naked body folding
into and about hers. His arms, which had slipped away as
she spoke, closed round her and his mouth nuzzled the taut
nipple on her breast. In a strange way he was like a child
who has been badly frightened and then, in his mother's
arms, has found security. He loved her. He needed her.
Their life together was to his liking and so he chose to
disregard the accusation Perry had made which he knew
was a load of nonsense anyway. To cast it from him, from
them as not worth another thought. He was safe in her love
and she felt him sigh, saddened perhaps that a small ripple
had appeared in the smoothness of the waters of their life,
but safe in the knowledge that it was no more than that,
a ripple that eddied to its edges and vanished.

✻   ✻   ✻

It was a fortnight later that Will Lucas, who, unaccountably, had not come home for his evening meal at the usual time, was found by his father, sent out by his anxious mother, badly beaten at the back edge of the coppice where three weeks previously he had given Perry Sutton a "bit of a licking" or so it was said. No one knew what over, though Annie Macauley's lass had been there at the time and there were many who remembered that before she wed that nice chap from foreign parts she had been in the thick of many a scrape. Always causing trouble of one sort and another and though they would not go so far as to say she was behind this, it was a bit odd, wasn't it.

Lord Sutton's son, at Phoebe Lucas's insistence, was questioned by the local constable as to his whereabouts at the time the beating took place but he had a strong alibi, having been in the sight of several gentlemen – and who was the constable to question their integrity? – at the home of one of them. Will could only mumble through his torn mouth, wincing from the pain of his broken kneecap that had received a hearty kicking, that there had been more than one attacker and if Perry Sutton was the gentleman he purported to be he would stand up and fight, man to man.

Lord Sutton's son had nothing to say to that, though he had smiled insolently, for a gentleman does not resort to fisticuffs, particularly with a man of a lower social position. His own damaged face was well healed by this time and the incidents, both of them, were soon forgotten by all but the two men involved, and Will Lucas's mother!

The year drew on. The tsar of Russia, Alexander II, was assassinated in March. President Garfield of the United

States was shot in July, dying of blood poisoning in September, and Mr Parnell was imprisoned in October over his objection to the Land Act. The Zulu war ground on, the Boers of the Transvaal refusing to fight their old enemy and the Battle of Isandhlwana was still unavenged along with the British troops who had died there. Discontent continued, according to *The Times* which Briar read every morning. War was imminent in the Transvaal but to those who farmed in the high fells of Westmorland and Cumberland, it all seemed very far away, for the decline in British agriculture was of far more importance than outbreaks of war and disaster in other men's countries. Cheap grain from the United States, due to the expansion of their railways and the sudden abundance of cheap ocean-going steamer transport and the improvement of marine engines, came flooding into the country and no agriculture in Europe could possibly meet the prairie prices on level terms.

Shearing time came round again, for the farmer's year ran in cycles which no man, nor government, nor world affairs could alter. As the year begins he and his men do the repairs, to dry-stone walls, tracks that have been worn, occupying their days in tasks that need to be done while they wait for the important work with the sheep which are their livelihood. In April comes lambing which is timed to coincide with grass growth, and for a month Hal and his men worked without respite. Eventually this hectic season of birth gave way to easier, early summer days when work among Hal's healthy flock became a pleasure, for they knew they had been successful. Hal and Briar, with Tom on Hal's shoulders, would walk up the fells, Hal's quiet dog at his heels, well trained as Blackie and Bonnie never had been, so they were left at home in the yard. Up and up towards Dead Craggs through the deep purple of the sweet-smelling heather, the golden brown of the bracken and the shoulder-high ferns until they reached a small plateau where they rested and Tom played with stones and picked the star clover that pierced the tufty grass. Shoulder to shoulder, their backs against a grey pitted rock, their hands clasped, for even after two years of marriage it seemed they had to touch and caress whenever they were alone. Her head would rest on his shoulder, her loose hair drifting in the breeze across his lips, sighing with the sheer magic content of their lives, watching their energetic young son who turned to smile at them with Hal's sweet smile. Hal's kiss would be warm, returned with love and Tom would shout that he wanted a kiss too, rushing to fling himself into their arms, sure of his welcome before leaping up on to his father's back ready for the journey home.

By midsummer day the sheep were ready for shearing and this time Briar was ready to play her part, not with the actual shearing but with the many jobs it entailed, helping Mrs Evans in feeding the men, moving about the yard with the other women, a proper farmer's wife now, accepted as such as Hal was accepted as a farmer. The lambs were almost as big as their dams, ready to be weaned, sold, or kept as part of the flock, and the whole of the autumn was spent in a succession of sales, journeys to Keswick market. And when the lambs were disposed of, one way or another, time for celebrations, parties, "merry-neets" the fairs that took place at this time of the year.

Then it was "tup" time when the instinct in the ewes and the rams, with the shortening days, comes into play and the mating, which must take place before winter sets in, begins.

At Christmas Briar had reason to hope that she was at last pregnant again. Well, she told Hal jubilantly, could you expect anything else when he was at her night and day like that big ram that had serviced all his ewes as though his very life depended on it.

"A ram, am I, well, we'll see about that," reaching for her with a glow in his eyes, for this woman of his never ceased to excite him.

"And what if I said that I do not care to be treated as he treated the ewes."

"You mean like this," he said, turning her on to her stomach and lifting her up into a kneeling position.

"Hal," she squealed, pretending to be shocked, and down in the kitchen Mrs Evans, panting with the heat from the enormous fire that roared in the range, cast her eyes heavenwards and clicked her tongue.

"Will tha' listen ter them two," she begged Nan, her voice indulgent, though she shook her head at Mary, the kitchen-maid, since really, such goings-on weren't fit for the innocent child's ears.

"Eeh, I think it's grand, really I do." Nan smiled. "Tha' can feel't 'appiness in this 'ouse minnit tha' come throught't door. Christmas is a time fer love, Mrs Evans, and by gow, I wish I'd a chap ter keep me warm the night. Frost's thick on't yard an' I nearly went on me bum."

"Nan, behave thissen in front o't lass." But Mrs Evans was inclined to agree with her.

Chapter Sixteen

Dobby was to say it was the hardest January he had ever known and in his long life he had known more than a few. For weeks on end during the short hours of daylight the sun was a blood-red orange in the sharp, brilliant blue of the sky. The wind was so cold it burned the faces of those who were intrepid enough to go out in it and the very breath that wreathed about their heads turned to frost so that the men all seemed to sport a white beard and moustache. The white world was tinted with a clear, cold rosiness and in the wind the frozen stalks of grass and flower and shrub, the stiff bracken on the fells, tinkled like crystal bells, producing a pleasing merry sound like a small orchestra. The black silhouettes of the denuded trees about the farmhouse were clothed in silvery white along every branch and down the sides of the trunks exposed to the wind, and at night the sky was lit with a million stars which were reflected in the crisp, silvery white of the earth: a strange, unnatural luminescence by which, if one had the stamina and inclination, one could read a newspaper. The sheep, brought down from the tops, huddled together on the inlands, their fleeces heavy with the frost that covered them each night so that they could hardly get to their feet as dawn broke. Hatted, wearing woollen mittens and leather jerkins against the keen air, the men fed them, since the grass was frozen and beyond even the sharp teeth of the animals, slinging down flaps of hay which they carried from the barn.

And yet the beauty of the land was breathtaking. At midday when the earth was at its warmest, which was still bloody cold Dobby remarked, Briar proposed taking Tom out for a short walk, since the child was fractious, not used to being shut up indoors.

"Nay, Miss Briar" — for she still got the name and title by which her old servants knew her — "tha's not tekkin bairn out in this. It'll flay skin from his poor face. I've just bin across ter't dairy an' near froze. Poor Janey's near crying wi' it, standin' on them flags wi' nought but clogs to 'er feet an' milk what she put out last night is froze solid."

"Oh, bring her in, Nan. What are we thinking about . . ."

"She's a job ter do, Miss Briar, same as everyone on't farm. Butter won't churn itsenn, nor't cheese neither, an' them chickens've ter be trussed. She knew it were a right cold job in't winter when she took on dairy-maid's job."

Nan was vastly disapproving, not only of Miss Briar's intention to take out the little lad in this weather but of her concern for the dairy-maid who was well used to the changes in the temperature in her dairy, which faced north-east from where the bleakest winds blew.

"That may be so but I've seen the chilblains on her fingers and though I know the goose grease helps she must be in need of respite. Ask Cook to make her a cup of hot chocolate, and Tom and I will have one before we go out. Then we must see if we can find her some stouter boots, oh, and a pair of those woollen socks you and Mrs Evans are constantly knitting for Mr Hal.

They ought to keep her warm and she could borrow that fur-lined ..."

Nan wasn't sure what the word "respite" meant but it made no difference. "Eeh, Miss Briar, lass couldn't work in no fur-lined *anything*. 'Ave a bit o' sense. I reckon it'd do no 'arm ter tekk 'er out a cup o' chocolate as long as t'others don't see, else they'll all be wantin' one."

"Nevertheless she is to have one and anyone else who is about in the yard."

Nan tutted as she wrapped Master Tom's warm scarf, one she herself had knitted, round his neck and pulled his little cap about his ears. His curls, such a lovely colour of coppery red, wisped round the edges and his bright, eager blue eyes, so like his pa's when he was excited about something he had done on the farm, beamed up into hers. He sat obediently on Mrs Evans's stool while she laced up his sturdy boots and submitted to being given a hearty kiss on his rosy round cheek. They all loved the lad, every last one of them, even the men who looked after his pa's sheep, the wallers and ditchers who moved from farm to farm, the shepherds and cowmen and their respective wives, for the boy had a warmth and kindliness which he had inherited, like his eyes, from his pa.

Janey was sitting with her toes up to the fire, her hands cupped round a steaming cup of chocolate, which would do her chilblains no good, Mrs Evans was saying reprovingly, when Briar, wrapped up as warmly as her son, came into the kitchen to collect him.

"Is that good, Janey?" she asked the dairy-maid and was rewarded with a shy, grateful bob of the head. "Right then, Tom, my lad," she said to her son. "Let's see if we can get as far as the lake."

"Eeh, never, Miss Briar," Nan made so bold as to argue. "That there's nearly a mile an' 'is little legs—"

"Are as strong as a little bull's, Nan, so let's have no more on the subject. If it should be too much for him I shall carry him. Now, does that suit you?"

"Well, Miss Briar . . ."

"I know, you don't approve but I promise we won't be more than half an hour."

They slipped and slid and crunched through the thick hoar frost that lay across the lawn and the grass that had frozen in the fields, past Browhead where Beth, so wrapped up she was barely recognisable, was collecting eggs in the yard.

"We're off to the lake, Beth. D'you want to come?" Briar shouted, as she had once done when she was off on some escapade.

"The lake! Never! Briar, not with young Tom. It's bitter out." Beth began to cross the yard as though to say more but Briar lifted Tom in her arms and continued down the track towards the white, shining stillness of the water. As she approached the little church of St Bridget's at its edge where she and Hal were married, she was open-mouthed with amazement when from the far side just below Castle How several small figures drifted out on to the water as though it were solid. Suddenly she realised that it *was* solid. The lake was frozen and there were skaters on it. So cold was it that Bassenthwaite Lake was frozen! She couldn't believe her eyes!

She and Tom stood on the water's edge, Tom's hand in hers, both of them silent, enchanted, since neither of them had seen this phenomenon before. In all the years she had lived here, although there had been spells of intense cold, not once had the great lake frozen over completely.

"Look, Mama." Tom pointed, his little rosy face a picture of bemusement. "Walk on lake ... see, lady and man walk on lake."

Though the boy was only just two years old he was able to put several words together and could speak clearly. "Darling, they're skating. The lake is so hard they are skating on it."

"Tom skate, Mama."

"We have no skates, my darling, but we could slide on it. We could try."

"Yes, Mama ... slide."

"Let Mama go first and then when I've made sure it's thick enough you can come too."

"Me too, Mama." He jumped up and down in his excitement and her insides moved in that mysterious way insides have when the heart is filled with melting love. This scrap of humanity was so precious to her, and to Hal, and one day, quite soon, the gladness in her would be doubled when the new baby arrived. Probably in June or July, she was not sure exactly, and she would love it as she loved this child.

She found a thick branch, half embedded in the frozen water, one end on the bank and with a great heave she released it from its frozen state.

"Now stand back, darling, while Mama tests the ice."

She prodded and banged the branch on the silvery-surfaced ice of the lake but could make no impression on it so, waving to Tom to stay where he was, she stepped gingerly on to its surface.

It was as solid as the setts in the farmyard. It made no peculiar sounds, no ominous cracks or groans or anything that could be called alarming. The water was probably only six inches deep, if that, on the edge of the lake so that should it give way she would be barely up to her calves, so, holding Tom by the hand, they began to slide their feet in a fair copy of the skaters on its frozen crust. She still held the branch. With a shout of glee Tom let go of her hand and grabbed the other end of the branch and for five glorious minutes he slipped and swung on the end of the branch though she was careful to keep near the water's edge where the trees that hung over the bank and into the water were held fast by the ice. They shrieked with laughter and were quite amazed when a cultured male voice called out to them from further out on the lake.

"Did you ever see such a wonder? Your boy seems to be enjoying himself."

It was a gentleman on skates and as she and Tom watched with breathless admiration he performed one or two graceful spirals.

"Me do," Tom chortled, pulling on her hand.

"Steady, lad." The gentleman smiled. "You must ask your mama to buy you a pair of skates."

"Me skates, Mama."

The gentleman, for he was a gentleman, since the common labouring man of the district could not afford to purchase such expensive and useless nonsense as skates, and if he could, hadn't the time to be larking about on the lake, skated over to where she and Tom stood, his eyes admiring her trim figure, her lovely, expressive face, the fall of her glorious hair, hanging loose as usual, and her golden-brown eyes which were as bright as her son's.

"I wasn't sure whether it was safe further out on the lake," she told him, not at all put out by his frankly admiring glance, since she had been used to the admiration of men ever since she was a girl.

"Safe as houses, madam. I have just skated across from

the other side and I have heard that a horse and cart are to venture over later."

"A horse and cart! Heavens above."

"Indeed. Now I suppose I must rejoin my party or they will think I have gone through the ice. Good-day to you, madam."

Tom could talk of nothing else when she carried him into the cosily glowing warmth of the kitchen an hour later — which was not the half-hour she had promised, Nan pointed out tartly — for the day was already beginning to darken at three o'clock. Nan took off his little coat and hat, and unwound his scarf, removing his boots and chafing his feet, unnecessarily since he was glowing with warmth. She and Mrs Evans exchanged amazed and anxious looks as he babbled on and they began to understand what he and Miss Briar had been up to. They couldn't believe their ears, really they couldn't, and Nan, with the familiarity of a servant who has been with the family for many years and feels she is entitled to speak out, rounded on her mistress with cries of reproach.

"'Ere, get this inside tha'" — putting a piping-hot cup of chocolate in her hand — "an' sit thi' by't fire. I can't believe me ears, really I can't and tha' should have more sense at your age, Miss Briar. Wait till I tell Mr Hal. Tha'll get what for, girl, goin' out on that lake and what if it 'ad broke up, what then, tell me that."

"Oh, Nan, it didn't. It was as safe as houses. Lord, there were people skating on it."

"That's as may be but ter tekk a wee bairn out there is wicked."

"Nan, I think you forget yourself. Tom is my son and I shall decide what is safe for him and what it not. It's Sunday tomorrow and with the weather as it is I'm sure Mr Hal can

take an hour off and come down to the lake with me. If he
says that it's safe I do believe I shall go into Carlisle and
see if I can buy some skates for Tom and me, and for Mr
Hal if he can find the time to accompany us."

"Hmmph," Nan grunted, pulling the boy on to her knee
and holding a cup of chocolate, cooled down with cold
milk, to his lips.

"Do you think you should try skating, my love?" Hal
said mildly as they drowsed peacefully in one another's
arms that night. "In your condition, I mean. What if you
should fall? You know how much this baby means to you.
To us both."

The fire, one of the many that were kept going night
and day during this cold spell, flickered on the whitewashed walls and the ceiling, colouring them to a pleasing
gold and apricot, the shadow of the flames creating
patterns which they both studied with dreamy interest.

"I won't fall if I have you to hang on to, will I?"

"Oh, I'm to be included in this expedition, am I?"

"Wouldn't you like to try your hand at skating? It looks
wonderful and since it might be years before the lake freezes
again I think we should do it."

"Try my *hand* at it? Don't you mean feet?" He smiled
into her silken hair and when she began to feel for his
manhood, the most vulnerable part of any man and
therefore an easy target with which to punish him, he
threw himself away from her, rolling about on the deep
bed, becoming entangled with the sheets and quilt with her
hand still attached to him, shouting for mercy, laughing, as
she laughed, until the servants, who were washing the last

pot and pan before going to their own beds, rolled their eyes and smiled too.

Hal carried Tom on his shoulders and insisted that Briar hold his arm on the slippery slope down to the lake. As it was Sunday the frosted track that led to the water had been well worn by the folk of the district who had made their way down to look at this marvel that few of them had ever seen before. It was a favourite Sunday stroll along the water's edge, particularly in the spring and summer months, families on their day of rest, children sliding and whooping with delight, and though today they were not strolling but walking briskly in the freezing temperature there were plenty of them to bid Mr and Mrs Saunders and their bonny lad a cheerful good-day. The Singletons, Mrs Singleton on the arm of her son, Jonty, and ahead of them her daughter Anne holding on to Sammy Garnett with whom she was walking out. Phoebe had been persuaded by her Charlie to walk to the lake to look at the skaters and with them was Will, still with a slight limp from the kicking he had received by what were still unknown assailants.

Will looked as though he was about to pass by without a greeting of any sort, and for a brief moment that scene in the coppice last year flashed across Briar's mind and she knew a fleeting sadness, for Will had been like this ever since that day. Gone were the easy smile, the banter, the comradeship they had once shared, and though the thought was gone in a flash, so quickly she barely got a grasp on it, she knew that it was all to do with the shame, the humiliation, the thrust to his pride that Perry Sutton had inflicted on him. Not then, but on the day he had been beaten by thugs Perry Sutton had undoubtedly set on him. The others nodded and smiled and Phoebe stopped to kiss Tom, managing to hold him to her for a moment before he ran off towards the whirling excitement of the skaters. His mama had promised him that the very next day she would take him into Carlisle and buy him some skates all of his own and that she would teach him how to whirl and dart like the ladies and gentlemen were doing this very afternoon. He was not to know that his mama had never in her life put on a pair of skates but with her usual belief that she could do anything she put her mind to was convinced that a couple of turns on the ice would teach her all she needed to know. She would then pass this on to Tom.

The wind was not as biting as it had been the previous day, or was it that it was more protected down here among the trees at the lake's edge? As the already low sun sank further in the sky the light all about them, which had been the blue of winter and the pale, pale pink cast by the sun on the snow, began to turn to a misty violet, almost purple among the stark trees. Darkness would not be far off on this day of mid-winter and those who had seen enough of the frozen lake and the graceful figures of the skaters began to make their way to their homes and the warm fires, the Sunday roast that awaited them.

Briar and Hal, her hand in the crook of his arm, strolled at the pace of their son's exhilarated dash backwards and forwards from them to the lake, turning frequently to watch him. Briar wore harebell blue, a simply cut but expensive fur-lined pelisse which reached to her ankle bone, fitted and trimmed about the neck with the same pale fur that lined it. Her small bonnet had cream silk tea roses on its brim, the outfit a Christmas present from her mother and father. She looked superb, the beginnings of her pregnancy already putting a bloom on her.

They were both smiling in those last moments before horror struck and when it did, when they turned for that last time, it was several frozen moments, as frozen as they had believed the edge of the lake to be in front of their smiling eyes, dazzled somewhat by the glint of the low red sun on the frosted lake, before they could assimilate what they saw.

There was a hole in the ice about a foot out from the edge of the lake, a small hole through which something, could it be bubbles, scraps of debris, disturbed water, was churning. They both stood rooted to the frozen grass, and as though it were really nothing to do with them, swung about to locate their son who must be on the path behind them, perhaps following Fancy who had come with them, into the stand of trees.

He was not there, only a black and white collie who, after a moment's hesitation, began to streak down to the water's edge, to the hole in the ice, to the horror which both of them suddenly knew was there. She began to bark frantically, ready to leap into the churning hole in the ice and at the same time Briar began to whimper, a low whimper of terror that mingled with her husband's hoarse cry.

"Tom ... Tom ... Dear sweet Jesus ... Tom," he was shouting as he flung himself on to the ice which immediately gave way beneath him, plunging him to his knees in the icy water. From behind them, where Phoebe and Charlie had just decided to turn back home since it was so bitter, came a bitten-off oath and at his parents' back Will sprang into action, flinging off his coat and racing like the wind to the spot where Hal was floundering in the broken ice, going further and further out in his distraught efforts to find his little son underneath the savage, inimical grasp of the ice. Hal still wore his heavy winter coat and as his feet hit the steeply sloping shelf of the lake, he too disappeared under the ice.

Phoebe was moaning, her face as white as the frost on the ground, her mouth open wide in terror.

"Not again ... Dear God, not again," she was saying, her arm still through that of her husband who was trying to draw away from her and get down to the lake.

But Briar was faster than Will and even before he reached her she had thrown herself at the spot where Tom had disappeared. She had begun to scream now and all about them men were shouldering their way to the same spot and women were beginning to weep, holding on tightly to their own children lest they follow poor little Tom Saunders.

Briar screamed again and again, her voice frantic as she thrashed about in the water, making the hole that had been caused by Tom and Hal bigger and bigger, the ice jagged, breaking up and floating wildly in the commotion she was making.

"Hal ... Tom ... Hal," she screeched, then, as Hal had done, she dived down under the water, under the ice, impervious to the cold and the pull of it and the darkness in which she could see nothing. Spluttering, she came to the surface, her mouth full of the murky, ice-choked water, her lovely little bonnet gone, her hair streaming like copper seaweed acoss her face, her mouth open in a wide scream of despair. With another howl she went under again, swallowing water, feeling her way blindly, feeling for her son, her husband, without whom she could not live, and when she felt strong hands grasp her and strong arms pull her up from the murky depths where Tom and Hal were, she struggled wildly.

"Let me go." And like an animal she snapped her teeth viciously into the hand that held her but it would not let her go. It fastened in her hair and pulled her upwards and backwards towards the bank where a dozen other hands reached out for her.

"Let me go ... let me go ... Tom ... Hal ... *let me go* ... let me go." But Will Lucas held her to his breast and when she raked him with her nails, leaving four bloody tracks down each cheek, he did not even flinch. There were men down at the lake now, Charlie and Jonty Singleton and Sammy Garnett, along with a dozen others who were eager to get to the little lad and his father. They smashed the ice all around the spot where they had gone, thrashing about in their good Sunday suits, desperate to find them both alive, but as the light began to fade, though they kept at it, they knew it was too late. They had been under the ice too long and the cold was too intense for any man, let alone a small child to survive.

She would not be drawn away, standing shivering and howling, a wounded animal that cannot bear the pain, in the circle of Will's arms, strong, resolute arms which prevented her from flinging herself into the muddy, ice-choked waters. She did not even feel the sticky residue of what had once been her child slide down the inside of her legs and it was not until the doctor came, brought by her frantic father who had been fetched by a passer-by, to force a sedative down her throat that she slowly sank into a death-like state.

She was carried home by Will Lucas whose own heart broke as hers did.

Chapter Seventeen

They had to watch her every minute of the day and night or she would have walked from the house and simply waded into the lake that had claimed not only her husband and son but her unborn child.

Nan and Mrs Evans had, on their own back doorstep, heard of the horrific event and had not believed it. The man, Danny Hutton, one of old Bracken's shepherds who had been drawn that Sunday like the rest of the community down to Bassenthwaite to marvel at the wonder of the frozen lake, had told them of it as he ran like the wind up to Long Beck for Mr Macauley, and for several minutes Nan and Mrs Evans stood in dithering horror on the kitchen doorstep, staring out into the white and bitter farmyard where Billy, Mr Hal's labouring lad, was busy shovelling manure. They refused steadfastly to believe Danny Hutton. Daft bugger, said Nan, the very words indicating her deepening sense of unease, for she never used bad language. He doesn't know what he's talking about, she added, and should be locked up, spreading rumours like that. Mr Hal and Master Tom ... Sweet Lord ... oh dear sweet ... it couldn't be ... it couldn't be true, could it, Mrs Evans? Mary, who believed anything anyone told her, began to cry silently, her rosy young face crumpling and awash with her easy tears, her nose dripping. She wiped it on her sleeve and it was perhaps this action that slithered its terrible message into the brains of the two older women and began to grow its canker. No man, not even one as half-witted as Dan Hutton, would tell such an awful lie, not if he didn't want the wrath of Reed Macauley to fall on him, which it surely would if he spread it about.

"Now, Mary, stop that row and put the kettle on." But neither of them drank the tea Mary made, and when the procession of shocked and stricken folk, with Will Lucas at its head, Miss Briar draped across his arms, her streaming hair hanging almost to the ground, straggled into the farmyard, they staggered against one another, clutching the doorpost for support and began to moan deep in their throats. Their moaning, taken up by Mary who put her hands to her face and began to back away, became cries of anguish, for it seemed what Danny Hutton had told them was true. Reed Macauley, looking for the first time as though life had been drained out of him, old suddenly, and him so handsome in his middle years, was led, stumbling, by the doctor to a chair before the fire and given a draught of something which he drank without a murmur, so deep in shock was he. Until Will spoke sharply to the maidservants they were ready to collapse into hopeless despair, for how was Miss Briar, and themselves who had loved the little lad, to bear it. It wasn't to be borne.

"You," Will snarled, savage in his pain, pointing to Nan, "go and warm her bed and you" – to Mrs Evans, who was reeling about, ready to faint – "go and help her. She'll need undressing and" – swinging round to the kitchen-maid who was crying helplessly into her apron –

"put the kettle on and make lots of tea. No, I'll carry her up."

He steadied them for the moment so that they were able to deal with the immediate crisis and though he knew that soon, when Briar was in her bed and they had time to dwell on it, they would be prostrate in their grief, for the moment, with something to do, they did it. His own mother was there, helping to undress Briar, to rub her cold and clammily wet body down with warmed towels, to fumble her into her nightgown and put her comatose figure in the bed that she had shared for two years and nine months with her beloved husband. Annie Macauley, strong as she had always been, for had not life made her that way, was silent in her agony having gone through this before with her own little daughter those many years ago, and she was well aware what her girl would suffer when she came round from the insensible state the doctor's potion had put her in.

It was a tradition in the district to invite representatives of the homesteads on the fells to attend a funeral, one person "bidden" from each farm, the corpse in its coffin being watched constantly until the day of the funeral. Visitors came to express condolences and to touch the body as was the custom, but where were the bodies of Hal Saunders and his little son? The answer to that was in the lake which, on the very night of the tragedy, froze solid again, leaving nothing but a churned-up mass of ice where the man and boy had gone under. Until the lake thawed, which could be as late as February or March, depending on the weather, there could be no funeral. No carrying of the coffins on the "corpse-way", no church bells to toll, nine times for the man, three times for the little lad, no funeral feast where the traditional "arvel bread" would be distributed. All the sad but comforting things that marked the end of the lives of those gone and which gave to those who mourned them the sense of the drawing together of their spirits, and the will to move on. A celebration of the lives of Hal and Tom Saunders which had been short but of the greatest sweetness. When the parson who had married Briar to Hal later tried to comfort her with the fact of their happiness, she spat in his face, leaving a great gobbet of spittle trickling down his outraged cheek.

When she came to the next day her cries rose in a growing, maddened crescendo, filling the house with her grief, her rage, her terror, and what was recognised later as her guilt, echoing round each room and spilling out into the yard where the men, who by then had resumed work, for the sheep needed attention no matter what had happened to the shepherd, covered their ears. It resounded up the fells, high and tormented, to where farm women with children and husbands of their own turned their faces to the wall and wept for her. The dogs cowered, their bellies flat to the ground, afraid of this dreadful sound like none they had ever heard, nosing for comfort into the hands of the men. Fancy was still down by the lake, waiting for her master and the child, her nose to the spot where they had vanished and nothing would shift her short of tying a rope on her collar and dragging her forcibly back to Bracken Ridge.

Again it was Will Lucas who took charge, for the men drifted about, waiting for someone to tell them what to do. He had expected Reed Macauley to take command but it seemed, for the moment at least, Briar's father, normally the strongest, proudest, most arrogant of men, was beaten. He had idolised his young grandson and had thought a great deal of his son-in-law. His love for his wife was, and always had been, the talk of the community, even before he married her, and though his one wayward daughter had given him more trouble than a baker's dozen of lads, his sorrow for her, for the grief she would suffer, had temporarily rendered him powerless.

Charlie Lucas begged his son to do what he could for the beleaguered family. He would manage at Browhead. It was no hardship to stay out of the cold by his wife's fire, for there was not a lot for two men to do so Will moved into the small room over the stable at Bracken Ridge where a fire in the grate kept him warm and the women in the kitchen of the farmhouse kept him fed. An experienced sheep farmer himself, he got the men on the go, for it did no good to hang about aimlessly. They all wanted to help, naturally, but what was there for them to do? Their master was gone and what was to happen next, not only to them but to their master's young widow?

"Keep them at it, Dobby," he told the old man. "Even if it's only clearing ditches or mending walls. Get them up on the fells to check on the sheep; anything to keep 'em occupied until . . . well . . ."

"Aye," was all the old man said. No one knew of it, but Dobby himself had wept in the stable, his face pressed to the flank of his master's bay, but he was calm now. He beckoned to his own dog who was as badly affected as he was. Not for the same reason, of course, since he was only an animal, but because he sensed the sadness in his master. His face was quite expressionless. "'Appen Mr Macauley'll let us know," was all he said.

Briar awoke to a familiar sense of ease and warmth. The firelight glimmered on the ceiling and walls as it always did on mid-winter days and she stretched, yawning, flinging out an arm for Hal.

Hal!

For what seemed an eternity, an aeon, the passage of time going on and on and on, she lay still, scarcely daring to breathe as she pushed back the memory of something that on no account must she allow to enter her mind. It was not a memory, for they could be good as well as bad. Hal was not lying beside her as he had done ever since they were married, nor was Tom in his little bed in the room next door. They were ... elsewhere in a place of horror so great she knew she could not, simply could not stand it. A nightmare then and when, at last, she could hold it at bay no longer, it flooded through her, hurting her so badly, so agonisingly, an actual pain that could have been caused by boiling water on her shrinking flesh or the thrust of a knife in her breast, she twisted about in the bed in an effort to escape it. She screamed for mercy, her screams like those of an animal, one that has been tormented beyond endurance and at once the room seemed to spring into action with a dozen people all converging on her bed at once. The screams continued to erupt from her throat, and she could taste blood in her mouth. They came from the very core of her soul, now empty without Hal in it, without her child, both of whom had ... had ...

They did their best to hold her down, for she was as strong as a horse in her determination to reach that place by the lake where she had seen them last, and where, if she couldn't find them on the surface, she would go beneath the ice and join them. A man, his face distraught, bent over her and put strong arms around her and for a blessed moment she was convinced it was Hal. He wept, his cheek against her cheek, his hair falling over her face, his voice calling her by all the lovely names Hal called her. "My love", "darling", "sweetheart", and one she hadn't heard, "lovely girl" and she knew then that it wasn't Hal; that they were trying to trick her. The man had scratches on his cheek and she did her best to put some more there, for if she didn't get down to the lake soon, Hal and Tom might not wait for her.

"Let me go . . . please . . . let me go to them," she wept. Someone held her nose and when she was forced to open her mouth poured something down her throat and the room grew misted and dim, and she sank into a lovely dream where she and Hal and Tom and another child, a little girl, played on the edge of the lawn with Fancy and Blackie and . . .

"If only they could be found," his mother wept. "Wi' a funeral 'appen she'd accept. Grieve, aye, we're all doin' that, but it's not 'avin' owt ter bury what mekks it worse. Six weeks an' that damn lake still frozen."

"And even then, my sweet, we may never find the bodies," Charlie said sadly.

Phoebe turned her back on them and put her face in her hands. "Nay, lad, don't say that. Lass'll never be right this road. She needs ter see't coffins goin' inter't ground. Eeeh, Will" – swinging round to her son – "is she never ter 'ave a bit o' peace?"

Patiently Will pulled his tormented mother into his arms while his father and sister, Beth in tears, looked on compassionately. They barely saw Will these days he was so busy up at the farm which now belonged solely to Briar Saunders. Well, it would when the body of her husband was found and his death established by a court of law. It was almost March and the land was beginning to thaw. Last night it had rained. A thin drizzle, no more, but soon the solid ground would soften. The pregnant ewes were all safely down on the inland pasture ready for the birth of their lambs which would not be long now and Will knew that his father needed him at Browhead. Reed Macauley, who had regained his senses which had fled when Hal and Tom died, was willing to offer the loan of men from his own place, or even pay for Will to hire extra. Will had kept the little farm that Hal had begun on its feet, directing Hal's shepherds, managing the farm, keeping it going in the hope that when Briar was ... well, the only word that could be used was *better*, for she would never completely recover, he and Annie had sadly decided, she would find the strength to continue the work her husband had begun.

For six weeks she had sat in a chair wherever they put her, silently distant. Her eyes, brown and dull, staring at nothing in particular, her face expressionless so that at first they had believed that, with time, she would come to herself. Not the Briar she had once been, of course, but recovered enough to get on with the life her husband had begun. Carry on his work, for what else had she?

They all came to see if there was anything, anything at all they could do for the stricken young woman, even Lady Sutton who had not really cared for the girl her nephew had married, coming to share her grief, for had not she herself been bereaved. Her own sister's son and grandson struck down in such a horrible manner and surely the widow would want to share her grief with her husband's aunt. She was somewhat put out by the look Briar gave her, her eyes moving slowly in her direction, not knowing her, not caring that Lady Sutton was suffering as much as she did.

Crazy, she told her husband later through her own tears, losing her mind, giving in, which was not something Lady Sutton, who had been brought up to be steadfast in the direst of tragedies, could admire.

Ally Sutton, her face puffed with crying, her tears brimming still, sat with her for ten minutes, then, not able to bear the dreadful silent grieving, the tearless agony of the woman she had called friend, left in her mother-in-law's carriage, and when she got home spent an hour in Perry's arms, something that had not happened for weeks but which gave her a small amount of comfort and him a great deal of satisfaction.

Maggie Singleton, who had many years ago sat with Annie when her girl was killed and now was prepared to do the same for Briar, helped in her quiet way, for had it not been for the Macauley family her Jake would never have aspired to be a farmer in his own right. Besides which she was a kind, good-hearted woman who would give a helping hand and warm concern to anyone in trouble.

Christy Buchanan drove over from Ambleside, offering any help she could, sitting on the opposite side of the bedroom fire from Briar, talking of anything that came into her mind in an effort to bring the senseless woman, who stared sightlessly at something over Christy's shoulder, from the deep dungeon of her agony.

But it was Nan, or Annie or Phoebe, sometimes Beth, who bore the brunt of it. She never spoke, ate little and that only when she was forced; and the first time she was left alone, for no more than two or three minutes while Phoebe went to answer a call of nature, she simply vanished. It was still bitterly cold, an east wind shrieking over the fells and she was without a coat or even decent shoes to her feet.

The sound of Phoebe screeching through the house

brought them all running, Nan and Mrs Evans and Mary, Mary still clutching the potato she was peeling in one hand, the paring knife in the other.

"She's gone, she's gone. Oh quick, Nan, set the men to search fer 'er. Down by't lake I shouldn't wonder. Oh, Will, I were only gone a minnit," to her son who appeared from the back yard where he was studying a sick sheep brought down by Dobby. "She'll catch 'er death, which we all know she'd not bother about. Poor lass ... no coat an' only 'er slippers on."

Will raced down the slope at the front of Bracken Ridge, jumping the wall into the yard at Browhead where his father watched him tear past in astonishment. Down the field, scattering his father's heavily pregnant ewes, the knee-cap that had been broken by Perry Sutton's thugs and which had left him with a slight limp not even noticed or, if it was, ignored.

She howled in tormented rage and pain when he dragged her from the ice which she had broken in her demented determination to get to Hal and Tom. She was soaked almost up to her waist, her heavy black skirt, the one the women dressed her in each morning, dragging her down to her knees. Her hands were bleeding as she struck at the lethally crested ice. Her hair was a wild tangle from beneath which her eyes peered out like an animal from its den and her face was a terrible sight, crazed, despairing, her flesh the colour of the dirty frost on the edge of the lake.

She knew him.

"Will, if you feel anything for me, let me go. Can't you see ... I can't live without Hal. Let me die ... for God's sake, have pity ... let me die."

"No ... no, I will not."

"My child ... I cannot bear it ... please ..."

She clawed at him, her nails raking at his eyes. She had nothing but her bare fists, her feet, her fingernails to tear at the vulnerable parts of his body in her effort to escape him, but though her agony was wild, giving her strength to fight him, he loved her and his love gave him a force that outweighed hers. He took a handful of her hair, forcing her back by it from the hole she had been enlarging, dragging her to the bank, dragging her up the bank away from the dangerous ice. He held her in his arms. Even so she continued to struggle, sinking her teeth into the fleshy part of his hand but he would not let her go as he tried to calm her, his voice soft and tender and loving, calling her "my lovely girl". And when his father, who had run after him to the water's edge, came upon them, his own face contracted with pain. And understanding. Charlie Lucas knew what it was to love a woman who did not return his love. So that was the way of it, the expression on his face said, and when his son stood up, still cradling Briar in his arms, he made no attempt to help him. Will needed to be alone in this moment. Briar had quietened. She was in a pitiable condition, a state of near collapse, and when, as before, Will lifted her into his arms, cradling her head on his shoulder and began to stagger up the woodland slope in the direction of Browhead, Charlie merely fell in behind.

Phoebe had reached Browhead when they got there, with Nan close on her heels. This time Will was forced to give up his burden to his mother who shooed him and Charlie from the house, and with the help of Nan and Beth stripped Briar naked. Wrapped in a warm blanket, her feet on a tuffet to the fire, she fell asleep, naturally this time, and when she awoke three hours later it was Will who carried her home, his mother, like a hen chivvying her chicks across the farmyard, only a step behind him.

The next time she escaped, as Nan described it, was at lambing time, late April when the last of the frost had finally thawed, and down on the water men were searching the lake for the body of a man and a small boy. She went in the other direction this time, climbing up Dead Crags to the summit at Bakestall, over two thousand feet high. Bakestall was a rough, raised platform on the sprawling north flank of Skiddaw. It was perched high above a steepening slope from which had been scooped an enormous hollow as though a giant hand had clawed at and ripped away the fellside, a horseshoe of cliffs, colourful even now with bilberry and brown and purple with ling. But grander even than this grand sight was a series of magnificent waterfalls which raced down a precipitous wooded ravine. The waters leaped exultantly, plunging over rocky lips in a mighty torrent of roaring and thrashing before racing down to gentler pastures. It was here that she and Hal used to swim, naked and alone, out of sight of every living creature but the gently moving sheep and the wild swooping of the eagle and kestrel.

Had she not sat for an hour living the past again, Fancy would not have found her, for it was up here that the dog had patiently watched her master and the woman frolic and splash and it was she who led Will to her. She was about to go into the water, jumping over the lip and into the abyss, for in her deranged mind, if she could not join Hal and Tom in the lake it seemed to her that to go from here, down, down to where the water met the lake, was as good a way as any.

She wept hopelessly, despairingly in Will's arms, begging him to let her go, begging him to tell her *why* he held on to her, why he would not let her die. She could not live without them. What was there to live for? And he could not tell her, for did she care who the hell Will Lucas loved, or why?

Lambing time was over when she finally went and this time it was evident that she had planned it. No desperate race to avoid the keen and watchful eyes of Will, Nan, Phoebe and her mother. No wild dash to the water that still held the bodies of her husband and son but a carefully orchestrated disappearance after every member of the household was in bed and asleep. A truckle bed had been pulled out from under Briar's bed and as Nan got into it, it being her night for keeping watch, her young mistress was fast asleep.

Something awoke the maidservant in the night but when she got up and put fresh coals on the fire, for the nights were still cold even if it was halfway through May, as the fire blazed up the sleeping form of Miss Briar was visible under the quilt.

Nan scurried back into her bed and burrowed under her own warm quilt, falling into an easy sleep from which the soft closing of a door somewhere in the house did not wake her. She awoke at six, stretching and yawning her way from sleep, glancing over at Miss Briar's bed, but her mistress was still sleeping so Nan took a chance and slipped downstairs to fetch a jug of hot water to wash in. Still Miss Briar slept and Nan sighed with relief, for a good night's sleep, according to Mrs Evans, did wonders for your health and Miss Briar's health had caused considerable worry over the past few months. She had to be forced to eat and in the night had been heard to weep desolately for hours on end, distressing whoever was attending her that night. Well, she'd certainly had a good night and soon, when the morning was a bit brighter, Nan would wake her and see if she could get a bit of

porridge inside her. Perhaps an egg in milk which was easy
to digest.

Mrs Evans dropped her frying pan and Mary fell over
the cat which had leaped up at the sound of Nan's
screeching, and when the maid pounded down the stairs
and burst into the kitchen they were both ready to scream
and jump up on the table in terror.

"She's gone. Dear good God, she's gone," Nan shrieked,
flapping her hands about as though warding off a swarm of
dangerous bees, her normally tidy hair all awry as though
she had run her hands frantically through it.

"Who?" quavered Mary.

"Miss Briar, tha' daft bugger," Nan exploded.

"Jesus and all 'is angels."

"Where's she gone then?" This from Mary who was
only just about getting over the last lot, as she called it.

"'Ow the 'ell do I know?" Nan was savage in her fear.
She wanted to smack Mary's silly face, really she did,
but there were more important things to think of than
daft Mary.

"Run and fetch Will."

"Me?"

"Yes, you, yer stupid . . ."

Mary began to cry but nevertheless she ran out into
the yard, screaming for Will, screaming that Miss Briar
had vanished, screaming into the faces of the astounded
men, Billy at the manure which was his usual job, Dobby
grooming his old dog and Janey the dairy-maid who'd run
out of the dairy to see what all the noise was about.

They searched every place they could think of, men from
other farms coming to lend a hand, going far up into the
fells and down round the lake, her father galloping up hill
and down dale on his mare while her mother sat in frozen

silence, somewhat as her daughter had sat for the past four months, and waited for them to tell her that her daughter was dead. No one did and the quiet woman in the deep bonnet and a plain shawl carrying a small portmanteau stared from the window of the train she had boarded in Keswick, stared with fixed unblinking eyes at the scenery beyond the window.

Chapter Eighteen

The door opened fiercely as though the woman with her hand on the doorknob had been interrupted in some task of weighty significance and was not at all pleased to be snatched away from it. She stared suspiciously at the figure on her donkey-stoned doorstep, the one she had finished only five minutes before, and her gaze dropped to the caller's boots which seemed to pass inspection.

"Yes?" she said, straightening her already straight back, her attitude saying that this had better be important, something that would be worth her while opening her front door. If there was anything she could not abide it was time-wasters.

"I'm looking for rooms," the plainly dressed young woman said. No more. No "good-day", or greeting of any kind, not that Jess Handy wanted any, for she was a woman of few words herself.

"Oh, are yer? And who said yer'd find 'em 'ere?"

"A gentleman at the dockside."

Jess Handy bristled as though deeply offended, for no respectable woman would be found wandering at the dockside, none that she'd care to know at any rate. It was well known that only women who were travelling, boarding ships for parts unknown, at least unknown to Jess Handy, or disembarking having been there, these, and whores, hung about down there.

"I don't *know* any gentlemen at dockside and I've no truck wi' anyone who does so yer'd best clear off."

The young woman squared what looked like weary shoulders and hitched up the portmanteau she carried, a decent bit of luggage, Jess decided, real leather if she was not mistaken, and Jess Handy rarely was.

"The gentleman said he was your brother-in-law. You *are* Mrs Handy, are you not? This *is* Peter Street, I believe."

Well, whoever she was she was not from round these parts. She spoke real "posh", like the gentry, not that Jess Handy had much to do with them but she knew they didn't have the thick, adenoidal tongue of Liverpool which was a combination of Welsh and Irish and the cosmopolitan population that had put down its roots by the river. The people of the world flowed through Liverpool's streets. Some remained and settled down; they bred, and their habits, their cultures, their thoughts, their speech and religion were assimilated into the life of the city. Jess herself was only a generation away from the green sod of Ireland and the faint brogue she had picked up from her parents in her childhood still remained.

"Potter sent yer!"

"I'm afraid he didn't tell me his name. I was looking for a passage to America and when I asked him—"

"A passage ter America! On yer own?" For once Jess was rendered speechless and for a moment she let her guard down. "No wonder Potter sent ya on 'ere. 'E musta thought ya were mad." She was clearly astounded, so much so she almost opened her door to allow the young woman in but she regained her composure and stood her ground.

"Mrs Handy, I do assure you I'm not mad and if there had been a ship sailing this day I would have been on it. But Mr ... Potter, did you say, told me there wasn't and I was to make for Peter Street, giving me instructions on how to get here where he said you would ... put me up until I sail. A day or two, no more."

"Queen, yer'd be berrer off at the Adelphi. That's where your sort stop." Mrs Handy made it sound as though the Adelphi, which was the best hotel in Liverpool and where royalty had been known to spend the night, was no better than a flophouse and far inferior to her establishment.

"I couldn't afford it."

Well, lass was honest if nothing else, Jess thought, looking her up and down with a steady gaze, which might have been insulting but the woman on the step met her eyes calmly, lifelessly, as if she cared neither one way or the other whether Jess let her in or not. Come to think of it she had a strange look about her. Not threatening, or anything like that, or Jess Handy would have shut the door in her face, but sort of *lost*, her eyes shuttered, the expression on her face ... well, *haunted* Jess would have said if she'd been a fanciful woman, which she wasn't. In fact she'd never seen such sadness in anyone and this lass could be no more than twenty or so. She wore gloves so Jess couldn't tell whether she wore a ring or not.

Jess dithered, which was not like her and she felt a certain annoyance with herself.

"I don't take females," she said finally, ready to shut the door but something stopped her and for the life of her she didn't know what it was. The woman just stood there, her thin face peeping from under the brim of her large, old-fashioned bonnet, her gloved hand clutching her plain black shawl about her. She was all in black, Jess noticed and curtly she asked, for it had just occurred to her, "Are ya a widder?"

The effect the words had on the woman was dramatic. Her face crumpled and every vestige of colour drained from her face. Her eyes were filled with an agony that Jess felt stab right through her own body as though the pain the woman suffered had been passed on to Jess, which was decidedly strange and something she had never before experienced. The woman didn't speak. Her mouth opened wide as though she were about to shriek then she clamped it shut. She swayed slightly and Jess put out a hand to her then withdrew it hastily.

But she had been moved against her will by the woman's obvious suffering which had, for a second, broken through her calm and frozen composure.

She stood back from the door. "Yer'd best come inside," she said grudgingly, "an' mind't cat. She sleeps on front door mat."

Briar Saunders followed Mrs Handy along a narrow passage with a closed door on one side, towards another that stood wide open. Beyond the door was a kitchen where she was told brusquely to "sit yersen down". It was small and steamy and very hot. It led into a narrow scullery with an open door, beyond which was a tiny walled yard. It was all painfully clean, the stone floor meticulously scoured, the walls washed white, the big, cast-iron range in the kitchen gleaming with black lead. If her front step, her kitchen table, which was as white as the frost at Bassenthwaite, and her kitchen floor were anything to go by, Jess Handy was a good housewife.

But she was something else as well. She liked things

that she called "nice". She and Albert had often bought little knick-knacks at the market in town, or a picture that took their fancy. Nothing expensive, mind, since Albert was thrifty, and so was she. They wanted to have enough to live out their old age in a modicum of comfort, which they would have done if her Albert had not been in the wrong place at the wrong time and been flattened by a heavy piece of timber that had fallen from a crane on the dockside. The pictures hung on the kitchen walls, pictures of mountains and lakes, dogs lying outside a door and horses flicking their tails in a meadow. There were more in her parlour which was now a small dining-room where her lodgers ate their meals, along with ornaments, Toby jugs and painted plates with "Wilful waste makes woeful want" written round the edge, Staffordshire figures of the royal family, some on horseback, painted in bold colours and much loved by Jess Handy, not only for their beauty, as she saw it, but for the lively memories of her and Albert that they evoked.

Though Briar had scarcely noticed, indeed did not even glance at her surroundings as she followed the instructions given her by Mrs Handy's brother-in-law, the streets through which she walked were narrow and dark, like canyons above which only a glimpse of the blue sky could be seen. The terraced houses on either side of the streets were identical, a front door with a window beside it, two windows above that and in the roof a tiny dormer window. Though it was still only May, the day was warm and in every open doorway women lounged, their arms folded across their chests, their shoulders leaning on their warped and rotting door frames. Each one wore a pinny, most of them grey with dirt, and on the broken pavements equally filthy children, barefoot, played games and shouted to one another. Girls skipped in and out of a whirling rope, chanting some incomprehensible words, while trundling between the cracked pavements a ramshackle cart drawn by an emaciated donkey was dragged along by what she was later to learn was a "rag and bone" man.

Every single person, children, women, the rag and bone man, stopped what they were doing to gawp at the tall, black-clad woman who walked carefully along the street, even the donkey seeming to turn his head for a look.

The houses in Peter Street were exactly like those in all the other streets she had traversed but number fifty-one, the address given her by the kindly man at the dockside, was in a much better condition. Indeed most of them were well looked after, just as though those with "a bit about them", as they called it, had banded together in an effort to drag their neighbourhood out of the general muck and muddle of the rest. Albert Handy, dead these five years, had been a careful man, a man who had saved and insured his own life to provide for his Jess whom he loved deeply and respected wholeheartedly. He had left her with a tiny income with which to rent the property he himself had restored and maintained. A fitter and carpenter he had been, well respected and sadly missed by his wife, though she let no one know it, not even her sister Elsie, who was married to Potter. And to keep her home, and herself, she took in lodgers. She was a woman who believed in giving value, a woman whose bed linen was snowy, whose meals were wholesome and filling and, wanting no complications, took in only gentlemen. Not real gentlemen, naturally, but men with decent jobs, steady and reliable regarding the question of rents. She was strong-willed and strong-backed, adapted by nature and circumstances for the carrying of burdens. Her own and no one else's! Heavy burdens, and she'd had plenty of those.

"Sit down then," she ordered and Briar did so, choosing a hard wooden chair by the spotless wooden table. She kept her portmanteau on her lap. Jess Handy did not sit. With a look about her that said she'd no time to waste on idle chatter, she removed a flat-iron from its rest on the fire and resumed the task with which she had evidently been occupied when Briar knocked on her door. She was ironing a shirt, a decent workman's shirt and as though she wasn't about to stand any nonsense, from it or her unusual caller, she thumped her iron up and down the blanket which was laid on the table where she worked.

She waited, glancing now and again at the young woman, the tragic young woman, she decided, then wondered why. Up and down the flat-iron banged and from the narrow hallway the cat wandered in, sniffing round Briar's skirts, rubbing herself in a sinuous way about the table leg before settling down on the rag rug by the range. From the street a male voice could be heard calling and at once Mrs Handy flung the iron back in its stand over the fire and reached for a jug.

"Damn, it's milkman," she muttered. "I nearly forgot what wi' one thing an' another," obviously meaning Briar. Darting down the hallway she flung open her front door.

"Fred," she screeched, "I want a couple a' pints; no, best mekk it three," she added, glancing back towards her kitchen where the still figure of the young woman was outlined against the open scullery door.

"You got visitors then, Mrs 'Andy?" a cheerful voice asked.

"Never you mind, Fred Jessop."

Carefully holding the jug which brimmed with frothy

milk, Mrs Handy re-entered the kitchen. Taking down a bowl from a shelf she filled it with cold water from a tap in the scullery, put the jug of milk in it and set the bowl on the cold marble slab which her Albert had picked up for next to nothing in one of his scavenging trips. A great one for scavenging, was Albert, picking up all sorts of useful – what other people would have called junk but which Albert always had a use for – objects over the years. Over the jug she placed a cloth, the ends of which hung down into the water. A grand way to keep milk fresh, Jess had proved time and time again. When others drank sour milk left over from yesterday, *her* lodgers didn't.

Jess sighed deeply. "Well, queen, if ya not ter tell me what ya want ya might as well gerron ya way. I've me lodgers comin' in soon an' a nice bit o' cod ter be cooked fer their tea."

Briar roused herself, glancing about the kitchen as though she were not awfully sure how she had landed up here. Here or in Liverpool for that matter. She had slipped out of Bracken Ridge in the middle of the night, leaving no note since it had not occurred to her to do so. She had one thought in her head, a repetitive thought that went round and round, coming back to where it started and then setting off painfully again. She had to get away. She didn't imagine for a minute that she would leave behind the deep and agonising emotion that was destroying her but perhaps in another part of the world, far away from where her happiest memories and her worst nightmares lay, she might be able to function at some level. She wanted to die and she had tried to die but they had stopped her. She hadn't given up the idea but perhaps ... perhaps ... She wasn't sure what the *perhaps* meant since she knew she would never be the same again but perhaps ...

She had walked and walked, heading down towards the lake that had taken her life away from her until she hit the road that led to Keswick from where she knew trains went to all parts of the country. Into her almost senseless mind had slipped the idea that she must wear something that was not part of her old life, not the fashionable, elegant, expensive outfits she had once worn and so she had put on her black dress, filled a portmanteau with something or other, underwear, her stunned mind seemed to tell her, taken Mrs Evans's bonnet and shawl which hung behind the kitchen door and set off.

At dawn a passing carter came upon her trudging mindlessly along the road by the lake and had given her a lift on his cart tail, dropping her off at the railway station in Keswick.

She had taken the first train that pulled into the station which happened to be going to Lancaster and there, for some reason she did not understand, she got off and waited until another train came in going, though she did not know it at the time since she was not really aware of her surroundings or the people who stared at her curiously, to Preston. By a somewhat circuitous route, getting on and off trains in a haphazard fashion, which she did not consciously think of as putting off any pursuers, she fetched up in the tumultuous turmoil of Lime Street Station in Liverpool.

When she ventured hesitantly out into the racket and din of Lime Street and then into Dale Street she felt something, not a conscious feeling of being in the right place but a sense of recognition, as though this was where she wanted to be.

For the first time in months she walked purposefully, her head erect, her portmanteau held with one hand, the other holding her shawl firmly about her shoulders. And when she reached the dock area and the great mass of ships that sped about the river, or stood proudly at berth, for several moments she felt a lift of her dead spirit, a sense of life and the feeling of being, at last, on the road to somewhere. It was all a bustle, a noisy, exuberant rush of people of all sorts, sailors, dock labourers, gentlemen hurrying she didn't know where, ladies holding their wide skirts out of the way of men carrying bales and boxes, men with huge hammers striking blows that made her head echo, dogs barking, men whistling, jutting figureheads of gaudily painted women, casks, horses, steam, smoke, great chains and ropes lying across her path. Over it all was the most wonderful smell. She could detect coffee, spices, tar, a salty smell that must come from the water, timber and others she couldn't recognise but which she thought were most pleasant. This was it, she thought, this is where I am meant to be, but where was she to start in this chaos? Her indecision must have showed, for when she swung about in confusion a squat, ruddy-faced, amiable gentleman with a pipe in his mouth spoke to her in a broad, nasal voice which she could barely decipher.

"Are ya lookin' fer summat, queen?" he asked genially, taking the pipe out of his mouth to smile at her.

"A ... a ship," she said hesitantly. She hadn't meant to say that but somehow it just came out and she knew it was right.

"A ship, lass, what kinda ship?"

He drew her out of the way of a cart loaded with casks, placing her behind an enormous contraption round which a rope was fastened.

"What kinda ship?" he said again. "Where ya goin'?"

"Anywhere."

He looked astounded, putting his hand on her arm as though to stop her from dashing off and climbing aboard the nearest ship by the dockside, which she would have done.

"Nay, lass. Ya must know where ya wanter go."

Behind him was a small shed and on the side of the shed were tacked leaflets. One was headed LIVERPOOL AND DOUGLAS, ISLE OF MAN, informing those who were interested that the steamship *Tynwald* was appointed to sail daily. Another announced that the *Minerva*, lying in George's Dock, was to sail to New York and another was off to Melbourne, Port Philip. Those wishing to secure passage on any of these ships, or indeed any of the many other destinations, could purchase their tickets at the office of the shipping line.

Briar tore her gaze away and looked into the man's kindly blue eyes, a faded blue which twinkled at her.

"New York," she told him, doing her best to smile but not quite succeeding.

"New York? On yer own?"

"Yes. If you please, and if you could direct me to the shipping office I would be grateful."

"Which shipping office, queen?"

"The one selling tickets to New York."

Ernie Potter said the first thing that came into his head. There was no doubt in his mind that there was something very wrong with this slender young woman whose eyes were not quite right. The lass looked mazed, not of this world. Just as though she were hanging on by the frailest thread to reality, to what was happening round her. What young woman, especially of her class, since she was obviously of the gentry, would take ship to New York unaccompanied? There were plenty of great Irish girls, buxom and ready to

give any man a piece of their mind, who were on their way
to make a new life for themselves on the other side of the
Atlantic. The famine of the forties and fifties had brought
the starving families over from Ireland in their thousands,
his own wife's family among them, and the number going
to the New World, as they called it, had steadily increased.
In the last decade two and three-quarter million of them
left England's shores via Liverpool and this decade there
would be even more, it was said. Large, transatlantic liners
could carry three hundred cabin passengers and twelve
hundred steerage, the latter costing just £5, the average
time of crossing a mere ten days.

"Well, queen," he said at last, "yer've just missed one.
They only sail twice a week but there'll be another in a
few days' time." The strangeness of it, the effect this tall,
thin and . . . yes, *haggard* young woman was having on him
was unreal, for he was not a man for fanciful ideas. He
was a river pilot, guiding smaller ships in and out of the
mouth of the Mersey as far as the bar light, a steady job
which needed a steady sort of a man, like himself, not given
to fanciful ideas. But some instinct, perhaps because he was
a male and it was a male's involuntary inclination to protect
a female or a child or some small creature that could not
defend itself, came to the fore, since it seemed to him this
lass fell into that category. God knows why, he was to say
to Elsie later, but somehow he did not like the idea of her
boarding a ship totally alone.

"So what will yer do until then, queen?" he asked her.

She stood and waited, not unduly concerned as though
a corner of the shed behind her would do, and if not she
would just sit here on a coil of rope and wait.

"P'raps our Jess could tekk yer in," he said hesitantly.
"She's a lodgin' 'ouse in Peter Street."

"Thank you, you've been most kind," the woman said politely, turning to walk away, towards Peter Street, he assumed, her face blank, only her eyes alight with some fierce emotion which made him put out his hand to stop her.

"Lass, wait a minnit."

She stopped and waited, her back to him and he was reminded of a puppet that jerks about when the puppetmaster pulls the strings, then dangles lifelessly when he stops.

"See, go to Mrs Handy's, that's me sister-in-law. It's in Peter Street. She's clean an' . . . well, yer can stop there fer a bit until . . ." Hoping to God their Jess would take her in because if she didn't, and Jess could be a tartar at times, only the good Lord knew what would happen to her in this town of sailors who would soon take advantage of her vulnerability.

"Until the ship sails?"

"Aye, until't ship sails."

"Will you let me know, sir?"

"I will that, chuck. Now see, go straight up here towards Custom 'Ouse and then . . ."

He gave her precise directions on how to reach his sister-in-law's house then watched her as she drifted, there was no other word for it, in the direction he had shown her.

Now Jess Handy studied her as she sat at her kitchen table, cursing their Ernie, for what the dickens was she to do with her. She was like a stray kitten, except a kitten would be doing its best to ingratiate itself in her kitchen, and this lass just sat there, uncaring, that dreadful look of suffering on her face, her eyes blank, not really looking at anything, her portmanteau clutched to her like a lifeline. She shivered once, though it was hot in the kitchen, and sighed so deeply it was more a moan than a sigh, but she continued to look at the wall, not at the pictures on it, Jess decided, but the blank wall itself, her face so sad Jess was convinced she saw pictures of her own that she could scarcely bear to contemplate.

Jess made a decision.

"Yer can stay fer a few days," she said shortly, waiting for the cries of gladness and gratitude but was not really surprised when none came. In fact the woman didn't seem to have heard her. She had never met anyone so disinterested in her own fate then remembered the woman's reaction when Jess had asked her if she was a widow. Perhaps she was, which was sad, for she was really only a girl but she'd best shape up if she was going to get on with her life as Jess and many another woman had had to do. "Did yer 'ear me?" she asked.

"I beg your pardon?" The woman turned her head slowly in Jess's direction.

"I said yer could stay fer a day or two." Jess banged the flat-iron once more for emphasis and the cat turned an offended eye on them both.

"That is most kind. Might I go to my room? I'm rather tired."

"Well, that's it, queen. There's no room right this minnit. I'll 'ave ter sort out the attic. Move a few things, like."

"Oh ..."

"I can't 'ave yer mixin' in wi't men so yer'll 'ave ter sleep an' tekk yer meals in't attic. Yer can gi' me a 'and wi't stuff. It'll not tekk long."

"Very well." Briar stood up stiffly, still lugging the

portmanteau with her as though she could not bear to part with it, Jess thought.

"Right then, but 'appen it'd be as well if I knew yer name."

"Of course. It's . . ." She hesitated. "It's Beth."

"Beth what?"

"Beth Smith."

"Right then, Beth Smith, fetch yer bag an' foller me." Jess was about to explain to Beth Smith that she wanted no fraternising with her other lodgers, for men could be frisky if given a bit of encouragement, but then she changed her mind. There was not a woman alive who was less likely to turn a man "frisky" and from the look of her she wasn't likely to try.

Chapter Nineteen

Will Lucas smashed his fist so fiercely on the counter of the ticket-office window the man selling tickets flinched away as though a mad dog had suddenly reared up and snarled at him. In fact the man addressing him, if such a mild word as *addressing* could be used, gave the impression of someone who had totally lost control and would, given the slightest provocation, drive the same fist through the glass of the window.

"Sir, there's no need ter tekk that attitude. I can't 'elp it if I've never seen no young lady o' that description passin' through the turnstile." He was seriously affronted. In fact, he had begun to glance at the station master who was parading importantly up and down the platform of the station at Lancaster. There was a train due any minute and behind the snarling, grim-faced man at the ticket-office window a restless queue of passengers was forming, peering over one another's shoulder, asking one another what the hold-up was.

"Surely to God you notice who buys tickets here?" Will exploded, leaning into the window and pressing his face against the glass. "This woman was ... she was ... she has a lovely face and her hair ... copper and long. She would have been wearing black ... she was recently widowed. A striking woman and hard to miss. You must have seen her." Will drew a deep shuddering breath and did his best to moderate his manner. The man in the ticket-office was ready to call another member of staff to do something about this difficult customer – himself – and so far he had found out very little regarding the whereabouts of Briar Macauley. A porter at Penrith, which was a busy, main-line station, thought he might have seen a tall lady in black wandering along the platform but she certainly had not fitted the description given by the slightly demented man – himself – for she had worn an old-fashioned bonnet and a shawl.

Not until the next day when Mrs Evans, who rarely went out, missed her shawl and bonnet was it realised that Briar must have taken them. Was the woman at Penrith Briar Macauley, Will had agonised, and if so, which way had she gone? Which train had she taken? North into Scotland, or south to practically anywhere? So they had split up, he and Reed Macauley, who really looked as though he were not long for this world and could you wonder with that lass of his, Reed taking the train for Glasgow, and Will following the railway track to Lancaster. In those first days they were just rattling about from place to place in total panic, Will realised that later, as did Briar's father, and it was only then that they became aware that they needed more qualified people than they to find her. The men from all the farms scoured the fells about the farmhouse, hoping to find her in some sheltered cranny where she might have crawled away to die like the wounded animal she was, but now the net had to be cast further. It was three days since she had slipped out of the farmhouse at Bracken Ridge, three days since those at Bracken Ridge, Long Beck and Browhead had been thrown into a panic-stricken chaos when it was discovered that Briar, who everyone had thought to be, at last, having a long and rejuvenating sleep, and about time too, was not sleeping, was not even in her bed, nor her room, nor the house.

The news that she was lost, whatever that meant, had run like wildfire from farm to farm and men, urged on by some unknown terror, remembering the terrible day her husband and son had drowned, rushed about from here to there and back again, chasing up the fells to where she had been seen in the past, in the happy days when Mr Hal had been alive, favourite haunts of theirs. Shepherds deserted their flocks, men dropped their tools, jumped over dry-stone walls they were repairing; cowmen abandoned cows about to calve, and Mr Macauley, his frantic face as grey as ashes, took horse to Keswick, shouting to anyone who would listen to tell him if they had seen his lass, to Carlisle and the railway station, to Ambleside to beg assistance from Alex Buchanan.

Will had been up at the summit of Bakestall, leaning back against the very stones that had once sheltered Hal and Briar Saunders, sadly contemplating his own bleak future which, if she did not recover, would never contain Briar Macauley. Even if she did, could she, *would* she, ever turn to him? He had loved her, he knew that now, from the days of their childhood, but his love had been concealed under the fickle maleness of a growing lad who despises any feelings that might be considered soft. It had taken her meeting with Hal Saunders, her flaring, explosive love for the man who became her husband to reveal to Will that he had always loved her, that she meant more to him than any living creature, and then it had been too late. Even had he realised earlier he doubted it would have made any difference, for Briar Macauley had wanted something more exciting than Will Lucas. He knew he was a quiet sort of a chap although he and Briar had found a certain pleasure, he didn't know how else to describe it, in one another's company. They had known laughter, shared a joke, teased one another and been easy together. It had come to nothing, of course. Indeed he had done nothing to further the relationship, since he had not been sure what that relationship might be. She was so wild, so rebellious, so defiant, flouting all the conventions, driving all who knew her, family, friends, servants, to a distracted sort of madness, then, tossing her long tangle of copper hair and flashing her coppery bronze eyes that looked as though sunshine shone behind them, she had gone striding away on her own business.

Would she ever return, that wildcat he had known, but been unaware he loved until it was too late? he mused, his eyes narrowing to stare into the distance, then, narrowing further, peering down the fell towards the yard at Bracken Ridge which looked like the hen run when the cat got into it. Dozens of scurrying figures running in every direction, all coming from the farmhouse, moving out in widening circles, to Browhead, to the Singleton farm, men, some on horseback, walking, some of them, beating the bracken and heather, and on the air, very faintly, the sound of their voices calling.

His heart plunged, knowing some dreadful thing, something that affected Will Lucas, had happened. It knocked so hard he shook from the blows and each pulse pushed a tide of blood deafeningly through his veins. It leaped and shook inside his ribcage as though it were doing its best to escape. To escape and fly to her, for it was *her*, wherever she was, and if it was the last thing he did on this earth he would convince her ... Dear God in heaven, what was he saying to himself, he had thought as he leaped down and down the side of the rock-strewn fellside, scattering sheep, his dogs behind him, his shepherd's crook, his "setting off" crook waving wildly as his arms flailed like the windmill at Orthwaite which helped to grind the corn.

"What ...?" he managed to yell as he burst into the yard at Bracken Ridge, too winded to speak, but the sad, old face of Dobby Hawkins was enough to tell him.

It was as though she was saying good-bye for the last time to the life she had known up to the moment she stepped into the carriage of the Keswick to Penrith Train and from there on to the Carlisle to Lancaster train which was to take her ... somewhere ... somewhere away from the past. The sights and sounds of Penrith which had been so familiar to her since she was a child when she had gone on exciting journeys with her mother and father, though her tired mind could not quite recall to where. The clattering of horses hooves on the cobbles of the yard, the barking of dogs, the cheerful whistles of grooms and coachmen from across the busy main street where The Fiddlers Arms stood, the sound of the clock sounding the hour – which hour? – on the monument which divided the street, the mighty shriek of the engine as it prepared itself for its thundering progress southwards.

There had been other passengers in the first class carriage for it had not occurred to her to hoard the small amount of money she had stuffed into the pocket of the handsome leather bag she carried. The Macauleys had always travelled first class and through habit she had done the same and if her fellow passengers wondered at the gaunt, lifeless woman dressed in the clothes of one of the lower orders she had certainly not noticed their sidelong glances, nor would she have cared if she had.

Through tiny village of Yanwath and Clifton, where, it was said, the Duke of Cumberland had caught up with Bonnie Prince Charlie … though she did not concern herself with such images while she gazed out unseeingly as her past slid further and further away. The train was still cutting through the land of the fells which she knew so well but at last the landscape became gentler, lush farm land where sleek cows grazed and small farms nestled comfortably in the low swell of the land, dropping into the busy market town of Kendal.

The 'auld grey town' … who had said that? … the southern gateway to the place of her birth. It was here that she had come with her parents to see Cumberland and Westmorland wrestling, although she shied away from that picture since it brought back the face of Jonty Singleton and the day when … when …

She shuddered so violently that a fellow passenger, a kindly looking woman in a bonnet as deep and drab as her own, put out a hand to her and asked her if she was unwell. She had been unable to answer.

Lancaster came and went, as did Preston, and if the other travellers sighed and fidgeted and wondered when the long journey was to end, she didn't for she had lost all capacity to measure time. When at last they had drawn up to the platform and the storm of activity which was Lime Street Station in Liverpool she might have left Penrith five minutes or five weeks ago.

She could not be said to be mentally reviewing her journey as she lay waiting for sleep in the bed where

Mrs Handy had placed her. Her thoughts drifted blindly like bats in a barn. Distorted images, vague and confused, which darted at her then swerved away when they proved too painful, but she finally slept well.

For the first time since her life shattered into so many pieces she had known it would never fit together again, she was free of the nightmares that were destroying her. The images in her head slid away as she placed it on Mrs Handy's crisp pillowcase. Images that had plagued her so that she could barely stop herself from screaming until her throat tore and bled. Hal, his heavy winter coat billowing out behind him in the water, trapping him, his head bumping up against the ice, holding him down as he reached for Tom's small hands. Did he reach him, did he get a firm grip on the small, struggling body, dragging him up towards the light and the life they should have had only to get to the surface and be unable to find the way through the ice? How long ... how long before ... before their breath went, before their lungs filled with the icy water? Oh, please ... please, let me escape from this terror, this pain, this agony she had pleaded again and again, she did not know to whom, let me die with them, escape the blame and the guilt, for, of course, it was all her fault. Was it not she who had taken Tom on to the frozen lake, encouraged him to play with her, sliding and shrieking his delight, told him she would buy him skates, and was it not she who had put the idea in his baby head that it was perfectly safe to run on to the ice whenever it pleased him? Which is just what he had done. All these months she had lived – existed – with these images carved into her brain, pictures of horror so great that her mind had become distorted and she had not known who she was or if she even existed. Briar Macauley had gone, changed by the love of Hal Saunders into a mature and happy woman, a wife, a mother, complete. Then in one devastating moment Briar Saunders had melted away leaving this lump of flesh like an open wound that never healed. She was no one. She no longer existed and she had, in a strange and almost senseless way, for there had been no coherent thought attached to it, become aware that if she was ever to be *someone* again, she must leave this place of memories, ecstatically happy and savagely tormenting memories, and go far away.

And so she had left them all behind, those who were part of her damnation, who kept it alive with their own sorrow, their sympathy, the compassion that constantly flowed from them, suffocating her, never letting her have a moment to forget. Not that she ever would, she was devastatingly aware of that, but maybe if she were with people who knew nothing about her, about her savage loss, she might be able to function on some level that was bearable. She knew that she, leaving without a note, without any intimation that she was to go, was as cruel to them as fate had been to her, but somehow she could not bring herself to care about that. What had happened to her had stripped her of any concern about what others might be feeling, or suffering. She could not cope with it so she simply ignored it, and them.

Mrs Handy had cleared a corner of the attic and made up an old-fashioned iron bedstead and striped mattress with snowy sheets so well starched and ironed that when the time came Briar had the utmost difficulty in forcing herself between them. A quilt of great beauty was thrown over it and even Briar, in her stunned state, noticed it. It was a warm cream with a pattern of flowers in all shades of pink, birds of the palest grey, and hearts of blue stitched into it, squares of vivid scenes which glowed in the dim light from the skylight let into the roof. Mrs Handy had opened it as she entered the room and a cool breeze drifted in, pleasant and redolent with the smells that had teased Briar's nostrils earlier in the day. For some reason, though the attic was cluttered with what must have been all the remnants unwanted but too good to throw away from Mrs Handy's past life, Briar found a certain peace seeping into her as she placed her portmanteau on the top of an old dressing-table then removed her bonnet, dropping it carelessly to a chair. She turned slowly to look at Mrs Handy as the woman gasped in shock. She said nothing, for at that precise moment her mind was occupied in a haphazard way with other things, vague things like tickets and times of sailing which must be attended to in the morning.

For a moment Jess Handy was incapable of speech. Her hand went to her mouth and her pale grey eyes which had imagined there was nothing in this world that could shock them, widened incredulously.

"Eeh, lass," she whispered. "'Ave yer bin poorly?"

"Not ... not really, Mrs Handy. Oh, you mean this," running her hand over what remained of her glorious hair. "I ... I wanted ... I wanted to ... it was easier to manage. Mrs Evans's bonnet was too small."

"Mrs Evans's bonnet ..."

"Yes."

"But ..."

Briar turned away abruptly. She could feel the dread despair welling up in her and she knew she must be on her own, for she was not equal to the task of explaining to Mrs Handy – had she wanted to which she didn't, for what was the point – why she had cut off all her hair. It was not just the fact that Mrs Evans's bonnet would not be crammed down on the tumbled mass of her thick, curling hair, which it wouldn't, but the necessity of keeping it tidy where she was going, wherever that might be. She had never been on a ship except the short ferry journey to France with her parents and then they had travelled in style and luxury. What would a steerage passenger on a voyage to the New World have to endure, a steerage passenger who would, without a doubt, have to share a cabin with other women? She wanted no unnecessary baggage, meaning the trouble of caring for her unruly hair. Mrs Evans's old shawl and bonnet and the carpet bag which she meant to purchase in exchange for her handsome leather portmanteau were all she needed where she was going.

Mrs Handy's face took on its normal grim expression, for this girl was telling her to mind her own business, which Jess usually did. She squared her shoulders, sorry in a way that she had been surprised by the girl's appearance which was nowt to do with her.

"There's a birra stew left over if yer fancy it." Her voice became casual, indifferent, as though it meant nothing to her whether Miss Smith cut off her head, never mind her hair, nor whether she ate or not, indeed lived or died.

"Thank you, but I'm tired. I've had a long journey."

Mrs Handy, as was her way, did not ask where that might be from. "Po's in't corner."

"Po?"

"In case yer want ter relieve yersen in't night."

"Oh, thank you."

"Aye, right, but yer've ter empty it yersen, so think on. I'll leave yer to it then." With a curt nod Mrs Handy bowed her head and left the room through the low doorway and her feet could be heard clattering down the wooden stairs that led to the landing.

It was barely six o'clock and not yet dark. The sky above the skylight was turning to a darker blue and Briar could see a star or two far over in the west where the smoke of the city did not reach. A ship's hooter sounded and in the street a door banged. There was no sound in the house and Briar wondered if speaking was allowed and then was amazed at herself, for it was a long time since she had managed a light, almost comical thought. At once, at the reminder, the clouds came down and enveloped her and the pain clamped her tight so that she could hardly breathe. She wanted to tear her hair, what was left of it, and scream out loud her anger at the God who had done this to her, if such a being existed. Then, carefully lowering herself to her knees, she stretched out her arms on the bed, burying her face in the lavender-scented quilt. She hadn't noticed the fragrance when Mrs Handy had thrown it over the bed but now it soothed her. Getting to her feet she took off her dress, clawed her way between the sheets, put her shorn head on the pillow and fell at once into a dark and bottomless pit.

It was the stable lad who had found her hair when he was mucking out the stable the next morning. It was buried under a pile of straw which had been swept up in readiness to go to the compost heap. Hal had been in the habit of collecting the horse manure and straw from the heap which he had then spread about his roses, and though he had been dead for four months the task was still continued since no one had told the stable lad to stop. He had put several forkfuls of the straw into the wheelbarrow when he began to babble and point, backing out of the stable in such a hurry he fell over his own feet and sat down on the cobbles.

"What the devil's up?" Chuckie asked him, then turned white with a dreadful thrill of horror, for had the lad found their missing mistress? Though naturally the stable and all the outbuildings had been the first places they had searched.

The lad pointed with a shaking finger towards the wheelbarrow and when they saw what was there they all backed away from it as though the hair were still on their mistress's head.

"Jesus!" one whispered and another, who had been brought up in a Catholic household, crossed himself.

"Will we tekk it in?" the first quavered.

"We'll 'ave ter. Mr Macauley'll 'ave ter be told. Hell's teeth, d'yer reckon someone's got 'er? Cut off 'er 'air, like an' then—"

"That's enough o' that," Dobby roared from the doorway where the men had gathered. "See, give it 'ere." But the men were strangely reluctant to handle the beautiful glossy curls, the long strands of copper tendrils which they had seen so often flaunting itself round the shapely head of their mistress. Magnificent it had been, as she had been and now would you look at it, brought down to the muck and stink of the stable yard, as she had been brought down to the wreck of womanhood they could hardly bear to contemplate. By God, she'd been a devil, a whirlwind in their lives and in the lives of the men who had loved her, but exciting, a breath of something invigorating in their lives. They had envied Hal Saunders without knowing it, for he had tamed her so that she was ready to eat off his hand like a dove but at the same time there was always something in her eyes that said it was all still there, the excitement, the wildness, just beneath the surface. Now all that was left of her was a hank of mucky hair.

Annie Macauley, when she was shown the hacked-off remainder of her daughter's copper curls, so like her own had been before they began to fade, took the hair from her husband's hand and looked into his eyes, her own haunted.

"Where is she? Where's my girl?" she begged him. "I lost one daughter and I'm damned if I'm going to lose another, Reed Macauley. You find her for me."

"There are men all over the country searching for her, my love. And she shouldn't be hard to spot with her bloody head shaved. Take comfort from the thought that she must still be alive. She'd not cut off her hair if she meant to . . . to do away with herself."

"Dear God, I hope you're right." Annie lifted the glowing tresses to her face then turned purposefully away.

"Where're you going, sweetheart?" For more than anything in the world, even more than finding his daughter, he wished to spare his Annie further pain.

"I'm going to wash her hair, just like I did when she was a little lass."

When she woke she didn't know where she was and didn't care. It was a long time since she had opened her eyes and found the day good, so what the hell did it matter where you were to experience it. She had slept well, she knew she had, for the day was bright, the sunshine falling through the uncurtained, still open skylight, touching the far wall, which was stacked with so much clutter she wondered for a moment how it managed to stay there without falling into the room. Whose room? she wondered vaguely. But whoever it belonged to it had afforded her the best night's sleep she had had since ... since ... She could smell bacon and feet clattered along a wooden floor and a door banged. She wasn't hungry. She hadn't felt hunger since ... but she supposed she had better get out of her bed, or whoever's bed it was. She remembered a woman, grim-faced but with something in her eyes that, though kept well hidden, spoke of kindness. Mrs Handy, that was her name and ... and Potter who had told her she was to go to the shipping office and book her passage on the next ship New York-bound.

There was a knock at the door and she lifted her head as it opened.

"Theer's breakfast on't table, madam, or d'yer want me ter fetch it up? 'Appen yer used ter breakfast in bed, well yer'll not gerrit 'ere so shape yersen. The men 'ave gone so yer can come down."

Mrs Handy stood over her, her arms folded over her chest, her pinny like the driven snow, every hair on her head severely dragged back. "An' if yer want a wash, which yer'd best do before yer come down, there's water in a basin outside door. An' a clean towel. I'll see yer in five minutes. Not that it'll tekk yer that long, not wi' that 'air." What might have been a smile twitched her lips. "Oh, an' Potter's 'ere."

"Mr Potter's here! Oh please, Mrs Handy, ask him to wait, would you?"

"'E is doin' so look sharp."

Mr Potter stood up when she sidled round the door of the room where Mrs Handy had taken her the previous evening. It was evidently his day off, for he wore a severe black suit, a celluloid collar with a black collar stud and a shirt as pristine as Mrs Handy's pinny and tablecloth. Evidently Mrs Handy's passion for cleanliness ran in the family.

"There y'are, chuck," he managed to say before his eyes fell on the ravages of her hair which was like a spiky russet cap on her skull. She had hacked it off with a pair of shears that Hal had once used on his roses and the result was quite disastrous, long and short tufts, patches where her white scalp shone through, the odd scrap of curl here and there at the back where she had been unable to reach it properly.

"Bloody 'ell!" Potter breathed, then watched with fascination the slow, surprised blink of the girl's eyelashes as though she had no idea what he might be astounded at. Now that she had removed her shawl he could see how drastically thin she was, the black dress she wore, or rather that seemed to wear *her*, for it hung on her tall body like a shroud, of obviously good quality. She must have once been a shapely young woman if the dress was anything to go by, but the bodice now pouched to her waist and the waist slid about round her body. Her face was still ... well, he had been about to say bonny, for she had the most magnificent eyes, large, tilted up at the outer corners, lashes an inch long tipped with gold, the eyes themselves a deep golden brown, like the malt whisky he liked to sip now and again. Her skin was without flaw and without colour but her mouth was like a child's, full and pouting and pink as a hedge rose, the bottom lip plump and shorter than the top.

She hesitated on the threshold of the kitchen, cautious, afraid even and he wondered why, for there was nothing to frighten anyone in Jess's warm and cosy kitchen. Jess was putting a couple of rashers of crisp, curling bacon on a plate that she'd removed from the oven, and beside the bacon was a perfectly fried egg and a slice of fried bread. The smell was lovely and he could have eaten it himself despite the good breakfast Elsie had put in front of him an hour ago.

The girl backed away from the table. "Oh, no, please, I couldn't eat that," she protested, looking at Jess with such horror Potter was bewildered. What was there in a good breakfast to arouse such feeling in the lass? But Jess was having none of that.

"Sit yer down, girl, an' get it inside yer."

"Oh, please, Mrs Handy, just a . . . a piece of toast and a cup of tea will suffice."

Jess put her hands on her hips in a gesture Potter recognised. "Yer'll eat that or Potter, who's come ter tekk yer ter't shippin' office'll go wi'out yer."

She sat down and picked up her knife and fork.

Jess exchanged a knowing look with Potter which again he recognised. If this lass reached New York it'd be over Jess Handy's dead body, it told him and he wondered why.

Chapter Twenty

Elsie Potter had been at work for three hours when Potter wheeled his bicycle from the back shed, opened the gate from the back yard to the alley and set off in the direction of their Jess's. It was no more than five minutes' ride from the corner of Bold Street and Colquitt Street, where Elsie had her thriving little business, to Peter Street. She watched him go then turned back into the bakery where Aggie was just taking a tray of bread from the brick oven. The loaves were perfectly cooked, the tops a lovely shade of brown, darker than the sides which were a golden colour. Aggie, though she knew they were done or she would not have opened the oven door, disastrous to the making of perfect bread, knocked the top of the loaves with her knuckle then, talking to herself as all cooks do, told herself they were just right.

At a table under the window that looked out on to the back yard Mabel was mixing the flour, the solid brewer's yeast, which Elsie considered the best, and the warm milk and water which would make up the next but one batch of bread. The next batch was standing on another table under a clean white cloth where it would remain for an hour or so until it was risen, when Mabel or Aggie, depending on who was free, would give it a "good old knead" as Aggie called it. Another three-quarters of an hour and it would then take its turn in the oven.

The room was stiflingly hot but none of the women seemed to be affected by it though their faces were beaded with sweat and their clean white overalls, which Elsie insisted upon, were stained at the armpits.

Cooling on a tray by the second window, which stood open, was a batch of sweet almond cakes, another of gingerbreads, a third of honey cakes and a fourth of plain tea-cakes.

The room was not large but so organised was the work of the three women, as planned by Elsie Potter herself, that not a moment or a space was wasted. They moved about the kitchen with swirling grace, never bumping into one another, not even touching one another as they reached for flour, butter, sugar or any of the hundred and one ingredients that went into Elsie Potter's cakes, pastries, sweet and savoury pies, scones and, of course, her bread. She was well known for the quality of her creative handiwork, the value of her products, for many of the women who shopped with her were not made of money and what they bought had to "go round". Naturally, ladies of quality, those from Everton and Wavertree, did not personally frequent her establishment, but their housekeepers did, rubbing shoulders with decent housewives whose husbands were in trade or were self-employed in a small way. A grand little business had Elsie Potter, who had been trained in the way of cooking and baking in the kitchens of a titled lady.

A head popped round the door that led into the shop, a neat and tidy head with not a strand of hair showing beneath a snowy cap. The young face beneath it was cheerful, ready to smile and have a "birr of a chinwag" with Aggie and Mabel who, poor things, were stuck in the back, but at the sight of Mrs Potter's steely-eyed expression she realised that this was no time for larking about and she became serious.

"We're runnin' shorta tea-cakes, Mrs Potter, an' there's a queue outside door. Me an' Dorcas're flat out."

"And what are them on't table, Rebecca?" Mrs Potter asked scathingly, nodding in the direction of the tray. She was the only one who called the girl by her full name which, as it was meant to, kept the girl from getting what Elsie called "skittish". Becky, she was known as by the other girls, and Becky now looked somewhat sheepish as she bent to lift the wire tray.

"Ta, Mrs Potter, an' will yer . . . ?"

"I'll be out in a minnit, Rebecca. An' what's that on yer pinny?"

Becky looked down guiltily. She was a right stickler for spotlessness was Mrs Potter and though it wasn't Becky's fault that a meat and potato pie had leaked a drop of gravy on to the pristine bib of her pinny, which she wore over her overall, she had hoped Mrs P wouldn't notice. Of course, she had. Eyes on her like a bloody cat, and it was well known that she could detect a flaw in anything from a hundred yards away.

Hefting the tray on to her hip Becky stood irresolutely in the doorway, waiting for further orders.

"What yer waitin' for? Tekk tea-cakes out ter Dorcas then go an' purron a clean pinny." Elsie tutted irritably. "See, give it 'ere. I'll tekk it in, then look sharp."

"Yes, Mrs Potter."

The expression on Elsie Potter's face changed as she

moved into the busy shop, the small bow window of which looked out on to the corner of Bold Street and Colquitt Street and the mad chaos that streamed up from Hanover Street, the Custom House and Salthouse Dock, and down in the other direction from Central Station, the Adelphi Hotel and Lime Street Station. She put on what her staff called her "customers" face, smiling, genial, not exactly servile, for, like her sister, Elsie would never be that, but polite, pleasant, ready to serve them to the best of her considerable ability.

Smiling at a stout, respectable, black-bonneted woman at the counter, whose basket and serviceable clothing proclaimed her to be of the better working class, indeed she was housekeeper to a doctor and his family in Duke Street, she moved forward. She placed the tray of tea-cakes on the wide counter and picked up a large white paper bag and a pair of tongs, ready to serve her. Nothing was touched by hand in her establishment. Hygiene was a god of Elsie Potter, for had not she and her sister been brought up in the religion by a mother who could not abide a speck of dirt.

"Good-day ter yer, Mrs Farmer. An' a nice day it is an' all. Now, what can I do for yer terday? Them tea-cakes is still warm from't oven and there's fresh bread just comin' from't kitchen."

For another three hours Elsie Potter worked, whisking from the kitchen to the shop and back again, giving a hand wherever it was needed, making sure that Rebecca and Dorcas didn't get flustered which, being young and rushed off their feet, they were inclined to do, keeping up a pleasant flow of small talk with her customers, most of whom shopped there daily, coping with the constant flow of bread, scones, cakes, biscuits which were put in her ovens, taken out when they were done, carried to the counter where it seemed a never-ending queue of customers couldn't get enough of them, tucking them into their baskets and hurrying out of the shop into the maelstrom of passers-by. It was a Saturday and women were stocking up for the weekend, and for the remainder of the morning and well into the afternoon Elsie had no time to dwell on the strangeness of the conversation she had had with Potter.

Well, she wasn't sure you could call it a conversation since she had told him in no uncertain terms, the daft bugger, that he must be out of his mind to take up with some young woman he had come across at the docks. What if someone had seen him, what would they have thought of him? He'd done no more than give her directions to a place of safety, her own sister's, he told her mildly, but Elsie was not to be appeased. She knew Potter was a right one for picking up strays, whether they be human or animal. Look at that mangy cur who even now lay on her hearth-rug in front of the good fire she kept in the sitting-room above the shop. Talk about ill-favoured! As tall as a donkey with legs on it like matchsticks, ears too big for its narrow head and a coat that, no matter how Potter brushed it, looked as though it were made of coconut matting. He'd found it foraging in a rotting tip of garbage down by the water and brought it home, whereupon she had made him bath the thing in a tin tub in the shed. It wasn't coming in her house, her *spotless* house, she had shrieked, but somehow Potter had got it over the doorstep and it was still with them. Patch, Potter called it, and that was just what it was, a patchwork of breeds and most of it mongrel. Potter loved the thing and said it had lovely eyes. Lovely eyes, indeed! It did not cross Elsie's mind that she was as soft-hearted as her husband. That if she'd really been incensed by the beast and its taking up residence in her parlour she could have had it out of the house in a minute. Elsie ruled!

So what did this lass whom he'd dumped on their poor Jess look like? And more to the point, what did their Jess feel about having the girl dumped on her like an unwanted kitten, or another Patch? And now Potter was to take the girl down to the shipping office and get her fixed up with a passage to New York. Which was probably the best place for her along with all the other miscellaneous misfits who poured through this great city searching for a place in the world, unable, it seemed to her, to get down to a job of work and make something of themselves, as she and Jess had done. And as soon as she had closed the shop at seven o'clock she meant to get round to Peter Street and find out what was going on.

Leaving his bicycle propped against the wall in Jess Handy's back yard, Potter steered the tall, lanky, strangely cautious young woman, who had been introduced to him by their Jess as Beth Smith, through the front door of the house, down the scoured step and into the street. She walked as though she were moving through a field in which potholes hid to catch an unwary step, lifting her feet higher than necessary and putting them down gingerly so that he was tempted to take her arm as though she were elderly. She had on her bonnet, and though the day was mild again her black shawl was wrapped tightly about her.

They crossed Victoria Street, passing behind the bulk of the General Post Office which was crowded with postmen looking exceedingly smart in their new navy blue uniforms and peaked caps, some of them going out on the third delivery of the day, others returning with empty postbags. Turning into Stanley Street and then left into the confusion of Dale Street which led directly down to the docks, Briar flinched at what seemed to be a lunatic madness as a fleet of enormous shire horses strained up the slight incline dragging drays and waggons piled to dangerous heights with bales and boxes, the contents of which she could scarcely guess at; at victorias and broughams, going at breakneck speed, all doing their best to find a space on the road unoccupied by any other vehicle; at horses whinnying, boys dashing in between their lethal legs sweeping the droppings into the gutter, men shouting to them to get the hell out of it, and a pavement crowded with men of every colour speaking languages from every corner of the world. Seamen from every sea-going nation who sailed in and out of the port of Liverpool, most of them looking for a woman, any sort of a woman, for anything that would make their short stay in this polyglot city more pleasurable.

They did not even glance at Briar who had once been the most beautiful woman in the parish of Bassenthwaite; nevertheless Potter took a gentle hold of her arm which she did not seem to mind or even notice until they reached the Pier Head. Ernest Potter had been used to piloting ships, both sailing and steamships in and out of the port of Liverpool for over twenty years now. He had undergone a long and exacting training before he was entrusted with a ship and its cargo, and the piloting of this fragile female from the Pier Head to the Cunard Steam Ship Company in Water Street was undertaken with the same calm benevolence with which he treated the vessels in his care. He loved ships, of any size or kind and indeed was well paid for the job he did. His Elsie had no need to work, as he frequently told her but it made no difference. "Can you see me sitting on me bum all day long?" she had asked him tartly, and to tell the truth he couldn't. They had not been blessed with a family, which he thought was why Elsie was as she was so he allowed her her head, though *allowed* was not quite the word Elsie would have chosen since no one allowed Elsie to do anything. Whatever she wanted to do she did it anyway! There was no more than ten months between Jess and her and they might as well have been twins they were so alike, in looks and character.

As on the previous day as they proceeded along Goree Piazza towards Water Street Briar felt a certain movement of her senses and something that bound her to harrowing grief loosened its grip momentarily. The river was like a great highway racing down towards the open sea, alive with craft of every size, shape and kind: sailing ships like birds flying across the moving waters, steamships trailing plumes of graceful smoke, some with spars that allowed them to transform themselves into ships of sail, small boats like dragonflies hovering on a lake, ferries chugging fussily from shore to shore, a teeming thoroughfare that led to the four corners of the world. It was all so lively, so filled with a cheerful restlessness, a headiness not just of sounds and smells but of the eye. Colour, the sun shining on the red and ochre of the brick buildings, the dancing silvery grey of the river, the flags of the nations flapping at mastheads on a hundred ships, sailing and steamships, patterns of stars, stripes, suns and moons woven into those flags, the neckerchiefs about the necks of sailors, a boiling, seething impression of life, of living, of something she had not known for months. She had lived in the most beautiful acres of this country, lakes and woods and mountains whose loveliness had once stopped her heart, caught her breath so that she had gasped, brought her to a frozen standstill to stare in wonder, but it had all gone, drowned in the black lake that had taken the two people who had meant most to her on this earth. She was surviving in some sort of way, she didn't know how, but when she left these shores on one of these magnificent ships, nudging at their berths as though longing to be loosened, she might find forgetfulness, a new beginning, if such a thing existed, and if she didn't then there was always the river, the water the ship ploughed through which seemed right somehow, for it was the water that had made her as she was now.

The kind man with her held her arm as they turned the corner into Water Street, hesitating outside an office that proclaimed itself to be the agency of the Cunard Shipping Line. Outside there was a restless crowd of people, most of them poorly dressed, the women clutching shawls about their bowed shoulders, a horde of children in their worn skirts, the men haunted by something that could scarcely be borne. There were posters on the windows of the office advertising the *Lancaster*, the *Prince Regent* the *Hibernia* and the *Thomas Hyde*, and many others, all sailing to New York via Queenstown, all of which offered berths that could be booked here. The rates varied in accordance with the steamer, date of sailing, position and number of passengers in each cabin. The passengers would disembark in North River, New York City, the notices informed them, and the men and women who waited patiently, one behind the other, to reach the counter and purchase their tickets, stared blindly at the words, for most could not read. Many of them seemed to be turned away, bewildered, still clutching the money they had offered, drifting out of the office and on to the street, looking this way and that as though not certain where to go next.

When it was her turn Potter guided her to the counter where the clerk nodded abruptly.

"Yes?" he asked her.

At the last moment she found herself to be without words. It was not that she had changed her mind. It was just that she was not sure how to ask for what she wanted. The man looked at her impatiently, for had he not already dealt with dozens of bog Irish who were as ignorant as the pigs they kept in their kitchens, or so it was said, and who stared at him uncomprehendingly as though he were speaking a foreign language.

"The lady wants a berth ter New York," Potter said politely, at the same time wondering how this tongue-tied lass was ever to support herself in New York, let alone get herself across the ocean.

"Promenade Deck, Upper Deck, Saloon Deck or Main?"

Potter turned to Briar enquiringly and smiled. "Which o' these is it, chuck?"

"Pardon?" Her eyes looked imploringly into his, begging him to decide for her and the clerk sighed loudly.

"Mekk yer mind up, madam. There's others waitin' ter be served."

Potter turned to glare at him and the clerk subsided, muttering under his breath.

"What sorta accommodation do yer want, lass? There's a difference in price, yer see."

"Oh, of course, yes, there would be." Briar could feel her heart banging against her ribcage and a pulse beat inside her head but she must get this done or she might . . . might . . . well, she didn't really know what she might do. About what? her dazed mind seemed to ask her, so, struggling with her confusion, or rather struggling to get herself out of it she opened the side pocket of her portmanteau which she had brought with her in case she was to get straight on a steamer, and drew out her purse. Fumbling with the catch she emptied the contents on to the counter. There was a pound note, a ten shilling note, three shilling coins, a sixpence, four pennies, two halfpennies and a farthing.

Both the clerk and Potter stared in amazement at the money, the clerk very obviously believing a joke was being played on him, then he looked up, not knowing whether to grin in disbelief or ask this simple woman – she could be nothing else – what the devil she thought she was playing at.

"What's this?" he asked her and the expression on Potter's face said he had the same question in his own mind.

"It's all I have ... whatever this will buy."

"It's all you have!" About to tell the silly cow to stop wasting his and the company's time and to take herself off, he suddenly became aware that the man with her might be her father or some relative with the wherewithal to buy her a ticket. A customer, in fact, and the company would not thank him for insulting a customer. The competition between shipping companies was fierce. With the advent of large, transatlantic liners that could carry three hundred cabin passengers and twelve hundred steerage, there were enormous profits to be made from the millions, five and three-quarter of them last year, the highest in decades, who crossed the ocean in search of a better life, but it seemed this woman was not to be one of them.

"I'm afraid £1.13s.11¼d. wouldn't ... er, it's not enough, madam. The cheapest fare at this time of the year and with four to a cabin is £13."

"Thirteen pounds!"

"I'm afraid so. Of course, there is steerage at four guineas."

"That will do."

"But you still 'aven't enough an' if yer 'ad we're booked up fer weeks."

"Please ..."

Potter suddenly regained his composure which had been shattered by the girl's apparent naïvety, simplicity, *stupidity*, call it what you will. He nodded apologetically to the clerk as though to say he was sorry to have wasted his time, took Briar's stick-like arm and practically dragged her from the office.

"Oh please, Mr Potter, I must get a berth, I must. Don't you see, if I don't ..."

"Don't be ser daft, girl. If I'd known yer only 'ad a few bob in yer purse I'd not've fetched yer. Yer medd me look a right fool. Me 'oo works on't bloody river an' all. It'll be all over't docks by't nightfall that ..."

He had hold of her arm, practically dragging her off her feet as he led her up Water Street towards Dale Street. He wanted to shake her, he really did, for despite his softness towards dumb creatures, he was a man who was proud of his achievements, a man who was well known in these part and she'd made a bloody fool of him.

She made no sound as he dragged her in the direction of Jess's, for where else was he to take her? It was not until he glanced at her, *up* at her, for she was taller than he was, that he became aware of her terrible distress. Her face, though she did not weep, was frozen in a rictus of such agony he stopped in the middle of the pavement, pulling her round to face him, to the considerable annoyance of those about them, believing that she was in physical pain. A sprained ankle perhaps, or was his savage grip on her arm hurting her, but it was none of these things, he realised instantly. It was something inside her, something that was racking her with a grief beyond tears, beyond the simple act of crying which was said to relieve, if not cure, any hurt. This was beyond words, impossible for her to rip out of her heart and reveal to the world. A deep, silent, savage, clawing grief that could only show itself at this moment in an entirely passive willingness to go with anyone, anywhere, thanking God that it was with him, for if any of the uncaring seamen who roamed the streets of Liverpool got hold of her she would have been in serious trouble. He realised in a moment of deep compassion that she was doing her best, her pathetic sense-bereft best to escape what was crucifying her by getting on a ship and sailing away from it.

"Come, chuck, 'old on ter me. Let's get yer back ter Jess's. She'll tekk care o' yer."

"New York, I must get to New York," she moaned just as though it was the answer to everything.

"Now, now, lass, New York'll still be there tomorrer. Now yer need ter rest a bit. Come wi' Potter," he said, urging her along Dale Street until they reached the Municipal Offices where they turned, crossing Victoria Street and into Peter Street.

Jess opened the door, the cat twining about her feet and for a fleeting moment her face creased into an expression of great pity, strangely like that of her brother-in-law, then it quickly changed to one of irritation.

"Now what?" she demanded, taking Miss Smith by the arm and almost carrying her over the front step.

"Don't ask, queen, just gerrer ter bed."

Later that evening they sat round Jess's fire, the three of them, drinking the rich, creamy cocoa that Elsie had made with her usual expertise. There was no one in the world who could make cocoa like their Elsie, they had all said it a dozen times. The lodgers had been fed and were even now either sitting round Jess Handy's parlour fire, for she believed in giving value for money and a decent fire was part of it, or off out for a pint at the Crown and Anchor on the corner of Preston Street and Whitechapel.

"What we ter do wi' 'er?" Jess pleaded. "I 'aven't time ter be lookin' after no woman 'oo's only elevenpence 'alfpenny in the shillin' ..."

"Nay, she's never that, our Jess," Potter remonstrated.

"What! Thinks she can get ter America wi' ... what were it?"

"One pound thirteen shillings and eleven pence farthing."

"I ask yer! What's ter become of 'er?"

"Appen she could gerrer a job." This from Elsie who had not as yet seen the mysterious Miss Smith, for the lass had been asleep in her bed when she got to Peter Street.

"A job!" Jess's voice was scathing. "She's 'alf-witted."

"She's not that, our Jess. I reckon summat bad's 'appened ter that lass an' she can't gerrover it. Give 'er time."

"Time! 'An then what?"

"We'll see."

Jess sighed exasperatedly, settled back in her chair and sipped her cocoa. *Men!*

Chapter Twenty-one

Phoebe Lucas laid a gentle, compassionate hand on her son's shoulder, feeling the shudders that rippled through his strong frame. Strong, aye, but she could feel, even on his shoulder, the amount of weight he had lost in the last few days. She knew for a fact that he'd never laid his head on his pillow since the day Briar had vanished and the amount of food he ate wouldn't fill a mouse. She should know, for of what she had put in front of him, when she could persuade him to sit down at the table, most had gone in the pig bucket. A mouthful here and there, a sup of tea standing up, and had she not insisted, almost stripping him where he stood, he would still be wearing the same shirt and undergarments he had put on that appalling morning. He'd been bedevilled ever since poor Hal and that babby had drowned and Briar had gone out of her mind. Wild and haggard he'd been with his need to ease her pain, but this last had virtually done for him. She was reminded of her Charlie, years ago before they were married and Charlie had been crazed about Annie Abbott, as she had been then. Annie had married Reed Macauley and Charlie had married her, Phoebe, and she'd pulled him through it and she prayed to God that Will would find some kind, wholesome lass to do the same for him. He was besotted with Briar, as Charlie had been besotted with Annie and in a way, though she knew it was a sin, she half hoped that Briar had gone for good, that her Will would accept it and look elsewhere. God forgive her, for Annie and Reed were nearly out of their minds and if Briar didn't return would Annie, who Phoebe loved with all her heart, ever recover? She didn't think so. Annie had lost one daughter, sweet Cat who had died in the heather, caught by the flames, when Annie and the old man, Natty Varty, had been burning it off. It had taken a long time before Annie could forgive herelf, and it was the same, apparently, with Briar, who had gone off her head shrieking that it was her fault that Hal and Tom had died. What sinister force worked in the lives of Annie and Briar that they should know such terrible loss? And now it was scourging Phoebe's son.

"Tha' must rest, lad," she said gently, doing her best to turn him to look at her but his face was buried in his arms which were crossed on the table. "Tha'll be poorly if tha' go on like this. If tha' don't keep up tha' strength tha'll not be able ter search fer 'er. Tha' know that, don't thi'?" She did not voice the fact that had not even occurred to her son that his father needed him on the farm as the new lambs and their mothers were sent off up the fells to the heaf where they would remain until July when clipping would begin. Already Charlie was dwelling on the possibility that he might have to employ a further shepherd to do the work Will was neglecting in his search for Briar. It was early days yet. The lass might be found hiding like a wounded animal in some nook or cranny on the fells above the farms, but until she was their Will was next to useless at Browhead.

"Ma, where the bloody hell is she?" His words were

muffled and she knew he was weeping for his lost love. Twice he had lost her. Once to another man and now vanished from the face of the earth which she supposed was worse. At least she had been safe and happy with Hal Saunders but the uncertainty, the black unknown, the horror of what might have become of her was driving her beloved son out of his mind.

"Nay, lad," she said sadly, "I wish I knew, but wherever she is, she'll survive. She's Annie Abbott's daughter, in't she? Now, get thi' ter tha' bed an' 'ave forty winks. I promise I'll wake thi'."

"Wake me! D'you think I could sleep?"

"Try, my son; besides, that there animal needs a rest," pointing to the horse tethered to the gate in the yard. It was Briar's mare, Flame, strong and enduring but standing with one of her back legs in a resting position, her head hanging in weariness. Will had been riding her, covering miles in his search for Briar, galloping from railway station to railway station, west to Penrith, north to Carlisle, to Windermere, east to Whitehaven, as far south as Kendal, then from farm to farm, from one isolated cottage to another in his desperate attempt to pick up Briar's trail. He was aware, or as aware as a man in his condition could be, that Reed had set men to travel to all parts of the country, men who were experts at tracing missing persons, but it meant nothing to the lad. Could he rest, or even work as usual when Briar was in danger, he was sure of it, since she was not in her right mind? So Reed Macauley had told him to use the mare, the best in the stable, for hadn't he picked her himself, but there was a limit to what any animal, any *man* can manage even with the maniacal strength Will dug from somewhere within him.

"Ma, where is she?" he groaned again, then allowed his

mother to turn his face into her shoulder and her arms to wrap around him as they had done as a hurt child.

"Lad, there's no way I can tekk on a half-wit. Them girls I've got wan' a birra watchin', I can tell yer, an' they're all normal ... well, as normal as daft lasses are these days. I dunno, when I were in service I'd o' got the rounds o't kitchen from Cook if I larked about way they do. D'yer know, that Becky—"

"I know, chuck, yer've told me a dozen times but I reckon this lass'll come out of it when—"

"When what, Ernie Potter?"

"When she's gorr over whatever's 'appened to 'er. She's gorrer work an' ... well, I dunno, it seems she were sent to us, like, an' ..."

"Give over, yer daft lummox." But Elsie Potter put her arm over the daft lummox who lay beside her in the bed, for hadn't he the kindest heart, the softest heart. She knew he had been mortified today, his dignity affronted when the lass had shown him up at the shipping office but he had come round and had given his opinion that she was suffering from some blow, not a physical blow, of course, but something that had disturbed her mind so that she had lost the reality of life. Jess had told her, before she had put her to bed, that the girl had sat in the rocking-chair by the fire with her face as blank as the kitchen wall, nothing in it of reason, of life, of sensible thought, just a mindlessness that was quite unnerving.

"I took 'er up t' dancers an' said what about a bit of a rest and she looked at me as if I were talking bloody Chinese. See, I said, let's get yer inter bed an' blow me if she didn't just stand there, our Elsie, an' let me undress 'er. She were like a kid, climbed inter bed as good as gold an' she's bin there ever since."

And now here was Potter suggesting that Elsie should employ the lass, put her in the shop, he said, let her earn a few bob to give to their Jess for her keep. It might bring the lass round, he said. Give her a few days to get over whatever it was that was bothering her and then see how she did in the shop!

The next day, being a Sunday, Jess was not surprised when the knock on the front door revealed their Elsie and Potter. She had fed her lodgers the good breakfast they had come to expect from her, thanking her profusely, for they knew they would not get such good service, nor such well-cooked and nourishing meals in most of the lodging houses in Liverpool. There were four of them, Mr Sampson, Mr Rourke, Mr Herbert and Mr Palmer, decent chaps with decent, steady jobs in offices connected with the shipping world, and they could afford to pay the slightly higher rents that Mrs Handy charged. Well worth it in their opinion. They shared two to a bedroom and the only disadvantage was Mrs Handy's insistence that after they had put away the bacon, eggs, mushrooms, tomato and fried bread, followed by toast, marmalade and best butter, all accompanied by as much tea as they could drink, they leave the house, not returning until their evening meal was put on the table at six sharp. A bit of an inconvenience, especially if it was raining, but there were plenty of places to spend the day: the reading room at the Free library in William Brown Street, the Billiard Rooms in Houghton Street, the Mechanics' Institute in Mount Street where they might learn astronomy, drawing, painting, modelling and vocal music, and the Art Gallery where, if you were that way inclined, you might take on a bit of culture. For enterprising young men who wanted to better themselves it was all there for the asking. And, of course, there were dozens of churches in Liverpool, of every denomination. So off they went, wherever it was they fancied, out from under Jess's feet, even on a Sunday.

Miss Smith, or Beth, as Jess had started to call her in the hope of some response, was sitting in the rocking-chair, the cat, who seemed to have taken a fancy to her, curled in her lap, her hand slowly smoothing the animal's glossy ginger coat. It purred ecstatically but she seemed not to notice nor did she look round as Elsie and Potter entered the room. She was dressed in her black gown and was clean and tidy.

"Mornin', chuck," Potter said, moving to stand in front of her. She lifted her gaze from her contemplation of the leaping flames in the grate and looked up into his face. She didn't answer but her eyes showed a glint of something that might have been recognition. He knelt down and put out a hand to the purring cat. Jess and Elsie watched them for a moment, waiting for her response, and when none came looked at each other and shrugged, then moved into the scullery, though why they bothered they didn't know. They could have discussed the lass and her condition in her hearing and it was doubtful she would have noticed.

"I reckon she's worse than ever, our Elsie. At least yesterday she 'ad a word fer't cat; now will yer look at 'er. D'yer think we should fetch doctor or summat? What we gonner do wi' 'er? She's nowt ter do wi' us, is she?" Jess picked up a cloth and began distractedly to give the draining-board a good going over, something she did unknowingly when she was worried. Her Albert had said he always knew when Jess was under increased strain by the enormous amount of work she put in, besides what she usually achieved.

Elsie pulled at her lip anxiously and shook her head, watching her sister slapping a snowy white dishcloth round the already spotless surface of the enamel sink. She could tell her sister was upset and as worried as she herself was. After all, the girl was a total stranger and perhaps, in the right hands, happen at the hospital, something might be done to bring her out of this witless state into which she seemed to be sinking ever deeper.

"Wharr about that place in Faulkner Street?"

"Yer mean the Magdalen?"

"Aye, it's fer females."

"Elsie, it's fer prostitutes. We can't tekk 'er there. She's a decent young woman, yer can tell that."

"Then what *are* yer ter do?"

"Me?" Jess bristled and her colour heightened. "It were your old man what picked 'er up an' sent 'er ter me. I reckon it's up to us all ter ... well, see to 'er."

Elsie bent her head in agreement, sighing gustily. She knew their Jess was right and her sense of fairness, strong in her, in them both, came to the surface.

"Yer right, chuck. It wouldn't be right ter just turn 'er out. Potter thinks I should tekk 'er on at shop."

"Doin' what, fer God's sake?"

"I dunno. 'E seems ter think she could serve in't shop."

"Give over." Jess's voice was scathing. "She can't even gerrout o' bed on 'er own. I 'ad ter gerrer up, wash an' dress 'er. Mind you, that 'air of 'ers is right easy ter do. I just ran't flannel over it."

They looked at one another and began to laugh, for, sad as it was, you couldn't help but be amused by the lass's almost bald head.

It seemed that for the moment things would be left as

they were. Give it a few days, seemed to be the unspoken agreement, and for the next couple of hours Potter sat opposite the silent girl, puffing on his pipe and reading last night's edition of the *Liverpool Echo* which one of the lodgers had left lying about. Jess leaned over him to put a nice piece of pork in the oven beside the fire, which they'd have for their dinner at one o'clock, what was left given cold to the lodgers at six. Elsie and she chatted companionably as Elsie washed the vegetables and Jess peeled the spuds, the pair of them, in this weekly ritual, once shared by Albert, that had taken place since the day the sisters had married and gone their separate ways, quite forgetting the still, speechless figure of the girl in the kitchen. Potter glanced at her over his newspaper now and again, shaking it out as though the rustle of it might bring her from her trance, but she just sat there, stroking the cat, only the slow rise and fall of the loose bodice of her gown showing that she was still alive.

Elsie bustled in and gave quite a start at the sight of her, then, rattling the cutlery, began to set the table, while in the scullery Jess made her superlative gravy from the juices of the meat.

It took a bit of persuading to get Beth to the table, since she didn't seem to know what the devil was expected of her and anyone looking in might have thought she had never sat down to eat a meal before. Jess even had to cut up her meat but, with a great deal of prompting and a few sharp words, slowly she began to eat and, as though she recognised good cooking when she ate it, even in her sad state, cleaned her plate and placed her knife and fork neatly side by side in the middle.

"Good lass," Elsie praised her, taking her plate.

"There's a nice syrup puddin' wi' a birra custard. See if

she'll 'ave a bit." And the sisters were inordinately pleased with themselves when she did.

"Well, she'll not starve."

While the washing-up was done, a woman's job after all, Potter went back to his pipe and his paper and was halfway down the list of missing persons when Elsie pulled it from his hands.

"Now then, lad, instead o' sittin' by't fire an' snorin' our 'eads off why don't we tekk a walk? It'll do 'er good," nodding in the direction of Briar. It was as though the girl's inclusion into their routine lives had stirred something in the sisters, perhaps a sleeping maternal instinct which had never been awakened. "It's a lovely day an' the spring flowers'll be out in Princes Park," Jess added, "and on the way we can go by't cemetery an' tekk our Albert a few flowers. I fetched a nice bunch o' tulips from St John's Market yesterday mornin'."

They agreed that it would be pleasant and though it seemed very odd to be treating the tall figure of the young woman who had come so strangely into their lives as though she were a kiddy, ordering her to stand up, to stand still while they wrapped her in her shawl and pulled her bonnet over her shorn head, almost leading her by the hand to the door, they were forced to do it, for it seemed she couldn't. She seemed to be lacking something, her manner suggesting that there was something she wanted to take with her and it was several minutes before they realised it was the cat!

And the cat was inclined to twine itself about her ankles as though it was as loath to part with her as she was unwilling to part from it!

At last they were all ready but just as she was about to bang the front door Jess darted back and retrieved the newspaper from where Potter had dropped it on the chair and returned it to the parlour, for it belonged to Mr Palmer and he might not have finished with it. When he had, in her thrifty, northern way, she would use it to make firelighters.

The notice among the "S"s, almost at the end of the column of missing persons, which Potter had not quite finished, went unread.

A reward is offered to anyone who knows the where-abouts of Briar Saunders, lately of Bassenthwaite in Cumberland. Her description is as follows. Tall and attractive with bright russet hair, long and curling. She will be dressed in black. Please contact her father, Reed Macauley of Long Beck in the parish of Bassenthwaite.

Obediently she walked between Jess and Elsie, with Potter a step or two behind so that the three of them looked like warders escorting an escaped prisoner back to his cell. Jess pulled her arm through her own, guiding her as though she were blind, which of course she was, blind to her surroundings, hidden safely in the secure place she had found for herself and where no one, at last, could hurt her. She had been looking for such a place ever since Hal and Tom had gone, searching for it on the fells, and lately in Liverpool, even contemplating crossing the ocean to find it. She had not realised that it was here, inside her, buried deep beneath the layers of agony, a small refuge, a resting place that held her in its warm, soft nest under a blanket where she was unseen and unheard. She had found it by accident when the cat had jumped on her lap and her hand had risen automatically to smooth its fur. At once she had felt calmer, relaxing into the rhythm that her hand took, rocking and stroking, the flames in the fireplace such a lovely harmony of colours, the cat a sort of key to the retreat she had found for herself. They had not let her bring it with her but it would be waiting back there, she was sure of it.

The day was mild, clouds gently moving across the city towards the river, driven by a breeze, parting now and again to reveal the pure blue of the sky and even a glimpse of the sun. They walked through several mean streets with houses on either side, flat terraced houses exactly like the ones she had passed on her way up from the river only the day before yesterday. Men lounged this Sunday in their open doorways, hands deep in their pockets, watching with sullen disinterest the play of their offspring, the skipping and hopping, the ball games, the "balls" rolled-up newspaper, a bat made from a bit of branch torn from a tree in St James Cemetery where Albert Handy rested and which the four reached after a ten-minute walk.

Jess and Elsie stood for a while beside Albert's grave, speaking softly of the man who was gone, though neither shed a tear for it was not their way. Potter strolled on, the girl's arm through his now, and he marvelled that this young woman, a perfect stranger to them, should put her trust, her innocent trust in their hands. As he had done yesterday, he shuddered to think what might have happened to her had she fallen into the wrong hands, and, looking ahead, wondered what was to be done with her if she did not recover. She was deep in some trance, some fixed tranquility which was quite frightening and he pondered on what could have happened to her to bring her to this state. Even yesterday she had been able to converse in a stumbling kind of way but ever since he had got her home and Jess had put her to bed she had tipped into this awful limbo.

Elsie and Jess caught up with them and within minutes they were out in what was almost open countryside. Princes Road ran between fields where crops were beginning to thrust up towards the spring sunshine and in the hedges beside the road honeysuckle and wild roses would soon be in bloom. In the ditches bordering the road were wild flowers, primrose, stitchwort, red campion and blue bugloss. There were carriages drawn along the roadside as they approached Princes Park, for this was a favourite Sunday walk for all classes of person.

The grand wrought-iron gates stood wide open and through them poured the citizens of Liverpool, men in cloth caps or silk toppers, women in shawls or elegant day dresses, children with bare feet or dressed in the finery of the middle classes, bowling hoops.

They walked in twos, Elsie and their Jess arm-in-arm and in front of them Potter and Beth, as they were all three calling her now. Beth had her arm passively through that of Potter, her other hand clutching her shawl about her protectively. It was a lovely park, the lawns mown to green perfection by the numerous gardeners, the flowerbeds that lined the paths bursting into colourful bloom. A massed bed of blue periwinkle and another of white, small and neat, were just ending their flowering. There were still the blazing trumpets of daffodils, a golden shout in the warming air, a shout that said, "look at me for I shall soon be gone". There was a wild garden ablaze with rose-purple "hardheads" which were something new, Potter said, and just introduced from Asia, so he had heard. The rhododendrons were in full bloom, curving along paths and directly ahead, surrounding the lake. There were hothouses through which visitors might stroll to see the exotic plants, gardenias, camellias, and those that could not be grown in the harsh northern climate, and there was a tea house where, Jess promised them, they would treat themselves to a cup of tea when they had circled the lake.

It was at the lake that disaster struck. As they strolled along the pathways that curled round its perimeter, moving in and out of the shadows of trees and the protection of newly greening shrubs, Potter began to notice the trembling of his companion's arm. She tried to pull away from him, turning towards the blue-grey dappled water and he put his hand on hers where it rested in the crook of his elbow.

"What's up, lad?" Elsie called out to him, for both she and Jess had noticed the beginning of her agitation.

"Nay, don't ask me, lass, summat—" But before he could finish the sentence Briar wrenched free from Potter's protective hand and began to hurl herself in the direction of the water, making for a man and a small boy who were sailing a boat at the edge of the lake. A woman with a perambulator in which a baby crowed, watched, smiling as the small boy placed his boat carefully in the water, held with a steadying arm by his father.

Briar began to shriek, her mouth opening on a long, wailing cry of terror, her arms outstretched, her shawl flying away like a bird on wing and her great bonnet falling to the back of her neck where it bumped in time to her step. Her shorn head was revealed, the scalp gleaming through and every man, woman and child who saw her flight, stepped back in panic. The woman with the perambulator turned her head, seeing the apparition making straight for her and began to scream in a high, shrill note of terror to match Briar's own.

"Hal . . . Tom," Briar shrieked, "be careful." And before

the father could steady himself against the onrush of the mad woman bearing down on him, she had snatched up his son and turned away from the gleaming, shiny, icy, treacherous water that was about to take him.

"Dear God," Jess whispered, rooted to the spot in horror but Potter, who was trained for emergencies and could react to them without even thinking, stepped in front of Briar, snatched the screaming child from her arms and passed him to his distraught mother.

"Lass . . . lass," he crooned, dragging Briar into his arms, holding her struggling figure, for she was still babbling about Tom and Hal and the ice, begging him to set her free, for they must be saved. Her voice rose higher and higher and about them there were mutterings of sending for the bobby on the corner of Rodney Street, for surely this woman must have escaped from the lunatic asylum in the city. The mother sobbed over her struggling son and the father did his best to calm them both while glaring at Briar and the man who held her.

"What's up with her?" he roared. "She wants locking up. She nearly had me in the bloody lake."

"I know, sir, an' I beg yer ter . . . she's bin poorly." For she must have been poorly, the horrified Elsie thought, to act as she had done. Out of her mind with some grief that was buried within her. Hadn't she known, she was to say to their Jess later when they had managed to calm the fright-ened father and mother, when they had managed to draw the suddenly silent, inert figure of their unwelcome visitor away from the curious crowd and out of the park. And why the devil hadn't Potter had the bloody sense to pass on at the Pier Head instead of stopping to give directions to this girl who sat in the rocker stroking the bloody cat and who was turning their humdrum existence on its ear?

Chapter Twenty-two

She sat in the chair by the fire and rocked, her wounded heart at peace, her crazed mind shut down, her hand smoothing the cat's fur. Her body began to mend, no longer controlled by the grieving, the suffering, the guilt which had stripped the flesh from her bones.

In the following weeks Jess was to say again and again that she daren't take her eyes off her for fear of what she might do. It was clear to them that this Hal and Tom had been people dear to the lass, people she'd lost, and her so young, but they couldn't question her, could they, in case it set her off again. Let her be calm, let her rest easy, for it was well known that rest was a remedy better than any medicine. Let her sleep deeply at night, which she appeared to do, for now and again Jess looked in on her, and she would recover.

"Imagine she's 'avin' a rest after a serious illness," wise Jess remarked to her sister and brother-in-law. "A body needs peace an' quiet when it's bin sorely afflicted an' so does t'mind. I reckon 'er mind's damaged wi' whatever 'appened to 'er an' nature'll cure 'er when she's ready."

She was no trouble. She never stirred from the kitchen

unless Jess was with her when they went out for a walk, and though Jess's gentlemen lodgers were now aware that Mrs Handy had a young woman to stay with her, presumably a relative, they never set eyes on her.

The cat was her constant companion. Jess had been astounded by its behaviour. It was a cat for God's sake, and in the way of its kind it allowed Jess to feed it and made her aware that it was doing her a favour by stretching out on her hearth-rug. It didn't mind a certain amount of fussing but now, under the lass's hand, it positively fawned. If it wasn't on her lap it was curled up against her side on her bed and should she take a step away from the rocking-chair the damned thing followed her, just like a dog. It had never had a name and Jess could hardly remember where the thing came from, probably one of Potter's strays! It was a handsome animal, the colour of marmalade, sleek and with eyes of the deepest blue in a pointed face. It was the funniest thing to see it walk behind the lass, its tail in the air, its back end swaying gracefully, as hers did, they began to notice. Wherever she was, it twined lovingly about her ankles. But strangest of all was the way it trailed in their footsteps when she and and the lass went out of the house. People stopped to stare and smile as it daintily picked its way at Beth's heels. At first Jess had tried to shut it in the house, tutting as it did its best to streak through the door after them.

"Come on, lass, yer know we can't tekk a cat fer a walk, don't yer. It'll be waitin' fer yer when we gerr 'ome." But Beth wouldn't "come on". She became distressed, pulling at Jess's restraining hand, turning back, her face crumpling, her mouth working though she made no sound. And she would not be moved, only calming and condescending to walk on when the cat was freed and following behind.

The first time it happened Jess didn't know where to put herself.

"Well, can yer imagine," she said to their Elsie. They had walked round to Elsie's place at the corner of Bold Street the Sunday after the incident in Princes Park. Potter was working that day which, since he worked a kind of shift system, he did sometimes. The shop was closed and after settling the lass in Elsie's rocking-chair, the cat on her lap, they were in Elsie's kitchen over the shop, making a brew.

"It were enough ter stop traffic an' folk were pointin', ready fer a good laugh but she never noticed. She 'eld me arm an' set off wi' bloody cat at 'er 'eels, 'appy as Larry, an' so was't cat. If I 'adn't seen it wi' me own eyes I'd never've believed it."

Elsie sniffed, not in disbelief but with further astonishment. "Well, talk about cat, 'ave yer seen way't dog's actin' wi' 'er an' all, daft 'apporth."

They both turned and looked at the girl in the chair. The cat was in its usual place and seemed not to mind the canine head that lay on the lap it occupied, and the girl, would you believe it, had a hand on each animal. On her face was that soft dreaming expression that had come over it last Sunday. After creating havoc in the park where she had screamed and wailed and frightened everyone to death she had suddenly fallen into this state of ... well what could you call it? Jess begged Elsie. Her face was calm, tranquil, like that of a madonna, peeping from under the brim of the hideous bonnet. She drifted about like a ghost, silent, impassive and obedient to Jess's hand and it made Jess want to cry, she who never shed a tear, even when their Albert died.

"It's as though they know she's ... not 'erself, cat an'

dog, I mean, an' they're sorry fer 'er." Elsie spoke with the voice of awe. She'd read about such things somewhere or other, she couldn't just remember where, of animals sensing pain or trouble in humans and extending their sympathy, and she could believe it now.

Very slowly, as week followed week, Jess began to put the girl to simple tasks. Wrapping her in a big apron, one of her own which fitted where it touched it was so large on her, she stood her at the sink in the scullery and led her through the task of washing the dishes. The sink was filled with warm, soapy water and very gently, plate by plate and cup by cup, the lass ran the dishcloth round the crockery, the cutlery, supervised by Jess who looked out for stains missed, pointing them out to her, putting the scouring brush in her hand, and instructing her on the proper way to stack the washed dishes, then how to wipe them and put them away in the cupboard.

"Good lass, good lass," she told her and was amazed with herself when she felt compelled to plant a kiss on the lass's cheek. She sometimes whispered to herself, though no one knew of it, that it was almost like having her own child, a daughter growing up and she had to admit that she was becoming right fond of her. She'd no idea it was like this, having a bairn of your own, though she never breathed a word of it to anyone, even their Elsie. She showed her how to dust, to make beds, to clean the windows with vinegar and water, to sweep the carpet in the parlour, spreading tea-leaves to get rid of the dust, to make firelighters with the lodgers' newspapers, twisting them into tight balls, placing them in the grate before heaping small pieces of wood and coal on top.

"I feel a bit funny, really," she told their Elsie.

"Why?" Elsie was clearly astonished.

"Well, yer can tell she's quality an' 'ere am I mekkin' a maid of all work of 'er. It don't seem right somehow."

"Jess 'Andy, that lass 'as you ter thank fer her life. An' if she can tekk a birr of a load off your back, let 'er. I reckon it's good for 'er ter be doin' summat instead o' sittin' on 'er bum in that rockin'-chair. 'Ave yer noticed 'ow much better she looks?"

It was full summer now and only a week or so ago Jess and Elsie had taken the lass, and the blasted cat, of course, along to St John's Market where anything under the sun could be bought. There, on a stall that looked as though every colour in the rainbow was scattered over it they had picked up a length of cotton. It was a warm cream, scattered with a pattern of primroses. Beside it was a roll of ribbon in the exact same shade of primrose yellow.

As though their minds ran on the same track, which they often did, they stopped, looking at one another before fingering the pretty length of material.

"A bargain tha'," the stall-holder told them, looking at the lass who stood there between them like a black-garbed survivor from some dreadful accident, which of course she was. "Suit the lass a treat," she added.

Again Elsie and Jess exchanged a look which said they agreed with her. Elsie was good with a needle, plain sewing which she and her sister had been taught when they were at the school their Irish mother had struggled to send them to. When she had been in service she had made her own plain working clothes and with Jess's help she reckoned she could make a dress for the lass. They both agreed they were sick to death of seeing her in the awful garment she had worn since Potter had fetched her from the docks and perhaps wearing something pretty might bring the lass out of her tranced state.

For several evenings, after the shop was shut, Elsie trailed round to fifty-one Peter Street and with the lass rocking and smiling and stroking the cat by the fire, they cut out and began to sew the dress. A pattern had been bought with the length of cotton, along with buttons and the ribbon, and though there was a bit of what Jess called "language", they contrived to make a passable, in fact a pretty dress. Beth had borne the pushing and pulling, the commands to stand still and give over fidgeting, the sighs of despair and the cries of triumph and when Potter came to pick up his Elsie, since he didn't like her walking the street alone at night, even if it was still light, it was a joy to see the look on his face when he saw Beth in her new attire.

She had put on weight. Well, could she help it with all the good food Jess shovelled into her three times a day. And her hair had grown, tumbling about her head in shining curls in which Jess had placed a knot of the yellow ribbon, a sash of which was tied about her waist. She was still slim but her body was supple and her breasts had filled out, pressing against the smooth bodice of the dress. They had taken her every Sunday either to Princes Park or down to the marine parade to look at the river, and the sunshine had tinted her cheeks with a wash of gold and put a spot of pink in them.

"By gum, she's a right pretty lass," Potter said, removing his everlasting pipe from between his lips. He stared, looking her up and down with a male interest in an attractive female, and they all failed to see the tiny light pierce her eyes. Her fingers trembled at her waist, wanting to be about something as though they would move to it if they knew what it was, or even how to manage it, then they stilled and her hand fell limply to her side.

Elsie and Jess surveyed their handiwork with proud, pleased expressions. They had created this attractive young woman, turning her from the haggard freak she had been when she came to them into this pretty creature who stood obediently where they had put her, as she always did. It was as though she were a puppet they had made, one that would do their bidding whenever they pulled her strings and it was as this thought occurred to all three of them that Potter became grave.

"Yer'll 'ave ter watch her, our Jess," he said quietly.

Jess bristled. "I allus do."

"I know, queen, but when she looked like a bloody guy she were in no danger from . . . blokes. They never gave 'er a second glance, which was good since she's nowt but a child in a woman's body. Not even that fer a child has a mind and will recognise danger. Now . . . she's still t'same, yer know wharr I mean – mindless – but wi' a look about 'er that'll fetch 'em round like bees ter t'oneypot."

Both Jess and Elsie sat down suddenly and Beth did the same, lifting the cat on to her lap and beginning to rock. Again they failed to notice her hand resting on the arm of the chair. It clenched then relaxed and moved to smooth the cat's rippling fur. Her eyes, such a lovely colour of brown, like burned syrup, watched the flames dancing about the coals and from one of them a tear slipped down her cheek. Tiny, it was, like a crystal, and as though it had a life of its own and was nothing to do with the girl from whose eye it fell it moved across her cheek and plopped on to the end of the cat's nose. The cat looked up at her and sneezed, slightly offended, then squirmed its way closer to her as though in the deepest sympathy.

"I wish we'd never medd damn frock now."

"Nay, don't say that. She looks a picture." Elsie sighed,

gazing at the silent figure in the chair. The room was warm and the tear had dried, leaving no more than a faint silvery track down the girl's cheek but as Elsie gazed at her she slowly turned her head and their eyes met. The girl stared, her eyes alive, the blank expression that had rested in them for weeks gone, leaving them clear, glowing, startled. She blinked and her hand clenched again on the arm of the chair.

"Jess," Elsie hissed afraid to look away from Beth in case she might lose her again. As though their linked gaze, if parted, might remain so for ever.

"Jess." Her voice was more urgent and when Jess turned to look at her it was with a bewildered expression.

"What?"

"Look ..."

"Look at what?" But she had turned her head to look at whatever her sister was staring at and when she did she clapped her hand to her mouth and rocked back in her chair as though someone had knocked her there.

"Don't she look ... different?"

Potter also turned his head to look at Beth, tutting as he did so, for of course she looked different. That dress they'd put her in made her look what she was, a pretty girl of nineteen or twenty, he supposed, though he was no good with females' ages.

"Look at her eyes," Elsie said in a hushed voice and as she did so the lass blinked again, a slow lowering and raising of her long eyelashes, then, like the sun coming hesitantly from behind a cloud, she smiled.

"Dear God ... oh sweet Lord, will yer ..."

It was Potter who recovered first, since his emotions were not as involved as the two women who had transformed the lass. He had grown fond of her and he knew that Elsie felt the same, but it was Jess who had cared for her. Who had undressed her at night, washed her and put her to bed, talking to her as though the girl might answer her. Who dressed her in the morning, sat her down to her breakfast and had taken it upon herself to train her to perform a few easy tasks. Who took her to the shops and down to see the ships. Who, in fact, had made a companion, a silent one, true, but a companion of her nevertheless. She it was who deserved the credit for the return to physical health of the girl in the chair.

"Well, chuck, it's grand ter see yer," he remarked conversationally, just as though she had popped out for a day or so and was now back with them again.

"Thank you," she answered politely, her voice husky. She looked about her at the room and the people in it as though she were not certain where she was or who they were. Her head moved stiffly on her neck and her breathing quickened as though she had been running. She swallowed violently then sprang to her feet, flinging the cat to the floor with so little regard it might have been a ball of the wool with which Jess endlessly knitted. Then, gracefully, bonelessly, she sank to her knees and began to wail. "No ... No ... No ... nooooo ... no. Where are they? Where? Hal ... Tom ... no, don't ..."

With a shout Potter was on his feet, his face an appalled mask and in their chairs both Elsie and Jess began to moan helplessly. Potter grabbed at Beth, catching her by the shoulders but she threw him off and began to beat at him with furious fists, doing her best to claw at his face.

"Please ... please ... let me go to them ..." But Potter had a good hold of her now, lifting her to her feet, dragging her into his arms as he had done in the park.

"Beth ... Beth, lass ... yer safe wi' us. See, Jess's 'ere, an' Elsie."

"Please, no ... no ... please ..." She struggled desperately with him, freeing herself, and again sank to her knees, rocking to and fro in a frenzy of despair, her head on her breast, her arms wrapped tightly about herself. Her agonised cries echoed round the kitchen and the cat slunk out into the scullery. Jess stood up hesitantly and would have gone to Beth but Potter waved her back, shaking his head, for surely this must come out. This girl, whoever she was, must scourge herself of the festering sorrow that was wrecking her life or she would never recover. For weeks, months, since it was now August, she had remained locked inside herself, healing, Jess said, but he was not so sure. Her sorrow was drowning her, but if she could just make an effort and swim for the shore would she not be what she needed to be: a survivor, stronger, living a life of some sort. She was young with so much ahead of her and though he was sure she had a sad tale to tell, with their help – and he was not surprised to hear himself say that – she could be led to something new. She could tell them who she was, where she was from, for surely someone was sorrowing for her?

Briar lifted her head and her eyes moved about the room in bewilderment. They widened, a deep golden brown, the flat look of burned syrup gone, replaced by dread. Where was she? She could feel her heart thudding sickeningly in her breast and she felt the rise of nausea fill her throat. She tried to stand but her legs appeared to have become boneless, refusing to support her. What was this place? It seemed only a moment ago that she had been shivering by a lake ... by *the* lake ... Oh God ... Hal ... Tom ... She shook her head, clamping her jaw together to stop the sound of agony from escaping, then looked about her wildly. She was in room, warm, cosy, comfortable, and looking at her were three total strangers. They were not threatening her at all, in fact they appeared to be as distressed as she was, the women, at least, crying freely. Her eyes darted about her jerkily, trying to make some sense of it all but her heart began to quieten as her mind recognised that she was in no danger, at least from them.

"Beth, chuck," the man said and she turned her gaze, like that of a trapped doe, in his direction. Her colour was mounting though and her face had lost its haunted look.

"My name is Briar," she said at last, her voice still cracked and hoarse.

One of the women spoke at last. "Briar! What the 'ell sort 'o name's that?"

"It's my name and what's wrong with it anyway? It's the one my mother and father chose."

Briar lifted her head in a fair imitation of the haughtiness her family had known. Her eyes snapped and she stood up, tossing her head. She seemed surprised to feel it so light and when she put her hand to it her mouth fell open.

"Where's my hair?" she asked them accusingly, as though they had stolen it while she slept.

Elsie came to with a sudden snap of temper, wiping away her tears with her hanky which she had snatched from the pocket of her apron. Her eyes glinted dangerously.

"Now listen 'ere, young lady, we'll 'ave none o' that. If it 'adn't bin fer my sister 'ere yer'd be in the bloody work'ouse, or 'appen in a brothel. She were't one what took care o' yer while yer were off in some trance."

"Trance?"

"Aye, a trance."

"Where am I? Please, tell me who you are and where I am. I seem to have forgotten." The spark of defiance appeared to have blown itself out and she turned about in evident confusion. Just for a few seconds she had regained her courage but now it had gone again, leaving only a terrified child who has misplaced its mother's hand.

"Yer where Potter took yer when 'e found yer wanderin'—" Elsie began in high dudgeon but Potter hushed her with a sharp word and a peremptory gesture of his hand, one that those whose ships he guided into the Mersey channel would have recognised.

"Well," she began, ready to stand up to this lass who seemed to have no gratitude for what had been done for her but she snapped her mouth shut, having the sense to know he was right.

"Beth ... or, what were it, Briar? Well, it's like this, lass. Yer were wanderin' about down't by't Pier 'Ead, askin' fer a passage ter New York but ... well, chuck, yer seemed poorly ter me, not quite right so I told yer to come t' our Jess's," nodding at Jess who in turn nodded at Briar. "She 'as this lodgin' house an' I knew yer'd be safe wi' 'er, an' so yer 'ave bin. Now, what 'appened to yer ter get yer inter this state, we didn't know. Now then, lass, don't upset yerself," as Briar bowed her head and sat down heavily in the rocking-chair where at once the cat returned to her lap. She stroked it and it purred.

"I ... my ... they were drowned." Her voice was soft and sad, no more than a whisper in the warm air and all three felt the hairs on the backs of their necks stir and rise. Jess made a choking sound in the back of her throat and her hand rose to her mouth as though to stifle it.

"Hal and Tom?" Potter's voice was filled with compassion.

She nodded and tears began to splash on to the cat's fur but it didn't move. "Hal was my husband and Tom was our son. He was two years old. It was my fault, you see ..."

"Your fault! Lass, how can—"

"I took Tom on to the ice and he ... it broke and he fell through. Hal tried to save him. It drove me out of my mind." The words were spoken simply.

"Oh, my poor lass ..." Jess began to sob out loud, turning to Elsie for comfort.

"When was this, chuck?" Potter asked her quietly.

"In January." She lifted her tear-stained face and though it was anguished Potter was relieved to see that it no longer held that dreadful expression of insensibility, that vague and distant look of the lost. She knew who she was and though as yet she did not recognise him and Jess and Elsie, she was not afraid. He had the idea that this lass would show herself to be a young woman of great valour when she was finally recovered.

"And now?" she asked tentatively.

"It's August, queen." As yet he could not quite bring himself to call her by the outlandish name she had given them.

"August," she breathed. "August. They have been gone seven months."

"Aye, lass." They might have sat there for a long time, Potter and Briar, contemplating the awfulness of it all but Elsie, the first to recover, moved somewhat jerkily towards the scullery.

"I reckon a nice cuppa tea is what's needed 'ere."

Jess dried her tears in relief. "Aye, an' 'appen ... Briar'd like one o' them scones yer fetched round."

Chapter Twenty-three

The man in the dark, crumpled suit worked his way slowly along the busy thoroughfare, stopping passers-by who didn't want to be stopped since they were always busy on market day. They'd no time to be exchanging pleasantries with a stranger when there was business to attend to, no matter how intense his manner, nor how grievous his troubles. Grudgingly they peered at the small miniature of a pretty young girl he held out to them before hurrying on, saying no, they had not seen her, and each time he smiled politely, a smile with no warmth in it, before patiently standing back to allow them to pass. He was a young man, probably in his late twenties, tall and lean with a face that was strained though he spoke pleasantly enough. His hair, if they noticed it at all, had once been dark as rich chocolate, curly and untamed, but now it was streaked with white, unusual in so young a man. His clever face was brown as though he worked outdoors and set in it were keen, silvery-grey eyes. A nice-looking young fellow in the opinion of the younger women, though he was very serious and did not respond to flirtatious quips from a buxom lass who stood behind a stall displaying farm produce.

"She yer sweet'eart, then? Run off wi't coalman 'appen. Well, I'm sure there's more'n a few'd tekk 'er place. Me fer one." She turned to wink at the woman behind the next stall who laughed and slapped her thigh.

"Have you seen her?" the man asked, unresponsive to her sly smiles and admiring glance.

"Nay, lad, not me. What about you, Aggie?"

"Can't say I 'ave."

"There ya' are then, but if yer want a . . . friend," winking again, "I'd be 'appy ter oblige."

The Market Place in Wood Green, a small market town several miles south of Preston, was crowded with stalls which were jammed along one side of the cobbled square, all set out with fresh produce brought from outlying farms early that morning. Women in their best black, bonnets firmly in place, most with a clean white apron tied about their waist, thronged between the stalls, studying each one before buying, for a Lancashire housewife likes value for money. Displayed on the stalls, protected from the weather by canopies, beside the dressed fowl, the eggs, the butter, the cream and the cheeses, were fresh vegetables, onions, potatoes, carrots, turnips, bright red and vivid green apples and pears, carefully piled into pleasingly artistic pyramids. There were stalls on which gingerbread, pin-cushions, lemonade, pies and muffins were set out alongside boot-laces, tea trays, cough drops and corn plasters, soap and mechanical toys, anything, indeed, that the busy housewife might require, the stall-holders shouting out to them to come and try their wares, for they were the best in the market. There were pot stalls selling sturdy earthenware, cups, saucers, dinner plates, soup tureens and vegetable dishes, for the folk who made their purchases here in Wood Green did not eat off bone china.

The crowds swirled round the square and between the stalls, bargaining for this and that, careful with their money, for it was not easily come by, every penny doing the work of two. Small carts were drawn to the edge of the market, each one pulled by a donkey or even a plough horse, their teeth crunching in the feed bags attached to their heads.

On the opposite side of the square stood those who had come for the "hirings", rows of men and women waiting with the patience of dumb animals. Though it was not yet Martinmas, which fell in November and was the traditional time for moving, there were servants who were desirous of changing their employment at other times in the year. Masters with walking sticks wearing good jackets, gaiters, sturdy boots and black bowlers walked between the rows, stopping to speak to one or the other. Now and again hands were struck and the hired man received a shilling as a token of his hiring.

Though it was August it was a cool day. The sun hid itself behind growing clouds which hung in great drapes almost down to the rooftops, and when it began to rain those who had made their purchases and were merely "looking" turned towards their carts and traps ready for the journey home.

The man with the miniature, which he had placed in his pocket for safe-keeping, sheltered for an hour in the porch of the public house, hoping the rain would let up, but instead it settled into a steady downpour and the stall-holders began to dismantle their stalls. His face expressionless, just as though it were nothing to him whether it rained or not, the man hurried from the market-place, turning in the direction of Preston town centre.

When he reached the town, which he had canvassed the

day before, he made his way to the railway station. When, an hour and a half later, the train for Penrith drew into the station he boarded it, settling down in the corner of a third-class carriage, staring out of the window as it chuffed its way through Lancaster, Kendal and into Penrith.

His horse, a fine chestnut mare which whickered and nuzzled his shoulder when he whispered her name, Flame, had been left overnight in the stable of the public house. He paid the lad who had saddled her and flung himself on her back and put her to the gallop, which she was glad to do after being stabled for two days and a night. Through Keldhead and on through the increasingly vile weather until he reached Keswick, where he forked to the right and on to the lake road and Browhead.

It took him two hours to reach his home and when his mother saw him coming up the track, his head bowed, his chin on his chest, she did her best to hold back her sorrowing tears, for it was evident he had been unsuccessful, as he had been unsuccessful for the past three months in his search for the woman he loved.

"Come in, lad, an' get them wet things off tha'," was all she said, flinging the door wide. She could feed him, keep him warm and as healthy as he would allow, but she could not deter him in his search for Annie's girl, as they called her in these parts, and never would, she suspected.

She still sat in the rocker, saying very little, the cat on her lap, rocking rhythmically as she had always done. She helped Jess in the house, wearing her old black frock as she swept and dusted, her bouncing hair wrapped decently in a duster. She washed pots and scoured pans, and her mother and father would have been horrified had they seen the state of her hands. She scrubbed floors and certainly took a great deal of the hard work from Jess's shoulders. She even learned to "donkey-stone" the front steps but she could not be said to be restored to herself. Not that Jess, Elsie and Potter had ever seen her before she came to them and it is doubtful they would have recognised the hoyden, the laughing wildness, the exuberance, the lively spirits of the girl who had once had the parish of Bassenthwaite by the ears. But when she looked at them there was intelligence in her eyes and she answered when spoken to, though it was not often she began a conversation.

She had been "normal", as Jess put it, for two weeks when, as delicately as she knew how, she who was always so blunt-spoken, she asked Briar if she would like to tell them what had happened to her and what had brought her to Liverpool.

"I'm not one fer pryin', lass. I believe a body's entitled to a birra privacy. Yer business is yer own an' if yer don't want ter tell me, then don't, burrit crossed me mind there's folks 'oo'd be glad ter 'ear from yer. Folks as'd be right worried about yer. Would it not be right ter send 'em a note, like, or ..."

Briar was becoming increasingly agitated. It was September now and the pretty summer dress had been put away in the wardrobe in the room in the attic which Briar called her own. The rubbish had been cleared away into a spare room at their Elsie's place, for though Jess called it rubbish, it wasn't to her. She and Albert had collected all sorts of things during their marriage and though Jess hadn't anywhere to put the boxes of gee-gaws, trinkets won at the fair that came to Liverpool, bright pictures and gaudy vases Albert had loved, she wouldn't throw them away for a gold clock. They were dear to her because they had been acquired when Albert was alive, but the lass couldn't sleep, now that she was "normal", in a room full of boxes and old bits of furniture. So they were cleared out and taken on a handcart to their Elsie's and in their place was the old iron bedstead, a low chest of drawers in which resided Briar's change of undergarments, brought from Bracken Ridge. On the chest of drawers stood a jug and ewer in a pleasing design of rosebuds and trailing fern. Above it, fastened to the wall, was a mirror, handsomely engraved and mounted on peacock-blue plush velvet, quite hideous but much loved by Jess. There was a chair of pine with cushions in red velvet, a low wardrobe which only just fitted under the slope of the roof, and a large, threadbare mat beside the bed. The only object of beauty in the room was the exquisite quilt which Jess insisted was taken off the bed at night, for she would not have that dratted animal stretching out on it, she told Briar.

Another length of material, this time of wool in a tawny shade of russet which exactly matched the lass's hair, had been purchased at St John's Market, along with a woollen shawl, second-hand, of course, in the mixed colours of autumn. Briar herself had chosen the material and the shawl, instinctively picking the colours that she knew suited her. Elsie and Jess had wanted emerald green with a purple stripe, which the stall-holder said was "all the go" but they had to admit she looked a treat when it was finished. She had even made an attempt to help them with a seam or two, though she admitted she was no seamstress. She did not embellish the remark with reminiscences of the teachers at school who had flung up their hands in horror at the sight of her sampler, which every young girl was expected to produce, nor her positive refusal to sit in the drawing-room with a bit of embroidery in her fingers. Her life as a rebel was buried beneath her grieving heart.

Now she was ready to scramble to her feet, causing the cat serious disquiet as she tumbled it to the floor. Jess put out a hand. They were sitting one on either side of the fire in the kitchen. The nights were drawing in and Jess had just been in to light the lamps in the "gentlemen's" parlour. The fires both there and in the kitchen had been stoked up and Jess had been attempting to show Briar the first steps in knitting. How to cast on had had the wool tangled round the lass's fingers and the cat hadn't helped, doing its best to play "footie" with the ball of wool.

"I can't. Please, Mrs Handy, I can't. Don't make me."

It was not the attempt to teach her to knit that Briar referred to.

"Nay, lass." Her hand was ready to take hold of Briar's as she struggled to get out of her chair, impeded as she was with knitting needles and wool. "I'll not mekk yer." Jess's face crumpled in distress, for this lass was as dear to her now as her memories of Albert. "Burr I thought 'appen it'd ease things a bit if yer was ter tell us . . ."

"Oh, no . . . no. The memories are too hard to bear. Please, Mrs Handy."

"Chuck, calm yersenn." For Briar was beginning to throw herself about the room, bumping into the table, wincing as her hip caught the corner. She stepped on the hem of her dress and almost fell and Jess stood up, her face growing stern, for this lass was ready to hurt herself if she wasn't stopped.

"Now see, give over or yer'll do yersenn a mischief. There's no need ter carry on like this. No one's gonner mekk yer do owt yer don't want but if yer were my daughter I'd like ter think yer'd 'ave the 'eart ter let me know yer were alive. Yer poor mam must be—"

"No ... no, don't you see? If I get in touch with them they'll come and get me and I can't go. I can never go back to ... to home. That's where it happened. Dear Lord, please ... the memories torture me. But here, with you and Mrs Potter and Mr Potter, I can manage. I ... I still dream awful dreams but when I wake up I'm here, not there where it happened and I can just about stand it. If I keep busy, wear myself out then I can sleep but—"

Jess interrupted her abruptly. "It's time yer did summat else beside help me, my girl." It sounded harsh and Jess felt sorry if she sounded uncaring. The lass hung about here, doing her weight in work, certainly, but she needed to be getting out, not just to the market with her, or a saunter down to the Marine Parade or Princes Park with Potter, but out and about on her own, strengthening herself, building some sort of life that was not to do with her or Elsie or Potter. The young men in the parlour were beginning to show a masculine interest in her, for they had caught a glimpse of her on occasion and you could see they were impressed. She was not just a pretty girl now, but a beautiful young woman, full-breasted, slim-hipped with a tiny waist in between, due no doubt to the manual work she did about the house. Her hair was quite glorious, short still, but full of life and colour like the autumn leaves that were falling from the trees. Her mouth was ripe and full and red and her eyes glowed with her renewed health, but this was no life for a lass like her. She was well bred, speaking with the cultured tones of her class and was as out of place in Peter Street as a rose on a dung heap. Not that Peter Street could be likened to a dung heap, for it was respectable, the houses occupied by families with mothers who were as houseproud as she was. And though Briar had improved since she came out of her tranced state, she was still not as she should be but happen if she got out a bit, met other people, she might be further restored.

Jess was a firm believer, for hadn't she done it herself, that there was no need to go through life feeling sorry for yourself at the blows the fates aimed at you. When her Albert died she could have brooded for the rest of her life on his loss, but though it had taken a long time for the pain to diminish, it had finally become bearable. That was how she put it to herself. Bearable. Enough to begin enjoying each day. Some of them were good, some were hell but the hellish ones began to be further and further apart until one day she had realised that not once during the day had she thought of Albert. That night she had wept as though it were the day on which he had just been lost to her. Cried in grief and cried in guilt that she should have forgotten him. But she hadn't, of course. She had *accepted*! That was what Briar must be made to do, somehow or other, and if that sounded heartless, then Jess Handy was a heartless bitch.

"I reckon yer could do wi' a job." Her voice was clipped, almost cold, and for a moment Briar stared at her in panic before sitting down abruptly in the chair. Automatically her hand reached for the cat which faithfully jumped on to her lap and curled itself into a ball.

"A . . . job?"

"Aye, a job. Summat ter keep yer occupied, besides which it's time yer brought in a few bob."

"A few bob!"

"Aye, I'm not medd o' money, yer know. I've mesenn ter keep and money don't grow on trees. That frock cost a bit an' it come outer me savings. An' wharrabout boots? Them's fallin' apart."

Briar looked down at her feet in consternation then up into Jess's grim face. She was not to know that the whole thing was a figment of Jess's imagination. That there was nothing Jess would have liked better than to keep the lass at home with her. She earned every penny Jess spent on her, the way she worked, but if there was some way to help her to recover, Jess was willing to try it. If Briar thought Jess was suffering hardships because of the added burden of feeding and clothing herself, perhaps she might be persuaded to get out and find a job. Of course, it couldn't be any old job and Jess had that sorted out entirely to her own satisfaction.

"I don't know what I could do, Mrs Handy. As you see, I'm not much of a hand with sewing and . . ."

"What can yer do then?"

"I can milk a cow."

"Milk a cow!" Jess gave a short laugh. "There's not many o' them round 'ere. Wharr else?"

"Sheep, I know about sheep. Not shearing, of course. Hal wouldn't . . ." Her face spasmed, then went rigid in an attempt to control something that was working to the surface of her mind. Jess longed to jump up and drag the girl into her arms, tell her to forget the whole bloody thing; she was safe here with her and could stop for ever as far as she was concerned but that was not the way to heal this lass of whatever it was that ailed her.

"Owt else?"

"Hens . . . and I've watched butter being made."

"Yer come from a farm, then." That didn't take much working out, Jess told herself with some irony.

"Yes." Briar's honey-brown eyes looked into those of Jess Handy. They were filled with a kind of agony. Her lips were tight clamped to stop their trembling and Jess

343

knew she had only to say a few kind words and the whole plan would be abandoned, but that was not her way. Cruel to be kind, she kept saying to herself though her heart hurt in her breast.

"Well, we could ask our Elsie, I suppose. D'yer know owt about bakin'?"

"I'm . . . I'm afraid not. I've watched our cook when . . . when she made biscuits but I've never actually . . ."

Jess sighed dramatically, just as though she couldn't believe there were women in this world who didn't know how to make a few biscuits, or a scone or two, then she got to her feet and began to walk about the kitchen. Briar watched her anxiously.

"I'm sorry, Mrs Handy, I didn't realise I was . . . I didn't think. You should have told me sooner that I was a burden. I still have the bit of money I was going to use for the berth to America."

Jess turned in surprise. "Yer remember that?"

"Oh, yes, Mrs Handy, I remember everything now – everything." Her head bowed and she sank a little in her chair then she straightened up, squaring her shoulders and lifting her head. "But I still mean to go."

"What!" Jess jumped to her feet and Briar reared back in her chair just as though she thought Jess might strike her.

"Don't be daft," Jess went on before she had time to think.

"It's not daft, Mrs Handy. There's nothing for me here and if I was to—"

"Oh, give over. See, get yer shawl."

"Where . . . where are we going?" For it was dark out beyond the scullery window.

"To our Elsie's."

✳   ✳   ✳

"Don't be daft." Elsie spoke the exact same words that Jess had when Briar had volunteered the information that she still intended taking ship to New York.

"And what's wrong wi' it?" Jess bristled up to Elsie and Elsie bristled up to Jess, and Briar, with no cat to cling to, turned for comfort to the dog which huddled at her knee. He was a timid dog, for he had known nothing but kicks and blows and harsh words until he landed up in Elsie's kitchen and the loud tension between the women frightened him.

"Yer askin' me ter tekk on a girl what knows nowt about bakin'."

"No, I'm not. She could serve in't shop. It don't tekk experience ter serve in a damn shop an'—"

"Oh, don't it? 'Ave yer ever tried it? No, yer 'aven't. Why that Becky's bin wi' me fer a year now an' she still needs watchin'."

"That's because she's half-witted. Our Briar's gorra bit about 'er." Neither noticed the use of the possessive "our" which was only used between members of a family. But Briar did and she jumped to her feet. It was not clear whether she felt indignation at Elsie's lack of enthusiam or Jess's assumption that she would accept a menial task like serving in a confectioner's, which she seemed to imply that Briar was to do, never mind Briar's feelings in the matter. From somewhere deep inside her where it had been buried for months, Briar Saunders's old spirited determination lifted its head, gave a yawn, and proceeded to exercise what it considered its rights.

"Excuse me, but am I not to be allowed some say in

this arranging of my life? You are both busy arguing over my future without asking me what I would want to do."

If the dog had turned round and spoken to them on the subject of his evening walk, they could not have been more surprised. They turned to stare at her, then at each other.

Jess was the first to recover. "Orlright then, what d'yer want ter do? What *can* yer do besides milk a bloody cow? Tell me that then. If there is summat, let's know about it. Me an' Elsie'd be glad ter ... well?"

"I want to earn a wage so that when I've saved up enough I can book a passage to America."

There was a lengthy silence. The three women stared at one another then looked away, Jess out of the window, the curtains of which had not yet been drawn, Elsie into the fire, and Briar from one sister to another. From beyond the window came the rattle of traffic from Bold Street. The room was warm and the window was slightly open and voices could be heard as workers hurried home from their ten-, or even twelve-hour day, shop girls, factory workers, those who worked in the city and were hurrying to catch the horse-drawn tramcar out to Aigburth, Everton, Old Swan and Wavertree. The clatter of feet on the pavement and the clamour of horses' hooves rang on the roadway.

At last Jess spoke and her voice bore no trace of the distress that she felt at the thought of losing this girl who had come to mean so much to her. She couldn't let her know, she *mustn't* let her know that she, Jess, would be broken-hearted to lose her. So her words were calm, rational, expressing only what she thought Briar would want to hear.

"Righto, queen, if that's what yer want yer'll 'ave ter convince our Elsie yer can serve in 'er shop. No one else'll employ yer." She made a warning gesture to Elsie who had been about to speak. "If yer want ter save up fer yer fare then there's only one way ter do it an' that's ter work 'ard an' learn ter do things proper. Elsie can't afford ter carry dead weight, can yer, chuck?"

Elsie shook her head wordlessly. She wondered what the hell their Jess was playing at. She already had two perfectly competent girls serving in the shop despite what she might have to say about Becky. Becky *was* flighty and she'd had to speak to her a time or two about laughing and joking with the young draymen on the corner when she was sent on an errand. But she was good in the shop, cheerful and helpful, and the customers liked her.

"So, Elsie'll give yer a week's trial, won't yer, our Elsie, an' if, at the end o't week she's not suited, yer'll 'ave ter look elsewhere. 'Ow's that?"

"That will do very nicely," Briar answered, standing up and reaching for her shawl. "Now, I'd best get to my bed if I'm to be up early."

Her mouth might be dry with fright and her heart banging like a drum inside her ribcage which suddenly seemed too small to contain it, but the courage, perhaps the bravado that had carried Briar Macauley through life, and through death and unendurable grief, was not about to flag now.

Chapter Twenty-four

She was afraid. She lay in the dark, the candle extinguished, and burrowed deeper beneath the warm blankets which smelled of the lavender Mrs Handy stored them in. Because the skylight in the roof had no cover and so let in the light from the deep purple sky she could see the faint outline of the wardrobe and, pale against the wall which Mrs Handy had persuaded Potter to whitewash, the shapes of the pictures Mrs Handy's Albert had been so fond of. The cat's body was warm at her side but for once it did not comfort her. She turned her face into the pillow and moaned softly, deep in her thoat. She didn't want to be here, meaning the real world, the world where she had to function as others did. It had been so sheltered in her cocoon. She had been aware of Mrs Handy and the others but their presence had not troubled her. Nothing had, even when she had returned, when she had crept out of the cocoon she had been safe in Mrs Handy's care. She didn't want tomorrow to come, an unknown tomorrow that terrified her. She wanted to creep back into that hidey-hole she had dwelled in for so many months, warm, safe, where no one could reach her, where nothing could reach her, where memories could not crucify her, but where she knew she would remain for ever if she didn't take this chance Mrs Handy and Mrs Potter were offering her. She longed to be mindless again, senseless, without pain, simply rocking by Mrs Handy's fire, cast into a hypnotic state by the cat's purring, by the movement of her hand on the cat's smooth fur, by the warmth, the comfort, not only of her rocking-chair by the fire but of the lack of need to plan her own life. What comfort that would bring. No fear of the future, since in that state she cared nought whether she had one, no fear of the present since she did not exist, only a fear of the past which was thankfully erased.

She did her best to sleep, to become unconscious of her surroundings, for only in that way could she prepare herself for tomorrow, but her dread of it kept her awake and in her wakefulness they came back to her, Hal and Tom. Minutes ticked by, hours, and the fear of what her life was to be sank deep into her heart. Painful memories scalded her, painful memories of her husband, her son and . . . a little girl. Whatever else happened to her in the future it seemed she was to have, she would never, even if she lived to be as old as . . . as old as Dobby Hawkins, she would never forget them, or those few years she had had with them. Time would never dim, nor heal her sorrowing pain, but she had been lost and now she must find a way to go on.

Despair, the most dreadful of emotions, ripped through her and she twisted painfully in her bed, disturbing the cat who raised its head to stare at her in the dark, but she could not escape it, whatever it was that was waiting for her. They were lost to her for ever, Hal and Tom and the little girl who had never had the chance to be born. The place in her heart that only they could fill was empty and would never be filled again and the thought was slashing at her in agonising waves, for she knew she would never love, or be loved, again. Though she was totally silent she was screaming inside, sunk in agonising, dry-eyed grief; would she ever weep again? She found herself biting on the sheet lest her cries escape and raise the household, and she lay rigid, waiting for sleep, for oblivion, for anything that would diminish her terror of the future. She had dealt with what had happened to her, if you could describe closing down all her senses as dealing with it, by simply withdrawing from life, but that was ended. She could get on, accept what Mrs Potter was offering her, or go down to the Mersey and throw herself in. She might as well, for she was only a burden to the two women, and don't forget Potter, her chaotic brain reminded her, but that would only be betraying them. So, to go on, that was her only option. Not to forget the beloved people who had left her behind but to allow them to slip into that part of her secret heart where their memory would for ever lie, safe and unseen by others.

Just as though the thought had comforted some wounded part of her, like a sweet-smelling balm smoothed over tortured flesh, she felt her body ease and relax and when the cat delicately shifted its body closer to hers she fell into a dreamless sleep.

They dressed her in her old black frock which fitted her now. It had been carefully cleaned and pressed by Jess, for she wanted the lass to look her best, and round the neck she had sewn a white muslin ruffle. Not exactly what Elsie's other employees wore but the lass was so lovely it seemed a shame to put her in drab, unadorned black. She was forced to wear her black boots until new ones could be bought for her, but round her waist was tied a snowy apron and on her tumultuous hair was jammed a snowy cap. Muslin cuffs were fastened at each wrist to protect her sleeves and, looking like a neat parlour-maid, or so she thought, remembering Nan, dear Nan, she was pushed into the shop.

"Now we've got five minutes before t'shop opens," Mrs Potter told her, bustling from the counter to the shelves that stood behind her and then back again, adjusting trays of biscuits and small cakes which did not need adjusting. To re-align slightly the trays her girls had already placed on the shelves was her way of showing that she had her eye on them and that she insisted on perfection.

The big, mahogany-encased clock on the wall of the shop ticked the minutes away to eight o'clock when the shop would open, and Elsie glanced at it in anticipation of the bell which would tinkle as the door opened. Already one or two ladies had collected on the pavement.

"Now as yer can see each tray is marked wi' what's on 'em an' prices. Fruit scones, almond biscuits, ratafias, coconut, shortbreads ... well, yer can read t'labels, an' 'ere's bread. There's not just ordinary bread but cottage loaves, tin, soda bread, rolls an' ... well yer can see't names, an' then cakes. We do plain buns, Victoria buns, iced buns, macaroons, almond cakes, honey cakes, ginger cakes, lemon, plum cake — them large 'uns in't winder — an' we tekk orders fer bride cakes an' at Christmas. See, you, Dorcas" — as a shout from the back kitchen stopped her in mid-flow — "show 'er t'way o' things until she picks it up. I've ter ..."

Elsie dashed back into what was really her domain, leaving the goggle-eyed Becky and Dorcas to eye up this young woman who had been, to put it mildly, thrust upon them ten minutes ago as they donned their own clean aprons and caps. "This is Briar," Mrs Handy had told them, hurriedly, as though she expected the strange name was going to cause a bit of a commotion. She shoved the tall and lovely girl at them, ignoring their slack-jawed amazement. "She's ter give yer a birra 'elp." And that's just what she looked as though she could give: a *bit* of help. The first time she opened her mouth to ask hesitantly if this was a lemon bun or a plain bun they knew she'd never worked in a shop before; indeed if she'd ever worked *anywhere* before they'd've eaten their freshly laundered caps. Her hair was enough to make you stare, all over her head in short curls until she had pulled her cap down to cover it. Had she been poorly then? Since that was what happened when you had a fever, Dorcas whispered to Becky. They cut off all your hair. And what a bloody name! Briar! Where in hell had she got that from? Dorcas told Becky on the quiet that she thought she'd made it up, but then Dorcas was a bit sharp and inclined to give her opinion on anything and everything under the sun when Mrs Handy wasn't there.

The shop filled up the minute the door was opened and at once Briar backed away from the counter, doing her best to sidle into the comparative safety of the kitchen where Mrs Handy, who had walked through the maze of streets from Peter Street to Bold Street with her, this being her first day, still waited.

"I can't do it. I really can't, Mrs Handy." Her face creased and her mouth opened wide on what might have been a wail of terror, but Mrs Handy took her arm and gave her a shake, watched by the equally open-mouthed Aggie and Mabel. There were scones in the oven ready to come out and a fresh batch of bread ready to go in, but for the moment the two women were mesmerised by the scene being played out against the background of their humdrum lives.

"Listen 'ere, girl." Mrs Handy put her face close to Briar's and her voice was harsh. "Yer goin' in there an' yer gonner show 'em that yer not medd o' bloody jelly. Remember what yer said. Off ter America, yer said, an' if yer want ter get there yer've to earn the cash fer a ticket. I'm not medd o' money, my lass, an' I can't keep yer fer ever. Yer a grown woman, not a babby, so gerrin there an' show 'em what yer medd of. Our Elsie's dependin' on yer." Which wasn't true. "She's willin' ter pay yer 12/6 a week so go an' earn it."

She gave Briar a push that propelled her into the shop where a steady stream of women were buying the fresh bread, more of which was baking in the ovens at the back, bags of buns, small iced cakes, biscuits, custard tarts and, though it was not apparent at the time, it was these last that were to start Briar on the slow, upward spiral towards recovery, for it was these that were the cause of what Elsie and Jess were to call "one of our Briar's inspirations"!

But now she trembled and hung back at the sight of all these women who stared at her curiously. Her eyes were enormous, like those of an animal trapped in a beam of light and her face was as white as the refined flour that Elsie insisted upon for her confections.

Elsie, who was not at this moment needed in the kitchen, was taking a turn at the counter. She turned and said curtly, unsmilingly, "Come on, girl, don't 'ang about in't doorway. We've customers want servin'. See to Mrs Mossop, will yer, an' then fetch the jam tarts from't kitchen."

Briar stared out into the sea of faces, wondering which

one was Mrs Mossop, then a woman with a patient, friendly smile spoke to her.

"I'll 'ave 'alf a dozen currant tea-cakes, queen."

She might have been speaking a foreign language. Briar stared at her in confusion while Becky and Dorcas and Mrs Potter swirled round her, tutting irritably since she was in everyone's way. But Mrs Mossop, thank God, Briar was to think later, was a kindly woman who had herself once been a girl beginning her first day of employment, many years ago now.

"Be'ind yer, queen. See, just ter yer left. That's it, 'alf a dozen. Good lass. A penny each; purrem in a bag. Thanks, love, an' good luck."

It was the start she needed and though she was slow, she began to recognise the different items on sale, the price of them, the change that had to be given. She found that if she shut out everything but the face she was serving, what that face said to her, concentrating fiercely on it, blanking out her mind from the two, sometimes three women serving behind the counter, she could do the work for which Mrs Handy was employing her.

She became quite adept by the end of the week at looking enquiringly at a customer – she could not quite bring herself to smile as Becky did – repeating an order and then finding what the customer asked for on the shelves behind her. The white paper bags, or the fresh sheets of paper in which a loaf was wrapped, were placed to hand where the three girls could easily reach them. After carefully watching what Becky and Dorcas did, her heart still beating sickeningly in her chest for fear one of the customers might address some remark to her, neatly side-stepping one or the other as they moved from counter to shelf to counter to till, she found she could do the same. She had to concentrate, wondering as she carefully wrapped a loaf or placed six iced buns in a paper bag how the other two, especially Becky, managed to serve the customers and at the same time hold some sort of conversation with them.

"And 'ow's your Tommy today, Mrs Earnshaw? Gorrover 'is cold, 'as 'e?"

"Saw your Nancy t'other day, Mrs Capstick, she in't 'alf shootin' up."

"You gonner watch Prince an' Princess o' Wales openin' new North Docks at weekend, Mrs Bentley? They say there's three o't young princesses ter be with 'em."

But it was the custard tarts that did it. They were fresh, just out of the oven, the pastry crumbling, fragrant, delicious, the custard, though set beautifully in its shell, inclined to crack if not handled with care. She spoiled half a dozen as she tried to ease them into their bags, and of course, she couldn't give Mrs Earnshaw or Mrs Capstick a broken tart so it had then to be replaced.

"All the more fer us," Becky whispered conspiratorially, winking at Briar, ready to be friends, for the new girl was young, not like Dorcas who was at least thirty and as old as the hills to perky little Becky.

"Oh!"

"Aye, Mrs Potter lets us eat what's broke or tekk it 'ome."

"They wouldn't break if they were properly packed in boxes," Briar retorted crisply, just as Mrs Potter came through from the back kitchen. "They could be placed four or six to a box, tied up with string and carried with perfect ease without breaking."

Well, the whole shop fell silent, for there was not one person in it who did not hear the remark. They all turned as one to look at Elsie Potter in order not to miss her reaction. The new girl, who moved about the small space behind the counter with a quiet dignity which pleased Elsie since Dorcas was too morose and Becky too chirpy, looked as though she might become a reliable member of staff but this was going a bit too far and Elsie's face flushed up angrily.

"I beg yer pardon?"

"I said if the custards—"

"I 'eard an' 'appen yer'd best work 'ere fer more'n 'alf an 'our before yer start givin' out yer opinions."

"It was just an idea, Mrs Potter, and one I thought was worth considering. I've spoiled a few myself and so have . . . well, it seems to me that if they were boxed they would not break so easily." She wished to God she'd never spoken as she felt the eyes of a dozen women fixed on her.

"I agree, Mrs Potter," a voice from the other side of the counter said, and again every head in the shop, including Briar's, turned to look at the speaker, a plain, no-nonsense, serviceably dressed woman. She had on a bonnet similar to the one in which Briar had arrived in Liverpool and a face underneath it that spoke of hard work, reliability and a speck of something that might have been humour. "Times I've carried home them custards only ter find a couple broke in me basket. Still worth eatin', o' course, since your bread an' confectionery's best in town, Mrs Potter, or I wouldn't come all this way ter fetch it, but not ter be served ter my mistress. She'd not tekk kindly ter broken custards."

"Well!" Elsie was ready to explode she was so outraged, but something in the way the customers were looking at one another and nodding their heads as though they agreed stopped her. She was not a woman to chuck away good custom and Mrs Jenkinson, housekeeper to one of

Liverpool's influential councillors, was a regular at the corner shop.

"Think about it, Mrs Potter," Mrs Jenkinson said, then turned to study the display on the shelves at the back of the three, four if you counted Elsie Potter, shop assistants.

"Now, young lady," she addressed Briar as though she had decided the lass was the only one in the shop with a bit of sense. "I'll 'ave six fruit scones, six fancies, no, lass, not them. Them ter yer left, two tins ... aye, them loaves an' a pound o' gingernuts. 'Ow much? Good lass, right first time."

Briar smiled then, for the first time, and Becky was to say later to Dorcas it was like a candle had been lit behind each golden-brown eye and had Dorcas noticed what lovely teeth the new girl had. Dorcas grunted irritably, for Becky could be the most aggravating creature at times. Good-hearted and willing to give a hand with anything but as daft and flighty as a butterfly.

The new girl was found to have the exact same disposition for hard work as Becky, despite her very obvious difference in what Dorcas called "class". Dorcas, like most northern-bred women, was not one to poke her nose into other folks' business but it was most intriguing, just the same. Where had she come from? She wasn't one of them, the way she spoke told them that, but Dorcas didn't care as long as she pulled her weight. And she was very serious which suited Dorcas a treat. She didn't mind a laugh, though there was not much time for larking about in their busy day, but she was often exasperated by Becky's light-minded attitude towards the serious business of earning their living. One of these days Mrs Potter would take exception to her giddy ways so happen the new girl, who had eased their load somewhat, had been brought in for a purpose.

Briar worked steadily through each day, becoming more confident as she began to recognise a lemon bun from a lemon tart. She found she had a head for figures, easily able to add up in her head the sum of a customer's purchases and to give the right change. She helped the two girls, if you could call Dorcas a girl, at the end of the day, taking a pride in the shining cleanliness of the shop and the kitchen where all the baking was done. Mrs Handy had taught her well. She was tired, weary to her bones but she was glad, for surely it meant that she might fall into a deep sleep as soon as her head hit the pillow, which she did and so was not privy to the conversation that took place between the sisters later in the week.

"Well?" Jess said, leaning forward in her chair and taking up the cup of tea she had just brewed. Potter was working and so Elsie had walked from the shop to their Jess's with Briar, sharing the good hotpot that Jess had made for the lodgers.

"Well what?"

Jess sighed. "Oh, don't give me that, our Elsie. Yer know wharr I mean. 'Ow did lass shape?"

"Not bad." Elsie sipped her tea, smacking her lips appreciatively. She had had a hard day. She wasn't as young as she once was, not that that bothered her for she still had the stamina, *and* the good sound sense both she and Jess had inherited from their spirited little Irish mother. But though the lass had incensed her the other day with her remark about packing custards in boxes she could see the practicalities of it. She wondered why she hadn't thought of it herself. There was a lot of wastage in her delicious custard tarts, she was the first to admit, but they were so popular she knew if she stopped making them her customers would be very disappointed. She'd never seen boxes of the sort Briar had spoken about and she wondered if such a thing was actually manufactured, but if they weren't she was sure they could be.

"Oh, stop it, our kid, summat 'appened, didn't it? Summat ter do wi' Briar?"

"Aye, she's not ser daft as she pretends, that lass."

"She never pretended ter be daft, you know that." Jess's voice was serious and Elsie leaned forward and patted her hand. She knew that their Jess was extremely fond of the lass who had just appeared out of nowhere and fitted into their lives so neatly. She had a past, relatives somewhere who must be mad with worry about her but she wouldn't divulge their names or where they were. Elsie thought it was cruel but Jess, probably relieved that the lass was not to go back from where she had come, wouldn't have a word said about her.

Elsie related the incident about the custard tarts and the boxes and Jess fell back, beaming. It was as though her own flesh and blood had done some wonderful thing of which she was extremely proud, as a mother would be proud.

"There, yer see, she's gorra 'ead on 'er an' I reckon yer'll find she'll be a right good little 'elper to yer. I know Dorcas is steady an' a good worker but that there Becky's not much cop, is she? Yer'll be glad yer took on our Briar."

"Oh, I dunno, Becky's bright an' cheerful an' willin'. Anyroad, we'll see. Shop's bin that busy I were glad ter 'ave extra 'elp be'ind counter. So let's wait an' see, shall us?" She paused, taking another sip of tea. "D'yer reckon she means it, goin' ter America, I mean?"

"She did, months back, but then she weren't in 'er right mind. She were runnin' away from losin' 'er 'usband an'

little lad but now she's got summat ter do I think she'll
stay put. I 'ope so, anyroad."

"Yer like 'er, don't yer, our Jess?" Elsie's voice was
soft.

"Don't you?"

"Aye, there's summat about 'er. Summat ... tragic
burr at same time yer've gorrer admire way she's picked
'ersenn up."

"Yer right. She's a brave lass." Jess gazed fondly into
the fire and sighed deeply.

By the end of the month Elsie was saying, privately,
of course, to Potter, that she didn't know how she
had managed without Jess's lass. Jess's lass, she repeated,
begging Potter to listen to the lunacy of that remark,
for the lass was no more Jess's than those bairns that
played out in the street. But Jess thought the world
of her, you could see that, and what was to happen
when Briar really came to her senses and decided it
was time for her to go home? She had been at Potter's
Bakery, as it was called, for no more than a month
but she fitted in with her own distinct way of dealing with customers, polite, helpful, but without that
certain subservience girls in her position adopted. At
first the customers were wary of her. It was like being
served by a bloody duchess, one was heard to say, but
nevertheless they seemed to like her and if one could
get a smile out of her or put a twinkle in her lovely
golden eyes, they went out of the shop feeling they had
really achieved something. They all knew by now that
some dreadful thing had happened to her, not what
it was, of course, but why would she be serving in

Elsie Potter's shop otherwise. Not a girl like her. But, like all things unusual she became accepted and there came a day when she was just one of the girls who served them.

Chapter Twenty-five

She had been there for two months that October day, a Saturday, when Becky, who had told Briar on her first day that she was sixteen and lived at home with her mam and dad, confided that she was walking out with the lad who drove a waggon for a tobacco company, and would Briar like to accompany her and Arthur on a walk along the Marine Parade the next day. Arthur had a friend and Becky thought it would be grand if they could all go out in a foursome. Becky's dad was very strict and if he knew Briar was to accompany his daughter he would be less likely to put his foot down.

Briar was astounded, for though she and Becky "gorron" as Becky described it, she often felt that she was older by many years than the blithe, sunny-natured girl. Surely she had friends of her own age and station, girls who were as frivolous-minded, who wanted the "good time" Becky talked of constantly. If Mrs Potter had told her off once she had told her off a dozen times since Briar had started at the bakery about chattering to the young men who drove the waggons and drays that lumbered up from the dock area, but Becky was like a child who could see no harm in having a "birra fun", a laugh and a joke with someone of the opposite sex. There was no harm in it, was there, she asked impishly and you couldn't help but smile at her.

"Well, I'd have to ask Mrs Handy," she replied hesitantly.

Becky tossed her cap into the basket where the soiled linen was kept for washing. Mrs Potter was very particular and insisted on washing their caps, aprons, overalls, cuffs and all the cloths used in the establishment herself. Each day they wore clean things, freshly ironed and each day Briar found she attained a certain satisfaction in the particular and pristine condition of the premises. She sometimes wondered if what had happened to her, shying away slightly from what it was, had altered her nature, for a year ago she had carelessly dropped her undergarments as she got out of them, giving no thought to what was to happen to them or where the fresh supply was to come from. A certain finickiness had rubbed off on her from Mrs Handy, she supposed, as now she studied Becky's cheerfully smiling face.

Becky was perching what was known as a Dolly Varden hat on to her pale crimped hair, tying a wide ribbon beneath her chin, adjusting the angle in the mirror which Mrs Potter provided. The hat was a leghorn with a small crown and a wide, limp brim and was worn with a very forward tilt. The crown was tied about with a broad red ribbon and "follow-me-lads" streamers which was exactly why Becky had put them there. Her cheap dress was of dimity, a stout cotton, in a loud shade of green and her shawl was black with long trailing points. She was pretty, with round, rosy cheeks which would, as she grew older, become coarse, florid, though now her very freshness, her cheekiness, was enormously attractive.

"Can't yer come wi'out askin' Mrs 'Andy?" she asked in astonishment. "It's only a birrof a walk down't by ships. There's all sorts goin' on there," and she winked provocatively. "An' Arthur's friend's a real toff. Yer'll like 'im. Gorra good job an' all. Go on, be a sport."

"Well, Mrs Handy might have something for me to do ..."

"Give over! On a Sunday? It's yer day off."

Briar knew Jess Handy would not approve of an outing with a girl who worked in her sister's confectioner's. In her way Jess was a snob. She was proud of the ladylike young woman whom she had raised, as it were, from the dead. She was proud of her success at their Elsie's. She was proud of her appearance, for with the money Briar earned at Potter's Bakery she had bought another length of material, an end of roll and therefore cheap, from the market and the three of them, Briar and Jess and Elsie, had spent many evenings making it up into a smart dress. A rich honey colour, plain, simple, for they were not experts, with a touch of cream at the neck and wrists and with a sash of honey-coloured ribbon about her waist. She also had a Dolly Varden hat in cream straw with a honey-coloured ribbon about the crown and streamers down the back. The dress was made from a rich woollen material and with the shawl she had bought earlier in the year she could have passed for one of the elegant ladies who promenaded along Bold Street. The sisters had to admit the lass knew what suited her. She turned heads wherever she went now, men's eyes drawn away from the females they accompanied to follow her progress. She didn't even give them a second glance! Her heart was firmly in the grave — the watery grave, they supposed — in which her husband and son lay. She never mentioned them, and neither did they. She never wept, at least in their presence, though sometimes when she got up in the morning there was an expression on her face of terrible pain, a calm and frozen look that spoke of nightmares.

Briar sighed and put her hand on Becky's arm, squeezing it to take the sting out of her words, smiling as she spoke.

"Can I postpone it for a week or two, Becky. Mrs Handy might have made other arrangements which I can't overturn."

Becky sighed too. Wasn't that just like Briar. "Postpone", "arrangements", "overturn". She had a lovely way of talking though sometimes she was hard to understand. More than anything in the world Becky would like to be the same as Briar, ladylike, genteel, quiet, refined. She would have been astounded to know that Briar had once been none of these, indeed there had not been a less ladylike creature in the whole of Bassenthwaite parish.

Briar was sorry that she couldn't bring herself to spend a few hours with Becky, but even as she imagined walking side by side with another man, no matter how much of a "toff" he was, smiling a little at Becky's choice of words, without warning, without giving her time to steady herself, another face imprinted itself inside her eyelids. A face that broke into a sweet smile, a warm and loving smile, a mouth that turned up humorously at the corners with clefts at each side, startlingly blue eyes in which there was so much love she had once drowned in them, and a tumble of thick, fair curls that fell over eyebrows raised in wry amusement. A tall, lean figure with arms that had folded her into his world, promising never to let her go and now he had gone himself and left her behind, taking her baby with him. Tom, his rosy mouth wide in a shout of sheer delight as he ran after her, his copper curls bouncing, his sturdy legs going ten to the dozen. Tom curled in her lap wrapped in a towel after his bath, smelling that special fragrance that belongs to a freshly bathed child, his body relaxing against her as she murmured to him and kissed the back of his neck and that spot beneath his chin that made him giggle. Tom who had ears as soft as a mouse, Tom … Tom … Tom … it was unbearable, her loss was unbearable and she could not at this moment hide her despair.

She bent over as the wild excruciating grief overwhelmed her, her arms round herself, holding on to her senses with a desperate grip, for she knew she was going to fall. Right here in the tiny room provided by Mrs Potter where the staff hung up their outdoor garments and where Becky was staring at her in consternation, her hand to her rosy mouth which hung open. Becky's hat, which was not yet firmly secure, tilted further over her forehead, covering her eyes and she pushed it back fiercely, then, with a lovely warmth and compassion, sprang forward and put her arms about the crouched figure of the woman with whom she had worked for a bare three months and whom she scarcely knew.

"Eeh, chuck, what's up? What did I say? I never meant ter upset yer. I know yer … yer come from a different world than me – better like, burr I just … Nay, don't upset yersenn. Come 'ere." And all the time she patted Briar's shoulder, bewildered, almost crying herself, for she had the softest heart in creation, her mam was always telling her so, adding that one day it would get her into trouble.

Gradually Briar relaxed. The stiffness seeped from her body and she struggled to escape Becky's hold but Becky wasn't sure she should let her go just yet, for surely something terrible had happened to this lass who had simply folded up like a stringless puppet at Becky's simple invitation to go "sparking" with her and Arthur and Arthur's friend the next day. If she wasn't interested in men, which Becky couldn't understand, then she'd only to say so. There was no need to crumple up and fall about as though Becky had just given her a sound thrashing. So she continued to hug her, murmuring words in which only "there, there" was comprehensible until Briar at last straightened up, slowly, painfully, and stood away from her. She turned to the wall for a full minute but Becky, whose simple soul had nothing but goodness in it, waited patiently, saying nothing until Briar swung round to face her.

"I'm sorry, Becky, I don't know what came over me."

"Aye, yer do, chuck, burrif yer don't want ter tell me then that's all right. Me an' Arthur . . . well, we can manage on our own," twinkling, her young face still uncertain. "Are yer sure yer all right, our kid?" For in Becky's eyes Briar was a friend and so was entitled to the latter address. Briar was pale, with a look about her eyes Becky wasn't sure she liked, drawn, old somehow and her usually so incredibly pretty.

"Yes, quite all right. Now, off you go and have a nice time with Arthur. Give his friend my . . . regrets. I'm not . . . perhaps you and I some time . . . one Sunday . . . I like to walk in Princes Park. We could have tea."

Becky's face brightened, for she admired Briar with all her young heart and the thought of them taking a Sunday walk, as friends do, then having a cup of tea in the pavilion, was quite intoxicating. She turned away to the mirror, tugging at her bonnet before swinging back and impulsively planting a hearty kiss on Briar's cheek.

"That'd be lovely," she said shyly. "I've always wanted a friend. A proper friend so 'appen . . ." She left the sentence unfinished, giving the hat another tug before making her way to the side door that led into Colquitt Street.

Again, as Briar followed her, she was spun back in time to the woman whom she had once thought would make a fine friend — aeons ago — but who had turned out to be brittle, bitter, self-centred. Perhaps she wronged Ally Buchanan who had married Perry Sutton, for any woman who had him to contend with must be weighed down by it, by his wildness, his unfaithfulness, his gambling, his drinking, his total lack of interest in her and their child. To be married for one's money must be hard, a sour pill to swallow, but her friendship had proved cursory, shallow, crumbling under duress. She could not remember much about those weeks after ... after ... but it seemed to her that Ally had been marked by her absence. For some reason she had the idea that the young girl who was at the moment rapturously clinging to the arm of the burly young man who waited for her on the corner would prove to be just the opposite. Staunch, loyal to a degree, compassionate, even loving. And yet she was merely a child, in years and in experience. She hoped this Arthur, whoever he was, treated her as she deserved to be treated. Becky turned and waved and for some reason Briar felt a cold clutch at her heart, then she dismissed it and began the walk back to the place she now called home.

The year moved on and before they knew where they were it was Christmas. The shop and the bakery were so pulled out with customers wanting Mrs Potter's mince pies, her Christmas plum puddings, individual and large, her beautifully decorated Christmas cakes that Mrs Handy had largely to leave her lodgers, the two who had not gone home due to the distance they would have to travel, to their own devices while she helped out in the shop. They had to make do with cold meats, rissoles, beef rolls, chicken cutlets, so they'd not starve, she said, as she rolled her sleeves up and plunged her arms up to the elbow in their Elsie's home-made mincemeat. And making the mincemeat wasn't the end of it by a long way. The raisins for the puddings had to be cut in half, a bloody fiddling job, Jess said on the quiet to Elsie, the currants had to be washed and dried, the suet minced finely, the candied peel cut into fine slices, the bread grated down into fine crumbs before the actual mixing of the ingredients for the cakes began. There were scores of eggs to be beaten, the brandy to be stirred in and when one pudding was done and put to boil for six hours, another had to be started. There were orders for two dozen large Christmas cakes, the raisins for which had to be stoned and cut into small pieces, and all this was on top of the usual baking, the orders for which were doubled and then doubled again.

By this time Elsie Potter had made enquiries at a cardboard manufacturer in Church Street and the cake boxes that had been Briar's brainchild had been created and, what's more, bore the name "Potter's Bakery" with "corner of Bold Street and Colquitt Street" printed just below. They were very popular with the customers. Elsie had wanted to charge a halfpenny each for them since she had to pay for the things, didn't she, but Briar had persuaded her against it.

"They won't like it, Mrs Potter. Most of them haven't got a halfpenny to spare and will make do with bags. Now if you let them have the boxes for nothing they'll buy more custards and, at Christmas, mince pies. And if they know they can carry them home intact they'll buy more. Nothing looks worse than a mashed mince pie so . . ."

"Eeh, yer'll ruin me wi' yer grand ideas," Elsie grumbled

but she was secretly pleased and proud of the splendid boxes with the shop's name on them. The lass had other ideas as well. They should advertise in the *Liverpool Echo*, she told the open-mouthed women who worked at Potter's Bakery, turning Elsie speechless. And why not in the better kind of magazines bought by ladies of quality? Every working-class household, those who had made something of themselves, purchased the *Echo*, the men for the sporting news, the women for the hints on good housekeeping, children's welfare, the recipes, patent medicines and help with simple sewing. There were those, of course, the families who lived in the squalid "courts" between Netherfield Road and the northern docks, those bounded by Park Lane, St James Street, Windsor Street and Northumberland Street, who barely had the coppers for the bread and potatoes they lived on, never mind a magazine. Their children died of fever, sore throats, consumption, coughs and colic and the simple remedies printed in the *Liverpool Echo* were of no use to them.

The *Ladies Illustrated News*, another source of aids to the housewife, was much sought after by those who lived in Toxteth, Everton and Walton-on-the-Hill where the better-off resided but they also advertised the fashions to be had at Lewis's and other smart and expensive shops: silks, furs, cashmeres. But on each page there was space for the "better" kind of provision shop and why should not Potter's Bakery be one of them?

"You've surely seen the advertisements for Lipton's teas and ... and Lea & Perrins sauce ..."

Elsie nodded her head, looking first at Jess, then at the others as though to say what would this girl think of next.

"Then there's Woodvilles at the other end of Bold

Street. An *Italian* warehouse he advertises himself as in all the newspapers and have you ever seen his place empty?"

"No, yer right. When I went past last week it were crammed."

"That's because folk know he's there. I went in last week and was told that he had started with a tiny shop in a back street."

"'Oo told yer that?"

"It doesn't matter. I pretended I was a customer of the sort they serve."

"Well, yer look like one, chuck, an' then there's the way yer talk."

"Mrs Potter, if you don't expand, if you stand still, which is what you're doing, you're going backwards."

"Listen 'ere, my girl," Elsie began, folding her arms across her bosom and drawing herself upright. After all this was her business and she'd built it up from a small market stall to this, which she thought of as a prestigious confectioner patronised by some of the better middle class. This girl who stood before her, her face flushed with excitement, an excitement she and their Jess had never thought to see when you looked back to the senseless creature she had once been, was only a shop assistant with no more idea of making a decent scone than the bloody dog who lay on her rug upstairs. But then anybody could learn to make a scone or a biscuit or a loaf of bread but there weren't many who had ideas, like the one about the boxes, and wasn't that what made a business grow? Both she and Jess had worked hard all their lives and had been successful in their own way. They had given good service along with the food they had learned to provide. They had had a modest, comfortable way of life which they were proud of and they had never asked for more, but here was this lass talking about *expanding*, for God's sake, whatever that might mean.

Jess stood quietly to one side. They had just closed the shop. It was nearly ten o'clock. Christmas Eve and they were utterly, totally exhausted; in fact young Becky, who should have been the liveliest being the youngest, was leaning wearily on the counter looking as though she might fall asleep. She had taken off her cap and her pale hair fell about her ashen face, but the others, Dorcas, Aggie and Mabel, were flushed, not exactly excited but intrigued by what was going on. Fancy having their shop printed in a newspaper, their expression said as they exchanged glances. They didn't know what it would mean to them if this advertisement Briar was talking about was printed in the *Liverpool Echo* and the *Ladies Illustrated News* but if it brought more customers in how were they to manage, for they already worked every hour God sent just to keep up orders.

Mrs Potter evidently thought the same. "Now listen 'ere. We've more than enough work fer these lasses as it is."

"You could employ more."

Elsie reared back in alarm and Jess watched it all happening and her heart, which was hidden but totally devoted now to the lass who had come into their lives, exulted.

"Eeh now, that's enough," Elsie shrieked. "There's 'ardly room ter move as it is."

"Bigger premises."

Jess stepped in before their Elsie could open her mouth on a louder shriek of horror. Elsie had a sharp mind. She had worked herself to a standstill to make this little business as it was, but their Briar was going too fast too soon and their Elsie was suddenly frightened. The boxes had been an enormous success. Such a small thing, bloody cake boxes so that Elsie's tarts would not fall apart before the customer got them home, but now, before Elsie could get used to the added custom, small but definite, these had brought in here was the lass talking of further innovations.

"Listen, let's stop this right now, Briar," she said. "We're all on us dead on our feet an' it's not time ter be discussin' business. It's Christmas Day termorrer an' we need the rest."

Becky sat down suddenly on the chair that was placed in the bakery for when Mrs Potter wanted a "birrof a sit down" and though they looked at her in surprise Elsie was too exhausted to remonstrate with her.

"We can talk about this another day," Jess continued. "It needs a good think an' we're none of us in a fit state. Come on, our Elsie, let's go upstairs an' 'ave us a brew. The lasses 've cleaned up and should gerr 'ome ter their beds."

"Aye, yer right. Now then, there's a bag each for yer," Elsie said, turning to the girls, "stuff fer Christmas tharr' I've purrup for yer. A puddin', some mince tarts an' that, oh, an' a birrof a bonus. Yer've all worked 'ard an' I'm grateful."

In the general tumult of "Ta, Mrs Potter", of "Goodbye" and "'Appy Christmas" nobody noticed how quiet young Becky was and if they did they put it down to the exhaustion they all felt. Nor did the three girls who linked arms to walk up Bold Street take note of the fact that instead of turning towards Ainsworth Street where she lived with her parents, Becky began to walk towards the docks. It had been a hectic week and they were glad that they were to get to their beds where Dorcas, at least, swore she meant to spend the next two days recovering.

Elsie and Jess sank into the chairs one on either side of

the fire, Potter having already gone up shoving the dog to one side while they sipped the tea Briar had made for them. They were both half asleep, Jess murmuring that she and their Briar had better get off before she *did* slip into the land of nod. She was glad she'd no cooking, for she and Briar were to eat their Christmas dinner with Elsie and Potter.

They did not notice that Briar was missing even though the dog stood whining at the bottom of the stairs that led to the front door, and when the commotion began, the dog barking, someone shouting, they both were so alarmed they shot up in their chairs and spilled their tea down their pinnies, convinced they were beset by burglars.

It was Briar and she was half carrying the hysterical figure of Becky up the stairs, the dog ahead of them as though leading them both to safety.

Chapter Twenty-six

"I should have gone with her. She asked me to go with her and . . . and Arthur and his friend; a foursome, she said, but you know I couldn't." Briar turned urgently to the two open-mouthed women. "Not after . . . what happened . . ." She gulped, close to tears. "So I said no. I let her go and now look at her."

The two women turned obediently to look at Becky who hung her head but they didn't know what they were looking for, so, their eyebrows raised, they turned back to Briar who ran her hand through her tangled curls.

"I knew something was wrong. I saw it and yet I *didn't* see it. D'you know what I mean?" She held out her hands appealingly but they didn't. Suddenly she leaped forward and took Becky by the arm and led her gently to the chair Jess had just vacated. "See, sweetheart, sit down, you must be exhausted after what you've done today and it's so cold out." She turned to Jess who still stood as though pole-axed, her mouth hanging open. "Is that tea still warm? Pour her a cup, will you, Mrs Handy." And Jess was so bewildered she did as she was told, putting the cup into the hands of the girl who was her sister's assistant.

"She's been ... strange for a while. I can't remember when I first thought she might be concerned about something but I didn't really *see* it if you know what I mean. Just now when they left I watched her go but it didn't register that she wasn't going home but in the other direction. Even then I made nothing of it until ... well, until suddenly it came to me that ... well ... So I took a chance and ran after her. I caught her just where Hanover Street runs into Paradise Street. If she hadn't been so tired and so ... so distressed I'd never have got her back. She struggled and cried so that several passers-by must have thought I was trying to kill her."

"I wish yer 'ad. Yer should've left me. Wharr else is there?" Becky put the cup from which she had barely taken a sip on to the plush-covered table, then bent her head into her hands so that the words she spoke were muffled. "Me dad ses ... mumble ... told me ter ... off an' tekk me ... but what's use ... Arthur don't wanter know." She began to weep broken-heartedly and the dog, in the way he had once done his best to console Briar, pushed his nose on to her knee and whimpered.

Briar knelt down before her, sharing Elsie's hearth-rug with the animal. She pulled Becky's hands away from her face and handed her one of Elsie's clean tea towels which were folded neatly on the table ready for the day when work in the shop and bakery would resume. The truth began to dawn on them but the two women continued to stare at Briar and Becky.

"Wipe your face, Becky, and blow your nose."

It might have been the idea that her clean tea towel was about to be used as a handkerchief by the girl who worked in her shop that brought Elsie to her senses, or was it that inborn instinct one woman has for another's troubles that exploded her into life? Whatever it was her face turned a deep puce and spittle sprayed from her mouth as she spoke.

"Yer not tellin' me this little slut's gorr 'erself in't family way?" she hissed venomously. "That she's led down an' dropped her knickers fer some lad an' decent women're expected ter sit in't same room as 'er." She had all the respectable woman's disgust and contempt for a fallen sister. "All this time she's bin lerrin some lad poke 'er an' workin' in *my* shop alongside decent women. Well, she can gerrout now, dirty little trollop, an' don't come back, d'yer 'ear me. Sittin' in *my chair* . . ." Just as though what Becky had allowed to be done to her might contaminate the place where Elsie sat every night.

"Please, Mrs Potter, can't you see how distressed Becky is. I think you might have some compassion for her predicament, and it doesn't help matters to call her names. Now then, Becky," Briar began, turning to Becky and stroking her hand, but Elsie Potter was outraged and was not about to be told off by this girl who had glared at her with an expression that Elsie had never seen before. At least on *her* face. Quiet, she was, withdrawn even, which was understandable in the circumstances, but that didn't give her the right to interfere in something that was none of her business.

"See 'ere, lady, don't you speak ter me like that. This . . . jade 'as disgraced 'erself an' this establishment, no' ter mention 'er family an' I don't want 'er in my 'ouse."

"So you're to turn her out on to the street."

"''Appen she'll find employment there. Employment more suited to 'er nature," Elsie sneered. "There's none 'ere fer 'er that's fer sure. D'yer think other lasses'll work alongside 'er? No, they won't so she'll 'ave ter go."

She turned on Becky. "Now, lady, gerrout an' tekk yer mucky ways wi' yer." Elsie turned her back on the sight of Becky cowering in the chair. It was as though she was not only shocked beyond measure by the revelation that sixteen-year-old Becky was "in trouble", but saddened, Briar thought, for she had been fond of the light-hearted, hardworking, sweet-natured, generous Becky, which had probably led to her downfall in the first place, and Elsie Potter wanted nothing more to do with her.

"'E said we was ter be married," a pathetic voice from the chair told them, followed by a hiccup that sounded as it might from a child. They all turned to look at her, the sisters' expressions suddenly softer. She still wore the Dolly Varden hat she was so proud of and beneath it her face was round and childlike, smeared with her tears. She wiped her nose, in fact she blew it and Elsie was once again incensed. She took great pride in the snow-white state of her tea towels and Becky wiping her snot on one was enough to inflame anyone.

"Yer a bad little bugger an' deserve everythin' yer got."

"I didn't mean ter ... be bad. It didn't feel bad, 'e were so ... I loved 'im, 'onest I did an' 'e promised we'd be wed ..." Becky's voice died away on a pitiful sob and once more the look on the two sisters' faces might have been one of sympathy, for every woman knows how easy it is to give way to the pleasures of the flesh. They had both loved a man, decent men who had not treated them as this child had been treated, but then they had both been virgins when they married, which was how it should be. Temptations must be overcome and Becky had not overcome the one put in her way.

Their faces were grim and Briar felt a moment of

despair. She had only just clambered back on to her own two unsteady feet and was finding it hard to remain there. Sometimes she wished she had the courage to chuck herself in the Mersey, for Hal and Tom had been lost to her in water and surely that was where she would find them. She did not realise that it was courage that was keeping her from doing so. Now here was Becky in the worst trouble an unmarried woman can find herself in and she had no one, *no one* who would help her to get through it. Not even the two sisters who had been so kind to herself.

"So, where is she to go?" Briar's voice and face had hardened. She got to her feet and swung round to Jess, for surely the woman who had been so good to Briar, so cherishing in her support, would not turn away from this young girl who was totally alone. Her own father – though Briar suspected her mother had been overridden in her maternal desire to help her child – had turned her from their doorstep which, Briar was well aware, was very often the case. The shame brought to a decent family, as Becky's was, could not be borne so it was cast out and the unfortunate girl with it, and she could go to the devil for all they cared.

"Mrs Handy, surely you don't agree with Mrs Potter. Becky has . . . she is in trouble."

"Aye, lass, so she ses."

"Her family have disowned her. The father of the child has turned away from his responsibility but I for one will not see her wandering the streets, prey to . . ."

"There's always t'work'ouse. No one else'll tekk 'er." An' neither will I, the expression on Jess Handy's face seemed to say. "Our Elsie's right, lass." Jess had seen what was in Briar's face and her own pleaded to be understood. A girl who had been "interfered with" was an outcast and it was not unusual for the "sinner" as she would always be known as to do away with herself, for what other choice had she. "The work'ouse is best place fer 'er. They'll look after 'er until babby's born. It's norra bad place. Big buildin' at top o' Brownlow Hill. There's nice gardings in front, flowers an' such. Inmates're taught a trade."

"Becky has a trade. One that Mrs Potter taught her," Briar said coldly.

"It'll do 'er no good. 'Oo's gonner employ 'er in 'er condition? No, best fer 'er ter gerrover there right now an' gerra bed."

Jess's face was as cold and set as Briar's. There was a right way to live your life and a wrong way and this girl, meaning Becky, had chosen the wrong one and must pay for it. Elsie had the exact same expression on her ruddy, still furious face. They might have been bookends, standing side by side, their backs straight to show their impregnable morals, their shoulders squared to show their determination, their heads high, for were they not blameless, their arms crossed over their jutting bosoms in defence against indecency.

Briar studied them for several moments, her own face without expression, then, with a resolute set of her own shoulders, she swung back to Becky.

"Right, sweetheart," she said gently. Jess was seen to wince at the endearment, for often enough she had longed to call Briar that but had never quite dared. It was not in her nature to be demonstrative, no matter how she felt, ask her Albert, but that didn't mean she didn't feel affection. Now the girl she had taken under her wing, spoon-fed, literally, cosseted and brought back from the dead into the land of the living, was flinging it about willy-nilly and at a girl who didn't deserve it. Her heart, which had treasured this lovely lass all these months as though she were her own child, was taking up for a little slut and it was like a stone in her breast and she didn't know what to do about it. She and Elsie were right, but Briar was ... was wrapping the wickedness of Becky Hamilton into her shawl as though she were the most precious thing in the world to her, and Jess ... yes, Jess was jealous.

"Where yer goin'?" she asked harshly.

Briar had lifted the still weeping Becky from the chair and with her arm about her shoulders was leading her towards the door and the stairs that led down to the side of the shop. The dog followed anxiously, his tail moving in the hope that someone might say a soft word and the tension ease.

Briar pulled her own shawl more closely about her then turned her head to say curtly, "I'm taking her to my room which I rent from you, Mrs Handy. She has nowhere else to go so she can share my bed for tonight. Tomorrow we will both look for lodgings elsewhere ... and jobs."

Both Jess and Elsie were dumbfounded. They had been amazed that the ladylike young woman who had been with them since May had not taken the same stance as themselves over Becky's fall from grace. Surely the wickedness of the girl, the shame of her actions which were not those of a "good" girl, were as frowned upon in her class as they were in theirs, but not only was she taking up for her defensively, she was determined to befriend her, support her and God knows what else. Not only was Jess to lose the young woman she was so fond of, Elsie was to lose two of her staff in one night. It was Christmas Eve and in two days' time Potter's Bakery was to open with only one lass to serve in the shop. How was she to manage?

"Now listen 'ere," Jess began, for the strong but befuddled heart of her was making itself felt in her chest. It pounded in the most hurtful way and yet at the same time it fluttered in great distress. In her eyes was a terrible, haunted look and as Elsie stared at her she was reminded vaguely of the way the lass, meaning Briar, had looked when they first came upon her.

Briar hesitated and turned her head in their direction, her arm still protectively about Becky.

"Yes." Her voice was still as frigid as the rain that fell outside. It was already turning to a cold, sleety downpour and would before dawn become a blizzard. Christmas Day tomorrow and where she and Becky were to find lodgings on such a day she couldn't imagine. She smiled ironically inside herself, for hadn't another woman bearing a child tramped looking for somewhere to lay her head on such a day?

"Yer can't just ..." Jess couldn't find the words. There was nothing she hated worse than a loose woman and in her eyes that was exactly what Becky was, but she just could not bear to see the young lass she had come to admire and ... and love ... yes, love, walk out of her life all on account of this simple and naïve child. She must have been both to trust some chap she'd picked up on the street corner. Briar had a great heart. She had suffered the worst torment inflicted upon a woman in losing not only the husband she loved but her own child, her flesh and blood and how did a woman recover from that? She didn't, not ever, Jess knew, for her child had been stillborn. She'd never even held the boy she and Albert had lost but she had loved him then and still did and it was perhaps this that made the difference between her and Elsie, who had never conceived a child.

"Yer can't." Her voice was anguished and Elsie turned to look at her in amazement.

"Jess," she said, ready to turn on her sister if she

gave way. She could see her dithering and again she was outraged, for she had expected their Jess to back her up on this important issue. She knew they both felt the same about girls, women, who were free with their favours. "Bad" girls were not employed in decent places alongside those who were virtuous, and the punishment for those who strayed was to be cast out. But Jess was looking at Briar with such distress Elsie began to be worried. Lines must be drawn or what would become of propriety? Sides must be taken, but to Elsie's horror she began to have the distinct feeling their Jess might not be on hers. The trouble was Jess had become so attached to the girl from nowhere, as Potter had named her, she was not thinking straight.

"Jess," she said again, uncertainty in her voice. "What d'yer think yer doin'?" Though at the moment Jess was just standing there, doing nothing, saying nothing except with her eyes. Briar turned round, her gaze on Jess, drawing Becky with her. Becky was in a stunned state with not the faintest idea what was going on, and, or so it seemed, she didn't much care now. Let her get down to the river and she'd be no trouble to anyone.

"Are you going to turn us out, Mrs Handy?" Briar said softly.

"Lass, lass, what are yer thinkin' of? Yer've enough troubles of yer own wi' out tekkin' on this ... this ..."

"Don't you dare call her a slut, Mrs Handy. You know she's not. She's just a young girl, a child really in her innocence, who has made a mistake. We've all made mistakes, you included. I nearly ... once ... well, a long time ago ..." Briar's eyes looked back into something the others couldn't see and her voice became vague. "A man ... I was a silly young girl who wanted to show the world, but I drew back." She shivered and lifted her head in what once had been a haughty gesture but was now something different. "I was older than Becky but not much and my father ..."

The two women and the young girl became as still as statues, their round, astounded eyes on Briar, for this was the first time she had ever uttered words about her past apart from when she had divulged the reason for her state when they found her. They all three held their breaths as they waited but Briar shook her head and cleared her throat.

"I won't let Becky go down the road to damnation, as you seemed determined she will. If you throw her out, I go too. We can both work, Becky until her condition is revealed and she is forced to give up. We shall find lodgings and we will survive. I'm not the weak creature you took in. Thanks to you both I am stronger – not recovered for I'll never be that – but quite capable of supporting myself and Becky *and* a child until ... well, until Becky is able to look after herself. It will be hard but we'll manage."

There was a long silence as the sisters digested this unforeseen announcement. They were thunderstruck, particularly Elsie, though in Jess was the realisation that she should have known this would happen. Briar was right. Becky was not a loose woman as she had first believed. No, not even believed, for the girl was as Briar said, more victim than culprit. She had been taken in by some glib-tongued bugger who had taken her down and the *right* thing to do, ignoring the concepts of the day, the Christian thing to do was to help the lass through her ordeal, for ordeal it would be. She would be shunned by the girls with whom she worked. They would draw aside their skirts in case she should contaminate them with the filth in which she had lain. And could she, after all these months of caring for Briar, let her simply walk away believing that she, Jess Handy, was as bad as the rest of the world? Their Elsie wouldn't like it but then Elsie was easily annoyed, easily roused, but she got over it and she'd get over this. She was a decent woman who'd harm no one. She'd had a shock but she'd soon see that to lose their Briar would be a disaster. Becky could be replaced but not Briar.

She reached for her shawl and bonnet, twisting about to look in the small mirror as she adjusted it. Elsie watched her in speechless amazement.

"What yer doin'?"

"Goin' 'ome before snow starts. I reckon us'll be stuck fast fer a day or two. Good job it's Christmas."

"What yer mean? Goin' 'ome? Wharr about these two?"

"If they've t'sense they were born with they'll gerrome an' all."

"What?"

Jess swirled round, her shawl flowing out from her set shoulders as though she were ready to do battle with their Elsie if necessary, but she'd not be moved, now or at any other time.

"I'm tekkin' 'em 'ome, pair on 'em an' if yer've owt ter say about it, don't. Sleep on it, our Elsie. If we can gerrover termorrer we will, that's if we're welcome, an' we'll 'ave us a chinwag. 'Appy Christmas, our kid."

The tall, extremely thin man opened the door of the third-class compartment and stepped down from the train which had just jolted into Lime Street Station and settled itself sedately beside the platform. There were a great number of passengers, for it was Christmas Eve and those who were travelling to spend the holiday with loved ones were rushing at the last moment into the city. People called out excitedly, meeting one another with delighted embraces, hurrying away on a tide of goodwill to start the festivities. The man stood for a moment in what seemed like desolation, for there was no one to greet him in this bustling city, no one to clasp him in a warm embrace.

He was carrying a small carpetbag. He wore a warm, double-caped coat and a flat cap and around his neck was an incongruously bright red knitted scarf, put there by his mam before he climbed aboard the small trap that was to take him to Penrith Station in Cumberland.

"When art tha' goin' ter stop this, our Will?" she'd said to him sadly, her hands lingering at his neck, for it broke her mother's heart to see what was happening to her beloved son. The deaths of Hal and Tom Saunders had as effectively ended his life as they had Briar's because she knew his journeying would, if he didn't find the woman he loved, slowly kill him. What was it about the lass that had taken such a hold on him? There were others, good girls, brought up in the farming community, any one of whom would make him an excellent wife, girls who were bonny, strong, good breeders, she thought, for she'd sized them all up in an effort to divert her lad from his endlessly painful search. Every moment he could be spared he was off, taking train to Carlisle, and even as far as Edinburgh once. To Penrith and across the mountains into Northumberland. To Whitehaven and Cockermouth, aimless searchings as she could be anywhere, or nowhere, which was more like it. South he'd gone during the summer and autumn, to the country fairs in Lancashire, and now he had the idea that she might have travelled to Liverpool where the liners took folk over the sea to a new life. Was he to do the same in his search? she'd asked him desperately, but he'd merely shaken his head, unsmiling, gone the merry, good-natured lad he'd once been. He was nearly twenty-nine years old and should have got himself a wife and children of his own by now. Grandchildren for herself to love and scold, for Charlie to spoil, which he surely would do, but would they ever get the chance?

Will Lucas strode swiftly down the platform, waiting at the turnstile for all the travellers to pass through, and when there was only himself left he handed his ticket to the collector and at the same time held up a miniature of a girl, the one he had hawked about the country for the past seven months.

"Have you seen this girl?" he asked the man politely, waiting with little hope, for he must have asked the question a hundred times and been met with a blank stare and a shake of the head.

The man delved into his pocket and brought out a pair of glasses in a wire frame. He attached them to his nose then wiped his hands down his trousers before delicately taking the miniature between his thumb and his forefinger. He studied it carefully and Will, for some reason, felt a small stirring of the pulse in his neck as it quickened. He was not to know that this particular man had once had high hopes of becoming a constable in the police force, but his poor eyesight had stopped him from achieving his aim. He had, before his hopes were dashed, made a point of closely observing faces, for who knew when the memory of one might solve a case. And though he did not appear to be doing so, indeed, hardly knew he was doing it himself, he noted every face that went past him at the turnstile.

He looked up at the man before him, then down again at the small portrait.

"I might've," he said at last.

Will's sad and lonely heart leaped like a salmon moving up river and his face worked in what might become tears. His voice was hoarse.

"Jesus Christ . . ."

The man was offended. "Now, sir, there's no need fer blasphemy."

"To hell with . . ." Will made a concentrated effort to compose himself. "I'm sorry, really, I'm sorry but I've been looking . . . Where did you see her? Here? At the station?"

"I reckon it were 'ere, like, burra while ago."

"May, she disappeared in May."

"Aye, it would be. But she weren't . . . well, she looked poorly, not like this 'un." The ticket collector, careful as a police constable has to be, took another look at the portrait. "Aye, it's 'er all right."

"Where . . . where did she go?" Will grasped the man by his lapels in his effort to get out of him the information he so desperately needed but the man shook him off.

"Nay, I don't know, do I? I only tekk tickets."

"Thank you, thank you." And grabbing the portrait from the man's hands Will Lucas ran out of the station and into Lime Street as though his love were waiting for him there.

Chapter Twenty-seven

Becky hadn't any idea when her baby would be born, she said apologetically. Well, she didn't know much about them really, she added naïvely, for she was the third of three daughters. Becky's father was one of those careful men, very rare in the class from which he came, who had not burdened his wife – and himself – with a child every year. They could manage three and though he would have liked a son – what man doesn't? – he and his wife had practised restraint. He worked on the docks, foreman of a gang of labourers and in comparison to many he was considered a well-set-up man. A proud man who had disowned his dishonoured daughter rather than suffer the jibes and sneers that he was sure would come his way because of her. A man who read his Bible, and the passage regarding eyes and plucking them out if they offened you was taken seriously.

Jess could see Becky only had the vaguest idea how she had come by the child. She had responded to the bugger's – meaning Arthur's – advances with the enthusiasm of a child who is deprived of affection, of the cuddles, the hugs, the kisses a child needs and this was the sorry result. By

God, if she could get hold of the sod, she said later to Briar, she'd cut off that part of his anatomy that had put the lass in this sorry plight. It seemed that Jess's feelings, which had at first condemned Becky, had turned around and though she was still not in agreement with Briar, that would take time, she could not bring herself to chuck the girl into the street as her father had done.

"Well, can yer say when ..." she asked the girl then turned her gaze on Briar in deep embarrassment. Becky gazed from one to the other, childishly eager to help if only she could and Briar took up the questioning.

"What Jess is asking is ... well, when did you and Arthur start having ... er, intimate relations?" She had begun calling Mrs Handy Jess from the moment she and Becky and herself had staggered back through the snowstorm to Peter Street. It was as though a new point in their relationship had been reached on this dramatic night. As though with Jess's support of her and Becky, the support that might cause a rift between the sisters, a deeper friendship had been formed. Not one of an older woman for a younger who needed guidance, though it had been that, but an equal partnership. Briar knew she was as old, if not older, in experience than even Jess and with her championship of Becky, going against both Jess and Elsie, she had broken out of the cosy dependence on them they had willingly given her and had stood for the first time on her own feet. Jess admired that.

"Pardon?" Becky said politely.

"When did you and Arthur begin to ..."

Jess sighed in exasperation, taking the matter in hand with her usual dogged determination. "What she means is when did yer first drop yer knickers fer 'im?"

"Please, Jess, can't you see—" Briar began, but Jess continued as though Briar hadn't spoken.

"I can see we're goin' bloody nowhere with this so we might as well come out wi' it in words lass understands. Dear Lord, don't yer know nuttin' about ... men an' women. Yer should, mess yer in."

Becky's face was on fire with shamed embarrassment and she hung her head, tears beginning to flow.

"An' there's no good cryin' again, lady. We gotter know when this child's comin' an' the only way ter do it is ter find out when Arthur first ... See, when did yer meet 'im?"

"Last summer," Becky whispered.

"Did 'e, yer know, do it right away?"

"Please, Mrs Handy."

"Don't 'please, Mrs Handy' me. See, when was yer last ..."

She turned to Briar who was kneeling at Becky's feet. "Ask her when she last saw ... you know ..." Her own face was as red as a brick, for she was of a generation that did not talk, not out loud at any rate, of such intimate details.

Briar took Becky's hands in hers. "Your monthlies ... when ..."

Becky's face cleared. "Oh, yer mean the curse."

"Aye," Jess said bitterly. "The curse an' there's norra word in't English language that's more ill-used. It's a curse when it *don't* come not when it do. Pity yer didn't think o' that when ..." She shook her head and sat back in her chair, leaving it to Briar.

"I don't know. I can't remember ..." Becky gulped on her tears. Her face was blotched and swollen and Jess had time to think it was a pity bloody Arthur hadn't seen her as she was now, for he'd not have fancied sticking his old feller in her with such enthusiasm.

"Weeks? Months?"

"More like months."

Jess tutted irritably, shaking her head at the daftness of some lasses, this one in particular. "So, best thing's ter 'ave a look at yer."

"What d'you mean, Jess?" Briar questioned doubtfully.

"Tell 'er ter tekk that pinny off an' . . . well, the rest of 'er gear."

"Mrs Handy!" Briar was deeply shocked and so was Becky, who had never undressed before another human being since she was a child, except Arthur, of course, who had insisted upon it, and her mam last night when her condition was revealed.

Silently weeping, she stripped down to her shift and when Jess Handy saw the curved swelling of her belly, which had told Becky's own mother the state of her daughter, Jess sat back in her chair and, as she had done so often this mad evening, shook her head and sighed.

"She must be six months. She's one o' them 'oo carry be'ind burr I've sin it before wi' a niece of Albert's. She were married, thank God, so it didn't matter. Now then, when did this 'appen, not that it makes no difference now?"

"I don't know. I . . . me an' Arthur 'ad . . . 'e 'ad a room in lodgin's in Neptune Street an' . . ."

"He took you there. When, sweetheart?" Briar's voice was soft.

"Right away. 'E said—"

"We don't wanter know wharr 'e said, the bastard. It's too late now burr I reckon this babby'll be along about March or April. 'As it . . . yer know . . . ?"

Becky looked bewildered.

"What Jess means is has the baby kicked, moved?"

Becky's face cleared. "Oh, aye, I reckon so. Talk about

lively." And even as they watched, the curve of Becky's belly under the thin shift moved perceptibly as though a small fist, or foot, had fluttered.

For the umpteenth time that evening Jess sighed in wonderment at young girls' folly. She pulled herself to her feet and began to damp down the fire with the ashes she kept in a bucket beside the fender.

"Well, an' there's you blamin' yersenn," she observed, glancing sideways at Briar, "sayin' yer should've gone wi' 'er when she asked yer an' it woulder done no good since she were already in' family way by't sound of it. But that's you all over, wantin' ter blame yersenn fer everythin'." This was a slanted reminder that Jess considered Briar should not feel guilty about the deaths of her husband and their son. "Sometimes it's God's will, lass, though why God should burden this child an' *us* with this babby, I can't think. Anyroad, that's enough o' that. Thank God them chaps is in their beds" – meaning the two remaining lodgers – "and I'm off ter mine. You two 'll 'ave ter share an' then termorrer, before we set off fer our Elsie's, that's if she lets us over't doorstep, we'll sort summat out."

It was the beginning of April when Becky went into labour. Since Christmas she had been living at Peter Street, sharing Briar's attic room. After that first night when she had sobbed on Briar's shoulder before slipping into a childlike sleep, a bed had been found for her, only a truckle bed which, during the day, was pushed under Briar's, but a warm, clean bed nevertheless and a damn sight better than the workhouse, Jess said tartly. Sleep in a coffin, they did there, or as near to a coffin as made no difference. Becky's eyes were like saucers in her horror-stricken face and Jess relented enough to say, "But yer not goin' there so tekk that look off yer face."

They settled down to a routine which was, on the whole, amicable. Well, as Jess said, it was hard to remain angry with someone like Becky whose sweet, generous nature, which had got her into trouble in the first place, never faltered. She'd work like a navvy at jobs that were often beyond her strength, and Jess had to watch her or she'd be scouring the very pavement in front of the house. She'd clean windows, balancing precariously on a chair, for she hadn't the sense she was born with, Jess told her. She would set to and scrub the scullery floor when Jess was out of the house, and had even moved all the furniture into the middle of the parlour with a view to "bottoming" the place, which her mam did at home once a week.

She had strict instructions never, *never* to go to what Jess called the "front" of the house since it offended Jess's sensibilities to allow her lodgers to see a pregnant woman wandering about and especially one who had no husband. The neighbours had had enough to say on the subject, speculating slyly with her on the relationship between her and Becky, just like they had when Briar came into her life, but Jess dealt with them like she dealt with all those she thought should keep their noses out of other folk's business. She nodded pleasantly and walked on by!

But the lass was willing, there was no doubt about it. She was company for Jess when Briar went out to work, taking Briar's place in a way, doing some of the work Briar had once done. She was cheerful, now she had got over her desperate fear of being abandoned, her only sadness the loss of her mother.

"'Appen she could come an' see yer," Jess told her gruffly, but when a message was sent it was intercepted by

Becky's father who thundered to the poor cowering little lad who was delivering it and who had nothing to do with it, being just the messenger, that he'd get a bloody good hiding if he came again. He *had* no daughter called Becky, he bellowed for half the street to hear, and to bugger off and tell whoever sent the message those very words.

Becky had cried sharply when she was told but, being the childish creature she was, the affection and kindness shown her by Briar, and to some extent by Jess, soon returned her to her old self again, chattering endlessly on what she and her baby would do. It would be a girl, of course, since she was looking forward to dressing her in all the little female garments, frilly dresses and such, that Briar helped her to make out of the oddments of material that they purchased at St John's Market. They cost next to nothing and "Alexandra" as she was going to call her, after the Princess of Wales who Becky had seen last year when she and the Prince opened the new North Docks, would look a treat in them. Yes, Alexandra. A beautiful lady and such a beautiful name, didn't Briar think so, she babbled artlessly as she stitched by the fire, her face rosy and content.

Briar was still working for Elsie who had said tartly that as long as that ... that trollop kept away, ignoring Briar's furious look, she was quite happy to keep Briar on. Briar should know that she would be expected to do the work of two women since Elsie had no intention of replacing Becky and if that didn't suit then she knew where the door was. Briar had no choice but to agree and to keep the sharp words that were on the tip of her tongue to herself. She needed this job. She was keeping herself and Becky out of the 12/6 Elsie paid her, the whole of which she gave into Jess's hand. She suspected that even so Jess was out of pocket, for Becky had a voracious appetite but then she did help out in the house.

It was the first of April, just before they were going to bed, when Becky put her hand to her belly and gave a gasp of pain.

"Oh, Lor', what were that?" she said in a surprised tone, then stared down at the growing patch of damp that had appeared on her skirt.

"What the . . . !" She stood up and a small pool formed at her feet. The cat also stood up and sniffed at it delicately, then sauntered into the scullery and settled herself on to a cushion under the sink as though to say this was where she was staying until it was all over and she could resume her usual place by the fire. She miaowed plaintively to let them know she was not pleased.

Both Briar and Jess got hurriedly to their feet. "Right," Jess said briskly. "Up them stairs, madam," speaking to Becky, "an' gerrin ter that old nightie I purrout fer yer. Briar, foller 'er up, strip bed an' spread them newspapers then run fer Margie Ainsworth. Now, there's no need ter panic, Becky," as Becky began to flap her hands, screwing up her face in fright. "Just do as yer told an' gerrup stairs, inter yer nightie, then lie down on't bed. Everythin's ready. I've only ter purron pans fer 'ot water an' fetch clean towels. Now, off yer go, pair o' yer," for even Briar who had borne a child was showing signs of alarm. But then she supposed the lass had been surrounded by experienced women, even a doctor, when her son was born and would remember little of the mechanics of it, except *her* part in the birth, of course. The end result, the baby placed in her arms, was all she would remember. For a second her face clenched in pain, for she had not had that joy but this was no time to be going back to the memory of sorrow.

"Oh, an' yer'd best tell them men ter ... I dunno ...
sleep wi' their 'eads under't pillow."

There was no need for the measure Jess had ironically
suggested, for the lass made little or no noise as she gave
birth to the little girl she had hoped for. Margie Ainsworth
said she'd never met a braver lass as she wiped Becky's
sweating face round with one of Jess's immaculate towels,
then moved to the other end of the bed to peer somewhat
anxiously between Becky's thighs.

The room was warm as though the energy produced by
the labouring mother, by the women who helped her, by
the movement of them all had created a heat which made
them sweat profusely. The window was open to allow in
some cool night air and through it came the sound of
footsteps, men who worked at the docks going on night
shift, wheels, horses' hooves, the faint sound of voices as
they passed beneath the window.

"Is summat up?" Jess murmured to the midwife while
Briar turned towards the cardboard box lined with towels
in which she had reluctantly placed the small bloody scrap
of humanity who lay so trustingly, so peacefully in her
arms. The baby's hand had fluttered against Briar's face,
a tiny crumpled shell with perfectly shaped oval nails.
Her eyes were as blue as the lapis lazuli in a brooch
she remembered her mother wearing, looking steadfastly
at her from beneath frowning eyebrows and a small
rosebud of a mouth sucking hopefully on nothing. No
fuss, no wailing, just a determined little face that seemed
to say she knew life would not be easy for her in the
circumstances, but she was ready for it and anything it
cared to chuck at her.

There was some drama happening at the bed, the
midwife urgently demanding that Mrs Handy "press this

towel ... see, 'old it tight. It's no good, gerr another ... no. Sweet God, press 'arder."

"What is it?" Briar moved to stand at the back of the two women who were sweating even more with the effort of staunching the birth blood and what she saw made her cry out with horror. Becky's blood was literally *pumping* in great pulsing waves from between her legs, forming a small lake on the newspapers, dripping through them and the mattress on to the floor where another pool formed.

She moved swiftly to the head of the bed, for she felt she must comfort and reassure Becky, tell her that everything would be all right, that the baby was fine and beautiful, but Becky, the Becky she had known and been fond of was gone and the face lying on the pillow was that of a stranger. It was the colour of the ash in Jess's bucket beside the fire, grey, with deep black sunken pits in which her closed eyes rested. Her long eyelashes were like spider's legs on her sunken cheeks and her mouth, once so red and rosy and childlike was a thin white line except where she had bitten it. Her breast rose and fell slowly, fractionally, and under the soiled sheet which they had not had time to change, Becky's body was as flat as a child's.

"What's wrong?" she quavered, wondering as she spoke why she was asking such a foolish question. It was obvious that Becky was bleeding to death.

Without turning from her task the midwife spoke in a voice that was hoarse and desperate. "D'yer know where Stanley Street is? Just past Post Office."

"Yes."

"Then run like t' wind, girl, an' fetch Doctor Benson. Tell 'im it's an emergency – life 'n' death."

"Oh dear God."

"Never mind God, lass, just fetch doctor. I'm at the end of me ... I don't know wharrelse ter do."

Without stopping to throw on a shawl or even change from her soft slippers into her walking shoes, Briar flung herself from the house and ran like a deer into Victoria Street then on until she reached Stanley Street. Folk turned to stare after her in astonishment, then looked back to where she had come from, certain that she was being chased but she did not stop, even when she crossed junctions where hansom cabs and horsemen threatened to run her down.

"Get home, girl, I'll follow on my horse as soon as I've got my bag," the young doctor told her. "I'll be there before you." His horse had to be saddled and his bag fetched but as she raced round the corner into Peter Street he was at the door of fifty-one. It stood wide open and in the hall, just about to mount the stairs which the doctor took three at a time, stood Jess. Her white apron was red from the neck to the hem. There was blood on her dazed face, in her disordered hair and her fingers dripped with it. She just stood there, seemingly unaware of her condition, or even of Briar's frantic hands pulling at hers.

"Jess ... Jess. Please, Jess, tell me she's all right," Briar began but she knew she wasn't.

"It's too late, lass, too late. She's gone, poor little bugger."

They all three wept, Elsie, Jess and Briar as they washed her. Elsie had come the moment she got Jess's message, not sure why she had been summoned except that Jess had thought it right, somehow. Elsie was anguished, for the lass had been no more than sixteen, or so Briar said, and it seemed worse somehow that she had no one to mourn her passing, only three women who were relative strangers. The terrible things she had said to the lass played on her mind, for she'd only been a bairn really, innocent, believing all that the sod had told her and could she be blamed for that? No, she was sorry and if there had been some way of taking it back then she would.

"If ... if that family of 'ers don't want nothin' ter do wi't babby, what'll yer do, our Jess?" she asked, wiping her nose with the back of her hand. Briar had moved away to stare into the makeshift cradle. The sisters stepped back from the bed, looking down at the peaceful face of the girl who had once had so much life in her, so much to give, and hadn't she given it, all of it? They'd brushed her hair and arranged it on the pillow. She had on one of Jess's nightgowns and a clean sheet was arranged across her breast.

"Don't worry about the child," a calm voice from beside the window told them. "I shall look after her."

The two sisters turned in astonishment, on their faces the exact same expression as though they couldn't believe their ears. Briar leaned one shoulder against the window frame and cradled in her arms, wrapped in the lacy shawl she herself had laboriously knitted, was Becky Hamilton's baby. She had been washed, not by the midwife whose job it was, but by Briar, and they could see the whorl of pale blonde curls that covered the child's head. Briar was gazing down at her, and round her forefinger was clutched the child's tiny hand. Briar was smiling, a smile they had never seen before, soft, loving, the smile she had once given to Tom Saunders and which had been waiting for this moment ever since he died. This was the little girl she had dreamed of. After Tom and Hal left her and she lost the child she was carrying, in her dreams it had been *that* child she had longed for. Tom's sister, she had believed. A little girl. A daughter, but it had not been so. This was her. Alexandra. The child Becky had given birth to but who would be Briar's daughter.

"Yer don't know what yer saying, lass," Jess whispered at last. "Yer can't keep 'er."

"Why not?" Briar's voice was dreamy and the sisters exchanged glances. Had she gone soft in the head again, their eyes asked one another and if so what the hell were they to do with her, *and* the babby?

"Because she's not yours, chuck."

"Then whose is she? Arthur's?"

"Who?" Jess looked puzzled, for they had all forgotten Arthur.

"Alexandra's father."

"Alexandra's father!"

"Yes, you know, the man who got Becky into trouble and who didn't want anything to do with her, *or* the child."

"Oh, 'im." Elsie sniffed disdainfully. "Norrim."

"Then who?"

"'Ave yer thought about Becky's mam and dad?"

"I thought they'd made it very plain they wanted nothing to do with her, or the baby."

"Aye, but 'appen things is different now." Jess shifted uncomfortably, turning to look sorrowfully at the still figure beneath the sheet. They'd not covered her face yet, since it seemed such a shame. She'd been so full of life before this had happened and now look at her, poor little blighter.

"Why should they be different?" Briar held the baby even closer to her and her face bore the fierce, protective expression even the mildest woman affects when her child is threatened.

"Well, their lass is dead so 'appen they—"

"I shall go and see them. Will that satisfy you? If they want the baby ... well ..."

"Listen, lass, even if they don't want it 'ow you gonner look after it? I'm not 'avin' it while you go ter work, an' if yer don't go ter work where yer gonner get money ter support you an' 'er?"

"Don't you worry about that, Jess. I have ... I shall get it somehow. No" – she laughed softly then dropped a kiss on the baby's cheek – "I shan't go on the streets."

"Then where?"

"Don't ask, but Alexandra shall want for nothing."

Chapter Twenty-eight

The sad little funeral was attended by just seven people: Briar, Jess, Elsie, Potter, and the three girls from the bakery. Elsie, still feeling remorse over the names she had called the girl whose funeral it was, names she admitted had not been deserved, made the unprecedented move of closing the shop for two hours.

The women wept for the artless little girl, for she had been no more than that, remembering her willingness to help, her cheerfulness even at the end of a wearying day, her capacity to charm the most grim-faced customer. They had missed her.

On a blustery April day they stood at the graveside doing their best not to dwell on what the coffin contained. She had barely lived, poor lass, and though it was a widely held notion that an unmarried female who gave birth to a child was coated with the filth of sin, how could you apply that to poor, naïve little Becky.

It grieved Jess that the lass's family were not present. A note had been delivered – not by the same lad who had protested vehemently that he wouldn't go there again for a golden guinea – to her parents and he, the messenger, the boy from next door but one who was afraid of no one, he said, was on fire to describe to them the woman, meaning Becky's poor mother, who had fallen to her knees and screamed when the note was read out loud. The man had blustered that he hadn't the faintest idea why they were informing him about this girl who, as he had already told them, was no daughter of his. He had no daughter called Becky and the lad had better bugger off before he got a clip round t'lug!

After the short funeral Elsie and the girls, escorted by Potter, had walked back from St James's Cemetery where the interment had taken place to the bakery to reopen the shop. Elsie had placed a notice in the window informing her customers that due to a bereavement the shop would be closed from one o'clock until three, and when they turned the corner from Berry Street there was a queue of patient women with baskets on their arms reaching round the corner into Colquitt Street. As she unlocked the shop door, smiling sadly at the women, Elsie remarked in an aside to Potter that that there idea of Briar's had certainly brought in a lot of new business and she wasn't sure they could cope much longer in these cramped quarters. It had given her no end of a kick to see her name in the advertising columns of the *Echo*: "Potter's Bakery" with underneath a long list of the goods she sold in her shop, all home-made, naturally, and at the bottom corner, "Proprietor, Elsie Potter". She had her head screwed on, did that lass and the conversation she and Jess and Briar had had the day after Becky died had reassured Elsie enormously, that's if what Briar had put to her worked out.

Briar was nursing the baby, a dear little thing who seemed to sense that she had had a poor beginning and barely raised her voice to protest that she was wet, or mucky, or even hungry. A feeding bottle had been purchased at the chemist in Bold Street plus a packet of Nestlé's Food which pronounced itself to be an entire diet for infants, the nearest equivalent to mother's milk. Alexandra took it placidly, sucking on the teat with her eyes closed and her small clenched fists, the thumbs tucked into the palms, folded neatly over the bodice of the tiny outfit her mother had made for her. Briar studied her rosy face, which had a look of Becky about it but which promised a beauty her mother had lacked. Becky had been pretty but the child had a delicacy, a refinement if you liked, and for the umpteenth time in the last twenty-four hours she had pondered on what the lecherous Arthur had looked like and where he had come from. Perhaps his mother had had a liaison with some sprig of the gentry, a parlour-maid seduced by the son of the house and Arthur had been the result; but whatever it was in his make-up it had been transferred to his daughter. *Her* daughter, Briar whispered to herself, for this was the little girl she had dreamed of and she meant to keep her. Becky's parents had disowned her once and, for the second time, the child Becky had given birth to. Nobody wanted her, only Briar and she meant to make sure she kept her legally.

She plucked the teat from the child's mouth with a sound like a cork coming from a bottle, putting her over her shoulder to wind her, and both Elsie and Jess watched, for it was evident that Briar knew what she was about. She had given birth to her own son and her manner with the infant showed confidence and experience. The baby burped and sank back at once into a deep sleep against Briar's breast.

Briar looked up and smiled. "Isn't she lovely?" Her voice was dreamy, her eyes soft and glowing, and the sisters were aware that this woman was herself again. This child had dragged her finally back from the void in which she had lived for over a year and though they were well aware that Alexandra – what a name – would never take the place of the dead Tom, she had found a corner of Briar's heart that needed filling.

Briar tore her eyes from the child's sleeping face and her smile deepened.

"Elsie, I wanted to have a word with you about the shop."

"Oh aye." Elsie was on the defensive, since she had no idea what she was to do about the shop. She certainly couldn't manage without Becky *and* Briar, and Briar looked set to do nowt but gaze at the babby for hours on end and where did that leave Elsie? She had to have at least two girls serving in the shop, probably more the way things were going what with the advertising and that, and happen another in the bakery. Sometimes she wished this lass had never come into their lives but then that wouldn't have stopped Becky from dropping her "kecks" for that bugger she had fallen for, would it?

"Yes, I wondered what you thought about my bringing Alexandra to the shop. I'm to buy a perambulator and if I was to wheel her round each morning, put the perambulator in the back yard or in a corner of the bakery if the weather is inclement, I could continue to work for you. Now I know—"

"Yer what?" Elsie was flabbergasted and so was Jess, who hadn't really got over the terrible tragedy of yesterday, never mind what was to be done with the baby. An orphanage, she had thought, believing that Briar couldn't possibly mean she was to keep the child, but would you look at her. Made up, she was, and with her sharp brain she had obviously got it all worked out, even to the buying of a perambulator. Where the money for that was to come from was a bloody mystery but it seemed Briar was about to enlighten them.

"I haven't told you about myself before. I've worked in the bakery and I hope I've earned enough to keep myself and Becky and not been a burden on the two of you. You have both been generous and now I hope to repay you. I'm ... not without money."

They both gaped speechlessly.

"My father is a wealthy man and my ... my husband was not without ... we had a farm. I had an allowance from my father from the age of eighteen and a cash sum when I married, which is sitting in a bank in Keswick gaining interest, I presume. So I am going to see a solicitor and ensure that Alexandra and I will be able to pay our way. I am hoping, if you agree, Elsie, that I might invest in your business. We did talk of expanding ..."

"Yer mean you did, lady," Elsie protested, her face a picture, for it took all her wits to keep up with this woman and she was feeling somewhat left behind.

"Can we talk about after I have seen the solicitor? I'll know more then."

Jess and Elsie exchanged glances, their faces almost a mirror image of one another. They shook their head in wonderment.

"Aye, I suppose so," Elsie said.

She wore black. Not the dress in which she had come to Liverpool, but a well-cut, elegantly simple gown of watered silk with a waterfall of narrow frills draped over a small bustle at the back. Her bonnet, worn at the back of her head and tied beneath her chin with wide ribbons, was decorated with ruched taffeta and tiny black satin roses. Over the gown she wore a black mantle edged with black fake fur with a muff to match, all purchased at Lewis's Department Store where such things were available already made up. Her outfit advised that she was a widow, which she was, and the gentleman into whose room she was shown by his respectful clerk rose at once to his feet, taking her hand and bowing over it.

"Mrs Saunders, do sit down," he begged and only when she was seated to his complete satisfaction did he return to his chair behind his enormous desk.

"Thank you, Mr Chancellor. You are most kind." She smiled warmly and he was quite taken aback by her loveliness, her graciousness, the perfection of her white teeth, the bloom on her smooth, flawless cheek, the rich fullness of her mouth, the colour of the pink carnations growing in his garden, and the deep, transparent golden brown of her eyes. She was quite magnificent and yet she was not wealthy. The fur on her mantle told him that. He was a man of money himself. His wife shopped at the best and most expensive dressmakers and milliners in town so he knew when a lady was well dressed. After all, he paid the bills.

"May I offer you tea, or perhaps coffee?" he asked her, reaching out for the bell on his desk.

"That would be splendid, Mr Chancellor, thank you." She placed her muff on her knee and began to draw off her gloves, and when the tea came, brought and poured by a small, neat and efficient lady of indeterminate age, she sipped it calmly with no effort to get to the reason for her visit. She and Mr Chancellor discussed the weather, her gratitude that he could see her so quickly, the loveliness of the spring flowers that had been planted in the city's parks and gardens, and the increasing traffic which made walking in the main streets so hazardous.

When they had exhausted all the topics that two strangers can successfully manage, she put her cup carefully in the saucer and lifted her head to look into his eyes.

"No doubt you are wondering what I am doing here, Mr Chancellor." He was surprised by a suggestion of tears in her eyes but then her outfit indicated that she was a widow, a very *young* widow which was sad, but she was not a client of his so he waited for her to tell him the reason for her visit. A patient man was Ernest Chancellor, as he had to be in his profession of solicitor.

"In your own time, Mrs Saunders." He smiled encouragingly.

"I have a task I would like you to perform, Mr Chancellor, somewhat strange perhaps but one that needs the utmost delicacy and ... discretion."

"I hope I can offer both, Mrs Saunders."

"I hope you can otherwise I must go elsewhere."

"Please, Mrs Saunders. In my work I must promise confidentiality and so ..."

"Thank you, sir, then I'll tell you what I want you to do."

"Please, Mrs Saunders—"

Again she cut him short as though she really hadn't a moment to spare even though she had just spent ten minutes drinking his tea and making small talk.

"I ... I have a child at home, sir. A little girl only a week old and—"

"Good heavens, Mrs Saunders." He rose to his feet in great consternation. "Should you be out so soon after ... after ..." He turned a bright crimson, embarrassed beyond measure, but Mrs Saunders waved him away, indicating that he should resume his seat.

"No, Mr Chancellor, she is not . . . not mine, really. It's a long story. No one wants her, only me."

"Please, Mrs Saunders, if I am to help you in whatever it is . . . well, perhaps you had best begin at the beginning."

Her face was calm but the expression in her eyes spoke of her anguish as she began with the day on which Hal and Tom were lost to her. She led him through the days that followed and her subsequent arrival in Liverpool.

"I was out of my mind, Mr Chancellor. I had determined I was to sail to New York. I needed to be as far away as I could from the area where . . . where it happened. I hoped that with distance between me and memories, that this aching that was, quite literally, withering me, would one day go away. But I had no money; some kind people, two sisters and the husband of one of them befriended me, took me in, helped me to better health and found me a job. This took place over many months, you understand. There was a girl, sixteen, with whom I worked who . . . got into trouble, you know?"

Mr Chancellor nodded gravely. He was totally fascinated by the impassive beauty of the young woman and her tragic tale, wondering as he watched her, noted the changing colour of her startling eyes, the flush of rose at her cheeks which deepened as she spoke, the curve of her lips, where this story would end.

"The girl, child, she was no more, gave birth to . . . to Alexandra." Here she smiled brilliantly and he was overcome by the splendour of her. Her smile slipped away. "But the girl, Becky, died. Her parents had disowned her. They wanted nothing to do with her or the child so . . . I want to adopt her. Alexandra, I mean. I want to do it legally. Her grandparents must be approached – I have their address – so I would like to retain you to act for me in this matter."

She leaned back in her chair, then sat straight again as though aware that she was not yet done with him, or he with her. The room was dim but the leaping flames of a good fire in the blackleaded grate warmed the panelled walls and lit the faces of the dour bearded gentlemen in the heavy framed portraits all about the room. It also lit her hair which curled up about the brim of her bonnet to a rich copper gold.

He put his elbows on the desk, hands together, steepling his fingers and tapping them against his mouth, his eyes on her, his expression thoughtful, doing his best to bring his mind back to a professional level. He said nothing for a minute or two then leaned back before speaking.

"Are you from these parts, Mrs Saunders?"

"No."

"May I ask where?"

She bit her lip, considering the question, considering whether she could trust him, he knew that, then looked down into her lap.

"I ran away, Mr Chancellor. I ran away from the agony of loss, the sorrow, not considering what I was leaving behind. Not caring, really. My mother and father, friends. I simply took a train to here and vanished."

"They don't know where you are, or even if you are still alive?"

She hung her head. "No."

"Please, Mrs Saunders, what you do, what you did is nothing to do with me unless you broke the law, which it seems you didn't, but what I want to know is: what do you want me to do?"

"I need money, Mr Chancellor. If I am to adopt Alexandra, which I am determined upon, I must have money to support her and myself. And I intend investing in a business."

Mr Chancellor looked quite horrified. Here was a gently bred woman talking of chucking her money about in some probably far-fetched scheme and without legal advice. Thank God she had had the sense to come to him. All this would need to be seriously gone into and he was just the man to do it. Such a lovely woman, and so tragic. He dragged his mind back to what she was saying.

"I cannot, not yet at any rate, go back to ... to ... I am not ready, but I need you to make enquiries about my husband's money. We had a successful farm. I have money of my own which my father gave to me when I married. I want to get my hands on it but ... without my father knowing."

"Mrs Saunders, I don't wish to interfere in your family problems but don't you think it is heartless, I can think of no other word, to keep your parents in the dark like this? I have daughters and the thought that—"

She rose to her feet with the grace of a young queen, reaching for her muff and gloves. "I'm sorry, Mr Chancellor, I feel that we cannot do business together. I shall have to go elsewhere. If you cannot simply advise and help me as a client without inflicting your opinion ..."

"Mrs Saunders, please." Mr Chancellor leaped to his feet and hurried round the desk to her. "I am ... I do apologise. I had no right to seem to criticise. I have no idea, none, of the suffering you ... nor what it might drive a person to. Forgive me. Please sit down and let us see what we can do. The adoption will be easy, from what you tell me. Please, do sit down, Mrs Saunders. May

I offer you more tea? I can see you're upset and then if you will give me details … No, please, I will not divulge your whereabouts to your father. You are of legal age and can do as you please with whatever monies are in … in … a bank in Keswick, you say. It should easily be arranged."

"The bank is not to know where it is forwarding cash, Mr Chancellor."

"Mrs Saunders, I have a partner; we have several branches in Lancashire and I can assure you that Liverpool will not be mentioned. Besides, the manager of the bank in Keswick is bound by confidentiality to his client, in this case, yourself."

"My father is influential in Cumberland, Mr Chancellor. I must be certain that he will not be informed. I was thinking – since you mentioned it and since it seems to trouble you – perhaps I could send a note to my parents through your firm to let them know I am well."

Mr Chancellor smiled warmly. "It would be my pleasure, Mrs Saunders."

It was Jess's money that had bought the outfit and paid Mr Chancellor's fees, though naturally Briar would pay her back as soon as her own money came from the bank in Keswick, she told her. Mr Chancellor was positive that she should have some cash available by the end of the week, by which time she and Alexandra would be ready to start work at Elsie's place, just as though Alexandra were to hold an important position there.

"Yer want ter borrow a few more quid, is that it?" Jess said tartly, holding Becky's child to her breast and looking down at her with the fond and doting expression which is the prerogative of a grandmother. That's how she felt, that her daughter had given birth to this lovely child and so she was entitled to spoil her as much as she liked. And she was lovely. God knows what Arthur looked like, she was to say to their Elsie, who fought with her to have a "go" at nursing the babby. Becky had been fair with blue eyes but this one's hair was like silver silk, curling round her shapely head in thick swathes and her eyes were the most incredible blue Jess had ever seen.

It was the same at the shop. The moment Briar pushed the elegant perambulator through the front door promptly at seven the following Monday everybody, including Elsie, dropped whatever they were doing. They crowded round the baby carriage, dying to have a look at Becky Hamilton's baby. Mind you, it was not to be Becky's baby but Briar's from what Mrs Potter had told them, since she was to adopt her for her own. They had never met a child who had been adopted, or a woman who had adopted one. In their class such things didn't happen. The women they knew had enough of their own without taking on any more. But you could see Briar doted on her and so did they all, even Mrs Potter.

Two months later they expanded their premises into the house next door which fell vacant, all the legal transactions being carried out by Mr Chancellor, who had proved to be worth his weight in gold. What had been the small parlour in the new house, which fronted on to Colquitt Street, was turned into a sort of nursery where Alexandra Saunders, as she was now called, always had one or other of the girls, eight of them now, who worked at Potter's Bakery, popping in to see her. It was an amazing room filled with toys and books and painted in lovely colours and the child was going a fair way to being totally ruined.

The shop took up the whole of the corner of the street

with one window in Bold Street and one in Colquitt Street with a smart windowed door over which hung a smart lamp in between. Another door in Colquitt Street led into what Briar called the "family" quarters. Elsie said she felt like the Queen, her place on the first floor was so smart, and on the second floor were bedrooms where three of Elsie's girls, who came from places in Lancashire that were too far away for them to go home at night, had a bedroom each. She and her girls, four of them in the much enlarged bakery at the back, turned out what Elsie described as "fancy" stuff, which appealed to the better class of lady, bringing in grand housekeepers who came in carriages to choose from the ever increasing choice of Elsie's delicacies. Her clientèle widened and it became clear that Briar Saunders, who still worked side by side with Dorcas and Maisie and Adah behind the gleaming glass counter of the shop, had turned what had been a successful but small business into what was rapidly becoming a large thriving concern that would need even more expansion if they were to keep up. If you didn't move on you were going backwards, she kept repeating, whatever that meant. A delivery van she was talking about now, with a smartly dressed man to drive it out to Everton, Knotty Ash, Toxteth and to the large villas of the wealthy along the waterfront, beyond the docks up towards Dingle and Garston.

It was a Saturday in June, the middle of the afternoon when business was beginning to slacken off, for most of the housewives and housekeepers had done their weekend shopping. Briar was leaning on the scrubbed table in the bakery sipping a welcome cup of tea, discussing with Elsie the advantages of one of them, herself, she thought, since Elsie would be frightened out of her wits, travelling up to London to have a look at Harrods Store in Brompton

Road. She had heard that Charles Harrod had in twenty years expanded a small business bought from his father into one that was now employing almost a hundred people, all of whom lived off the premises.

"Eeh, lass, wharrever next?" Elsie said absently, thumping her scrubbing brush down on the already immaculate table, prior to giving it another good "go".

Briar laughed, determined to get Elsie's full attention one of these days and go into the scheme further. She was fully aware that at Elsie's age everything she herself suggested was frightening. Elsie had been the proprietor of Potter's Bakery for many years and had become used to running it, confident in her talent of confectioner, baker, and turning out all the plain, wholesome food her customers required. She had been delighted by the success of the square cardboard boxes and by the advertisement which had drawn more customers to her shop. She had hesitatingly agreed to the expansion of her premises only because of the cash Briar herself was putting into it and had even acknowledged, since she had no option, that Briar now had a share in the profits. But Briar knew she was not awfully sure she wanted to go any further. She was a small shopkeeper at heart, too old to extend her vision beyond what she already had.

Briar smiled as she tucked Alexandra into the baby carriage, knowing that Elsie would have a purple fit if she knew what plans Briar had evolving in her mind.

"We're off now, Elsie," she called out as she manoeuvred the carriage down the steps into the street. "I want to call in at the chemist on Bold Street before it closes. Will we see you tomorrow?" Knowing the answer would be yes, for, like Jess, the elder woman doted on the baby.

"Aye, we might tekk us a walk over. Now you mind the traffic wi' that babby."

Late Saturday afternoon in Bold Street was busy. Last-minute shoppers were rushing to and fro, hurrying along the pavements, gentlemen carrying their lady companions' parcels, chattering, laughing, window-shopping. This was Liverpool's most fashionable shopping street. The ladies for the most part were expensively dressed in the vivid colours that were fashionable, the gentlemen almost in uniform, equally smart in their black frock coats, light grey trousers, plain grey silk waistcoats, immaculate shirt fronts and silk top hats. They stepped aside politely as Briar pushed the baby carriage along the pavement, barely glancing at them or the windows, her whole attention on the sleeping baby whose rosy face, framed in a white frilled bonnet, lay on the pillow.

A hansom cab drew up outside the gentlemen's club, a gambling club she had heard, halfway along Bold Street and from it stepped a tall, extremely handsome gentleman dressed exactly like all the others but in his neck cloth was a pearl, on his finger was a heavy gold ring and across his waistcoat lay a thick gold watch chain. He carried his top hat and the lights from the shop windows which were just being turned on fell on his thick, curling fair hair.

He turned away from the cab, his destination the doorway of the club and almost bumped into the perambulator. At once he began to apologise, recognising a pretty woman when he saw one and instantly responding, then he fell back in some confusion. His face registered his shock, then he began to smile.

"Well damn me, if it isn't Briar Saunders," he said smilingly.

It was Perry Sutton!

Chapter Twenty-nine

He was the first to recover. The pavement was becoming increasingly crowded with shoppers and as Briar stood there, unable to move her limbs, unable to take the few steps needed to get her past the insolently grinning figure of the man who was her dead husband's cousin, he put his hand on the handle of the baby carriage as though, should she take it into her head to bolt, she would have to fight him to achieve it. She stared into his face, hypnotised as a rabbit might be by a snake, and about them passers-by began to tutt and mutter, for she and the baby carriage effectively blocked the pavement. Perry Sutton did not give a damn, since when had others' inconvenience concerned him?

"Well, I'll be damned," he said softly, his eyes roving over her from the crown of her leghorn hat to the tips of her high-heeled boots. She had abandoned her black gown only last week, feeling that her mourning for Becky, though her death still saddened her, should come to an end. Besides, if she was honest, the black had been initially donned to impress Mr Chancellor. She was a widow and the outward trappings of mourning must be observed even if the inner grief would never be seen by a living person. She wore a fawn-coloured afternoon dress of durable "corde lorraine", high-necked and tight-sleeved, the skirt swathed across her stomach into a small draped bustle at the back, cascading into narrow frills. It was simple, smart and yet, with a full white apron, covering her from neck to hem, the white cotton cuffs and the pretty, frilled white mobcap they all wore, was eminently suitable for the shop. The others still wore black but it was understood that as a partner in the business she was allowed to wear a different dress to the employees. Binding each frill and about the neck and wrist was a narrow band of apple green in the same fabric. Her straw hat, which dipped down attractively over her forehead, was bound about the crown in apple-green ribbon which tied in a large bow under her chin and had streamers down her back. Her boots were of fawn kid with heels so high she was almost as tall as Perry. It was made very evident by his expression that Perry considered her to be just to his taste.

The baby made a mewing sound as she awakened and the sound drew Perry's obviously admiring glance down into the baby carriage and at once, just as though he had barely noticed it in his interest and sudden shock at seeing her, he smirked, his mouth drawing up into a knowing grimace.

"My dear, you *have* been busy. Hal gone less than eighteen months and already you have a new family. And all of Bassenthwaite thinking you to be dead. Your parents are a shadow of their former selves and still, so I have heard, employing men to search for you. And here you are, in the best of health and looking lovelier than ever. Alice will be pleased when I tell her. Mind you, we don't see a lot of one another these days. She has her interests and I have mine." He paused and raised his eyebrows quizzically. "Are you not to speak to me, Briar? After all we were once good friends."

They were like a small island in the sea of people who were forced to swirl round them in eddying currents, and still she could not speak, nor even move. The shock was so great her mouth had dried up, her mind had gone blank, empty of all thoughts beyond repugnance, but at the word "friends" she broke out of her shell of shuddering horror.

"When were you and I ever friends? You were my husband's cousin so I was forced to be polite but by no stretch of the imagination could we be called friends. So, take your hand off the perambulator, if you please, and allow me to pass," she told him icily. "I am in a hurry to get the baby home."

"Ah yes, the baby, and what a pretty baby it is, to be sure," not even giving Alexandra a second glance. "She has a look of Hal about her, don't you think? The same colouring."

She had indeed thought so herself and was perhaps aware that that was why she loved the child so much, but she was not about to allow Perry Sutton to lay his filthy mouth about the name of her much loved husband, no matter what their relationship might be, nor to spout his nasty insinuations about her and her child. She was not even sure what she meant by that but whatever it was she didn't like it, and she loathed him.

"*Get your hand off the perambulator,*" she hissed, "or I shall call that constable over there and tell him that you are interfering with me and my child. Now step out of my way."

He smiled his insolent smile but took his hand away from the carriage, stepping back from her, bowing in an exaggerated way.

"My dear, far be it from me to prevent a wife from hurrying home to her husband but as I am in Liverpool indefinitely ... I have business within" – nodding at the entrance to the club – "I shall watch out for you. Perhaps you and your husband will do me the honour of dining with me. We could catch up on the news. You might be interested to hear of the service – what do they call it? – a *memorial* service that was held for Hal and young Tom. Ah, I see I have your attention now. Your father has—"

"Where ... where ... when did ... have they found the ...?" Her frantic hand plucked at his coat sleeve but he stepped back from her, laughing.

"Dear Briar, I'm so sorry but I have an important engagement within, but later perhaps we might meet and talk about old times. Now, I must bid you good-day, or rather good evening since it will soon be dark."

"Please, Perry, for the love of God tell me ..."

"Tell you what, my pet?" He raised his eyebrows and she could see he was enjoying every moment of her distress but she was beyond caring. She was desperate to know if ... if Hal and Tom had been found and at the same time she fully understood at last that what she had done, leaving behind her distraught family, disappearing without a thought for their plight, did not entitle her to anyone's sympathy.

"I would love to stay and ... chat," he went on, "really I would. Perhaps if you were to leave your address I might call and bring you up to date on the news. Now, I must go."

"Peter Street. Fifty-one Peter Street. Please, Perry ..."

"Peter Street. How quaint. And won't your husband mind?"

"I don't have a husband."

"I see. No husband." He looked at her speculatively before glancing into the perambulator, then grinned audaciously, giving her breasts a last lingering look. With another slight bow and a grin, which revealed his white and gleaming teeth, he crossed the pavement and entered the doorway of the club, taking the stairs two at a time.

She stood for several minutes on the darkening street unaware of the passers-by and even the one or two anxious voices that asked her if she was all right. The baby began to grizzle, for it was long past her supper time and still Briar stood like a statue, aware that had she not the perambulator to cling to she would have fallen. It all came rushing back at her, the past in which so much pain lurked, hammering blows that almost brought her to her knees. She had not forgotten, how could she? But her new life, the joy of the baby, the friendship of Jess and Elsie which warmed her every day, comforted her, upheld her, the satisfaction of her success with Potter's Bakery, slipped away on a tide of grief for the lovely man and child who had once been hers. He had brought it back, not kindly but doing it in such a way as to hurt her, deliberately. A memorial service: what did that mean? Had they found Hal and Tom or was it something to honour and remember them as they deserved? Dear, dear God, why had this happened, why? She was just getting her life back together again. Mr Chancellor had, as he had promised, sent a note on her behalf to let her parents know that she was alive and well and had received a desperate plea in return for her to come home. They had been elated, overjoyed, was how Mr Chancellor had put it, to hear from her, or at least from him, but they wanted her home and she was not ready for that yet. How could she walk those paths, climb those hills, walk the lake where she had known such happiness and such despair? One day, one day when the healing begun with Alexandra was complete she would go home, wherever that was, and visit them all but her *real* home was here now, with Jess, with Elsie and the shop she loved, with Potter, bless him, and with her daughter.

She suddenly came out of the stunned trance into which Perry Sutton had spiralled her, wondering how long she had been here. Alexandra was howling – why hadn't she heard her? – and the constable on the corner of Concert Street was beginning to make his way towards her, his attention caught by her absolute stillness and the crowd of concerned passers-by who had collected round her.

With a great effort she put one foot in front of the other and began to move, throwing off the hands of the anxious women, pushing the baby carriage, which felt as though it weighed a ton, along Bold Street, ignoring all those who stared at her. She must get home. She must get back to Peter Street, to Jess, to the comfortable warmth of the kitchen, to the safety she had made for herself.

She was almost running as she turned into Peter Street. Mrs Foster who lived at the end house and who always took a great interest in the beautiful baby who lived at Jess Handy's was just coming out of her front door.

"'Ello lass," she said. "Yer in a 'urry. Where's t'fire?" And was taken aback when Briar galloped past her as though she didn't exist. The baby was screaming her head off so that when Briar reached the door of fifty-one, Jess, who had been hanging about waiting for her, since it was almost dusk, nearly fell off the top step in her attempt to get to her.

"Jesus God, where've yer bin? I've bin outer me mind. An' what's up wi't babby? See, come ter Jess, lambkin," she crooned, plucking the red-faced baby from the perambulator, cradling her in one arm while the other whipped off the pretty bonnet and smoothed back Alexandra's silver-gilt curls. It was only then, after she had soothed the baby, that she gave her full attention to Briar who stood trembling, white-faced, teeth chattering with shock, still clinging for support to the perambulator.

"Chuck ... lass, what's up? What's 'appened? Yer look like yer've sin a ghost."

"I have," Briar managed to stutter.

"Yer what?" Jess blundered down the steps and put her free arm round Briar's shoulders, urging her up the steps and into the lamp-lit passage.

"The perambulator ..." Briar protested feebly.

"Bugger t' perambulator. Come inside and sit yer by't fire an' tell us what's 'appened." She kissed the baby on her forehead then placed her in the lined cradle which stayed in the kitchen or went upstairs to the attic where Alexandra slept with her mother. Alexandra was not pleased. She was hungry and the promise of her feed which had been implied when Jess picked her up was suddenly slipping away. She protested loudly.

"I'd best feed 'er then." Jess hurried out into the scullery, returning with the bottle, and once more picking up the baby popped the teat in her mouth before settling them both in the chair opposite Briar's. Briar was staring blankly into the fire, her face like chalk, her eyes big, the pupils dilated so that they looked almost black. Her hands twisted themselves about one another, like two squirming animals and Jess leaned over and gently put one of hers over them.

"It's all right, chuck, really it is. Stop mitherin' an' tell Jess what's up."

The hands stilled and Briar turned her gaze away from the fire and looked at Jess. Her expression was harrowed.

"I saw Perry Sutton."

"'Oo the 'ell's Perry Sutton?"

"He's ... he is Hal's cousin."

"Your Hal?"

"Yes."

"So ...?" Jess prompted.

"He's the worst kind of libertine, the exact opposite to Hal. You could hardly believe that they were related. He's a gambler, a womaniser, with a cruel streak that—"

"A sod, in other words?"

Briar smiled for the first time. "Exactly."

"But what's 'e ter do wi' you?"

"He ... I met him just now in Bold Street. He was going into that gambling club there. He believed that I had married again and that Alexandra was ... He sneered at me, saying that with Hal ... gone less than eighteen months it had not taken me long to find consolation. Then ..."

"What, queen?"

"He said there had been a memorial ... service for ..." Her words ended on a choking gulp as the tears began to flood to her eyes and coursed down her cheeks, "Oh, Jess," she wailed, and in Jess's arms the baby's eyes stared in wonder at Briar and the bottle teat became unplugged. Her bottom lip trembled.

"Nay, lass, don't upset yersenn, nor't babby," Jess said stoutly.

"But I must know, don't you see? The ... the bodies might have been recovered. Jess, what am I to do?" She dropped her face into her hands and sobbed broken-heartedly.

"About what, lass? There don't seem ter be a lot yer *can* do. Wharrever's 'appened, 'as 'appened, if yer see whar I mean. Yer can't go back, lass. I mean yer can go back ter yer family, find out what's gone on, but yer can't turn back t' clock. If ... if ... eeh, lass, I don't like ter see yer upset burrif they've found your Hal an' the little 'un it don't mekk any difference ter yer life, do it? Aye, I know yer'd like ter ... ter know about it but ..." Jess shrugged philosophically.

"If it had been anyone else but him," Briar wept.

"Yer mean this Perry Whatsit?"

"Yes. He's such a ... a troublemaker. You see I gave him this address ..."

"Yer did what?" Jess reared up and the baby gave a little hiccup of protest.

"He wouldn't tell me, you see. I begged him then he said he'd call."

"Call?"

"Yes. At the house."

"This 'ouse?"

"Yes, that's what they do in our ... in his society."

"Do they indeed." Jess humphed contemptuously.

"Yes, to tell me what ... if ... if Hal and Tom ..."

"Right, queen, lerrim call an' 'e'll 'ave me ter deal with."

Jess Handy had not got where she had by allowing others to outwit or victimise her. Many had tried. She was a widow and fair game to those men who preyed on women alone but her strong character, her determination to be a winner and not the loser many women became when they lost their breadwinners, had dragged her up from the grief she had known when her Albert died. She might have given up and moved in with their Elsie. Elsie had offered but Jess had stood on her own two, well-shod, earthbound feet and got on with life. She earned her own living in the only way she knew how and had succeeded. Just let any man interfere with her, or those she loved and she'd give them what for. This bastard who had upset their Briar would be sorry he'd been born. Call, indeed! Let him call and see what that got him.

It was the following Sunday when Mrs Foster's lad, who was ten and had been the first messenger to take a note to Becky Hamilton's family, knocked on the door of fifty-one, out of breath, red-faced, his hair standing on end, his boy's face terrified.

"Mrs 'Andy, can yer come? Me mam's tipped pan o' boilin' watter ower 'ersen an' me dad's at work an' there's only me 'cos our Lilly's gone off wi' her bloke an' please Mrs 'Andy, I don't know what ter do . . ."

"Calm down, lad, calm down. It'll not be as bad as all that. See, Briar, pass me that butter an' them clean cloths. Now, lad, stop that snifflin'. If them chaps come back afore me, our Briar, give 'em that cold meat an' pickles, will yer," shouting over her shoulder to Briar who was taking the opportunity to give the scullery floor a good scrub while Alexandra was sleeping peacefully in her cradle.

So when Perry Sutton knocked distastefully on the gleaming brass knocker of Jess Handy's front door Briar was alone in the house. He had never been in a mean street such as this one before and as he waited for the door to open he glanced about him. There were men lounging against the walls of the houses, this being a Sunday, some smoking cigarettes, others a pipe. There were children playing hopscotch and swinging ropes off the street lamps. There were others kicking a ball about and some sitting on the steps of their homes nursing tattered dollies. He had come in a hansom cab which had stopped all movement in the street as it drew up at the door of fifty-one, for there were not many who travelled in such conveyances in Peter Street. They watched him as avidly as spectators at a pantomime and when the door opened and he moved inside they sighed as one.

It was Briar who opened the door and for a moment she was tempted to bar it. She had waited in fear and at the same time with urgent anticipation since a week yesterday for this moment, shuddering at the thought of meeting this man again and yet longing for him to come so that she might hear if the bodies of the two she loved had been found. She had such mixed feelings. It was as though as long as Hal and Tom were not found they were not, as it were, dead, but at the same time if their bodies had been recovered and given a decent, reverent burial with those who loved them to mourn their passing, would it not at last give her the chance to accept their loss and slowly build the life she envisaged for herself and Alexandra.

She was wearing her old black dress, the one she had worn when she came to Liverpool, and over it a sacking apron. Her hair was tied up in a cotton duster but wisps escaped and stuck to her cheeks and forehead in wet strands soaked with perspiration. Since it was a hot day the top buttons of her bodice were undone. In her hand she held the scrubbing brush.

"Well, well, well," Perry murmured, his eyes roaming over her body in a nasty way, coming to rest on the deep cleft between her breasts. "What have we here? The divine Briar taking a turn at the scrub bucket and, if I might say so, looking quite ravishing. I've always liked a bit of rough, my dear, so it seems I have come at the right time."

He could not have said anything more likely to stiffen her spine and bring back to life the Briar who had once strode over the hills with the men chasing the fox, the Briar who had ridden hell for leather on the back of her mare in hot pursuit of any mad escapade that intrigued her, who had accompanied himself and others of like mind to illegal cock-fights and bare-knuckle prizefights and who, he had heard had been more fun than any woman had a right to be.

"You can go to hell, Perry Sutton, and the sooner the better as far as I'm concerned." Her golden eyes flashed to copper red and her cheeks flamed. She was so maddened her magnificent bosom strained to escape its bonds, flaunting itself in Perry's fascinated eyes, and before she knew what he was about he had stepped inside and pushed the door to behind him which was when the interested spectators all sighed sadly.

"Go to hell, is it, my little wildcat? Well, you're not the first one to say that to me. My wife tells me to go there with tedious regularity but, as you see, I'm still here."

"Poor Alice, she still has you tied to her then. I thought she would have left you a long time ago."

"No, with two children a woman finds it awkward to—"

"She has two . . ."

"Oh, yes, despite her protestations that she hates the bloody ground I walk on she still finds me irresistible."

They were crowded together in the narrow passage. She could feel the heat coming from his body. His eyes had narrowed and his breath was rasping in his throat as it quickened. He reached out a hand to her, prepared to put it to the back of her neck and pull her closer but she knocked it down with the scrubbing brush, hurting his wrist with the hard back. He dropped it with an oath.

"By God, madam, if you're not the most infuriating, magnificent woman I've ever come across. I told Hal so many times which he didn't care to hear—"

She spat in his face, watching him recoil in disgust. "Don't mention my husband's name with that foul tongue of yours, you bastard. He was a gentleman."

"But did he satisfy you in bed, my pet?" He grinned as he reached for his pocket handkerchief and fastidiously wiped the spittle that ran down his face. "Gentlemen seldom do. Now me, I've had a fancy for you since before you married my cousin and if you're prepared to be . . . friends with me I'll tell you all you want to know about that husband and brat of yours."

She screamed and sprang for his face, her fingers bending into lethal claws, ready to take his eyes out, but she misjudged the space between them and before she could steady herself he had her wrists in his strong, horseman's hands. He pressed her up against the wall, forcing her hands behind her back and though she fought him with every ounce of strength in her, he was as incensed as she was and his strength overcame hers. With both her hands behind her he grasped them in one hand and with the other hooked his fingers in her bodice, ripping it down. Her breasts fell out, the peaks of her nipples thrusting themselves in his face and with a hoarse, animal-like cry he fastened his teeth on one of them. The pain was excruciating. She squirmed in agony which seemed to please him. When he lifted his head there was blood on his mouth. His eyes were clouded with his lust, unseeing, blank, unfocused. His mouth searched for hers while his free hand scrabbled at her skirt, dragging it upwards until it was about her knees, then higher and higher until it reached her waist.

Her voice was demented as she freed her mouth and screamed out one name and even afterwards, when it was all done with she could not understand why, for the man whose name it was had gone.

"Hal ... Hal ..."

Her eyes were closed against the sight of the foul expression of the man who was trying to rape her and suddenly, on the inside of her eyelids swam the calm, reassuring face of the man she loved and she was instantly reassured, for Hal was with her. Perry's fingers scratched between her thighs and up the wide leg of her drawers until they reached the soft, secret part of her that no man had touched except Hal. Hal ... Dear sweet Hal who had loved her, made a woman of her, a decent woman, and with Hal settled peacefully and for ever in the heart of her was she to let this man dirty his memory?

With a scream that turned every head in the street she tore herself free. She brought up her knee as a voice told her to do and plunged it between his thighs at the juncture where they met his belly, at the same time clawing at his face, dragging her nails down each cheek, leaving eight bloody trails from his eyes to his chin. The blood began to flow and Perry Sutton didn't know whether to clutch at his genitals which were in flames of agony or put his hands to his face to stop the blood.

The front door crashed open and into the passage flew the lioness who was Jess Handy, the lioness who would die to protect her cubs and wasn't one of them Briar Saunders.

She stopped in her tracks at the sight that met her eyes and began to smile. Their Briar looked a wreck with blood on her bared breasts and her mouth but the groaning man on the floor looked even worse as his blood dripped into her clean strip of drugget. She smiled triumphantly before shouting for one of the chaps in the street to come and help her throw this piece of rubbish into the street, which they did with great eagerness. The horse that had delivered him had also left a pile in the gutter, which seemed appropriate and the men made sure that Perry Sutton landed in it.

Chapter Thirty

"Lad, eat tha' porridge. Tha' can't go out wi'out summat inside thi'."

Phoebe Lucas hovered anxiously about her son who was perched on the edge of a chair pulling on his boots. She held a pan in one hand from which wisps of appetising steam rose and in the other a large ladle. At the table her husband and daughter, obeying her as they always did, for it made life easier and they loved her, spooned the admittedly delicious porridge into their mouths. They exchanged glances, for this conversation took place at almost every meal, Phoebe beseeching her son to "eat up" and her son arguing with her.

"I'm not hungry, Mother. Make me up a sandwich and I'll eat it later. I've to check on those ewes on the tops. Dobby Hawkins passed me yesterday and told me he thought some of them were hobbling. If we've got foot rot in the flock I want to treat it immediately."

"Will Lucas, either tha' get some o' this porridge down thi' or I'll hide tha' breeches an' tha'd look a right cut climbin' tops in tha' underwear."

They all smiled, even Will, but Phoebe was not in a

mood to be amused. She cursed the day Briar Saunders had caught the eye of her son, for ever since Will had mooned about like a lovesick boy. At first it didn't matter, since the lass was here in Bassenthwaite and Will did his daydreaming under his mam's eye. She had been the only one to recognise what was in her son, and though she hadn't liked the idea, for Annie's girl was as wild as an unbroken pony, she was prepared to take the lass as her daughter-in-law for the sake of her friendship with Annie. But Briar had married Hal Saunders and settled down a treat, which Will had finally accepted. She had thought he might look favourably on the daughter of a local farmer, a sensible lass whose work in the dairy was the best in the parish. She had spoken of it to Charlie in their bed at night, telling him of her hopes that at last might come to fruition, planning the changes she would make in Will's bedroom to accomodate his bride, dwelling on quilts and new curtains and even on the cradle in which her own children had slept.

But for the past year, ever since Briar had disappeared, Will had been obsessed with just one fixed thought and that had been finding her, dashing Phoebe's hopes to the ground, and not only that but her son's health was suffering. He was rake thin and looked ten years older than he was, gaunt and totally without that guarded but winsome smile which had flashed out on occasion. He had not been what Phoebe called a merry lad but he had been good-humoured, like her Charlie. Clever, somewhat bookish, again like his father, but never dour, which was how she would describe him now. And spending so much time away from the farm as he did, if he had worked for anyone but his own father he would have been chucked out on his ear months ago. Charlie, though, was a gentle, compassionate man who perhaps saw in his son shades of himself as a young man when he had loved, hopelessly as it turned out, Annie Abbott who had married Reed Macauley. And so he was indulgent of Will's frequent journeying about the country in his search for Briar. He did not, as Phoebe herself was wont to do, tell him to leave it to the men Reed Macauley employed, men who were experienced in such matters, but she knew that Charlie was as worried as she was about their son. Surely it was not healthy to carry on like this. At first they had all believed she was dead, lying deep in the waters of some tarn where she had chucked herself in her devastating grief, but then Will had found a chap who said he had seen her in Liverpool and since then he was forever going off to walk the streets of the city on the lookout for her.

Now Annie and Reed had received an official-looking letter from some solicitor who refused to reveal his whereabouts telling them that Briar was alive and well but did not, at the moment, want to be found, begging them to respect her wishes for the time being. What joy there had been at Long Beck, and yet what sadness, for what was the state of mind of their daughter when she didn't want to see her own parents?

"Mother, I don't want to eat my porridge like a good boy and I swear if you—"

"Will . . ." his father said warningly.

"I'm sorry, Mother, but please . . . make me up something and I promise I'll eat it later. I must get up to those ewes."

Phoebe sighed and turned away. She packed him enough food to last him a week, despite his objections, praying that he would eat at least some of it. He was fading away before her eyes, his good clothes hanging on him so that she had been forced to take in even his shirts, the collars of which stood out from his neck. His eyes, each week that passed, seemed to look further and further into the distance, as though he were searching in his mind for something in another world, barely alive in this one. Dear sweet Lord, what was it in a woman that could arouse such devotion in a man? Like mother, like daughter, for Annie had been the same, with Reed and with Charlie. Charlie had settled for second-best, herself, and she had loved him, fed him, carefully skirted about his feelings for Annie, and their marriage had been successful.

She stood at the door of the farmhouse, shading her eyes from the rays of the sun which struck a million diamond sparkles on the lake, watching Will as he trudged wearily up the hill. Why, he looks like an old man, she thought, his shoulders bent under the impossible strain he put on himself. When he was out of sight she turned back into her kitchen where Beth was siding the table.

"Charlie," Phoebe said to her husband, stepping into the comfort of his arms.

"I know, love, I know. But give him time. Perhaps now that we know she's alive he'll stop looking and wait until she comes home."

"Oh, Charlie ..."

Will sat with his back to a rock in the shelter of a tumble of others. There was a fine veil of rain in the air, a pale grey sky with a patchy mist beneath it so that he felt as though he were sitting in the clouds, clouds that moved lazily to reveal in the gaps between them the roof of Long Beck and, below that, the solid shape of Browhead. The sheep moved slowly about him, cropping peacefully, aware of his presence but not threatened by it, since he and his dogs were so still. The dogs lay at his feet, glancing up at him now and again, waiting for orders, alert to his every move, even to his eyebrows. The ground was heavy with water and he could feel it soak through his breeches and undergarments to his skin and he knew his mother would give him the rounds of the kitchen when he got home. But it didn't matter to him apart from the worry he knew he caused her. He could feel the heaviness inside him as though he were weighted down with rocks as unkind as the ones he leaned against, wondering idly, without too much interest, whether he would ever feel content again. He had achieved a kind of peace, if you could call the nothingness in which he existed peace, but he was tired, bone tired. He felt old, all the youthfulness gone out of him and he knew that if he didn't do something about it he would simply fade away and become an old man, older than his father, withering on the winter branch of his life. Perhaps he should give in to his mother and start to court one of the willing young women hereabouts who would make good farmers' wives. Have a family, sons to work with him on the farm that would one day be his, daughters to fill his heart with love, cut Briar Macauley from him with a sharp and painful knife and . . .

He was roused out of his reverie by the sound of a galloping horse, the clatter of its hooves as it struck the stones and small rocks embedded in the tufted grass echoing across the small plateau. It was coming from the north where the head of the lake lay and as it got closer the sheep began to scatter. He had time to think that he hadn't even examined their feet and now they were all over the bloody place and he'd have to get his dogs to bring them back, when the horseman came thundering into view, crashing up the rocky track, going God knows where unless it was over the tops to Keswick.

It was Perry Sutton. For a moment, until Will rose to his feet, Perry did not see him and when he did he was considerably startled. Then he reined in his grey with what seemed to be pleasure, his eyes sparkling in anticipation of something only he was aware of.

"Well, I'll be damned if it isn't the local yokel. It must be a real exertion on the brain watching sheep all day long. Do you actually see their fleeces grow or does that make too much demand on the old grey matter? Myself, I don't think I could stand the excitement." He grinned insolently. His animal moved beneath him, dancing from side to side in its aristocratic way, for it was an expensive thoroughbred bought with his wife's money, but he controlled it easily, since he was a superb horseman.

Will leaned his back against the rock, wondering why he didn't leap for the arrogant fool's throat, or pull him from the animal's back and beat him to a pulp which, not long ago, he might have done, but it was just too much trouble. He somehow couldn't get up the energy to care very much.

"Bugger off, Sutton," he said wearily, preparing to turn to his dogs and give them the command to fetch the flock, but he suddenly became aware of the eight half-healed tracks down the other man's face, four to each cheek and he began to smile. Not much of a smile but he found it amused him to think that some hell-cat had done her best to put her mark on him. She had succeeded too! So there were women about who found Perry Sutton's advances not to their liking?

"You been in a fight, lad?" he remarked, his lip curling contemptuously. "Some woman said no to you, did she, and backed up her refusal with her fingernails? Or have you been interfering with a playful kitten?" He turned away but not before he saw the hot rage flare in Perry's eyes.

"No, *lad*, it was no kitten who did this to me but a full-blooded woman. And you would never believe who it was."

Something in his voice made Will turn sharply, his heart beginning to quicken with some emotion, some terrible dread that told him he was not going to like what he heard. Afterwards he wondered what it was that warned him, for Perry Sutton was well known for his womanising and it could have been any female between the borders of Scotland and the outskirts of Kendal.

"I've just come back from Liverpool, laddie. A ... a business trip, I suppose you could call it, and really, you'd never guess who I ran into."

Will took a step forward, a faltering step, for suddenly his legs felt like jelly.

"Ah, I see you're interested. Shall I tell you?"

"You bastard ..." Will's voice was thick, hoarse.

"Am I? Well, that's as may be but nothing to do with ... Briar Saunders who I met while I was there."

"Briar ..."

"Yes, Briar Saunders, though I don't think Saunders is her name now. She was pushing a perambulator. A delightful child about three months old though I must admit I'm not the sort of man to take interest in such things. I have two of my own, you know, but if you were to put me to the torture I couldn't say how old they are. Well, I must be off. Glad to see you're so interested. Now you take care of those sheep and mind they don't outwit you."

He laughed as he put his heels to the grey's side, turning

to shout over his shoulder. "She lives in the most appalling house, no more than a slum really, in Peter Street, just in case you might be interested, but if the men thereabout are anything to go by her husband must be the worst kind of lout. He has her scrubbing the floor, would you believe. Briar Saunders scrubbing the floor!"

The day was so fine, one of those rare September days at the tag end of summer when the rose-scented gardens of Princes Park drew in even those who were on their way somewhere else and had no intention of lingering. Just for a few moments, they told themselves, finding a spot somewhere to collapse on the grass. Every seat lining the broad paths was filled, with females fanning themselves, the better class with pretty fans, the lower orders with anything that came to hand, males with their hats or caps which they had removed. There was a band playing and the noise, a delicate air that did not disturb the slumbrous warmth of the day, floated across the park, and not a few gentlemen nodded off, for it was a Sunday. The only ones not to be affected by the heat were the children who bowled their hoops, whipped their tops to a frenzy, or sailed their boats – some of them only made of paper – on the lake. Mothers took their toddlers from their baby carriages and let them scuttle about the grass, fetching them patiently back when they wandered, while their fathers dozed on their backs, the Sunday newspaper over their faces.

The flowerbeds were a kaleidoscope of colour from the delicate salmon of the pinks to the deep scarlet of roses. There were tall delphiniums, blue as the sky, and giant sunflowers as bright and golden as their namesake. Edging the borders were white alyssum and vivid begonias. Shrubs of varying degrees of green, hebe, viburnum, glossy-leaved rhododendron, their spring blooms over, lilac at its best, had been planted round the lake in which a small island floated, joined to the lakeside by a small bridge.

The woman crept diffidently between the large ornate wrought-iron gates that led into the park from Rodney Street. Though it was so warm she had a clean but well-darned, worn grey shawl wrapped tightly about her. On her head was a nondescript bonnet with a stuffed bird to one side. Her skirt was grey, her hair was grey and so was her careworn face. She might have been pretty once but hard work, sorrow and the troubles that come to the lower classes had taken it from her.

Keeping her head down and tucked into her shawl in the manner of a tortoise, she began to sidle along the pathways, her eyes darting from side to side, her step slow and careful. She seemed to keep to the shade cast by the groups of trees that stood along the paths, mingling with those who sat or sprawled there, keeping out of the heat of the sun. There was a rug spread against the trunk of an oak tree and on it sat three women, two of them older than the third who was a lovely, smiling young woman with a baby on her lap. The young woman was dressed in a pale shade of apple-green muslin, the sleeves short, the neckline demure, about her waist a velvet sash in a deeper shade of green. She wore no hat and her bright copper hair fell in a loose curling tumble about her head and neck, dipping to her eyebrows. She held the baby under its arms, a baby with quite exquisite colouring, silver-gilt curls, almost transparent blue eyes and a bloom on its cheeks that was the palest peach. The baby was doing its infant best to stand, laughing into the woman's face, reaching out its plump hands to her and beside her the two older women watched with the fond and indulgent expressions of grandmothers.

But they weren't the baby's grandmothers. From her hiding place behind the trunk of another oak tree she watched, her face wretched, in her eyes a strange expression; one, if it had been seen by the three women, that would have given cause for alarm.

One of the women produced a wicker basket and from it took a snowy-white cloth which she spread on the rug. She arranged plates and glasses, cutlery, placing small pies on the plates, a bowl of salad, another package which seemed to contain sandwiches, scones and dainty cakes on the cloth and a big glass bottle with a cap containing a colourless liquid which she poured into the glasses. A baby's feeding bottle with a teat was next which the woman handed to the baby's mother – only she wasn't its mother – and with a sigh of pleasure the baby settled down in her arms, the teat plugged firmly between its rosy lips.

They chatted and laughed, a happy picture, eating the good food, talking to the baby who had finished the bottle, putting snippets of biscuits in its eager, bird-like mouth, which it sucked on with its two baby teeth, then opened wide for more. It held out its arms to one of the women and she reached forward and settled it on her lap, kissing its cheek, giving it a spoon to play with which it studied with great interest before putting it in its mouth. There was a baby carriage and when the child began to doze, it was placed tenderly in it where it went to sleep. The two older women closed their eyes and with their backs to the tree trunk cat-napped, while the younger shook out a newspaper and began to study it, keeping an eye on the child. The woman in the grey shawl continued to watch them, her eyes unblinking.

It was about half past three when the baby awoke, doing its best to pull itself into a sitting position and at once the young woman picked it up and held it to her, loving it, kissing its cheek, smiling, whispering into its ear so that it chuckled and the watching woman felt her heart break. The older women sat up abruptly at the sound of the child's voice and began to pack up the remains of their picnic, rearranging their hats which had slipped to the side while they dozed, smoothing down their skirts as they stood up, shaking out the rug and placing the whole lot with the crowing infant into the baby carriage. With a last look round to see if they had everything, they began to trundle the perambulator across the grass to the path and the gate that led out into Rodney Street. Many of those who had picnicked and played and lounged in the park were beginning to move, and the watching woman was able to mix with those who were homeward bound, unnoticed by anyone.

When the women and the baby carriage containing the baby turned into Park Road she watched them go for a moment then continued along Warwick Street, her footsteps dragging, her head bent with weariness.

When the alterations for the new shop had been done, extending it into the house next door, a door had been knocked through from the new kitchen of what had once been the cramped quarters in which Elsie had done all her baking, into the passage in the new house. This meant that Briar didn't have to run out of the shop, round the corner and in through the front door of the house in Colquitt Street to check on her daughter. Alexandra slept in a well-barred cot and when she woke there was always one or other of the women to hear her and run through the new doorway to pick her up.

"Yer'll ruin 'er," was Elsie's prophecy but she was the worst of the lot, pushing aside anyone who got in her way as she fought to pick up the baby who had settled herself in all their hearts.

She was Briar's daughter by law now, Mr Chancellor having gone through the family courts to arrange the adoption. Apparently Becky's father had shut the door in Mr Chancellor's face when he had worked out what the solicitor was talking about, shouting that if he had to say it again he'd get his *own* lawyer to stop them harassing him. He had no daughter called Rebecca and had no interest in anyone of that name who had given birth to a child. Was that clear? He didn't give a bugger what happened to the bloody kid, was *that* clear? Mr Chancellor had been somewhat distressed, for at the back of Mr Hamilton had been a distraught woman pleading with him at least to see the child but he had swept her away with a backhander that had knocked her to the floor before shutting the door.

Now, at last, Briar's life was calm, there was content in it, fulfilment, for her child was loved, she was loved by her child, she had friends, not only the two women who had put her life back together again, but women who shopped at Potter's Bakery and who chatted to her, asked after the baby, even begged to have a peep, and when they did she often offered one or the other a cup of tea. The success of the shop, which had a lot to do with her, gave her immense satisfaction, and she had begun to think of expanding again, though she had not mentioned it yet to Elsie who was only just about coming to terms with what they had already achieved. She had her eye on a shop down by the docks. A different class of women, certainly, women who barely had two halfpennies to rub together but a small business in which they could employ a decent cook, one able to supply the dockers' wives with what they wanted and, after all, she had said to Mr Chancellor who had become a staunch friend and adviser, they must do *something* with the profits they were making. Elsie was quite happy to put it away in the bank and watch it grow, amazed at the size of her account, which was her choice but Briar had her eye on a bigger prospect.

Mr Chancellor had persuaded her to write to her mother and father, and with the joy she now found in Alexandra and her friends she had felt able to re-establish the bond she had known with them years ago. She had explained, and apologised for her actions, and promised that soon, when she was able, she would come north and visit them. She had been adamant about that word "visit". Her life was here now with her new family, though Mr Chancellor had begged her not to put that in her letter, but she told him she must be honest and not raise their hopes that one day she would return for good. In the night, when Alexandra's soft breathing sighed through the attic bedroom the sound would remind her of the nights she and Hal had spent hanging over Tom's cradle, listening to him breathe, their joy and love, for him and each other, so great and wonderful it could scarcely be contained. Then she would weep, knifed by a terrible pain, a deep and agonising emotion which, but for the child in the cot beside her, would have tipped her back into that black pit from which she had been hauled. There seemed to be no way she would ever get over her terrible grief but at least in this place she had found for herself she could live again and know peace and security. Never again would she have that passionate love, that total commitment to one person who had been the focal point of the life she had shared with Hal, but this was good, this life, and she was safe from harm in it, or so she thought.

It was a Saturday in October when the horror struck and even as she screamed and ran up and down Bold Street she was calling on a terrible God who had done this to her again, cursing Him and at the same time begging Him to be merciful.

She had helped Elsie and the girls to clean and tidy the shop and the kitchen, for she had become as firmly fastidious as Elsie in her demand for absolute and total cleanliness. It could not be left until Monday. It could not be left at all and the place had to be immaculate before any of the girls were allowed to leave. The window was set out with white lacy doilies on which tins of biscuits, home-made naturally, were set out, with arrangements of flowers, *fresh* flowers which Elsie would check on, a list of prices written in gold letters on a white background, a neat stack of cardboard boxes, artistically arranged, and two china figures, both dressed in aprons and caps which were supposed to denote a couple of cooks. All very pleasing to the eye, the china figures becoming a symbol of Potter's Bakery.

Briar dressed Alexandra in her recently knitted white woollen matinee coat and a bonnet edged with swansdown, smiling at the eager little face, for there was nothing the baby liked better than an outing in the baby carriage. Heaving it through the door and down the couple of steps into Colquitt Street, Briar put on the brake with her foot, then ran back inside.

"I'm off now, Elsie. We'll see you and Potter about noon tomorrow, will we?" Since it was their custom to have Sunday dinner together, taking it turn and turn about. A roast dinner of a saddle of lamb, a shoulder of pork or, Potter's favourite, a nice piece of topside of beef. "Don't forget that apple pie, will you?" For there was nothing better in the world than one of Elsie's apple pies.

"Rightio, chuck." Elsie's voice floated down the stairs. "D'yer wanna 'and wi't baby carriage?"

"No, I've managed thanks. See you tomorrow."

"Right, queen."

Briar stepped out though the open door, ready to bang it to behind her. Her hand was still on the door knob which was set in the middle of the door, gleaming with polish and elbow grease as all Elsie's things gleamed, when her heart gave a leap of such gigantic proportions it reached her throat and she gagged on it. She looked frantically up and down the street and even ran to the corner which was daft, for was she likely to leave the most precious thing in the world to her where she couldn't see her?

She began to scream and upstairs Elsie dropped the cup of tea she had just made for herself. She screamed so fiercely she felt the flesh tear, tasting blood as she looked at the spot where she had left Alexandra but she was not there. She and the perambulator had vanished.

Chapter Thirty-one

Will Lucas stood in the doorway of the New Law Courts on Victoria Street looking directly down the length of Peter Street. Peter Street had roughly twenty-five houses on each side and the one Will was interested in was almost at the end, which led into Victoria Street. He had a good view of the comings and goings of its occupants and standing in the doorway of the Law Courts through which a constant flow of people passed, he was inconspicuous, arousing no interest. He was decently dressed in a tweed Norfolk jacket, trousers to match and a cap with a button on top, the peak of which he kept pulled down over his forehead. He was neat and presentable, with a clean shirt and unobtrusive tie, the only inconsistency his hair, which needed a cut and fell over the collar of his coat. He had been there on and off for the past three days.

It was October and since the day in June when Perry Sutton had told him that Briar had remarried he had done his utmost to cut her not only out of his heart, which he knew was impossible, but out of his mind, which was also proving tricky. No matter how hard he tried to turn it to other things, his father's farm, which would one day be his, the exhausting job of shearing the sheep, the mating of the ewes, the tramps up and down the fells, all the strenuous tasks that he hoped would help him to sleep; the gathering in of the crop of hay for the animals' winter feed, the coppice wood, all the hundred and one tasks he shared with his father, yet despite this he still lay in his bed of a night, wide-eyed, longing for sleep and oblivion, but it still eluded him.

He had even begun to dally with the idea of courting the girl his mother had picked out for him, since it made no difference to him who it was he took to wife. Anne Singleton, a bonny lass whose family farmed Upfell which lay alongside Browhead, and but for the fact that she was Jonty Singleton's sister he might have made a move in her direction by now. But he knew that was not the real reason. He must sever that part of him that had held Briar Saunders firmly in the sum and substance of him for the past ... well, to be honest he couldn't remember when she had not been as much a part of him as his eyes or his good right arm. Even as a child she had maddened him with her waywardness and yet at the same time a coil of tenderness had come to rest inside him making him want to hug her even when she was being her most obstreperous, which was not a thing a lad did. Not if he wanted to keep his self-respect among other lads.

"I saw Anne today," his mother would say casually. "She looked a fair treat in 'er new winter frock. She do suit blue. I thought 'appen I'd ask 'er fer 'er tea one day. What dost think, our Will?" Her eyes rested hopefully on his face which was becoming increasingly austere with every passing day.

"If you like, Mother," he would answer indifferently, seeing no connection with the custom that once a lass was asked to tea it was almost a declaration of marriage.

"What dost *thou* think, lad?" she persisted.

"Whatever you want, Mother."

"No, lad, it's what *tha'* want."

"I really have no preference, Mother," he would answer her, nearly driving her mad. He was like that, was Will. He used big words, for he never had his nose out of a book, just like his pa, while Phoebe, who had learned to read and write with Cat, Annie Macauley's first daughter, and her a woman grown at the time, could only just pick out the news in Charlie's newspaper. It was the same with the way Will spoke, he and his sister. Phoebe hadn't the faintest idea where she came from, having been rescued when she was about twelve or fourteen, she thought, by Annie Abbott, from some chap at the hiring fair in Keswick who had been intent on interfering with her. She had spoken with a broad northern accent then as she did today. But Charlie came from good stock down south somewhere, an educated family and his children had picked up *his* accent rather than her own.

Now she took a chance, ignoring her husband's words of warning, inviting the lass for Sunday tea and was delighted when Anne, as though she knew she were on trial, fetched over a batch of the lightest scones Phoebe had ever tasted, a remark she repeated again and again. Will was pleasant with Anne, even walking her home as dusk fell, not saying much but as Anne was a bit of a chatterer it didn't seem to matter. Her voice filled the silences that might have been awkward. She was a kind lass, a merry lass and had fancied Will Lucas for a long time. She was the right sort of wife for him, or so Phoebe thought.

Before the end of the week the news was out that Will

Lucas, who was known to be a bit strange, was courting Anne Singleton. The only one who didn't recognise the fact was Will himself.

"You're stirring up trouble here, my lass," Charlie said grimly to his wife. "Don't you realise that? Will's a deep one, and clever."

"Like thee, Charlie."

"That's as may be, but despite his cleverness he doesn't realise what people are speculating. You shouldn't have taken it upon yourself."

"I had to do summat, Charlie." Phoebe's voice was desperate. "Lad's pikin' away an' a good lass like Anne'll bring 'im a bit of comfort. If Briar's wed again then he'll turn to Anne, don't tha' see."

"I hope so."

Will liked Anne. He had to make no effort to entertain her, laugh or make jokes. She seemed to be content to walk by his side when they met on the fell above the farms, her bonny face smiling, and after a month or two in his heart a kind of peace settled, an acceptance perhaps, but he knew, if he was to take Anne, which his mother slyly hinted at, he must, for the last time, make sure that Briar Saunders, or whatever her name was now, was safe and herself again after the death of her husband and child. Perry had said that she was married to a lout who had her scrubbing floors, but Will knew that he must, for one last time, see her in the setting she had chosen for herself.

His mother had flown into a furious rage when he had told them where he was going.

"Leave it, leave it, our Will," she had shrieked. "When are thi' ter learn she don't want thi'. She's medd her life an' why tha've ter go traipsin' off ter Liverpool every five minutes checking up on 'er I don't know. Tell 'im, Charlie," turning her angry face appealingly to her husband. "There's Anne, as nice a lass as tha' could find an' thinkin' tha' like 'er."

"I *do* like her, Mother, but that's all. At least for the moment. Perhaps ..."

"Yes? Yes, p'raps what?" his mother asked eagerly.

"When I've seen that ... when I come back from Liverpool ..."

"Promise me. Lad, please promise me. I can't bear ter see thi' mothetten."

"I'm all right, Mother and I promise to think about it."

His mother went to bed happy that night.

The first day he had taken up his post in the doorway of the New Law Court he had watched as Briar bounced the perambulator down the steps of a house further up Peter Street, turning left towards what he knew was called Whitechapel. Dear God, didn't he feel he knew the streets of this city like the back of his hand. Ever since the ticket collector at Lime Street Railway Station had admitted that he had seen Briar, he had tramped up and down the main thoroughfares with his little picture, shoving it in people's faces, going down side streets, radiating out further and further from the station until he had hit the river itself, the docks, the quays and piers and parades against which the great ships lay, but on that first day when he had actually seen her he had thought he would faint like some great daft girl. She had looked as beautiful as he remembered her when she was a young lass. Her smile as she looked down into the baby carriage had closed like a fist about his heart and with a part of his brain that was not wholly absorbed with the wonder of Briar Macauley, he said a sad farewell to Anne Singleton. Indeed to any woman he might meet in the future, for this woman had him in a grip of iron. She had worn a rich shade of russet which matched exactly the mass of curly hair that bounced upon her head. There was a bonnet in her hand which she threw carelessly into the baby carriage and with that gesture he knew that she was still at heart the enchanting rebel she had always been. No decent woman left home without a hat on her head and gloves on her hands but Briar wore neither.

Briskly she set off up the street, turning into Whitechapel, cutting across through a maze of streets until she reached Bold Street. Will followed, keeping a distance between them, not knowing why he was doing this, acting on an instinct that forced him to discover what the life of this intriguing woman might be. She was not for him and never would be, but perhaps if he could see what she had done with her life since she disappeared, who her friends were, the nature of her husband and his work, where she went so early in the morning he might be better able to leave her alone. *For ever.*

She turned the corner of Bold Street and Colquitt Street and at a smartly painted door she put the brake on the perambulator, ran up the steps, opened the door and ran down again. Struggling, she hauled the perambulator up the steps and Will almost leaped forward to help her but he restrained himself, watching as she pulled the baby carriage inside and closed the door.

He was startled when five minutes later she appeared in the window of the bakery on the corner and began arranging platters of fancy cakes, pies, tarts, custards, scones, biscuits, with baskets of what was obviously freshly baked bread. She wore a pretty frilled cap on her head and was enveloped in a snowy apron.

He stood for over an hour watching her as she bustled

about the shop, and it was not until a suspicious police constable tapped him on the shoulder and asked politely if he needed help that he turned away and began to walk back the way he had come.

What did he have in his mind? he wondered as he walked slowly along Peter Street. To look again at the house that was now home to Briar. Perhaps a sight of the man who was her husband, though what that would achieve apart from tormenting himself, he didn't know. To take a picture back to Briar's parents of the area in which their daughter had settled, which was a far cry from Long Beck and the luxury in which she had been brought up. Would they be pleased to hear, no matter how content she was, that she lived among the working classes and actually had a job in a bakery? They wouldn't believe it, not the girl who had scorned the mundane life she had believed she led in the land of the lakes. The girl who had wanted to travel, to be entertained, to be excited, not to be a housewife, now with a child, with a job that kept her chained to a counter from where she served other women with bread and confectionery.

When his hand lifted the gleaming brass knocker on the door of fifty-one he was as surprised as the woman who popped her head out of the next-door window.

"Lookin' fer Mrs Handy, lar?" she asked him.

He supposed he was. "Er, yes," he answered.

"She's norrin, lad. I saw 'er go out nor'alf an 'our since."

Mrs Handy! Briar Handy! He wasn't sure how to respond to the woman who stared at him curiously, nor did he know what the hell he was doing here when he should be at the railway station waiting for a train back up north.

"Well, thank you." He turned away, moving down the steps which he noticed even in the depth of the despair that filled him, were the whitest he had ever seen.

"Can I tell 'er 'oo called?" the woman asked helpfully.

"No, thanks. I'll try again." And even as he spoke the words he realised that, just one last time, he had to look on the face of the woman he loved. Say goodbye, he supposed. Say goodbye to the dream he had nurtured within himself, a foolish dream, he knew that now, but one that had upheld him for months and months. What would he do now, he thought hopelessly, without that dream to sustain him? And though a small voice inside whispered that it was now time he got on with the life he had been born for, perhaps with Anne Singleton at his side, no matter how his heart sank at the idea, he felt the light go out in his world.

He didn't know how long he walked the streets of Liverpool. He found himself down at the docks, staring at a small iron, full-rigged schooner on which seamen scrambled like monkeys. There was a three-masted barque being unloaded in Salthouse Dock, one of the smaller docks where the sailing ships were now confined. The dock road was filled with the hullabaloo of continuous motion, horse buses, carts and team waggons constantly shifting goods to and from the quayside, and through the chaos he walked as though he were on the quiet, deserted slopes of the fells behind his house, oblivious to the irritated shouts of the men in whose path he wandered. St Nicholas's Church, which marked where the original shoreline of Liverpool used to be, soared on his right, the clock set in its graceful and delicate spire striking five, and with a shudder that seemed to come from the strike of his own heart he realised the passage of time. Five o'clock and though he had no idea what time the bakery where Briar worked closed for the day, it must be soon. He must go at once if he was to catch a glimpse of her beloved face.

He quickened his stride, turning into Chapel Street which led into Tithebarn Street, jostling among the crowds that thronged the pavements outside Exchange Station, his heart beginning to race in case he missed this last sight of her. He must catch the evening train out of Lime Street Station and as he sped northwards he would begin the process of cutting Briar ... Briar ... he could not bring himself to call her by her married name; his dearest girl she would always be, cutting her out of his life.

If any of the homeward-bound workers in the centre of the city thought it strange that a plain, working woman should be trundling an elegant baby carriage which contained a well-dressed squalling infant through the tumult, they were too concerned with fighting their way on to trams to Bootle, to Kirkdale, to Netherfield and other districts on the edge of the city to take any notice.

She caught the attention of only one solitary man and if it had not been for the baby carriage, which seemed to ring a bell in his clouded brain, she would have passed him by as she did all the others. It was very smart, a rich navy blue, slung between high wheels with a hood which was folded down and what looked like a mother-of-pearl handle. The baby who was struggling to sit up was dressed in white, a beautifully knitted matinee coat threaded with pink satin ribbon and a bonnet edged with swansdown. From beneath the bonnet wisped curls the colour of silver gilt. Across the carriage lay a fluffy white blanket, again edged with satin ribbon, this time in white.

He hesitated, he didn't know why, since it was nothing

to do with him. Wasn't he on his way to catch a glimpse of the woman he would never see again. He had no time to be dithering over a woman and a baby, probably the woman's grandchild, though it did seem odd that such a poorly dressed woman should be pushing a baby carriage which only a wealthy family could afford, inside which was a well-dressed, *expensively* dressed child. Perhaps she was the ... well, the nursemaid, but the nursemaids he had seen, and he admitted there were not many of those that he had actually noticed in any particular way, were plainly but neatly dressed. This woman had grey drifting hair, a shawl his mother wouldn't feed the chickens in, down-at-heel shoes and a face which looked ... well, not quite right though he didn't even know what he meant by that.

Acting on an impulse, he turned and followed her, weaving between the home-going crowds along Church Street, Whitechapel, Lord Street, James Street and on to Strand Street where she continued in the direction of Princes Dock and on to Waterloo Road. The baby had fallen into a doze, hiccupping at regular intervals, still crying in its sleep and Will, who was not a father and knew nothing of children, realised that the child was deeply distressed. A vague recollection of the baby carriage still flitted about on the edge of his memory, but then he knew nothing of baby carriages either so what the hell was he doing here, following a complete stranger on what was probably a perfectly legitimate outing?

Halfway down the shabby street which butted on to the dock area the woman stopped and, taking a key from a pocket in her skirt, fitted it into the lock of a door which proclaimed itself to be number fourteen. The door opened and after looking up and down the street the woman smiled. Will could distinctly see it and it was a smile of triumph, then she began to haul the carriage backwards into the house.

She had the thing halfway in and halfway out when there came a roar from inside the house which lifted the baby from its cowering position at the back of the perambulator and at once it began to cry.

"What the bluddy 'ell's this?" Will heard a male voice shout, and at once the woman began to blubber, pushing the perambulator out into the street again but losing her hold of it so that it trundled across the pavement and would have tipped into the road, the baby with it, had not Will been there to catch it.

"Dan ... please, Dan, don't shout at me."

"Don't shout at yer? I'll bluddy well throttle yer, woman."

"Dan, it's our Becky's. I can't lerrer go ..."

"Wharr'ave I told yer, yer daft bitch. She's nowt ter do wi' us. She's dead ... dead, d'yer 'ear, an' even afore she were in 'er grave she were dead ter us."

"Please, Dan, don't say that. Let's keep 'er. No one'll know. I'll look after 'er. See ... look at 'er, Dan, she's the image of our Becky when—"

"Gerrinside ..." For by this time half the street was at their doors, women in pinnies, men just returned from work, children excited as they are at anything out of the ordinary, and Will was aware that if he calmly walked away, pushing the baby carriage before him, though it would look odd, for there wasn't a man in Liverpool who would be seen pushing a baby carriage, no one in the street would notice, or particularly care. They had eyes only for the man and woman who were struggling on the doorstep of number fourteen.

The woman fell to her knees, clutching at the man about

his legs and several women moved forward in pity, for they all knew the story of Nell and Dan Hamilton and their wayward Becky. This must be her child that Nell had brought home but they had heard that the kid had been adopted so what was Nell doing with it, and in that magnificent baby carriage an' all, the likes of which they had only seen grand nursemaids pushing in Princes Park.

"Gerrin, yer daft bitch," Dan Hamilton said through gritted teeth, hauling his wife to her feet and dragging her into the narrow passage behind him. "Yer know full well it's bin adopted ... solicitor sed so ... you 'eard 'im." He turned away from his frantic wife, though he still held her in a grip of steel.

"Your't father, are yer? Well, get that baby outer 'ere," he snarled at Will. "Yer wanner keep yer eye on it, lerrin anybody" – meaning his wife – "cart the thing off. Now clear out before I fetch bobbies." He smashed the door to in Will's face.

What he had done to produce such aggression Will could not imagine. Fetch the bobbies! If anyone should have the bobbies fetched to her it was the old woman with the grey face and hair, the one who had taken the baby in the first place, or so it seemed from the exchange between the furious man and sobbing woman. The man had been livid with rage and yet underlying it was something so sad it took Will a moment or two to recognise it as sorrow, as though the child who lolled against its pillow, its thumb firmly plugged in its rosy mouth, staring at him with enormously alarmed eyes, had some connection with him, though what it could be Will was at a loss to understand.

He stood for several seconds, still not quite able to grasp the significance of the man's remarks. Everything had happened so quickly and yet in the slow, deliberate way of dreaming. First the strange recognition of the baby carriage which he realised now he had seen Briar pushing only that morning. Watched her grasp the handle, striding out, confidence brimming in her, a half-smile touching her lips every time she looked at the child, which she seemed to do every few seconds, going towards what was obviously her place of work. His own wandering through the streets of Liverpool, just as though he were saying goodbye to the city that had become so familiar to him, as he was saying goodbye to the woman who had become one of its polyglot citizens. His final, agonising decision to see her face one more time had led to the woman, the crazy woman, she had seemed, whom he had followed to this house, this street, where it was very obvious the child did not belong. This was Briar's child, though its colouring was very different from hers. The hair so fine and silvery pale, the eyes of an incredible blue, eyes that he had seen somewhere but for the life of him he could not have said where. He didn't even know whether it was a girl or a boy though the woman who had taken it had said *her* and what with pink ribbons and that pretty fluffy stuff round its bonnet it could only be female, surely?

Still, this wasn't getting the steps fettled, as his mother often said, standing here with a daft look on his face, he was sure. Briar must be frantic at the loss of the child and there was only one person to return it to her and that was himself. Bloody hell, he dreaded the very idea. It had been his plan to slip out of Liverpool without her even knowing he had been *in* Liverpool. Without her knowing that he had been looking for her for well over a year. Without having to admit what a daft bugger he had been, and he was, mooning over another man's wife, and not for the first

time, either. Perhaps he could just push the carriage up to
the front door in Peter Street, ring the bell and then run
like the wind for the end of the street?

But first he had to do just that. Push the baby carriage through the streets of Liverpool, turning heads
and inviting bewildered glances, for what man would
push his child about in a perambulator when it was a
well-known fact that men, *real* men did not get up to
such antics. He might even get stopped by a suspicious
policeman!

It was almost dark when he turned into Peter Street
which in a way had been a godsend. The falling dusk and
the rushing crowds who were concerned only with getting
themselves home on this chill autumn evening didn't give
a damn about him, or the baby carriage. Lights were on in
all the shops, horse-drawn vehicles flung themselves up and
down the streets, the busy bustle of a big city enveloping
him and the withdrawn child until he reached the Law
Courts which were now closed.

He hesitated at the corner, for there she was, minus her
coat and hat, struggling with a policeman who seemed
intent on forcing her back indoors.

"I can't just sit on my bum and wait," she was shrieking,
and he had time to smile at the word "bum" thinking of
Reed Macauley who would have a fit if he heard her. She'd
picked up more than a husband and child since she left
Bassenthwaite.

"Madam, please . . . yer can't just roam about in't dark,"
the policeman was saying. "There's constables all over
lookin' . . ."

"I don't give a damn . . . oh please, please let me go . . ."
And it was then that she saw him, or rather saw the
baby carriage.

With a shout which brought an older woman to the door, she began to run towards him, her arms outstretched with joy, not for him, not for Will Lucas who loved her, but for another man's child.

Chapter Thirty-two

Jess Handy glared suspiciously at the man who stood awkwardly holding the handle of the baby carriage as though he were not awfully sure what to do next, which was not surprising the way their Briar was acting. Cavorting about on the pavement, their Alexandra clasped in her arms so that the poor mite could hardly breathe. The lass was crying and laughing at the same time, tears pouring down her cheeks so that all those who had come out into the street to see what was going on could only stand and stare.

"Look, Jess, look, she's back, thank God ... thank God. I thought I'd lost her. I couldn't have borne it, not another, not after ... Oh, thank God. Whatever would I have done if she hadn't been brought back. Thank God, thank God." She twirled about, performing a little dance of jubilation. Her hair, which had grown since she had arrived on Jess's doorstep, swung about her head in a curtain of copper, the street gas lamps, newly lit, putting a vivid glow in its shining, tangled length. During the past few hours she had run her fingers through it time and time again, on the brink of despair, but now she was radiant, radiant with love, and the man who watched her, it seemed to Jess, was stunned by it, stunned and frozen.

"'Appen it's this chap what yer should be thanking, lass," Jess said drily, coming down the steps to take the handle of the perambulator from him and it was then and only then that Briar looked at him. Up until that moment she had had eyes for no one but the child, not really caring who had brought her daughter back as long as she was home safe and well which, of course, they had yet to check but by the sound of her, yelling her displeasure at the top of her lungs, there was not much wrong with her.

Ever since that horrifying, unbelievable moment when she had returned to the door of the house in Colquitt Street to find the baby carriage gone, with Alexandra in it, vanished as though the very ground had opened up and swallowed her, she had been like a woman demented, just as she had been after Tom and Hal had vanished under the ice. She had screamed and screamed, seriously startling passers-by and frightening the girls in the shop half out of their wits. She had flung herself up and down the steps, into the shop and out again, back into the street, knocking shoppers almost to the ground as she galloped madly to the corner, causing an uproar that had fetched the constable from Bold Street. For more than four hours she had, quite literally, gone off her head, lost her mind, she supposed, as imagination of the worst kind had taken her over and squeezed her in its malevolent grip. Now she had her baby back again, and looking at her with a wary expression on his face was the last person she had ever thought to see again.

Will Lucas!

"Will?" she said hesitantly. "Will?"

Will managed a slight smile, barely a lifting of the corners of his mouth, for truth to tell he had almost lost the knack of smiling over the past eighteen months or so. Besides, the sight of Briar, vibrant, ecstatic, overflowing with joy and love and thankfulness was almost more than he could bear. He wondered idly where Mr Handy was. Surely the disappearance of his child would warrant sending for him from wherever he worked but the only person who seemed to be involved was the elderly woman on the step who was hovering at Briar's elbow. She had parked the baby carriage to the side of the steps and was now trying to get a hold of the baby.

Reluctantly, kissing the child's flushed cheek, Briar allowed the woman to take the child from her arms. Grandmother, he supposed, for it was evident she doted on the baby, making as much fuss as Briar, crushing the small, indignant body to her in a plethora of love.

Briar took a step towards Will, on her face such an expression of amazement his smile deepened involuntarily. The perambulator was suddenly no longer between them. Another woman had appeared from the house, fussing about the baby, almost fighting the first to have a turn at cuddling it, and again he wondered where the child's father had got to.

He just stood there, knowing he was, later, going to be plunged into the worst sort of agony a man can suffer, but at that moment he was mesmerised by the sheer, incandescent beauty of Briar Macauley, Briar Saunders, Briar *Handy*, the woman he loved, had loved, would love until the end of his days.

"Will," she breathed and before he could set himself to steady her she flung herself at him, her body pressed against his, her arms about his neck, her cheek to his, while her sweet breath brushed against his lips. Without conscious thought his arms rose and enfolded her within them and before the fascinated gaze of the street's inhabitants they were nailed together for a full minute. Briar was murmuring incoherent words, thanks, Will supposed, for the return of her child, while his body, doing what it had longed to do for years, clung to hers, closer and closer and she didn't seem to object. The baby had quietened, nestling against the shoulder of the woman who had taken it and who now stood open-mouthed at the foot of the steps beside the other, obviously her sister. Later Will was to smile to himself that in the midst of the exhilaration, the desire, the joy, the sheer bloody wonder of holding Briar in his arms as he had dreamed of doing for years, he had time to take note of such unimportant things.

"I can't believe it's you," Briar was murmuring. "Will Lucas, of all people to be the one to bring my baby back. The last person in the world. Dear Lord ... Will, if you knew ..."

"Briar, it's over now, she's safe." He didn't know what else to say, he only knew he wanted to stand here with his arms about the woman he loved for ever. He didn't care if the whole street was out staring at him as long as she stayed here within the circle of his arms, but the woman on the steps had other ideas.

"Yer'd best fetch yon lad inside, our Briar," the voice said from the doorway, but it seemed Briar had no inclination to let him go, pressing herself even closer, and though Will told himself it was no more than a mother's gratitude for the return of her child he felt a certain *something* between them he was disinclined to put into words in case he was wrong.

At last she stepped back, keeping her hands against his chest and looking up into his face. Her eyes were brilliant with tears, the colour of the waters in the tarn above Browhead, a happiness in them which threatened to spill over and flood her face again. She dashed one hand across her cheeks then wiped it under her nose, laughing when he pushed his hand into his pocket and handed her the clean handkerchief without which Phoebe would not let him leave the house each day. They still held each other with one hand and when she turned him towards the steps she kept her arm about his waist and it seemed natural to keep his about her. As they closed the door behind them there was a concerted and collective sigh of disappointment from the watching crowd. It was not often such excitement happened in their drab lives. The constable, after watching the couple go up the steps with their arms about one another, moved the crowd on with great importance. He would have to come back, naturally, to question the young man whom the distraught mother had embraced, but for the moment let them have their moment, he thought good-naturedly.

Will was seated with great ceremony in Jess's chair by the fire. A cup of tea was put in his hand though he didn't remember being asked if he would like one. Briar sat opposite him, the baby on her lap and neither seemed able to utter a word. They continued to look at each other, she with astonishment, he with his love shining from him like a beacon and if Briar didn't recognise it, Jess did. She and Elsie sat at the table, sipping their tea. Jess was the first to speak.

"Well, you an' this chap seem ter know each other, our lass. 'Appen yer'd best introduce us, like. I reckon there's a lot needs explainin', don't you, our Elsie?"

Elsie nodded her agreement, her eyes round with excitement. After the few hours she and Jess, and of course, Briar, had just put in it was time they had a bit of summat to make up for it.

"This is Will, Jess. He and I grew up together back in

Bassenthwaite." Briar laughed softly. "I plagued the life out of him when I was a girl, didn't I, Will?"

And still do, Jess thought.

"Aye, that she did." Will's voice sounded rusty, as though he hadn't spoken for weeks, which is what it felt like to him. Not just weeks, but months, for every conversation, every sentence, every word he had uttered to those around him had been nothing, because they had not been spoken to this woman. This woman who had put her arms about him, had clung to him, had been ready to kiss him, he was certain, and his body was still imprinted with the feel of hers.

"But never mind that, Will, we can talk about old times later. Tell us what you are doing in Liverpool, and how you came to find Alexandra? And how did you know where I lived?" A sudden light of understanding lit her face, and it became grim, her mouth thinning. Her eyes, which had been looking so fondly at Will, took on an expression of what might be loathing and, dumbfounded, Jess and Elsie watched breathlessly. "Unless it was . . ." She did not finish what she was saying, since she could not bring herself to speak the name of the man who had tried to force himself on her in this very house. It would be just the sort of thing he would do, boast to another man of his conquest of Briar Saunders, even if it wasn't true.

"Aye. It was." Evidently Will felt the same distaste.

"But Alexandra? How did you find her?"

"Oh, I was just passing," he stammered, for he had had no time to rehearse the reason why he should be in the vicinity when the woman had helped herself to Briar's child.

"Just passing! What, on the way from Browhead to Long Beck?" Briar held the child closer to her, rubbing her cheek against the soft curls, smiling down into the rosy face.

"Well, there's a lot to ... It would take all night to explain and really ..." He stood up abruptly, managing to set his cup and saucer precariously on to the table. "I've a train to catch, you see, and ..."

"Never mind your train, Will. Surely you don't mean just to dash off after what you've done for me." She turned to the two women. "For us. Jess and Elsie love Alexandra as I do. Sit down and tell us what ... well, just sit down and tell us what's been happening to you. I want to know what brings you to Liverpool. I want to hear about Phoebe and Charlie and Beth and—"

Suddenly Will's face hardened. "I see, you want to know about my family but what about your own, Briar Macauley? Have you any idea what your parents have suffered since you slipped off in the night and were never seen again? They have heard nothing from you in all this time."

Briar's face snapped into a familiar expression of rebellion, familiar to Will, at least.

"I sent them a letter ... well, I wanted them them to have word."

"Word! *Word!* They didn't know whether you were alive or dead and you *Wanted* them to have a word! Mind you, that was always your way, wasn't it. Go your own way and devil take the rest. You were the most self-willed, self-absorbed lass in the county of Cumberland and still are by the sound of it. Married with a child and not a bloody word to anyone. Annie and Reed Macauley were heartbroken when they lost their grandson and now, when they have a granddaughter you haven't even the grace to tell them of her. You don't deserve their love and sorrow, nor anyone else's, and why I've traipsed about this bloody city all these months I'll . . ."

He missed the surprised expression on Briar's face. He was only concerned with the realisation that he was saying far more than he intended. As always she had goaded him into words he had not meant to speak. He should have handed her the child and legged it back to the station before there was time to question him. Instead, in the enchantment of seeing her, speaking to her, holding her in his arms, he had hung about hoping for more and God only knew what that might be. Hell's teeth, her bloody husband would probably be coming through that door any minute, for surely it was long past the time when the working man gets home.

But she was speechless, which wasn't like her. Staring at him with her mouth hanging open, an expression of total disbelief on her face, her marvellous eyes wide and incredulous.

"Well?" he queried, belligerently. "Isn't it true?"

"What?" And it was at this point that Jess stood up, took the baby who had fallen asleep, put a hand on Elsie's arm and silently drew her from the room. She shut the scullery door behind them.

"What d'yer wanner do that for?" Elsie hissed, peeved beyond measure, since this was as good as one of the penny novelettes she bought at the bookshop in Church Street.

"Shurrup, our Elsie. Now, run up and get babby's little duds then put yer coat on."

"Why, where we goin'?"

"Back to your place."

"What for?" Elsie was annoyed by their Jess's tone, besides being agog to hear what was going on in Jess's kitchen.

"That chap needs ter talk to our Briar an' she needs ter listen."

"But . . ."

"Oh, give yer gob a rest an' get yer bloody coat on."

The woman, whoever she was, with the other one peering inquisitively over her shoulder, had put her head round the door and told Briar in a hoarse whisper that she and Elsie were taking the baby to Elsie's place for a bit of a walk and though Briar had looked somewhat perplexed she had made no objection. Well, she wouldn't, would she, since any child was safe with its grandmother!

For what seemed an aeon Will stood by the table, longing to go and get away from the pain this woman was causing him, wanting to stay and suffer some more, wondering at the madness of men who scourged themselves in the name of love. He stared at the picture on the wall of a man with a plain but kindly face whose sideburns gave him the look of a hound, wondering with that part of his mind not split asunder by what Briar was doing to him who he was.

"Do sit down, Will," Briar's quiet voice told him and something in it made him obey. "Tell me, please."

"Tell you what?"

"I don't know, really. It's all such a muddle. You're a farmer. Your farm is far to the north and yet here you are, wandering about the streets of Liverpool and what's more astonishing, in the very place where Alexandra happens to be when whoever it was took her. Why? What possible reason can a farmer from the parish of Bassenthwaite have for being in this great seaport?"

"The same reason that brought you here, I suppose."

She looked astonished. "You know . . . you must know

why I left Bracken Ridge. I was not myself; out of my mind with grief and the only way to escape it, I thought, was to get away from the place where it happened." She smiled sadly, turning her gaze to the bright fire and studying the flames that danced in the grate. "I had the mad idea that I would go to America. Oh yes, you may look confounded. God knows what would have happened to me if I had not met these good people, but I thought . . ." She shook her head and her hair swayed and rippled about her face and Will Lucas stood up, for he really didn't think he could stay in this room, in this house that Briar shared with another man. He had done it once, suffered it once when she married Hal Saunders, but twice, surely that smacked of insanity.

She watched him struggle to the door, then stood up to take hold of his arm, determined not to let him go until she had an explanation for his sudden intrusion into her new life, but even as she touched him he turned fiercely. His face twisted in the strangest way and before she knew what he was about, before she could evade him, had she wanted to, he dragged her into his arms and sank his lips into hers. His virile male energy, dammed up for all these years, was violently released, spreading through his body like ripples on a quiet lake, communicating itself to her, so that she began to shake with something she barely recognised though her starved body did. His lips moved, caressed, folding hers into his and his hand moved to the back of her head, holding her so that she could not tear herself away. She felt something start to thump and shake inside her as if her heart had come loose. He lifted his head for a moment and his strong, handsome face was stern and uncompromising as it looked down into hers. Then his mouth took hers again and she made no resistance. Was she so amazed by his impertinence, he had time to think, that she had as yet not offered resistance, or was there a response in her that a woman shows when she was not averse to what was happening? His free hand smoothed her shoulder, moving down her arching back, reaching her buttocks, gripping them strongly, pressing her even closer to him, knowing she must feel the rock hardness of his manhood and still she did not resist.

Again he lifted his mouth from hers as she swayed against him. Her face was pale, her lips were a vivid poppy and her eyes unfocused.

"So it was love, or the loss of it that brought you here, was it, Briar Macauley. Well, it's the same for me, woman. I love you. I've loved you for years and for the past eighteen months I've been searching this bloody city to find you." His voice was hoarse, with despair, with passion, with hopelessness, or was it triumph, for at last he had her in his arms and she was making no objection, but he was wrong!

With a strangled cry, she sprang away from him, and with a look of what might be horror, or was it guilt, or even shame, she wiped the back of her hand across her mouth which so recently had lifted eagerly to his. Pressing herself up against the wall as far from him as she could get, just as if she were afraid of another assault, her eyes glared into his with what seemed to be loathing.

"I don't know what you're talking about, Will Lucas, and I don't think you do, either. Love, you don't know the meaning of the word. You're all the same, you bloody men. First Perry Sutton comes sniffing round me like some tomcat on the tiles and now you're the same."

"Don't you compare me to Perry Sutton, my fine lady. It didn't seem to bother you a moment ago when I put my hands on you. Perhaps that bastard was telling the truth when he intimated that he and you——"

473

"How dare you. You make me sick."

"Make you sick, is it?"

"Yes, sick to my stomach. You talk of love but what you mean is lust. That's all."

"Bloody hell, is this what I've been searching for all these months? A foul-mouthed bitch who thinks, just as she always did, that she's irresistible to every man who glances at her. Well, I've finished with it, d'you hear? I'm off home and you can go to the devil in a handcart for all I care. All these months . . . and you're not worth another moment of my time."

All of a sudden it was over, that familiar tirade of rage which in the past had often driven them almost to blows. That youthful need to strike out, her at him for what she saw as his pomposity, him at her for her outrageous and wilful defiance.

He eased himself away from the door, his hands held up in a gesture of yielding, and she relaxed, ready to slide down the wall to a crouch.

"Sit down, Briar," he told her gently and was surprised when she complied. He sat opposite her, his hands resting on his knees so that she might recognise he would not touch her again. It seemed he had given offence, he could think of no other word, and yet his body still remembered that certain submission, even eagerness as he held her close to him.

"I meant what I said, about loving you, I mean. I don't *lust* after you though I must admit if you were willing I would take you up those stairs, lay you on the nearest bed and make love to you for the rest of the night. You see I love you, and want you. I know you don't feel the same, how could you now, but I couldn't rest until I'd seen you. Seen that you were well and happy and it seems you are, so I'll be on my way."

Briar watched his face with eyes which were wide and somewhat incredulous. It was as though she were seeing him for the first time, not just as Will Lucas who had been her brother, her friend, her companion, her foe, her teacher in many things, but as a *man*. She recognised, though she was reluctant to admit it, that her body had responded to his right willingly but it was, of course, only the natural response of a woman who has known physical love and has been deprived of it for a long time. That was all. He was telling her that he loved her, that he had never stopped looking for her, not as a man hoping for the things a lusty man wants from a woman but for the simple reason that his concern for her would not let him rest. A caring man. A compassionate man, a strong, reliable man and if that made him sound stuffy, self-righteous, then it was not true. She could hardly get her mind round the thousand things she wanted to ask him ... What about for God's sake? her astounded brain asked, for didn't she know Will Lucas better than any man in the whole of her life, even her beloved Hal. Will had been in her life ever since she had taken her first toddling steps between her mother and Phoebe in the kitchen of Browhead, she a baby scarcely older than Alexandra, he a gruff lad of six or seven. She had taken him for granted, but she had loved him. As a brother, perhaps, but love just the same.

"Have you nothing to say, Briar?" he asked her gravely. "I've spent enough time away from the farm and must get back, now that I've found you and can tell your mother and father ... how you are. My own father has been patience itself, doing my work as well as his own and at his age it can't be easy. He's been ... well, he knows what it is to love a woman to distraction."

"Phoebe?" She was dumbfounded.

"No, not my mother, though he loves her tenderly. Someone . . . well, it's not my tale to tell."

He became brisk, reaching for his coat which he did not remember taking off. His heart was a cold lump of stone in his chest, lying so heavily he thought he might never get to the railway station but collapse in a corner somewhere, but he would not let her see it. Not again.

"So, I'll get off before your husband comes home and finds you entertaining a strange man, even if he is an old friend. It wouldn't do to . . ."

He stopped, one arm in his coat sleeve, the other doing its best to struggle into the garment. He looked at her, at her open-mouthed, amazed expression, her widening eyes, the sudden tension of her body as she slowly rose to her feet.

"My . . . husband?"

"Yes . . . and those ladies will be back soon with your child . . ." His voice faltered, for she looked so strange, so wild and thunderstruck he could not go on.

"My husband!"

"Yes."

"I have no husband, Will."

"Your child?" His voice was weak, sounding foolish, unsure, even to his own ears.

"Is adopted. One of the girls in the shop . . . she died when Alexandra was born. The father didn't want her but I did."

He lifted his face to the ceiling and into his silvery-grey eyes came an expression of such joy Briar felt her own mouth curve into a smile. He looked exalted and when he turned to look at her there was what could have been moisture clinging to the heavy sweep of his lashes.

"Oh, you beautiful girl," he whispered. "You beautiful, beautiful girl."

Chapter Thirty-three

"I don't know. Yer say yer not ter go 'ome ter wherever it is yer come from. What? Right, Bassenthwaite. An' yet ever since that chap went off wi' 'imself yer've bin moonin' round't place like some love-sick lass."

"Don't be ridiculous. I'm doing no such thing. Will's just ... unsettled me, that's all. When somebody turns up out of your past as he did, it brings back memories, some good, some you don't want to remember and you can't help but ... but ..."

"Think on 'em."

"Yes, that's right. Think of them." Briar's reply was eager, as though she wanted nothing more than to be persuaded that that was exactly how she felt and nothing else. Overcome with memories of the past which were slightly upsetting and nothing, absolutely *nothing* to do with the sudden appearance of Will Lucas himself. She was astonished and loath to admit to Jess, or indeed even to herself, that the sight of him had affected her so strongly. He had, of course, brought Alexandra back to her which in itself was a miracle and her gratitude to him had made her act in an unguarded, warm and welcoming manner, or

so she told herself. But ever since he had left her, striding
off up the street shouting that he'd be back, she had been
troubled by feelings of unusual intensity. Gladness had
been one of them, gladness that he had reappeared into
her life though she could not really analyse why that should
be. Sadness had been another, since he had reminded her of
so many things that she had tried, with this new life of hers,
to put from her and at the same time to cherish secretly
in her heart. There had been curious need to hold on to
him, a physical thing, which had been disturbing since Will
had been like a brother to her and what she had felt in his
arms was *not* sisterly. She was inclined to be troubled by the
knowledge that she had found his embrace pleasing, that
his kisses had evoked a response in her when she had firmly
believed that with Hal gone she would never feel that way
again. It was as though she had been guilty of unfaithfulness
to her husband's memory. She had welcomed Will's hands
on her body and the feeling had left her breathless.

He loved her, he had told her, and the thought of being
loved by Will Lucas awoke some sleeping thing in her
that had been dormant for many months. Even as he sat
opposite her his glance heightened her awareness of his
manly beauty, which she had never noticed before or if
she had it had not concerned her. His slow smile brought
an echoing smile to her own lips and she found that her
eyes lingered on the lines of his face, his firm chin and
well-shaped mouth and within her something stirred, and
she knew it was deeply sensual and at the same time softly
grieving for the man who had first brought it to life. Hal
was gone but Will was here, demanding something of her
that she was not sure she wanted to give. He had looked for
her, never given up hope of finding her, he had told her. He
was wordlessly asking for some commitment from her, his

last glance had promised her that, and yes, it had excited her and yet it had grieved her, for how could she entertain the thought of any other man taking Hal's place?

But it had been a joy just the same. Will's descriptions of what was happening in Bassenthwaite had made her lean forward with interest at the news of the place that had once been her home. He had made her smile with his talk of his mother who, it seemed, would never change but who, just lately, had not been well. It was not that that had made her smile, but his humorous account of Phoebe's absolute refusal to admit that she was not as spry as once she had been, her sharp irritation when her family did their best to take little tasks from her which she was convinced no one could manage as well as she did. If you want something doing right, do it yourself, had been Phoebe's adage and it seemed it was still so. She had been surprised to hear that Jonty Singleton, that most single-minded bachelor of the parish, was to marry Will's sister, Beth, before Christmas. And at last, when she had thought he would not mention them, he spoke of her own parents who longed for her return. Would she not come home with him, he had begged, if only to show them their new granddaughter, but at that she had taken fright, for he was going too fast for her. The day had been one of terrifying intensity, flinging her down into the familiar pit of despair with Alexandra's disappearance and then lifting her again to the heights of joy on her return. The sight of a man from her past had frozen her, then released in her, and not just because of Alexandra, a surge of delight that had amazed her; and as for the way her body had responded to his closeness, well, she must have time to brood on its meaning, though she did not say so to Will.

When he left he had kissed her again and she had let him.

His hands had rested gently on her shoulders, keeping space between their bodies and his mouth had been soft against hers. There had been none of the passion his first kiss had shown. He had gazed at her for a long time and she had been aware with that look of an inexpressible tenderness, a love that went far deeper than sexual desire. That she had been wrong when she accused him of lust. That this man truly loved her and when he left she must deal with the knowledge and where it was to go.

And Jess had been right, of course. She *had* been mooning but not in the way Jess meant. If she was mooning over anyone it was Hal and her memories of him. He had been her first love, that special love that comes only once to a woman, but when it came Briar had not been a woman, but a girl. Hal had been older but still a boy. Despite this their love had been deep and fulfilling and her sorrow and loss would never leave her. But now it had become something that was bearable. Her despairing misery had been made up equally of guilt and shame, since she had believed that it had been her fault. She it was who had led Tom on to the ice in that far-away game between mother and son, and because of it he, and his father, had died. But she had learned to forgive herself, for if she hadn't she would never be able to love her daughter as she deserved to be loved. Hal and Tom were a beautiful, unspoiled memory with a special place in her heart. They had come into her life and slipped out again but the affection and respect she had earned with Jess and Elsie and Potter, not as Briar Macauley whose father was a wealthy man, but as herself, had gradually healed her. That, and Alexandra.

She had been less than useless at the shop since Will had left, her normal efficiency vanishing with every passing hour until the girls looked at one another in amazement and Elsie became so sharp with her she felt like snatching up her sleeping child and running back to Jess. She made up the customers' orders, those who sent their coachmen to pick up their their goods rather than shop personally, wives of rich and influential businessmen who lived on the outskirts of Liverpool in the splendid villas and mansions being built there. Important customers who did not like to be told by their housekeepers that Potter's had sent pork pies instead of the oyster patties the mistress had ordered. She fumbled about in the shop, getting in everybody's way as though she were a new girl just starting, tripping over her own feet, forgetting the price of the most ordinary things and even the names of old, favoured customers.

"I'm sorry, Elsie," she said a dozen times a day. "I don't know what's wrong with me."

"Oh, don't yer, well, yer must be daft as well as 'andless. See, gi' me that fruit cake before the thing gets mashed ter pieces. It's supposed ter go in a box, yer daft 'apporth. Don't yer know that by now."

It was three weeks since Will had come so explosively into her life and the run-up to Christmas was just getting into full swing. Elsie, with Jess's help, was slaving for hours each day in the kitchen, making the dozens of plum puddings, the exquisitely decorated Christmas cakes which had been ordered for weeks. Anything that would keep was made far in advance of the Christmas season, As the day drew near they would turn to baking that would need to be fresh on Christmas Eve, such as the mince pies which were made to Elsie's special recipe. The storeroom was packed from floor to ceiling with boxes of fruit, sugar, candied citron and orange peel, bottles of brandy, eggs and suet, butter and flour and sugar. Elsie became more and more irritable, as she did every Christmas, but somehow this one was made worse by the growing group of customers, not just the working women who still bought from her, but the more discerning ladies of Everton and Walton-on-the-Hill. Last year the work had not been so intense and if it had she had Briar, solid, reliable, efficient Briar to soothe her worries, and would you look at the lass now. Her bloody head in the clouds over some chap who seemed to have turned her from what she had been, Elsie's right-hand woman whom she relied on, to the level of the youngest recruit who was no more than a scullery-maid.

He came back two days before Christmas and when she opened the front door letting in a draught of snow-laden wind, he stepped over the doormat and swept her into his arms as though he had every right to do so. And the amazing thing was, she clung to him with equal ferocity before she remembered who she was, who *he* was and what had gone before. For an instant she had been overjoyed, so much so that his arms about her, his warm mouth on hers seemed as natural as the very air she breathed. Then Jess's voice from the kitchen demanding who it was brought her back from the dizzying heights his kisses had swept her to.

The gentlemen lodgers had gone only that afternoon back to their families at this season of the year and there was only her and Jess in the house. The baby was fast asleep in her cradle which was tucked closely beside Jess's chair where, should she stir, a soothing hand could be laid on her. When Briar went to bed they would would carry it upstairs between them and place it next to her bed.

His shoulders had a thin ledge of snow on them and his hair had a cap of white, and for a moment she had time to wonder what he had done with his hat as his eyes searched her face, then she was in his arms again, she didn't know how, for God's sake, and their mouths fused, hot and wanting, before she tore herself away and put a trembling hand to her hair.

"'Oo is it, lass?" Jess asked querulously, for tomorrow was going to be an absolute bugger in the shop where she had promised to help out and she needed to get to her bed. Visitors at this time of night were an unlooked-for nuisance.

Briar opened the door wide into the cosy kitchen, leading Will by the hand, again she didn't know why, into Jess's astonished presence.

"It's Will, Jess. Do you remember him?" Briar asked her breathlessly, scarcely noticing the sudden sharp look on Jess's face. It was more than eighteen months since this lass had dragged herself, dazed and wandering, over Jess's doorstep looking as though she had just been released from the workhouse, her head shorn, her face grey and so thin her cheekbones stuck out like two narrow shelves. It had taken some doing and, though she said it herself, it was thanks to her and Elsie that she was now as lovely and bright as the Christmas star on the tree in the corner. Afterwards she was to confess to herself that the thought was unjust, for Briar Saunders had brought herself back to life with her own inborn strength come from her mother and father, and that she and Elsie had been merely on the sidelines, so to speak, there in case she should falter, which, once she had got going, she never did.

Now would you look at her. Her face was flushed and her hair escaping from its carelessly tied ribbon in curly tendrils over her ears and she was holding the hand of the chap ... oh aye, she remembered Will all right. Her heart sank, then fluttered pathetically, for staring her in the face, she knew it then, as she had vaguely known it the last time, was the knowledge that as sure as eggs are eggs she was about to lose this woman who meant so much to her, and not only her but the beautiful child she had come to think of as her own granddaughter.

She was cool in her greeting.

"Oh aye, an' what brings you 'ere at this time o' night? Me an' Briar's just off to us beds. Busy day termorrer in't shop."

"Please, Mrs ... er ..."

"Handy."

"Mrs Handy, don't let me keep you up. I shan't be long. I've yet to find a place to stay but I came straight here from the station." And all the time his eyes were on Briar and his hand was in Briar's until, suddenly, she let it go and sat down abruptly in the chair opposite Jess, then, just as abruptly, stood up.

"Sit down, Will, and let me offer you ... tea ... coffee ..."

It was no bloody pot of tea, nor coffee this lad wanted, Jess told herself despairingly, but when Briar moved into the scullery and his eyes followed her, the rest of him longing to do the same, Jess had a moment's self-disgust, for could any mother have wished for any man as well set up as this one for her much loved daughter.

They did not mean to exclude her, but they seemed to have a lot to say to one another about folk she didn't know. Someone called Phoebe who was confined to her bed after a slight stroke. A wedding between Beth and Jonty which his mother, who turned out to be Phoebe and also Beth's mother, could not attend, to her own great disappointment. Briar's mother and father who had longed to come to her but, on Will's advice, had stayed away until she was ready. They had sent these letters, he added, handing Briar a thick package which she took gingerly, though her eyes were bright with tears.

"I was not prepared to do that, my darling," he said, "stay away, I mean," with a glance at Jess which told her that he wished her anywhere but here. He reached out and took Briar's hand, bending his head to kiss the inside of her wrist and Jess saw Briar shiver then snatch her hand away as though his lips burned her flesh. She turned to look guiltily at Jess, and Will knew that she was going back to the time when another man had done just that, and though he could sense that his love for her was not unwelcome she was far from ready to forget Hal Saunders.

They spent Christmas Day at Peter Street. Jess and Elsie and Potter, Briar and the baby, with Will an uneasy guest, and it was obvious to him that her first reaction when he stepped over the threshold was one she regretted. She was pleasant, friendly, accepting his Christmas presents for her and the baby with a smile that smote his heart, and he wished he had not come. It was far from easy effecting a courtship from so far away and it was going to get harder. It was winter on the fells and the white bowl of the great valley below the farm was filled with snow so that he had had great difficulty getting to the station at Penrith. The sheep had been brought down and fed with hay from the barn, and he and his father had been busy keeping an eye on the pregnant ewes which had been mated at "tup" time. The lambs would not be dropped until April so the pressure on him and his father was not, at this time of the year, unduly heavy. But he wanted Briar back with him at Browhead, his wife and partner, before then. His father had persuaded him to come, saying that Phoebe had many friends in Maggie Singleton, Annie Macauley and others who would help him in the care of his mother, not to mention the newly wed Beth Singleton who now lived over at Upfell Farm with her new husband.

He had allowed himself to be persuaded, but as he watched Briar in the company of these friends of hers, heard her speak of her work in the shop where she was a partner, saw her love and fulfilment with her baby, he began to despair, the initial triumph he had known, last time and this, beginning to dribble away. It seemed she was happy and settled in her new life.

He was not to know of the confusion in Briar's mind, and had he been aware of the muddle she had got into in the business which had once been her pride and joy, and her saviour, he might have felt more hopeful. Neither Jess nor Elsie helped him out, though Potter said later in the privacy of the bed he shared with Elsie that he thought the lad was a proper gentleman and that their Briar could do a damn sight worse than wed him! Elsie gave him a right piece of her mind, leaving him wondering, and not for the first time, on the bloody contrariness of the female sex.

He did not come again and she found she missed him, which was ridiculous when you considered how long they had been parted before his first visit, and in that time she had never given him a thought. That was not strictly true, for the people in her past life were often in her thoughts but he had been included as a part of them, her mother and father, Phoebe, Charlie, Beth, Will, Jonty Singleton, even Alice Sutton and her family. They were all there in her memory, dear Nan, old, cantankerous Dobby Hawkins, ghosts from the past who came to smile at her and remind her of happier times.

"That lad's not bin again then," Jess said delicately one fine Sunday morning at the beginning of March.

"No," she answered shortly and Jess knew when to leave a thing alone. They were lifting the baby carriage down the steps, one at each end, Jess smiling at the babble that came from the baby as though she were giving instructions on the best way to go about it. She was nearly a year old and already playing havoc with everything in her way as she crawled about the kitchen. The cat had found a safe shelf on which to perch, for it was not inclined to allow her to chuck it about as she would have liked.

A shadow of something that might have been sadness passed across Briar's face, for though she did not admit it, even to herself, she had looked for Will in the past ten weeks. Yes, she had counted the weeks and as they passed she had unhappily come to the conclusion that he had given up and was probably wooing Jenny Bracken from Hilltop Farm or one of the other pretty, unwed girls who had cast their glance in his direction. But at the same time she knew that was unfair of her, since Will was not a man to flit lightly from one woman to another. So why had she not heard from him?

They sauntered slowly in the pale sunshine towards Bold Street where they were to pick up Elsie, this time, as a change, for a walk round Sefton Park which was also further out beyond Princes Park. Elsie was full of the great honour done the shop on the previous day when the housekeeper who served the household of His Worship the Mayor, John Hughes, Esq., had descended from a carriage, swept into the shop and ordered four dozen scones, a lemon sponge, three fresh plum tarts, two dozen Victoria buns, and three of Elsie's special tipsy cakes for one of the Mayoress's official teas. What an honour, and what a grand help in the shop and on the baking side that new girl Briar had hired was turning out to be, she added. A good head on her shoulders and, though it was left unspoken, someone to step into Briar's shoes if, as seemed likely, this chap was to whisk her off back home. At least that was what had been thought last Christmas!

The park was filling with the usual Sunday morning strollers, those who had done their duty to God in the many churches that lay about the broad stretch of gardens which were just coming into their fresh spring beauty. Daffodils, golden-headed, trumpeted the glory of the loveliness of the day, carpets of crocus, purple, white and yellow, quilted the grass, and children were warned not to step on their delicate beauty as they ran and shrieked in their boisterous games. Alexandra yelled her displeasure at being confined to the perambulator when she wanted to romp on the grass, and Briar felt her spirits sink and was afraid, since she knew quite simply that she was not in her rightful place any more. Where was her rightful place? her logical mind asked. And though she knew the answer in her heart where it whispered his name, she was still afraid, for she was convinced that she had lost him.

When they turned the corner into Peter Street she was amazed to see him waiting at the bottom of the steps, his face like thunder as though her prevarications were not to his liking, which was unfair since he had asked for nothing. Jess took the perambulator from her without a word, lifting the baby from it and taking her inside, shutting the door behind her.

"I don't know why I'm here," he said, striding irritably along the pavement in the direction of Victoria Street. "I don't understand myself any more and I certainly don't understand you. You seem to welcome me ... and my advances but then you turn about and show me a face as cool as the ..." He had been about to say "as the ice on the lake" when he stopped himself in time.

Stopping in his tracks he put hard, heavy hands on her, forcing her to stop too. The man who had been so tender, gentle, patient, had come to the end of all that, it seemed, and she swayed slightly towards him, causing great consternation to the passing pedestrians.

Suddenly the anger died in his eyes and his shoulders slumped. He turned away and began to walk again. She fell in beside him, silent, compliant.

"I could say anything to persuade you to come home with me. Words come cheap but I think I've said enough. I love you. I want you to marry me and come as my wife to Browhead. You are needed, Briar."

"By Phoebe and Charlie?"

"By me, Goddammit. I've missed you but I'll not keep crawling back here every few weeks in the hope you'll soften that locked-up heart of yours."

He turned again, causing a hold-up in the pedestrian traffic as he stopped. He took her wrist with a tenderness that calmed her and filled her, at the same time, with great excitement, kissing it lightly, then crushed her in his arms and kissed her with great urgency.

"Will you marry me, Briar?"

And there in the soft spring sunlight, face to face with him, she knew her answer.

"Marry you, Will?"

"Yes, damn it, marry me and put me out of this bloody misery."

"Can I let you know, Will?" For there were Jess and Elsie and the business to consider.

He almost threw her from him. "Devil take you, you

heartless ..." But she was smiling and her hand came to rest lovingly on his cheek so that he turned his mouth into the palm of it. The crowd who had gathered were delighted.

"Go on, chuck, marry't poor sod," some wag said as they drew apart.

"I'll come soon, Will, I promise."

"I'll wait until ..."

"Please, Will, be patient with me."

She saw him on to his train at Lime Street, sighing like a young lass as she watched it out of the station, seeing his dark head which he had out of the window at last merge into the smoke and steam at the end of the platform.

She walked back to Peter Street through the warm sunshine, smiling, languorous, wanting to stretch herself in the soft air like a cat, sleekly purring. And in the doorway of the house, Jess was waiting with Alexandra in her arms. The baby held out eager hands to Briar, and she took her, and Jess knew then, but she gave no indication of the breaking of her heart.

"Yer'll be goin' 'ome then, 'appen termorrer?" she said.

Briar walked past her, her smile growing, spreading from her lips until her whole body seemed to be smiling and when she turned to Jess it transferred itself to the woman who had given her life and hope and love, and Jess smiled too, this time with genuine pleasure.

"I love you, Jess. I can't bear to part with you so I shan't. Don't think you've seen the last of me. I shall bring Alexandra and if I can persuade you, you shall come and stay with me."

"Wha', all that way up there ..." as if Bassenthwaite

were in the wastes of Siberia, which to Jess, Liverpool born and bred, it was.

"It's beautiful, Jess, you'll love it. Promise me."

"Gerraway, what do I want wi' . . ."

"Promise me." Briar's voice was urgent. "I cannot go unless you promise me."

"Righto, yer daft 'apporth. 'Ere, gi' me't babby. I reckon yer'll want ter pack fer termorrer."

"Yes, I suppose so, but . . . if there's a train I think I'll go tonight."